THE
CONGO ROVERS

A Story of the Slave Squadron

HARRY COLLINGWOOD

1ˢᵗ WORLD
LIBRARY
Literary Society

The Congo Rovers

Harry Collingwood

© 1st World Library, 2009
PO Box 2211
Fairfield, IA 52556
www.1stworldlibrary.com
First Edition

LCCN: 2009923398

Softcover ISBN: 978-1-4218-8844-6
Hardcover ISBN: 978-1-4218-8943-6
eBook ISBN: 978-1-4218-8745-6

Purchase *"The Congo Rovers"*
as a traditional bound book at:
www.1stWorldLibrary.com/purchase.asp?ISBN=978-1-4218-8844-6

1st World Library is a literary, educational organization
dedicated to:

- Creating a free internet library of downloadable ebooks

- Hosting writing competitions and offering book publishing scholarships.

Interested in more 1st World Library books? contact:
literacy@1stworldlibrary.com
Check us out at: www.1stworldlibrary.com

1st World Library Literary Society

Giving Back to the World

"If you want to work on the core problem, it's early school literacy."

- James Barksdale, former CEO of Netscape

"No skill is more crucial to the future of a child, or to a democratic and prosperous society, than literacy."

- Los Angeles Times

"Literacy... means far more than learning how to read and write... The aim is to transmit... knowledge and promote social participation."

- UNESCO

"Literacy is not a luxury, it is a right and a responsibility. If our world is to meet the challenges of the twenty-first century we must harness the energy and creativity of all our citizens."

- President Bill Clinton

"Parents should be encouraged to read to their children, and teachers should be equipped with all available techniques for teaching literacy, so the varying needs and capacities of individual kids can be taken into account."

- Hugh Mackay

CHAPTER ONE

MY FIRST APPEARANCE IN UNIFORM

"Um!" ejaculated my father as he thoughtfully removed his double eye-glass from his nose with one hand, and with the other passed a letter to me across the breakfast-table—"Um! this letter will interest you, Dick. It is from Captain Vernon."

My heart leapt with sudden excitement, and my hand trembled as I stretched it out for the proffered epistle. The mention of Captain Vernon's name, together with the announcement that the subject-matter of the letter was of interest to me, prepared me in a great measure for the intelligence it conveyed; which was to the effect that the writer, having been appointed to the command of the sloop-of-war *Daphne*, now found himself in a position to fulfil a promise of some standing to his dear and honoured friend Dr Hawkesley (my father) by receiving his son (myself) on board the sloop, with the rating of midshipman. The sloop, the letter went on to say, was commissioned for service on the west coast of Africa; and if I decided to join her no time should be lost in procuring my outfit, as the *Daphne* was under orders to sail on the—; just four days from the date of the receipt of the letter.

"Well, Dick, what do you think of Captain Vernon's proposal?"

inquired my father somewhat sadly, as I concluded my perusal of the letter and raised my eyes to his.

"Oh, father!" I exclaimed eagerly, "I *hope* you will consent to let me go. Perhaps I may never have another such an opportunity; and I am *quite sure* I shall never care to be anything but a sailor."

"Ah! yes—the old, old story," murmured my father, shaking his head dubiously. "Thousands of lads have told their fathers exactly the same thing, and have lived to bitterly regret their choice of a profession. Look at my life. I have to run about in all weathers; to take my meals when and how I can; there is not a single hour in the twenty-four that I can call my own; it is a rare thing for me to get a night of undisturbed rest; it is a hard, anxious, harassing life that I lead—you have often said so yourself, and urged it as one of the reasons why you object to follow in my footsteps. But I tell you, Dick, that my life—ay, or the life even of the poorest country practitioner, for that matter—is one of ease and luxury compared with that of a sailor. But I have said all this to you over and over again, without convincing you; and I hardly dare hope that I shall be more successful now; so, if you are really quite resolved to go to sea, I will offer no further objections. It is true that you will be going to an unhealthy climate; but God is just as well able to preserve you there as He is here; and then, again, you have a strong healthy constitution, which, fortified with such preservative medicines as I can supply, will, I hope, enable you to withstand the malaria and to return to us in safety. Now, what do you say—are you still resolved to go?"

"Quite," I replied emphatically. "Now that you have given your consent the last obstacle is removed, and I can follow with a light heart the bent of my own inclinations."

"Very well, then," said my father, rising from the table and pushing back his chair. "That question being settled, we had better call upon Mr Shears forthwith and give the order for your uniform and outfit. There is no time to lose; and since go you *will*, I would very much rather you went with Vernon than with anyone else."

The above conversation took place, as already stated, in the breakfast-room of my father's house. My father was at that time—as he continued to be until the day of his death—the leading physician in Portsmouth; and his house—a substantial four-storey building—stood near the top of the High Street. The establishment of Mr Shears, "Army and Navy Tailor, Clothier, and Outfitter," was situated near the bottom of the same street. A walk, therefore, of some ten minutes' duration took us to our destination; and at the end of a further half-hour's anxious consultation I had been measured for my uniform—one suit of which was faithfully promised for the next day—had chosen my sea-chest, and had selected a complete outfit of such clothing as was to be obtained ready-made. This important business concluded, my father departed upon his daily round of visits, and I had the remainder of the day at my own disposal.

My first act on emerging from the door of Mr Shears' establishment was to hasten off to the dockyard at top speed to take another look at the *Daphne*. I had often seen the craft before; had taken an interest in her, indeed, I may say, from the moment that her keel was laid—she was built in Portsmouth dockyard—and had watched her progress to completion and her recent launch with an admiration which had steadily increased until it grew into positive *love*. And now I was actually to have the happiness, the *bliss*, of going to sea in her as an officer on her first cruise. Ecstatic thought! I felt as though I was walking on air!

But my rapture received a pretty effectual damper when I reflected—as I soon did—that my obstinate determination to go to sea must certainly prove a deep disappointment, if not a source of constant and cruel anxiety, to my father. Dear old dad! his most cherished wish, as I knew full well, had long been that I, his only son, might qualify myself to take over and carry on the exceedingly snug practice he had built up, when the pressure of increasing years should render his retirement desirable. But the idea was so utterly distasteful to me that I had persistently turned a deaf ear to all his arguments, persuasions, ay, and even his entreaties. Unfortunately, perhaps, for the fulfilment of his desires, I was born and brought up at Portsmouth; and all my earliest recollections of amusement are, in some way or other, connected with salt water. Swimming and boating early became absolute passions with me; I was never quite happy unless I happened to be either in or on the water; *then*, indeed, all other pleasures were less than nothing to me. As a natural consequence, I soon became the intimate companion of every boatman in the harbour; I acquired, to a considerable extent, their tastes and prejudices, and soon mastered all the nautical lore which it was in their power to teach me. I could sail a boat before I could read; and by the time that I had learned to write, was able to hand, reef, and steer with the best of them. My conversation—except when it was addressed to my father—was copiously interlarded with nautical phrases; and by the time I had attained the age of fourteen—at which period this history begins—I was not only acquainted with the name, place, and use of every rope and spar in a ship, but I had also an accurate knowledge of the various rigs, and a distinct opinion as to what constituted a good model. The astute reader will have gathered from this confession that I was, from my earliest childhood, left pretty much my own master; and such was in fact the case. My mother died in giving birth to my only sister Eva (two years my junior); a misfortune which, in consequence of my father's absorption in the duties of his practice, left me entirely to the care of the servants, by whom I was shamefully neglected. But for this I should doubtless have been trained to obedience and a respectful deference to my father's wishes. The mischief, however, was done; I had acquired a love of the sea, and my highest ambition was to become a naval officer. This fact my father at length reluctantly recognised, and by persistent entreaty I finally prevailed upon him to take the necessary steps to gratify my heart's desire—with the result already known to the reader.

The sombre reflections induced by the thought of my father's disappointment did not, I confess with shame, last long. They vanished as a morning mist is dissipated before the rising sun, when I recalled to mind that I was not only going to sea, but that I was actually going to sail in the *Daphne*. This particular craft was my *beau-ideal* of what a ship ought to be; and in this opinion I was by no means alone—all my cronies hailing from the Hard agreeing, without exception, that she was far and away the handsomest and most perfect model they had ever seen. My admiration of her was unbounded; and on the day of her launch—upon which occasion I cheered myself hoarse—I felt, as I saw her gliding swiftly and gracefully down the ways, that it would be a priceless privilege to sail in her, even in the capacity of the meanest ship-boy. And now I was to be a midshipman on board her! I hurried onward with swift and impatient steps, and soon passed through the dockyard gates—having long ago, by dint of persistent coaxing, gained the *entree* to the sacred precincts—when a walk of some four or five hundred yards further took me to the berth alongside the wharf where she was lying.

Well as I knew every curve and line of her beautiful hull, my glances now dwelt upon her with tenfold loving interest. She was a ship-sloop of 28 guns—long 18-pounders—with a flush deck fore and aft. She was very long in proportion to her beam; low in the water, and her lines were as fine as it had been possible to make them. She had a very light, elegant-looking stern, adorned with a great deal of carved scroll-work about the cabin windows; and her gracefully-curved cut-water was surmounted by an exquisitely-carved full-length figure of Peneus' lovely daughter, with both arms outstretched, as in the act of flight, and with twigs and leaves of laurel just springing from her dainty finger-tips. There was a great deal of brass-work about the deck fittings, which gleamed and flashed brilliantly in the sun; and, the paint being new and fresh, she looked altogether superlatively neat, in spite of the fact that the operations of rigging and of shipping stores were both going on simultaneously.

Having satisfied for the time being my curiosity with regard to the hull of my future home, I next cast a glance aloft at her spars. She was rigged only as far as her topmast-heads, her topgallant-masts being then on deck in process of preparation for sending aloft. When I had last seen her she was under the masting-shears getting her lower-masts stepped; and it then struck me that they were fitting her with rather heavy spars. But now, as I looked aloft, I was fairly startled at the length and girth of her masts and yards. To my eye— by no means an unaccustomed one—her spars seemed taunt enough for a ship of nearly double her size; and the rigging was heavy in the same proportion. I stood there on the wharf watching with the keenest interest the scene of bustle and animation on board until the bell rang the hour of noon, and all hands knocked off work and went to dinner; by which time the three topgallant-masts were aloft with the rigging all ready for setting up when the men turned-to again. The addition of these spars to the length of her already lofty masts gave the *Daphne*, in my opinion, more than ever the appearance of being over-sparred; an opinion in which, as it soon appeared, I was not alone.

Most of the men left the dockyard and went home (as I suppose) to their dinner; but half a dozen or so of riggers, instead of following the example of the others, routed out from some obscure spot certain small bundles tied up in coloured handkerchiefs, and, bringing these on shore, seated themselves upon some of the boxes and casks with which the wharf was lumbered, and, opening the bundles, produced therefrom their dinners, which they proceeded to discuss with quite an enviable appetite.

For a few minutes the meal proceeded in dead silence; but presently one of them, glancing aloft at the *Daphne's* spars, remarked in a tone of voice which reached me distinctly—I was standing within a few feet of the party:

"Well, Tom, bo'; what d'ye think of the hooker *now*?"

The man addressed shook his head disapprovingly. "The more I looks at her the less I likes her," was his reply.

"I'm precious glad *I* ain't goin' to sea in her," observed another.

"Same here," said the first speaker. "Why, look at the *Siren* over there! She's a 38-gun frigate, and her mainmast is only two feet longer than the *Daphne's*—as I happen to know, for I had a hand in the buildin' of both the spars. The sloop's over-masted, that's what *she* is."

I turned away and bent my steps homeward. The short snatch of conversation which I had just heard, confirming as it did my own convictions, had a curiously depressing effect upon me, which was increased when, a few minutes afterwards, I caught a glimpse of the distant buoy which marked the position of the sunken *Royal George*. For the moment my enthusiasm was all gone; a foreboding of disaster took possession of me, and but for very shame I felt more than half-inclined to tell my father I had altered my mind, and would rather not go to sea. I had occasion afterwards to devoutly wish I had acted on this impulse.

When, however, I was awakened next morning by the sun shining brilliantly in at my bed-room window, my apprehensions had vanished, my enthusiasm was again at fever-heat, and I panted for the moment—not to be very long deferred—when I should don my uniform and strut forth to sport my glories before an admiring world.

Punctual almost to a moment—for once at least in his life—Mr Shears sent home the uniform whilst we were sitting down to luncheon; and the moment that I decently could I hastened away to try it on.

The breeches were certainly rather wrinkly above the knees, and the jacket was somewhat uncomfortably tight across the chest when buttoned over; it also pinched me a good deal under the arm-pits, whilst the sleeves exhibited a trifle too much—some six inches or so—of my wristbands and shirt-sleeves; and when I looked at myself in the glass I found that there was a well-defined ridge of loose cloth running across the back from shoulder to shoulder. With these trifling exceptions, however, I thought the suit fitted me fairly well, and I hastened down-stairs to exhibit myself to my sister Eva. To my intense surprise and indignation she no sooner saw me than she burst into an uncontrollable fit of laughter, and was heartless enough to declare that I looked "a perfect fright." Thoroughly disgusted with such unsisterly conduct I mustered all my dignity, and without condescending to ask for an explanation walked in contemptuous silence out of the room and the house.

A regimental band was to play that afternoon on Southsea

Common, and thither I accordingly decided to direct my steps. There were a good many people about the streets, and I had not gone very far before I made the discovery that everybody was in high good-humour about something or other. The people I met wore, almost without exception, genial smiling countenances, and many a peal of hearty laughter rang out from hilarious groups who had already passed me. I felt anxious to know what it was that thus set all Portsmouth laughing, and glanced round to see if I could discover an acquaintance of whom I might inquire; but, as usual in such cases, was unsuccessful. When I reached the Common I found, as I expected I should, a large and fashionably dressed crowd, with a good sprinkling of naval and military uniforms, listening to the strains of the band. Here, for the first five minutes or so, I failed to notice anything unusual in the behaviour of the people; but the humorous item of news must have reached them almost simultaneously with my own arrival upon the scene, for very soon I detected on the faces of those who passed me the same amused smile which I had before encountered in the streets. I stood well back out of the thick of the crowd; both because I could hear the music better, and also to afford any friend of mine who might chance to be present an opportunity to see me in my imposing new uniform.

It was whilst I was standing thus in the most easy and nonchalant attitude I could assume that a horrible discovery forced itself upon me. I happened to be regarding with a certain amount of languid interest a couple of promenaders, consisting of a very lovely girl and a somewhat foppish ensign, when I suddenly caught the eye of the latter fixed upon me. He raised his eye-glass to his eye, and, in the coolest manner in the world, deliberately surveyed me through it, when, in an instant, a broad smile of amusement—the smile which I by this time knew so well—overspread his otherwise inanimate features. I glanced hurriedly behind me to see if I could discover the cause of his risibility, and, failing to do so, turned round again, just in time to see him, with his eye-glass still bearing straight in my direction, bend his head and speak a few words to his fair companion. Thereupon she, too, glanced in my direction, looked steadfastly at me for a moment, and then burst into an uncontrollable fit of laughter which she vainly strove to stifle in her pocket-handkerchief. For a second or two I was utterly lost in astonishment at this unaccountable behaviour, and then all the hideous truth thrust itself upon me. They were laughing at *me*. Having at length fully realised this I turned haughtily away and at once left the ground.

I hurried homeward in a most unenviable state of mind, with the conviction every moment forcing itself more obtrusively upon me, that for some inconceivable reason I was the laughing-stock of everybody I met, when, just as I turned once more into the High Street I observed two midshipmen approaching on my own side of the way, and some half a dozen yards or so behind them a certain Miss Smith, a parlour boarder in the ladies' seminary opposite my father's house—a damsel not more than six or seven years my senior, with whom I was slightly acquainted, and for whom I had long cherished a secret but ardent passion.

With that sensitiveness which is so promptly evoked by even the bare suspicion of ridicule I furtively watched the two "young gentlemen" as they approached; but they had been talking and laughing loudly when I first caught sight of them, and although I saw that they were aware of my presence I failed to detect the sudden change of manner which I had dreaded to observe. Whether they were speaking of me or not I could not, of course, feel certain; but I rather fancied from the glances they cast in my direction that they were.

As they drew nearer I observed that the eyes of one of them

were intently and inquiringly gazing into mine, and they continued so to do until the pair had fairly passed me. Being by this time in a decidedly aggressive frame of mind I returned this pertinacious gaze with a haughty and contemptuous stare, which, however, I must confess, did not appear to very greatly intimidate the individual at whom it was levelled, for, unless I was greatly mistaken, there was a twitching about the corners of his mouth which suggested a strong, indeed an almost uncontrollable disposition to laughter, whilst his eyes fairly beamed with merriment.

As they passed me this individual half halted for an instant, passed on again a step or two, and then turning abruptly to the right-about, dashed after me and seized me by the hand, which he shook effusively, exclaiming as he did so:

"It *is*—I'm *sure* it is! My *dear* Lord Henry, how are you? This is indeed an unexpected pleasure!"

At this moment Miss Smith passed, giving me as she did so a little start of recognition, followed by a bow and a beaming smile, which I returned in my most fascinating manner.

I was once more happy. This little incident, trifling though it was in itself, sufficed to banish in an instant the unpleasant reflections which a moment before had been rankling in my breast, for had not my fair divinity seen me in the uniform of the gallant defenders of our country? And had she not also heard and seen me mistaken for a lord? If this had no power to soften and subdue that proud heart and bring it in sweet humility to my feet, then—well I should like to know what would, that's all.

I allowed my fair enslaver to pass out of ear-shot, and then said to the midshipman who had so unexpectedly addressed me:

"Excuse me, sir, but I think you are mistaking me for someone else."

"Oh, no, I'm not," he retorted. "I know you well enough— though I must say you are greatly altered for the better since I saw you last a year ago. You're Lord Henry de Vere Montmorenci. Ah, you sly dog! you thought to play a trick upon your old friend Fitz-Jones, did you? But what brings you down here, Montmorenci? Have you come down to join?"

This was a most remarkable, and at the same time gratifying occurrence, for I could not keep feeling elated at being thus mistaken for a noble, and greeted with such enthusiasm by a most agreeable and intelligent brother officer, and—evidently —a scion of some noble house to boot. For a single instant an almost invincible temptation seized me to personate the character with which I was accredited, but it was as promptly overcome; my respect for the truth (temporarily) conquered my vanity, and I answered:

"I assure you, my dear sir, you are mistaken. I am *not* Lord Henry de Vere Montmorenci, but plain Richard Hawkesley, just nominated to the *Daphne*."

"Well, if you persist in saying so, I suppose I must believe you," answered Fitz-Jones. "But, really, the resemblance is most extraordinary—truly remarkable indeed. There is the same lofty intellectual forehead, the same proud eagle-glance, the same haughty carriage; the same—now, tell me, Tomnoddy, upon your honour as an officer and a gentleman, did you ever in your life before see such an extraordinary resemblance?"

"I never did; it is really most remarkable," answered the other midshipman in a strangely quivering voice which, but for his solemn countenance, I should have considered decidedly indicative of suppressed laughter.

"It really is most singular, positively *marvellous*," resumed Fitz-Jones. Then he added hurriedly:

"By the way, do you know my friend Tomnoddy? No! Then allow me to introduce him. Lord Tomnoddy—Mr Richard Hawkesley, just nominated to the *Daphne*. And I suppose I ought also to introduce myself. I am Lord Montague Fitz-Jones. You have, of course, heard of the Fitz-Jones family— the Fitz-J-o-h-n-e-s's, you know?"

I certainly had not; nor had I, up to that moment, any idea that Lord Tomnoddy was other than a mythical personage; but I did not choose to parade my ignorance in such matters, so I replied by a polite bow.

There was silence between us for a moment; and then Fitz-Jones—or Fitz-Johnes, rather—raised his hand to his fore-head with a thoughtful air and murmured:

"Hawkesley! Hawkesley! I'm *positive* I've heard that name before. Now, where was it? Um—ah—eh? Yes; I have it. You're the handsome heartless fellow who played such havoc with my cousin Lady Mary's affections at the state ball last year. Now, don't deny it; I'm positive I'm right. Do you know," he continued, glaring at me in a most ferocious manner—"do you know that for the last six months I've been looking for you in order that I might shoot you?"

Somehow I did not feel very greatly alarmed at this belligerent speech, and vanity having by this time conquered my natural truthfulness, I determined to sustain my unex-pected reputation as a lady-killer at all hazards. I therefore drew myself up, and, assuming my sternest look, replied that

I should be happy to give him the desired opportunity whenever he might choose.

Fitz-Johnes' ferocious glare continued for a moment or two; then his brow cleared, and, extending his hand, he grasped mine, shook the member violently, and exclaimed:

"That was spoken like a gentleman and a brave man! Give me your hand, Hawkesley. I respect you, sir; I esteem you; and I forgive you all. If there is one thing which touches me more than another, one thing which I *admire* more than another, it is to see a man show a bold front in the face of deadly peril. Ah! *now* I can understand Lady Mary's infatuation. Poor girl! I pity her. And I suppose that pretty girl who passed just now is another victim to your fascinating powers. Ah, well! it's not to be wondered at, I'm sure. Tomnoddy, do you remember, by the by—?"

But Lord Tomnoddy was now standing with his back turned toward us, and his face buried in his pocket-handkerchief. His head was bowed, his shoulders were heaving convulsively, and certain inarticulate sounds which escaped him showed that he was struggling to suppress some violent emotion.

Lord Fitz-Johnes regarded his companion fixedly for a moment, then linked his arm in mine, drew me aside, and whispered hastily:

"Don't take any notice of him; he'll be all right again in a minute. It's only a little revulsion of feeling which has overcome him. He's frightfully tender-hearted—far too much so for a sailor; he can't bear the sight of blood; and he knew that if I called you out I should choose him for my second; and—you twig, eh!"

I thought I did, but was not quite sure, so I bowed again, which seemed quite as satisfactory as words to Fitz-Johnes, for he said, with his arm still linked in mine:

"That's all right. Now let's go and cement our friend ship over a bottle of wine at the 'Blue Posts,' what do you say?"

I intimated that the proposal was quite agreeable to me; and we accordingly wheeled about and directed our steps to the inn in question, which, in my time, was *the* place of resort, *par excellence*, of all midshipmen.

Lord Tomnoddy now removed his handkerchief from his eyes; and, sure enough, he *had* been weeping, for I detected him in the very act of drying his tears. He must have possessed a truly wonderful command over his features, though, for I could not detect the faintest trace of that deep feeling which had overpowered him so shortly before; on the contrary, he laughed uproariously at a very feeble joke which I just then ventured to let off; and thereafter, until I parted with them both an hour later, was the merriest of the party.

We arrived in due course at the "Blue Posts," and, walking into a private parlour, rang for the waiter. On the appearance of that individual, Fitz-Johnes, with a truly lordly air, ordered in three bottles of port; sagely remarking that he made a point of never drinking less than a bottle himself; and as his friend Hawkesley was *known* to have laid down the same rule, the third bottle was a necessity unless Lord Tomnoddy was to go without. Lord Tomnoddy faintly protested against the ordering of so much wine; but Fitz-Johnes was firm in his determination, insisting that he should regard it as nothing short of a deliberate insult on Tomnoddy's part if that individual declined his hospitality.

After a considerable delay the wine and glasses made their

appearance, the waiter setting them down, and then pausing respectfully by the table.

"Thank you; that will do. You need not wait," said Fitz-Johnes.

"The money, if you please, sir," explained the waiter.

"Oh, ah! yes, to be sure. The money." And Fitz-Johnes plunged his hand into his breeches pocket and withdrew therefrom the sum of twopence halfpenny, together with half a dozen buttons (assorted); a penknife minus its blades; the bowl of a clay tobacco pipe broken short off; three pieces of pipe-stem evidently originally belonging to the latter; and a small ball of sewing twine.

Carefully arranging the copper coins on the edge of the table he returned the remaining articles to their original place of deposit, and then plunged his hand into his other pocket, from which he produced—nothing.

"How much is it?" he inquired, glancing at the waiter.

"Fifteen shillings, if you please, sir," was the reply.

"Lend me a sovereign, there's a good fellow; I've left my purse in my other pocket," he exclaimed to Lord Tomnoddy.

"I would with pleasure, old fellow, if I had it. But, unfortunately, I haven't a farthing about me."

Thereupon the waiter proceeded deliberately to gather up the glasses again, and was about to take them and the wine away, when I interposed with a proposal to pay.

"No," said Fitz-Johnes fiercely; "I won't hear of it; I'll perish at the stake first. But if you really don't mind *lending* me a sovereign until to-morrow—"

I said I should be most happy; and forthwith produced the coin, which Fitz-Johnes, having received it, flung disdainfully down upon the table with the exclamation:

"There, caitiff, is the lucre. Now, avaunt! begone! Thy bones are marrowless; and you have not a particle of speculation about you."

The waiter, quite unmoved, took up the sovereign, laid down the change—which Fitz-Johnes promptly pocketed—and retired from the room, leaving us to discuss our wine in peace; which we did, I taking three glasses, and my companions disposing of the remainder.

Fitz-Johnes now became very communicative on the subject of his cousin Lady Mary; and finally the recollection came to him suddenly that she had sent him her miniature only a day or two before. This he proposed to show me, in order that I might pronounce an opinion as to the correctness of the likeness; but on instituting a search for it, he discovered— much to my relief, I must confess—that he had left it, with his purse, in the pocket of his other jacket.

The wine at length finished, we parted company at the door of the "Blue Posts;" I shaping a course homeward, and my new friends heading in the direction of the Hard, their uproarious laughter reaching my ear for some time after they had passed out of sight.

CHAPTER TWO

I QUIT THE PATERNAL ROOF

On reaching home I found that my father had preceded me by a few minutes only, and was to be found in the surgery. Thither, accordingly, I hastened to give him an opportunity of seeing me in my new rig.

"Good Heavens, boy!" he exclaimed when he had taken in all the details of my appearance, "do you mean to say that you have presented yourself in public in that extraordinary guise?"

I respectfully intimated that I had, and that, moreover, I failed to observe anything at all extraordinary in my appearance.

"Well," observed he, bursting into a fit of hearty laughter, notwithstanding his evident annoyance, "*you* may not have noticed it; but I'll warrant that everybody else has. Why, I should not have been surprised to hear that you had found yourself the laughing-stock of the town. Run away, Dick, and change your clothes at once; Shears must see those things and endeavour to alter them somehow; you can never wear them as they are."

I slunk away to my room in a dreadfully depressed state of mind. Was it possible that what my father had said was true! A sickening suspicion seized me that it *was*; and that I had at last found an explanation of the universal laughter which had seemed to accompany me everywhere in my wanderings that wretched afternoon.

I wrapped up the now hated uniform in the brown paper which had encased it when it came from Shears; and my father and I were about to sally forth with it upon a wrathful visit to the erring Shears, when a breathless messenger from him arrived with another parcel, and a note of explanation and apology, to the effect that by some unfortunate blunder the wrong suit had been sent home, and Mr Shears would feel greatly obliged if we would return it per bearer.

The man, upon this, was invited inside and requested to wait whilst I tried on the rightful suit, which was found to fit excellently; and I could not avoid laughing rather ruefully as I looked in the glass and contrasted my then appearance with that which I remembered it to have been in the earlier part of the day. Later on, that same evening, my sea-chest and the remainder of my outfit arrived; and I was ready to join, as had been already arranged, on the following day.

The eventful morning at length arrived; and with my enthusiasm considerably cooled by a night of sleepless excitement and the unpleasant consciousness that I was about, in an hour or two more, to bid a long farewell to home and all who loved me, I descended to the breakfast-room. My father was already there; but Eva did not come down until the last moment; and when she made her appearance it was evident that she had very recently been weeping. The dear girl kissed me silently with quivering lips, and we sat down to breakfast. My father made two or three efforts to start something in the shape of a conversation, but it was no good; the dear old gentleman was himself manifestly ill at ease; Eva could not speak a word for sobbing; and as for me, I was as unable to utter a word as I was to swallow my food—a great lump had gathered in my throat, which not only made it sore but also threatened to choke me, and it was with the utmost difficulty that I avoided bursting into a passion of tears. None of us ate anything, and at length the wretched apology for a meal was brought to a conclusion, my father read a chapter from the Bible, and we knelt down to prayers. I will not attempt to repeat here the words of his supplication. Suffice it to say that they went straight to my heart and lodged there, their remembrance encompassing me about as with a seven-fold defence in many a future hour of trial and temptation.

On rising from his knees my father invited me to accompany him to his consulting-room, and on arriving there he handed me a chair, seated himself directly in front of me, and said:

"Now, my dear boy, before you leave the roof which has sheltered you from your infancy, and go forth to literally fight your own way through the world, there is just a word or two of caution and advice which I wish to say. You are about to embark in a profession of your own deliberate choice, and whilst that profession is of so honourable a character that all who wear its uniform are unquestioningly accepted as gentlemen, it is also one which, from its very nature, exposes its followers to many and great temptations. I will not enlarge upon these; you are now old enough to understand the nature of many of them, and those which you may not at present know anything about will be readily recognisable as such when they present themselves; and a few simple rules will, I trust, enable you to overcome them. The first rule which I wish you to take for your guidance through life, my son, is this. Never be ashamed to honour your Maker. Let neither false pride, nor the gibes of your companions, nor indeed *any* influence whatever, constrain you to deny Him or your dependence upon Him; never take His name in vain, nor countenance by your continued presence any such thing in others. Bear in mind the fact that He who holds the ocean in the hollow of His hand is also the Guide, the Helper, and the defender of 'those who go down into the sea in ships;' and make it an unfailing practice to seek His help and protection every day of your life.

"Never allow yourself to contract the habit of swearing. Many men—and, because of their pernicious example, many boys too—habitually garnish their conversation with oaths, profanity, and obscenity of the vilest description. It *may* be—though I earnestly hope and pray it will not—that a bad example in this respect will be set you by even your superior officers. If such should unhappily be the case, think of this, our parting moments, and of my parting advice to you, and never suffer yourself to be led away by such example. In the first place it is wrong—it is distinctly *sinful* to indulge in such language; and in the next place, to take much lower ground, it is vulgar, ungentlemanly, and altogether in the very worst possible taste. It is not even *manly* to do so, though many lads appear to think it so; there is nothing manly, or noble, or dignified in the utterance of words which inspire in the hearers—unless they be the lowest of the low—nothing save the most extreme disgust. If you are ambitious to be classed among the vilest and most ruffianly of your species, use such language; but if your ambition soars higher than this, avoid it as you would the pestilence.

"Be always *strictly* truthful. There are two principal incentives to falsehood—vanity and fear. Never seek self-glorification by a falsehood. If fame is not to be won legitimately, do without it; and never seek to screen yourself by a falsehood—this is mean and cowardly in the last degree. 'To err is human;' we are all liable to make mistakes sometimes; such a person as an infallible man, woman, or child has never yet existed, and never will exist. Therefore, if you make a mistake, have the courage to manfully acknowledge it and take the consequences; I will answer for it that they will not be very dreadful. A fault confessed is half atoned. And, apart from the *morality* of the thing, let me tell you that a reputation for truthfulness is a priceless possession to a man; it makes his services *doubly* valuable.

"Be careful that you are always strictly honest, honourable, and upright in your dealings with others. Never let your reputation in this respect be sullied by so much as a breath. And bear this in mind, my boy, it is not sufficient that you should *be* all this, you must also *seem* it, that is to say you must keep yourself far beyond the reach of even the barest suspicion. Many a man who, by carelessness or inexperience, has placed himself in a questionable position, has been obliged to pay the penalty of his want of caution by carrying about with him, to the end of his life, the burden of a false and undeserved suspicion.

"And now there is only one thing more I wish to caution you against, and that is *vanity*. It is a failing which is only too plainly perceptible in most boys of your age, and—do not be angry, Dick, if I touch the sore spot with a heavy hand; it is for your own good that I do it—you have it in a very marked degree. Like most of your compeers you think that, having passed your fourteenth birth-day, you are now a *man*, and in many points I notice that you have already begun to ape the ways of men. Don't do it, Dick. Manhood comes not so early; and of all disagreeable and objectionable characters, save me, I pray you, from a boy who mistakes himself for a man. Manhood, with its countless cares and responsibilities, will come soon enough; whilst you are a boy *be* a boy; or, if you insist on being a man before your time, cultivate those attributes which are characteristic of *true* manhood, such as fearless truth, scrupulous honour, dauntless courage, and so on; but *don't*, for Heaven's sake, adopt the follies and vices of men. As I have said, Dick, vanity is certainly your *great* weakness, and I want you to be especially on your guard against it. It will tempt you to tamper with the truth, even if it does no worse," (I thought involuntarily of Lady Mary and my tacit admission of the justice of Lord Fitz-Johnes' impeachment of me with regard to her), "and it is quite possible that it may lead you into a serious scrape.

"Now, Dick, my boy—my dear son—I have said to you all that I think, even in the slightest degree, necessary by way of caution and advice. I can only affectionately entreat you to remember and ponder upon my words, and pray God to lead you to a right understanding of them.

"And now," he added, rising from his seat, "I think it is time you were on the move. Go and wish Eva good-bye, and then I will drive you down to the Hard—I see Edwards has brought round the carriage."

I hurried away to the drawing-room, where I knew I should find my sister, and, opening the door gently, announced that I had come to say good-bye. The dear girl, upon hearing my voice, rose up from the sofa, in the cushion of which she had been hiding her tear-stained face, and came with unsteady steps toward me. Then, as I looked into her eyes—heavy with the mental agony from which she was suffering, and which she bravely strove to hide for my sake—I realised, for the first time in my life, all the horror which lurks in that dreadful word "Farewell." Meaning originally a benediction, it has become by usage the word with which we cut ourselves asunder from all that is nearest and dearest to us; it is the signal for parting; the last word we address to our loved ones; the fatal spell at which they lingeringly and unwillingly withdraw from our clinging embrace; the utterance at which the hand-clasp of friendship or of love is loosed, and we are torn apart never perhaps again to meet until time shall be no more.

My poor sister! It was pitiful to witness her intense distress. This was our first parting. Never before had we been separated for more than an hour or two at a time, and, there being only the two of us, our mutual affection had steadily, though imperceptibly, grown and strengthened from year to year until now, when to say "good-bye" seemed like the rending of our heart-strings asunder.

It had to be said, however, and it *was* said at last—God knows how, for my recollection of our parting moments is nothing more than that of a brief period of acute mental suffering—and then, placing my half-swooning sister upon the couch and pressing a last lingering kiss on her icy-cold lips, I rushed from the room and the house.

My father had already taken his seat in the carriage; my luggage was piled up on the front seat alongside the driver, and nothing therefore remained but for me to jump in, slam-to the door, and we were off.

It seemed equally impossible to my father and to myself to utter a single word during that short—though, in our then condition of acute mental tension, all too long—drive to the Hard; we sat therefore dumbly side by side, with our hands clasped, until the carriage drew up, when I sprang out, hastily hailed a boatman, and then at once began with feverish haste to drag my belongings off the carriage down into the road. I had still to say good-bye to my father, and I felt that I *must* shorten the time as much as possible, that ten minutes more of such mental torture would drive me mad.

The boatman quickly shouldered my chest, and, gathering up

the remainder of my belongings in his disengaged hand, discreetly trotted off to the wherry, which he unmoored and drew alongside the slipway.

Then I turned to my father, and, with the obtrusive lump in my throat by this time grown so inconveniently large that I could scarcely articulate, held out my hand to him.

"Good-bye, father!" I stammered out huskily.

"Good-bye, Dick, my son, my own dear boy!" he returned, not less affected than myself. "Good-bye! May God bless and keep you, and in His own good time bring you in health and safety back to us! Amen."

A quick convulsive hand-clasp, a last hungry glance into the loving face and the sorrow-dimmed eyes which looked so longingly down into mine, and with a hardly-suppressed cry of anguish I tore myself away, staggered blindly down the slipway, tumbled into the boat, and, as gruffly as I could under the circumstances, ordered the boatman to put me on board the *Daphne*.

CHAPTER THREE

THE TRUTH ABOUT FITZ-JOHNES

"Where are we going, Tom?" I asked, as the boatman, an old chum of mine, proceeded to step the boat's mast. "You surely don't need the sail for a run half-way across the harbour?"

"No," he answered; "no, I don't. But we're bound out to Spithead. The *Daphne* went out this mornin' at daylight to take in her powder, and I 'spects she's got half of it stowed away by this time. Look out for your head, Mr Dick, sir, we shall jibe in a minute."

I ducked my head just in time to save my glazed hat from being knocked overboard by the jibing mainsail of the boat, and then drew out my handkerchief and waved another farewell to my father, whose fast-diminishing figure I could still make out standing motionless on the shore, with his hand shading his eyes as he watched the rapidly moving boat. He waved back in answer, and then the intervening hull of a ship hid him from my view, and I saw him no more for many a long day.

"Ah, it's a sorry business that, partin' with friends and kinsfolk when you're outward-bound on a long cruise that you can't see the end of!" commented my old friend Tom;

"but keep up a good heart, Mr Dick; it'll all be made up to yer when you comes home again by and by loaded down to the scuppers with glory and prize-money."

I replied somewhat drearily that I supposed it would; and then Tom—anxious in his rough kindliness of heart to dispel my depression of spirits and prepare me to present myself among my new shipmates in a suitably cheerful frame of mind—adroitly changed the subject and proceeded to put me "up to a few moves," as he expressed it, likely to prove useful to me in the new life upon which I was about to enter.

"And be sure, Mr Dick," he concluded, as we shot alongside the sloop, "be sure you remember *always* to touch your hat when you steps in upon the quarter-deck of a man-o'-war, no matter whether 'tis your own ship or a stranger."

Paying the old fellow his fare, and parting with him with a hearty shake of the hand, I sprang up the ship's side, and—remembering Tom's parting caution just in the nick of time—presenting myself in due form upon the quarter-deck, where the first lieutenant had posted himself and from which he was directing the multitudinous operations then in progress, reported myself to that much-dreaded official as "come on board to join."

He was a rather tall and decidedly handsome man, with a gentlemanly bearing and a well-knit shapely-looking figure, dark hair and eyes, thick bushy whiskers meeting under the chin, and a clear strong melodious voice, which, without the aid of a speaking-trumpet, he made distinctly heard from one end of the ship to the other. As he stood there, in an easy attitude with his hands lightly clasped behind his back and his eye taking in, as it seemed at a glance, everything that was going forward, he struck me as the *beau-ideal* of a naval officer. I took a strong liking to him on the spot, an instinctive prepossession which was afterwards abundantly justified, for Mr Austin—that was his name—proved to be one of the best officers it has ever been my good fortune to serve under.

"Oh, you're come on board to join, eh?" he remarked in response to my announcement. "I suppose you are the young gentleman about whom Captain Vernon was speaking to me yesterday. What is your name?"

I told him.

"Ah! Hawkesley! yes, that is the name. I remember now. Captain Vernon told me that although you have never been to sea as yet you are not altogether a greenhorn. What can you do?"

"I can hand, reef, and steer, box the compass, pull an oar, or sail a boat; and I know the name and place of every spar, sail, and rope throughout the ship."

"Aha! say you so? Then you will prove indeed a valuable acquisition. What is the name of this rope?"

"The main-topgallant clewline," I answered, casting my eye aloft to note the "lead" of the rope.

"Right!" he replied with a smile. "And you have the true nautical pronunciation also, I perceive. Mr Johnson,"—to a master's mate who happened to be passing at the moment— "this is Mr Hawkesley. Kindly take him under your wing and induct him into his quarters in the midshipmen's berth, if you please. Don't stop to stow away your things just now, Mr Hawkesley," he continued. "I shall have an errand for you in a few minutes."

"Very well, sir," I replied. And following my new acquaintance, I first saw to the hoisting in of my traps, and then with them descended to the place which was to be my home for so many months to come.

This was a tolerably roomy but very indifferently lighted cabin on the lower or orlop deck, access to which was gained by the descent of a very steep ladder. The furniture was of the most meagre description, consisting only of a very solid deal table, two equally solid forms or stools, and a couple of arm-chairs, one at each end of the table, all securely lashed down to the deck. There was a shelf with a ledge along its front edge, and divisions to form lockers, extending across the after-end of the berth; and under this hung three small book-cases, (which I was given to understand were private property) and a mirror six inches long by four inches wide, before which the "young gentlemen"—four in number, including myself—and the two master's mates had to perform their toilets as best they could. The fore and after bulkheads of the apartment were furnished with stout hooks to which to suspend our hammocks, which, by the by, when slung, left, I noticed, but a very small space on either side of the table; and depending from a beam overhead there hung a common horn lantern containing the most attenuated candle I ever saw—a veritable "purser's dip." This lantern, which was suspended over the centre of the table, afforded, except at meal-times or other special occasions, the sole illumination of the place. Although the ship was new, and the berth had only been occupied a few days, it was already pervaded by a very powerful odour of paint and stale tobacco-smoke, which made me anxious to quit the place with the least possible delay.

Merely selecting a position, therefore, for my chest, and leaving to the wretched lad, whom adverse fortune had made the attendant of the place, the task of lashing it down, I hastened on deck again, and presenting myself once more before the first lieutenant, announced that I was now ready to execute any commission with which he might be pleased to intrust me.

"Very well," said he. "I want you to take the gig and proceed on board the *Saint George* with this letter for the first lieutenant of that ship. Wait for an answer, and if he gives you a parcel be very careful how you handle it, as it will contain articles of a very fragile character which must on no account be damaged or broken."

The gig was thereupon piped away, and when she was in the water and her crew in her I proceeded in my most stately manner down the side and flung myself in an easily negligent attitude into the stern-sheets.

I felt at that moment exceedingly well satisfied with myself. I had joined the ship but a bare half-hour before; yet here I was, singled out from the rest of the midshipmen as the fittest person to be intrusted with an evidently important mission. I forgot not only my father's caution against vanity but also my sorrow at parting with him; my *amour propre* rose triumphant above every other feeling; the disagreeable lump in my throat subsided, and with an unconscious, but no doubt very ludicrous, assumption of condescending authority, I gave the order to—

"Shove off, and get the muslin upon her, and see that you crack on, coxswain, for I am in a hurry."

"Ay, ay, sir," returned that functionary in a very respectful tone of voice. "Step the mast, for'ard there, you sea-dogs, 'and get the muslin on her.'"

With a broad grin, whether at the verbatim repetition of my

order, or in consequence of some pantomimic gesture on the part of the coxswain, who was behind me—I had a sudden painful suspicion that it might possibly be *both*—the men sprang to obey the order; and in another instant the mast was stepped, the halliard and tack hooked on, the sheet led aft, and the sail was all ready for hoisting.

"What d'ye say, Tom; shall us take down a reef!" asked one of the men.

"Reef? No, certingly not. Didn't you hear the gentleman say as how we was to 'crack on' because he's in a hurry? Give her whole canvas," replied the coxswain.

With a shivering flutter and a sudden violent jerk the sail was run up; and, careening gunwale-to, away dashed the lively boat toward the harbour.

It was blowing fresh and squally from the eastward, and for the first mile of our course there was a nasty choppy sea for a boat. The men flung their oil-skins over their shoulders, and ranging themselves along the weather side of the boat, seated themselves on the bottom-boards, and away we went, jerk-jerking through it, the sea hissing and foaming past us to leeward, and the spray flying in a continuous heavy shower in over the weather-bow and right aft, drenching me through and through in less than five minutes.

"I'm afeard you're gettin' rayther wet, sir," remarked the coxswain feelingly when I had just about arrived at a condition of complete saturation; "perhaps you'd better have my oil-skin, sir."

"No, thanks," I replied, "I am very comfortable as I am."

This was, to put it mildly, a perversion of the truth. I was *not* very comfortable; I was wet to the skin, and my bran-new uniform, upon which I so greatly prided myself, was just about ruined. But it was then too late for the oil-skin to be of the slightest benefit to me; and, moreover, I did not choose that those men should think I cared for so trifling a matter as a wetting.

But a certain scarcely-perceptible ironical inflection in the coxswain's voice, when he so kindly offered me the use of his jumper, suggested the suspicion that perhaps he was quietly amusing himself and his shipmates at my expense, and that the drenching I had received was due more to his management of the boat than anything else, so I set myself quietly to watch.

I soon saw that my suspicion was well-founded. The rascal, instead of easing the boat and meeting the heavier seas as he ought to have done, was sailing the craft at top speed right through them, varying the performance occasionally by keeping the boat broad away when a squall struck her, causing her to career until her gunwale went under, and as a natural consequence shipping a great deal of water.

At length he rather overdid it, a squall striking the boat so heavily that before he could luff and shake the wind out of the sail she had filled to the thwarts. I thought for a moment that we were over, and so did the crew of the boat, who jumped to their feet in consternation. Being an excellent swimmer myself, however, I managed to perfectly retain my *sang-froid*, whilst I also recognised in the mishap an opportunity to take the coxswain down a peg or two.

Lifting my legs, therefore, coolly up on the side seat out of reach of the water, I said:

"How long have you been a sailor, coxswain?"

"Nigh on to seven year, sir. Now then, lads, dowse the sail smartly and get to work with the bucket."

"Seven years, have you?" I returned placidly. "Then you *ought* to know how to sail a boat by this time. I have never yet been to sea; but I should be ashamed to make such a mess of it as this."

To this my friend in the rear vouchsafed not a word in reply, but from that moment I noticed a difference in the behaviour of the men all round. They found they had not got quite the greenhorn to deal with that they had first imagined.

When at last the boat was freed of the water and sail once more made upon her, I remarked to the coxswain:

"Now, Tom—if that is your name—you have amused yourself and your shipmates at my expense—to your heart's content, I hope—you have played off your little practical joke upon me, and I bear no malice. But—let there be no more of it—do you understand?"

"Ay ay, sir; I underconstumbles," was the reply; "and I'm right sorry now as I did it, sir, and I axes your parding, sir; that I do. Dash my buttons, though, but you're a rare plucky young gentleman, you are, sir, though I says it to your face. And I hopes, sir, as how you won't bear no malice again' me for just tryin' a bit to see what sort o' stuff you was made of, as it were?"

I eased the poor fellow's mind upon this point, and soon afterwards we arrived alongside the *Saint George*.

I found the first lieutenant, and duly handed over my despatch, which he read with a curious twitching about the corners of the mouth.

Having mastered the contents, he retired below, asking me to wait a minute or two.

At that moment my attention was attracted to a midshipman in the main rigging, who, with exaggerated deliberation, was making his unwilling way aloft to the mast-head as it turned out. A certain familiar something about the young gentleman caused me to look up at him more attentively; and I then at once recognised my recent acquaintance, Lord Fitz-Johnes. At the same moment the second lieutenant, who was eyeing his lordship somewhat wrathfully, hailed him with:

"Now then, Mr Tomkins, are you going to be all day on your journey? Quicken your movements, sir, or I will send a boatswain's mate after you with a rope's-end to freshen your way. Do you hear, sir?"

"Ay ay, sir," responded the *ci-devant* Lord Fitz-Johnes—now plain Mr Tomkins—in a squeaky treble, as he made a feeble momentary show of alacrity. Just then I caught his eye, and, taking off my hat, made him an ironical bow of recognition, to which he responded by pressing his body against the rigging—pausing in his upward journey to give due effect to the ceremony—spreading his legs as widely apart as possible, and extending both hands toward me, the fingers outspread, the thumb of the right hand pressing gently against the point of his nose, and the thumb of the left interlinked with the right-hand little finger. This salute was made still more impressive by a lengthened slow and solemn twiddling of the fingers, which was only brought to an end by the second lieutenant hailing:

"Mr Tomkins, you will oblige me by prolonging your stay at the mast-head until the end of the afternoon watch, if you please."

As the answering "Ay ay, sir," came sadly down from aloft, I felt a touch on my arm, and, turning round, found my second acquaintance, Lord Tomnoddy, by my side. As I looked at him I felt strongly inclined to ask him whether *he* also had changed his name since our last meeting.

"Oh, look here, Hawksbill," he commenced, "I'm glad you've come on board; I wanted to see you in order that I might repay you the sovereign you lent us the other day. Here it is,"—selecting the coin from a handful which he pulled out of his breeches pocket and thrusting it into my hand—"and I am very much obliged to you for the loan. I *really* hadn't a farthing in my pocket at the time, or I wouldn't have allowed Tomkins to borrow it from you—and it was awfully stupid of me to let you go away without saying where I could send it to you."

"Pray do not say anything further about it, Mr—, Mr—."

"I am Lord Southdown, at your service—*not* Lord Tomnoddy, as my whimsical friend Tomkins dubbed me the other day. It is perfectly true," he added somewhat haughtily, and then with a smile resumed: "but I suppose I must not take offence at your look of incredulity, seeing that I was a consenting party to that awful piece of deception which Tomkins played off upon you. Ha, ha, ha! excuse me, but I really wish you could have seen yourself when that mischievous friend of mine accused you of—of—what was it? Oh, yes, of playing fast and loose with the affections of the fictitious Lady Sara, or whatever the fellow called her. And then again, when he remarked upon your extraordinary resemblance to Lord—Somebody—another fictitious friend of his, and directed attention to your 'lofty intellectual forehead, your proud eagle-glance, your—' oh, dear! it was *too* much."

And off went his lordship into another paroxysm of laughter, which sent the tears coursing down his cheeks and caused me to flush most painfully with mortification.

"Upon my word, Hawksbill—" he commenced.

"My name is Hawkesley, my lord, at your service," I interrupted, somewhat angrily I am afraid.

"I beg your pardon, Mr Hawkesley; the mistake was a perfectly genuine and unintentional one, I assure you. I was going to apologise—as I *do*, most heartily, for laughing at you in this very impertinent fashion. But, my dear fellow, let me advise you as a friend to overcome your very conspicuous vanity. I am, perhaps, taking a most unwarrantable liberty in presuming to offer you advice on so delicate a subject, or, indeed, in alluding to it at all; but, to tell you the truth, I have taken rather a liking for you in spite of—ah—ahem—that is—I mean that you struck me as being a first-rate fellow notwithstanding the little failing at which I have hinted. You are quite good enough every way to pass muster without the necessity for any attempt to clothe yourself with fictitious attributes of any kind. Of course, in the ordinary run of events you will soon be laughed out of your weakness—there is no place equal to a man-of-war for the speedy cure of that sort of thing—but the process is often a very painful one to the patient—I have passed through it myself, so I can speak from experience—so *very* painful was it to me that, even at the risk of being considered impertinent, I have ventured to give you a friendly caution, in the hope that your good sense will enable you to profit by it, and so save you many a bitter mortification. Now I *hope* I have not offended you?"

"By no means, my lord," I replied, grasping his proffered hand. "On the contrary, I am very sincerely obliged to you—"

At this moment the first lieutenant of the *Saint George* reappeared on deck, and coming up to me with Mr Austin's letter open in his hand, said:

"My friend Mr Austin writes me that you are quite out of eggs on board the *Daphne*, and asks me to lend him a couple of dozen." (Here was another take-down for me; the important despatch with which I—*out of all the midshipmen on board*—had been intrusted was simply a request for the loan of two dozen eggs!) "He sends to me for them instead of procuring them from the shore, because he is afraid you may lose some of your boat's crew." (Evidently Mr Austin had not the high opinion of me that I fondly imagined he had.) "I am sorry to say I cannot oblige Mr Austin; but I think we can overcome the difficulty if you do not mind being delayed a quarter of an hour or so. I have a packet which I wish to send ashore, and if you will give Lord Southdown here—who seems to be a friend of yours—a passage to the Hard and off again, he will look after your boat's crew for you whilst you purchase your eggs."

I of course acquiesced in this proposal; whereupon Lord Southdown was sent into the captain's cabin for the packet in question; and on his reappearance a few minutes later we jumped into the boat and went ashore together, his lordship regaling me on the way with sundry entertaining anecdotes whereof his humorous friend Tomkins was the hero.

We managed to execute our respective errands without losing any of the boat's crew; and duly putting Lord Southdown on board the *Saint George* again, I returned triumphantly to the *Daphne* with my consignment of eggs and handed them over intact to Mr Austin. After which I dived below, just in time to partake of the first dinner provided for me at the expense of His Most Gracious Majesty George IV.

For the remainder of that day and during the whole of the next, until nearly ten o'clock at night, we were up to our eyes in the business of completing stores, etcetera, and, generally, in getting the ship ready for sea; and at daybreak on the second morning after I had joined, the fore-topsail was loosed, blue peter run up to the fore royal-mast head, the boats hoisted in and stowed, and the messenger passed, after which all hands went to breakfast. At nine o'clock the captain's gig was sent on shore, and at 11 a.m. the skipper came off; his boat was hoisted up to the davits, the canvas loosed, the anchor tripped, and away we went down the Solent and out past the Needles, with a slashing breeze at east-south-east and every stitch of canvas set, from the topgallant studding-sails downwards.

CHAPTER FOUR

A BOAT-EXCURSION INTO THE CONGO

Our skipper's instructions were to the effect that he was, in the first instance, to report himself to the governor of Sierra Leone; and it was to that port, therefore, that we now made the best of our way.

The breeze with which we started carried us handsomely down channel and half-way across the Bay of Biscay, and the ship proving to be a regular flyer, everybody, from the skipper downwards, was in the very best of spirits. Then came a change, the wind backing out from south-west with squally weather which placed us at once upon a taut bowline; and simultaneously with this change of weather a most disagreeable discovery was made, namely, that the *Daphne* was an exceedingly crank ship.

However, we accomplished the passage in a little over three weeks; and after remaining at Sierra Leone for a few hours only, proceeded for the mouth of the Congo, off which we expected to fall in with the *Fawn*, which ship we had been sent out to relieve. Proceeding under easy canvas, in the hope of picking up a prize by the way—in which hope, so however, we were disappointed—we reached our destination in twenty-three days from Sierra Leone; sighting the *Fawn* at daybreak and closing with her an hour afterwards. Her skipper came on board the *Daphne* and remained to breakfast with Captain Vernon, whom—our skipper being a total stranger to the coast—he posted up pretty thoroughly in the current news, as well as such of the "dodges" of the slavers as he had happened to have picked up. He said that at the moment there were no ships in the river, but that intelligence—whether trustworthy or no, however, he could not state—had reached him of the daily-expected arrival of three ships from Cuba. He also confirmed a very extra-ordinary story which had been told our skipper by the governor of Sierra Leone, to the effect that large cargoes of slaves, known to have been collected on shore up the river, awaiting the arrival of the slavers, had from time to time disappeared in a most mysterious manner, at times when, as far as could be ascertained, no craft but men-o'-war were anywhere near the neighbourhood. At noon the *Fawn* filled away and bore up for Jamaica—whither she was to proceed preparatory to returning home to be paid off—her crew manning the rigging and giving us a parting cheer as she did so; and two hours later her royals dipped below the horizon, and we were left alone in our glory.

On parting from the *Fawn* we filled away again upon the starboard tack, the wind being off the shore, and at noon brought the ship to an anchor in nine fathoms of water off Padron Point (the projecting headland on the southern side of the river's mouth) at a distance of two miles only from the shore. The order was then given for the men to go to dinner as soon as that meal could be got ready; it being understood that, notwithstanding the *Fawn's* assurance as to there being no ships in the river, our skipper intended to satisfy himself of that fact by actual examination. Moreover, the deserted state of the river afforded us an excellent opportunity for making an unmolested exploration of it—making its acquaintance, so to speak, in order that at any future time, if occasion should arise, we might be able to make a dash into it without feeling that we were doing so absolutely blindfold.

At 1:30 p.m. the gig was piped away; Mr Austin being in charge, with me for an *aide*, all hands being fully armed.

The wind had by this time died away to a dead calm; the sun was blazing down upon us as if determined to roast us as we sat; and we had a long pull before us, for although the ship lay only two miles from the shore, we had to round a low spit, called, as Mr Austin informed me, Shark Point, six miles away, in a north-easterly direction, before we could be said to be fairly in the river.

For this point, then, away we stretched, the perspiration streaming from the men at every pore. Fortunately the tide had begun to make before we started, and it was therefore in our favour. We had a sounding-line with us, which we used at frequent intervals; and by its aid we ascertained that at a distance of one mile from the shore the shallowest water between the ship and Shark Point was about three and a half fathoms at low water. This was at a spot distant some three and a half miles from the point. Half a mile further on we suddenly deepened our water to forty-five fathoms; and at a distance of only a quarter of a mile from the point as we rounded it, the lead gave us fifteen fathoms, shortly afterwards shoaling to six fathoms, which depth was steadily maintained for a distance of eight miles up the river, the extent of our exploration on this occasion. On our return journey we kept a little further off the shore, and found a corresponding increase in the depth of water; a result which fully satisfied us that we need have no hesitation about taking the *Daphne* inside should it at any time seem desirable so to do.

Immediately abreast of Shark Point is an extensive creek

named Banana Creek; and hereabouts the river is fully six miles wide. On making out the mouth of this creek it was our first intention to have explored it; but on rounding the point and fairly entering the river, we made out so many snug, likely-looking openings on the southern side that we determined to confine our attention to that side first.

In the first place, immediately on rounding Shark Point we discovered a bay at the back of it, roughly triangular in shape, about four miles broad across the base, and perhaps three miles deep from base to apex. At the further end of the base of this triangular bay we descried the mouth of the creek; and at the apex or bottom of the bay, another. The latter of these we examined first, making the discovery that the mouth or opening gave access to *three* creeks instead of one; they were all, however, too shallow to admit anything drawing over ten feet, even at high-water; and the land adjoining was also so low and the bush so stunted—consisting almost exclusively of mangroves—that only a partial concealment could have been effected unless a ship's upper spars were struck for the occasion. A low-rigged vessel, such as a felucca, would indeed find complete shelter in either of the two westernmost creeks—the easternmost had only three feet of water in it when we visited it; but the shores on either side consisted only of a brownish-grey fetid mud, of a consistency little thicker than pea-soup; and the facilities for embarking slaves were so utterly wanting that we felt sure we need not trouble ourselves at any future time about either of these creeks.

The other creek, that which I have described as situated at the further end of the base of the triangle forming the bay, was undoubtedly more promising; though, like the others, it could only receive craft of small tonnage, having a little bar of its own across its mouth, on which at half-tide, which was about the time of our visit, there was only seven feet of water. Its banks, however, were tolerably firm and solid; the jungle was thicker and higher; though little more than a cable's length wide at its mouth, it was nearly a mile in width a little further in; and branching off from it, right and left, there were three or four other snug-looking little creeks, wherein a ship of light draught might lie as comfortably as if in dry-dock, and wherein, by simply sending down top-gallant-masts, she would be perfectly concealed. Mr Austin would greatly have liked to land here and explore the bush a bit on each side of the creek; but our mission just then was to make a rough survey of the river rather than of its banks, so we reluctantly made our way back once more to the broad rolling river.

A pull of a couple of miles close along the shore brought us to the entrance of another creek, which for a length of two miles averaged quite half a mile wide, when it took a sharp bend to the right, or in a southerly direction, and at the same time narrowed down to less than a quarter of a mile in width. For the first two miles we had plenty of water, that is to say, there was never less than five fathoms under our keel; but with the narrowing of the creek it shoaled rapidly, so that by the time we had gone another mile we found ourselves in a stream about a hundred yards wide and only six feet deep. The mangrove-swamp, however, had ceased; and the grassy banks, shelving gently down to the water on each side, ended in a narrow strip of reddish sandy beach. The bush here was very dense and the vegetation extremely varied, whilst the foliage seemed to embrace literally all the colours of the rainbow. Greens of course predominated, but they were of every conceivable shade, from the pale delicate tint of the young budding leaf to an olive which was almost black. Then there was the ruddy bronze of leaves which appeared just ready to fall; and thickly interspersed among the greens were large bushes with long lance-shaped leaves of a beautifully delicate ashen-grey tint; others glowed in a rich mass of flaming scarlet; whilst others again had a leaf thickly covered with short white sheeny satin-like fur—I cannot otherwise describe it—which gleamed and flashed in the sun-rays as though the leaves were of polished silver. Some of the trees were thickly covered with blossoms exquisite both in form and colour; while as to the passion-plant and other flowering creepers, they were here, there, and every-where in such countless varieties as would have sent a botanist into the seventh heaven of delight.

That this vast extent of jungle was not tenantless we had frequent assurance in the sudden sharp cracking of twigs and branches, as well as other more distant and more mysterious sounds; an occasional glimpse of a monkey was caught high aloft in the gently swaying branches of some forest giant; and birds of gorgeous plumage but more or less discordant cries constantly flitted from bough to bough, or swept in rapid flight across the stream.

We were so enchanted with the beauty of this secluded creek that though the time was flitting rapidly away Mr Austin could not resist the temptation to push a little further on, notwithstanding the fact that we had already penetrated higher than a ship, even of small tonnage, could possibly reach; and the men, nothing loath, accordingly paddled gently ahead for another mile. At this point we discovered that the tide was met and stopped by a stream of thick muddy fresh water; the creek or river, whichever you choose to call it, had narrowed in until it was only about a hundred feet across; and the water had shoaled to four feet. The trees in many places grew right down to the water's edge; the roots of some, indeed, were actually covered, and here and there the more lofty ones, leaning over the stream on either side, mingled their foliage overhead and formed a leafy arch, completely excluding the sun's rays and throwing that part of the river which they overarched into a deep green twilight shadow to which the eye had to become accustomed before it was possible to see anything. A hundred yards ahead of us there was a long continuous *tunnel* formed in this way; and, on entering it, the men with one accord rested on their oars and allowed the boat to glide onward by her own momentum, whilst they looked around them, lost in wonder and admiration.

As we shot into this watery lane, and the roll of the oars in the rowlocks ceased, the silence became profound, almost oppressively so, marked and emphasised as it was by the lap and gurgle of the water against the boat's planking. Not a bird was here to be seen; not even an insect—except the mosquitoes, by the by, which soon began to swarm round us in numbers amply sufficient to atone for the absence of all other life. But the picture presented to our view by the long avenue of variegated foliage, looped and festooned in every direction with flowery creepers loaded with blooms of the most gorgeous hues; and the deep green—almost black— shadows, contrasted here and there with long arrowy shafts of greenish light glancing down through invisible openings in the leafy arch above, and lighting up into prominence some feathery spray or drooping flowery wreath, was enchantingly beautiful.

We were all sitting motionless and silent, wrapped in admiration of the enchanting scene, all the more enchanting, perhaps, to us from its striking contrast to the long monotony of sea and sky only upon which our eyes had so lately rested, when a slight, sharp, crackling sound—proceeding from apparently but a short distance off in the bush on our port bow—arrested our attention. The boat had by this time lost her way, and the men, abruptly roused from their trance of wondering admiration, were about once more to dip their oars in the water when Mr Austin's uplifted hand arrested them.

The sounds continued at intervals; and presently, without so much as the rustling of a bough to prepare us for the apparition, a magnificent antelope emerged from the bush about fifty yards away, and stepped daintily down into the water. His quick eye detected in an instant the unwonted presence of our boat and ourselves, and instead of bowing his head at once to drink, as had evidently been his first intention, he stood motionless as a statue, gazing wonderingly at us. He was a superb creature, standing as high at the shoulders as a cow, with a smooth, glossy hide of a very light chocolate colour—except along the belly and on the inner side of the thighs, where the hair was milk-white—and long, sharp, gracefully curving horns. We were so close to him that we could even distinguish the greenish lambent gleam of his eyes.

Mr Austin very cautiously reached out his hand for a musket which lay on the thwart beside him, and had almost grasped it, when—in the millionth part of a second, as it seemed to me, so rapid was it—there was a flashing swirl of water directly in front of the deer, and before the startled creature had time to make so much as a single movement to save itself, an immense alligator had seized it by a foreleg and was tug-tugging at it in an endeavour to drag it into deep water. The deer, however, though taken by surprise and at a disadvantage, was evidently determined not to yield without a struggle, and, lowering his head, he made lunge after lunge at his antagonist with the long, sharply-pointed horns which had so excited my admiration, holding bravely back with his three disengaged legs the while.

"Give way, men," shouted Mr Austin in a voice which made the leafy archway ring again. "Steer straight for the crocodile, Tom; plump the boat right on him; and, bow-oar, lay in and stand by to prod the fellow with your boat-hook. Drive it into him under the arm-pit if you can; that, I believe, is his most vulnerable part."

Animated by the first lieutenant's evident excitement, the men dashed their oars into the water, and, with a tug which made the stout ash staves buckle like fishing-rods, sent the boat forward with a rush.

The alligator—or crocodile, whichever he happened to be—was, however, in the meantime, getting the best of the struggle, dragging the antelope steadily ahead into deeper water every instant, in spite of the beautiful creature's desperate resistance. We were only a few seconds in reaching the scene of the conflict, yet during that brief period the buck had been dragged forward until the water was up to his belly.

"Hold water! back hard of all!" cried Mr Austin, standing up in the stern-sheets, musket in hand, as we ranged up alongside the frantic deer. "Now give it him with your boat-hook; drive it well home into him. That's your sort, Ben; another like that, and he *must* let go. Well struck! now another—"

Bang!

The crocodile had suddenly released his hold upon the antelope; and the creature no sooner felt itself free than it wheeled round, and, on three legs—the fourth was broken above the knee-joint, or probably *bitten* in two—made a gallant dash for the shore. But our first lieutenant was quite prepared for such a movement, had anticipated it, in fact, and the buck had barely emerged from the water when he was cleverly dropped by a bullet from Mr Austin's musket. The boat was thereupon promptly beached, the buck's throat cut, and the carcass stowed away in the stern-sheets, which it pretty completely filled. We were just about to shove off again when the first lieutenant caught sight of a banana-tree, with the fruit just in right condition for cutting; so we added to our spoils three huge bunches of bananas, each as much as a man could conveniently carry.

The deepening shadows now warned us that the sun was sinking low; so we shoved off and made the best of our way back to the river. When we reached it we found that there was a small drain of the flood-tide still making, and, the land-breeze not yet having sprung up, Mr Austin determined to push yet a little higher up the river. The boat's head was accordingly pointed to the eastward, and, four miles further on, we hit upon another opening, into which we at once made our way.

We had no sooner entered this creek, however, than we found that, like the first we had visited, it forked into two, one branch of which trended to the south-west and the other in a south-easterly direction. We chose the latter, and soon found ourselves pulling along a channel very similar to the last one we had explored, except that, in the present instance, the first of a chain of hills, stretching away to the eastward, lay at no great distance ahead of us. A pull of a couple of miles brought us to a bend in the stream; and in a few minutes afterwards we found ourselves sweeping along close to the base of the hills, in a channel about a quarter of a mile wide and with from three to four and a half fathoms of water under us. Twenty minutes later the channel again divided, one branch continuing on in an easterly direction, whilst the other—which varied from a half to three-quarters of a mile in width—branched off abruptly to the northward and westward. Mr Austin chose this channel, suspecting that it would lead into the river again, a suspicion which another quarter of an hour proved correct.

The sun was by this time within half an hour of setting, and Shark Point—or rather the tops of the mangroves growing upon it—lay stretched along the horizon a good eleven miles off, so it was high time to see about returning. But the tide had by this time turned and was running out pretty strongly in mid-channel; the land-breeze also had sprung up, and, though where we were, close inshore, we did not feel very much of it, was swaying the tops of the more lofty trees in a way which I am sure must have gladdened the hearts of the boat's crew; so the oars were laid in, the mast stepped, and the lug hoisted, and in another ten minutes we were bowling down stream—what with the current and the breeze, both of which we got in their full strength as soon as we had hauled a little further out from the bank—at the rate of a good honest ten knots per hour.

The sun went down in a bewildering blaze of purple and crimson and gold when we were within five miles of Shark Point; and, ten minutes afterwards, night—the glorious night of the tropics—was upon us in all its loveliness. The heavens were destitute of cloud—save a low bank down on the western horizon—and the soft velvety blue-black of the sky was literally powdered with countless millions of glittering gems. I do not remember that I ever before or since saw so many of the smaller stars; and as for the larger stars and the planets, they shone down upon us with an effulgence which caused them to be reflected in long shimmering lines of golden light upon the turbid water.

Presently the boat's lug-sail, which spread above and before us like a great blot of ghostly grey against the starlit sky, began perceptibly to pale and brighten until it stood out clear and distinct, bathed in richest primrose light, with the shadow of the mast drawn across it in ebony-black. Striking the top of the sail first, the light swept gradually down; and in less than a minute the whole of the boat, with the crew and ourselves, were completely bathed in it. I looked behind me to ascertain the cause of this sudden glorification, and, behold! there was the moon sweeping magnificently into view above the distant tree-tops, her full orb magnified to three or four times its usual dimensions and painted a glorious ruddy orange by the haze which began to rise from the bosom of the river. Under the magic effect of the moonlight the noble river, with its background of trees and bush rising dim and ghostly above the wreathing mist and its swift-flowing waters shimmering in the golden radiance, presented a picture the dream-like beauty of which words are wholly inadequate to describe. But I am willing to confess that my admiration lost a great deal of its ardour when Mr Austin informed me that the mist which imparted so subtle a charm to the scene was but the forerunner of the deadly miasmatic fog which makes the Congo so fatal a river to Europeans; and I was by no means sorry when we found ourselves, three-quarters of an hour later, once more in safety alongside the *Daphne*, having succeeded in making good our escape before the pestilential fog overtook us. Our prizes, the buck and the bananas, were cordially welcomed on board the old barkie; the bananas being carefully suspended from the spanker-boom to ripen at their leisure, whilst the buck was handed over to the butcher to be operated upon forthwith, so far at least as the flaying was concerned; and on the morrow all hands, fore and aft, enjoyed the unwonted luxury of venison for dinner.

Mr Austin having duly reported to Captain Vernon that the river was just then free of shipping, we hove up the anchor that same evening, at the end of the second dog-watch, and stood off from the land all night under easy canvas.

CHAPTER FIVE

THE "VESTALE"

About three bells in the forenoon watch next morning the look-out aloft reported a sail on the larboard bow; and, on being questioned in the usual manner, he shouted down to us the further information that the stranger was a brig working in for the land on the starboard tack under topgallant-sails, and that she had all the look of a man-o'-war.

By six bells we had closed each other within a mile; and a few minutes afterwards the stranger crossed our bows, and, laying her main topsail to the mast, lowered a boat. Perceiving that her captain wanted to speak us, we of course at once hauled our wind and, backing our main topsail, hove-to about a couple of cables' lengths to windward of the brig. She was as beautiful a craft as a seaman's eye had ever rested on: long and low upon the water, with a superbly-modelled hull, enormously lofty masts with a saucy rake aft to them, and very taunt heavy yards. She mounted seven guns of a side, apparently of the same description and weight as our own—long 18-pounders, and there was what looked suspiciously like a long 32-pounder on her forecastle. She was flying French colours, but she certainly looked at least as much like an English as she did like a French ship.

The boat dashed alongside us in true man-o'-war style; our side was duly manned, and presently there entered through the gangway a man dressed in the uniform of a lieutenant in the French navy. He was of medium height and rather square built; his skin was tanned to a deep mahogany colour; his hair and bushy beard were jet black, as also were his piercing, restless eyes; and though rather a handsome man, his features wore a fierce and repellent expression, which, however, passed away as soon as he began to speak.

"Bon jour, m'sieu," he began, raising his uniform cap and bowing to Mr Austin, who met him at the gangway. "What chip dis is, eh?"

"This, sir, is His Britannic Majesty's sloop *Daphne*. What brig is that?"

"That, sair, is the Franch brigue of war *Vestale*; and I am Jules Le Breton, her first leeftant, at your serveece. Are you le capitaine of this vaisseau?"

"No, sir; I am the first lieutenant, and my name is Austin," with a bow. "Captain Vernon is in his cabin. Do you wish to see him?"

At that moment the skipper made his appearance from below, and stepping forward, the French lieutenant was presented to him with all due formality by Mr Austin.

It being my watch on deck I was promenading fore and aft just to leeward of the group, and consequently overheard pretty nearly everything that passed. The *Vestale*, it appeared from Monsieur Le Breton's statement, had just returned to the coast from a fruitless chase half across the Atlantic after a large barque which had managed to slip out of the Congo and dodge past them some three weeks previously, and she was now about to look in there once more in the hope of meeting with better fortune. And, judging from the course we were steering that we had just left the river, Monsieur Le Breton had, "by order of Capitane Dubosc, ventured upon the liberte" of boarding us in order to ascertain the latest news.

The skipper of course mentioned our exploring expedition of the previous day, assured him of the total absence of all ships from the river, and finally invited him into the cabin to take wine with him.

They were below fully half an hour, and when they returned to the deck the Frenchman was chattering away in very broken English in the most lively manner, and gesticulating with his hands and shoulders as only a Frenchman can. But notwithstanding the animation with which he was conversing, I could not help noticing that his eyes were all over the ship, not in an abstracted fashion, but evidently with the object of thoroughly "taking stock" of us. It struck me, too, that his English was too broken to be quite genuine—or rather, to be strictly correct, that it was not always broken to the same extent. For instance, he once or twice used the word "the," uttering it as plainly as I could; and at other times I noticed that he called it "ze" or "dee." And I detected him ringing the changes in like manner on several other words. From which I inferred that he was not altogether as fair and above-board with us as he wished us to believe. I felt half disposed to seize an early opportunity to mention the matter to Mr Austin; but then, on the other hand, I reflected that Monsieur Le Breton could hardly have any possible reason for attempting to deceive us in any way, and so for the moment the matter passed out of my mind.

At length our visitor bowed himself down over the side, throwing one last lingering look round our decks as he did so, and in another five minutes was once more on board his own ship, which, hoisting up her boat, filled her main topsail, and, with a dip of her ensign by way of "good-bye," resumed her course.

"Thank Heaven I've got rid of the fellow at last!" exclaimed Captain Vernon with a laugh, when the brig was once more fairly under weigh. "He has pumped me dry; such an inquisitive individual I think I never in my life encountered before. But I fancy I have succeeded in persuading him that he will do no good by hanging about the coast hereabouts. We want no Frenchmen to help us with our work; and I gave him so very discouraging an account of the state of things here, that I expect they will take a trip northward after looking into the river."

We continued running off the land for the remainder of that day, the whole of the following night, and up to noon next day, with a breeze which sent us along, under topsails only, at a rate of about six knots an hour. On the following day, at six bells in the forenoon watch (11 a.m.), the look-out aloft reported a something which he took to be floating wreckage, about three points on the port bow; and Mr Smellie, our second lieutenant, at once went aloft to the foretopmast crosstrees to have a look at it through his telescope. A single glance sufficed to acquaint him with the fact that the object, which was about six miles distant, was a raft with people upon it, who were making such signals as it was in their power to make with the object of attracting our attention. Upon the receipt of this news on deck Captain Vernon at once ordered the ship's course to be altered to the direction of the raft, a gun being fired and the ensign run up to the gaff-end at the same time.

It was a trifle past noon when the *Daphne* rounded-to about a hundred yards to windward of the raft, and sent away a boat to pick up those upon it. It was a wretched make-shift structure, composed of a spar or two, some half-burned hen-coops, and a few pieces of charred bulwark-planking; and was so small that there was scarcely room on it for the fourteen persons it sustained. It was a most fortunate circumstance for them that the weather happened to be fine at the time; for had there been any great amount of sea running, the crazy concern could not have been kept together for half an hour. We concluded from the appearance of the affair that the castaways had been burned out of their ship; and so they had, but not in the manner we supposed. As we closed with the raft it was seen that several sharks were cruising longingly round and round it, and occasionally charging at it, evidently in the hope of being able to drag off some of its occupants. So pertinacious were these ravenous fish that the boat's crew had to fairly fight their way through them, and even to beat them off with the oars and stretchers when they had got alongside. However, the poor wretches were rescued without accident; and in a quarter of an hour from the time of despatching the boat she was once more swinging at the davits, with the rescued men, most of whom were suffering more or less severely from burns, safely below in charge of the doctor and his assistant. Later on, when their injuries had been attended to and the cravings of their hunger and thirst satisfied—they had neither eaten nor drunk during the previous forty-two hours—Captain Vernon sent for the skipper of the rescued crew, to learn from him an account of the mishap.

His story, as related to me by him during the second dog-watch, was to the following effect:—

"My name is Richards, and my ship, which hailed from Liverpool, was called the *Juliet*. She was a barque of three hundred and fifty tons register, oak built and copper fastened throughout, and was only five years old.

"Fifty-four days ago to-day we cleared from Liverpool for Saint Paul de Loando with a cargo of Manchester and Birmingham goods, sailing the same day with the afternoon tide.

"All went well with us until the day before last, when, just before eight bells in the afternoon watch, one of the hands, who had gone aloft to stow the main-topgallant-sail, reported a sail dead to leeward of us under a heavy press of canvas. I have been to Saint Paul twice before, and know pretty well the character of this coast; moreover, on my first trip I was boarded and plundered by a rascally Spaniard; so I thought I would just step up aloft and take a look at the stranger through my glass at once. Well, sir, I did so, and the conclusion I came to was, that though it was blowing very fresh I would give the ship every stitch of canvas I could show to it. The strange sail was a brig of about three hundred tons or thereabouts, with very taunt spars, a tremendous spread of canvas, and her hull painted dead black down to the copper, which had been scoured until it fairly shone again. I didn't at all like the appearance of my newly-discovered neighbour; the craft had a wicked look about her from her truck down, and the press of sail she was carrying seemed to bode me no good. So, as the *Juliet* happened to be a pretty smart vessel under her canvas, and in splendid sailing trim, I thought I would do what I could to keep the stranger at arms'-length, and when the watch was called, a few minutes afterwards, I got the topgallant-sails, royals, flying jib, main-topgallant, royal, and mizen-topmast-staysails all on the old barkie again, and we began to smoke through it, I can tell you. That done, I set the stranger by compass, and for the first hour or so I thought we were holding our own; but by sunset I could see—a great deal too plainly for my own comfort—that the brig was both weathering and fore-reaching upon us. Still she was a long way off, and had the night been dark I should have tried to dodge the fellow; but that unfortunately was no use; the sun was no sooner set than the moon rose, and of course he could see us even more plainly than we could see him. At seven o'clock he tacked, and then I felt pretty sure he meant mischief; and when, at a little before eight bells, he tacked again, this time directly in our wake, I had no further doubt about it. At this time he was about eight miles astern of us, and at midnight he ranged up on our weather quarter, slapped his broadside of seven 18-pound shot right into us without a word of warning, and ordered us to at once heave-to. My owners had unfortunately sent me to sea with only half a dozen muskets on board, and not an ounce of powder or shot; so what could I do? Nothing, of course, but heave-to as I was bid; and we accordingly backed the main topsail without a moment's delay. The brig then did the same, and lowered a boat, which five minutes later dashed alongside us and threw in upon our decks a crew of seventeen as bloodthirsty-looking ruffians as one need ever wish to see. We were, all hands fore and aft, at once bound neck and heels and huddled together aft on the monkey-poop, with two of the pirates mounting guard over us, and then the rest of the gang coolly set to work and ransacked the ship. The fellow in command of the party—a man about five feet six inches in height, square built, with deeply bronzed features and black hair and beard—made it his first business to hunt for the manifest; and having ascertained from it that we had amongst the cargo several bolts of canvas, a large quantity of new rope, four cases of watches and jewellery, and a dozen cases of beads, he first ordered me, in broken English, to inform him where these articles were stowed, and then had the hatches stripped off and the cargo roused on deck until he could get at them. When the beads, rope, canvas, and other matters that he took a fancy to, amounting to six boat loads, had been transferred to the brig, he informed me that I must point out to him the spot where I had concealed the money which he knew to be on board. Now it so happened that I had *no* money on board;

my owners are dreadfully suspicious people, and will not intrust *anybody* with a shilling more than they can help—and many a good fifty-pound note has missed its way into their pockets through their over-cautiousness; but that's neither here nor there. Well, I told the fellow we had no money on board, whereupon he whipped out his watch and told me out loud, so that all hands could hear, that he would give us five minutes in which to make up our minds whether we would hand over the cash or not; and if we decided *not* to do so he would at the end of that time set fire to the ship and leave us all to burn in her. And that's just exactly what he did."

"He actually set fire to the ship!" said I. "But of course he cast you all adrift first, and gave you at least a *chance* to save your lives?"

"I'll tell you what he did, sir," replied the merchant-skipper. "When the five minutes had expired he called for a lantern, and, when he had got it, went round and examined each man's lashings with his own eyes and hands, so as to make sure that we were all secure to his satisfaction. Then he ordered half-a-dozen bales of cotton goods to be cut open and strewed about the cabin; poured oil, turpentine, and tar over them; did the same down in the forecastle; and then capsized a cask of tar and a can of turpentine over the most inflammable goods he could put his hand upon down in the main hatchway; had the bottoms of all the boats knocked out; took away all the oars; and then set fire to the ship forward, aft, and in midships; after which he wished us all a warm journey into the next world, and went deliberately down the side into his boat. The brig stood by us until we were fairly in flames fore and aft, and then filled away on the starboard tack under all the canvas she could show to it, leaving us there to perish miserably."

"And how did you manage to effect your escape after all?"

I inquired.

"Well, sir," the skipper replied, "the ship—as you may imagine, with a cargo such as we had on board—burned like a torch. In less than five minutes after the pirates had shoved off from our side the flames were darting up through companion, hatchway, and fore-scuttle, and in a quarter of an hour she was all ablaze. Luckily for us, the ship, left to herself, had paid off before the wind, and the flames were therefore blown for'ard; but the deck upon which we were lying soon became so hot as to be quite unbearable; we were literally beginning to roast alive, and were in momentary expectation that the deck would fall in and drop us helplessly into the raging furnace below. At last, driven to desperation by the torture of mind and body from which I was suffering, I managed to roll over on my other side; and there, within an inch of my mouth, was a man's hands, lashed, like my own, firmly behind his back, and his ankles drawn close up to them. The idea seized me to try and *gnaw* through his lashings and so free him, when of course he would soon be able to cast us adrift in return. I shouted to him what I intended to do, and then set to work with my teeth upon his bonds, gnawing away for dear life. When my teeth first came into contact with the firm hard rope I thought I should never be able to do it—at least not in time to save us—but a man never knows what he can do until he tries in earnest, as I did then; and I actually succeeded, and in a few minutes too, in eating my way through one turn of the lashings. The man then strained and tugged until he managed to free himself, after which it was the work of a few minutes only to liberate the rest of us. We then hastily collected together such materials as we could first lay our hands on, and with them constructed the raft off which you took us. It was a terribly crazy affair, but we had no time to make a better one. And of course, as the ship was by that time a mass of fire fore and aft, it was impossible for us to secure an atom of provisions of any kind, or a single drop of water."

"What a story of fiendish cruelty!" I ejaculated when Richards had finished his story. "By the by," I suddenly added, moved by an impulse which I could neither analyse nor account for, "of what nationality was the leader of the pirates? Do you think he was a *Frenchman*?"

"Yes, sir, I believe he *was*, although he addressed his men in Spanish," answered Richards in some surprise. "Why do you ask, sir? Have you ever fallen in with such a man as I have described him to be?"

"Well, ye—that is, not to my knowledge," I replied hesitatingly. The fact is that Richards' description of the pirate leader had somehow brought vividly before my minds' eye the personality of Monsieur Le Breton, the first lieutenant of the French gun-brig *Vestale*; and it was this which doubtless prompted me to put the absurd question to my companion as to the nationality of the man who had so inhumanly treated him. Not, it must be understood, that I seriously for a single instant associated Monsieur Le Breton or the *Vestale* with the diabolical act of piracy to the account of which I had just listened. We had at that time no very great love of or respect for the French, it is true; but even the most bigoted of Englishmen would, I think, have hesitated to hint at the possibility of a French man-of-war being the perpetrator of such a deed.

The mere idea, the bare suggestion of such a suspicion, was so absurd that I laughed at myself for my folly in allowing it to obtrude itself, even in the most intangible form, for a single moment on my mind. And yet, such is the perversity of the human intellect, I could not, in spite of myself, quite get rid of the extravagant idea that Monsieur Le Breton was in some inexplicable way cognisant of the outrage; nor could

I forbear sketching, for Richards' benefit, as accurate a word-portrait as I could of the French lieutenant; and—I suppose on account of that same perversity—I felt no surprise whatever when he assured me that I had faithfully described to him the arch-pirate who had left him and his crew to perish in the flames. Indeed, in my then contradictory state of mind I should have been disappointed had he said otherwise. The man's conduct—his stealthy but searching scrutiny of the ship; his endeavour, as I regarded it, to mislead us with his broken English; and his excessive curiosity, as hinted at by Captain Vernon, had struck me as peculiar, to say the least of it, on the occasion of his visit to the *Daphne*. I had suspected *then* that he was not altogether and exactly what he pretended to be; and *now* Richards' identification of him from my description seemed to confirm, in a great measure, my instinctive suspicions, unreasonable, extravagant, and absurd as I admitted them to be. My first impulse—and it was a very strong one—was to take Mr Austin into my confidence, to unfold to him my suspicions and the circumstances which had given rise to them, frankly admitting at the same time their apparent enormity, and then to put the question to him whether, in his opinion, there was the slightest possibility of those suspicions being well-founded.

So strongly, so unaccountably was I urged to do this, that I had actually set out to find the first lieutenant when reflection and common sense came to my aid and asked me what was this thing that I was about to do. The answer to this question was, that with the self-sufficiency and stupendous conceit which my father had especially cautioned me to guard against, I was arrogating to myself the possession of superhuman sagacity, and (upon the flimsy foundation of a wild and extravagant fancy, backed by a mere chance resemblance, which after all might prove to be no resemblance at all if Richards could once be confronted with Monsieur Le Breton) was about to insinuate a charge of the most atrocious character against an officer holding a responsible and honourable position—a man who doubtless was the soul of honour and rectitude. A moment's reflection sufficed to convince me of the utter impossibility of the same man being in command of a pirate-brig one day and an officer of a French man-o'-war the next. I might just as reasonably have suspected the *Vestale* herself of piracy; and *that*, I well knew, would be carrying my suspicions to the uttermost extremity of idiotic absurdity. I had, in short—so I finally decided—discovered a mare's nest, and upon the strength of it had been upon the very verge of proclaiming myself a hopeless idiot and making myself the perpetual laughing-stock of the whole ship. I congratulated myself most heartily upon having paused in time, and resolved very determinedly that I would not further dwell upon the subject, or allow myself to be again lured into entertaining such superlatively ridiculous notions.

Yet only four days later I was harassed by a temporary recurrence of all my suspicions; and it was with the utmost difficulty that I combated them. I succeeded, it is true, in so far maintaining my self-control as to keep a silent tongue; but they continued persistently to haunt me until—but steady! Whither away, Dick, my lad? You are out of your course altogether and luffing into the wind's eye, instead of working steadily to windward, tack and tack, and taking the incidents of your story as you come to them.

The incident which revived my very singular suspicions was as follows:—

Upon learning the full details of Richards' story, Captain Vernon had come to the conclusion that the brig which destroyed the *Juliet* was a vessel devoted to the combined pursuits of piracy and slave-trading; that she was, in all probability, one of the three vessels reported by the *Fawn* as daily-expected to arrive on the coast from Cuba; and that it was more than likely her destination was the Congo. He therefore determined to make the best of his way back to that river, in the sanguine hope of effecting her capture; after which he intended to run down to Saint Paul de Loando to land the crew of the *Juliet*, Richards having expressed a desire to be taken there if possible.

It was on the fourth day after we had picked up the *Juliet's* crew, and we were working our way back toward the mouth of the Congo, making short tacks across the track of vessels running the notorious Middle Passage, when the look-out aloft reported a sail about three points on the weather-bow, running down toward us under a perfect cloud of canvas. It was at once conjectured that this might be Richards' late free-and-easy acquaintance outward-bound with a cargo of slaves on board; and the *Daphne* was accordingly kept away a couple of points to intercept him, the hands being ordered to hold themselves in readiness to jump aloft and make sail on the instant that the stranger gave the slightest sign of an intention to avoid us. At the same time Mr Armitage, our third lieutenant, proceeded aloft to the main topmast crosstrees with his telescope to maintain a vigilant watch upon the motions of the approaching vessel.

All hands were of course in an instant on the *qui vive*, the momentary expectation being that the stranger would shorten sail, haul upon a wind, and endeavour to evade us. But minute after minute passed without the slightest indication of any such intention, and very shortly his royals rose into view above the horizon from the deck; then followed his topgallant-sails, then his topsails, his courses next, and finally the hull of the ship appeared upon the horizon, with studding-sails alow and aloft on both sides, running down dead before the wind, and evidently going through the water at a tremendous pace.

Every available telescope in the ship was now brought to bear upon the craft, and presently her fore-royal and fore-topgallant-sail were observed to collapse, the yards slid down the mast, and the sails were clewed up, but not furled. The next instant the French tricolour fluttered out from her fore-royal-mast-head, the only position from whence it could be made visible to us; and simultaneously with its appearance the conviction came to us all that in the approaching vessel we were about to recognise our recent acquaintance the *Vestale*. Our ensign, which was already bent on to the peak-halyards, was promptly run up in response, whereupon the French ensign disappeared, to be instantly replaced by a string of signals. Our signal-book was at once produced, our answering pennant run half-mast up, and we then began to read off the following signal:

"Have you sighted?—"

Our pennant was then mast-headed to show that we understood; the flags disappeared on board the Frenchman, and another batch was run up, which, being interpreted, meant:

"Brig—"

This also was acknowledged, and the signalling was continued until the whole message was completed, thus:

"Same tonnage as—"

"Ourselves—"

"Hull—"

"Painted—"

"All black—"

"Steering west-north-west?"

The final string of flags then disappeared, and the *Vestale's* answering pennant directly afterwards showed just above her topgallant yard, indicating that she had completed her signal and awaited our reply.

The entire signal then, freely interpreted, ran thus:

"Have you sighted a brig of the same tonnage (or size) as ourselves, with hull painted all black, steering a west-north-west course?"

We answered "No;" and, in our turn, inquired whether the *Vestale* had seen or heard of such a craft.

The French gun-brig was by this time crossing our bows, distant about half a mile; her reply was accordingly made from her gaff-end, the fore-topgallant-sail and royal being at the same time sheeted-home and mast-headed.

It was to the following effect:

"Yes. Brig in question sailed from Congo yesterday, six hours before our arrival, with three hundred slaves on board."

By the time that this message had been communicated—by the slow and tedious process then in vogue—the two vessels were too far apart to render any further conversation possible, and in little more than an hour after the final hauling-down of the last signal the *Vestale's* main-royal sank beneath the verge of the western horizon, and we were once more alone.

CHAPTER SIX

IN THE CONGO ONCE MORE

I have not yet, however, stated what it was in connection with our encounter with the *Vestale* which served to fan my fantastic suspicions into flame anew, and, I may add too at the same time, mould them into a more definite shape than they had ever before taken.

It was Richards' peculiar conduct and remarks. He had manifested quite an extraordinary amount of interest in our *rencontre* with the *Vestale* from the moment of her being first reported from the mast-head, evidently sharing the hope and belief, which we all at first entertained, that the strange sail would turn out to be the brig which had served him so scurvy a trick a few days before.

It was easy to understand the excitement he exhibited so long as this remained a matter of conjecture, but when the conjecture proved to be unfounded I fully expected his excitement, if not his interest, would wane. It did not, however. He borrowed my telescope as soon as the brig became fully visible from the deck, and, placing himself at an open port, kept the tube of the instrument levelled at her until her topsails disappeared below the horizon again. I remained close beside him during the whole time, and his excitement and perplexity were so palpable that I could not refrain from questioning him as to the cause.

"I'll tell you, Mr Hawkesley," he replied. "You see that craft there? Well, I could almost stake my soul that she and the pirate-brig were built on the same stocks. The two craft are the same size to a ton, I'll swear that; and they are the same model and the same rig to a nicety. It's true I was only able to closely inspect the other craft at night-time, but it was by brilliant moonlight, and I was able to note every detail of her build, rig, and equipment almost as plainly as I now can that of the brig before us; and the two are sister-ships. They carry the same number of guns—ay, even to the long-gun I see there on the French brig's forecastle. The masts in both ships have the same rake, the yards the same spread, and the running-gear is rove and led in exactly the same manner. The only difference I can distinguish between the two ships is that yonder brig has a broad white ribbon round her, and a small figure-head painted white, whilst the pirate-craft was painted black down to her copper, and she carried a large black figure-head representing a negress with a gaudy scarf wrapped about her waist."

"Um!" I remarked. "Lend me the glass a moment, will you? Thanks!"

The *Vestale* was, at the moment, just about to cross our fore-foot, and was therefore about as near to us as she would be at all I focused the telescope—a fine powerful instrument—upon her, and could clearly see the weather-stains and the yellowish-red marks of rust in the wake of her chain-plates upon the broad white ribbon which stretched along her side. Evidently that band of white paint had been exposed to sun and storm for many a long day. Then I had a look at her figure-head. It was a half-length model of a female figure, beautifully carved, less than life-size, with one arm drooping gracefully downwards, and the other—the right—outstretched, with a gilded lamp in the right hand. That, too, was weather-stained, and the gilding tarnished by long exposure. Those pertinacious, half-formed suspicions, which Richards' words had stirred into new life were refuted; and yet, as I have said, I could *not* shake them off, try as I would, and argue with myself as I would, that they were utterly ridiculous and unreasonable.

"Look here, Mr Richards," said I; "if you really *are* as positive upon this matter as you say, I wish you would speak to Captain Vernon about it; it might—and no doubt *would*—help us very materially in effecting the capture of the pirate-brig. We have seen the *Vestale* twice, and have had so good an opportunity to note her peculiarities of structure and equipment that we shall now know her again as far off as we can see her. If, therefore, we should ever happen to fall in with a brig the exact counterpart of the *Vestale* in all respects, except as to the matters of her figure-head and the painting of her hull, I should think we may take it for granted that that brig will undoubtedly be the pirate which destroyed the *Juliet*. And you may depend upon it, my good sir, that it is that identical craft that the *Vestale* is now seeking."

"Ye-es, very likely—quite possible," he replied hesitatingly, and evidently still labouring under the feeling of perplexity I had noticed. Then, straightening himself up and passing his hand across his forehead, as though to clear away the mental cobwebs there, he added: "I'll go and speak to Captain Vernon about it at once."

And away he accordingly walked to carry out his resolve.

We stood on as we were going until eight bells in the afternoon watch that day, when the ship was hove round on the larboard tack and a course shaped for Saint Paul de Loando, our skipper having come to the conclusion that the brig referred to in the *Vestale's* signal was undoubtedly the craft which we had been on our way back to the Congo to look for, and that as, according to the gun-brig's statement, she was no longer there, we were now free to proceed direct to Saint Paul to land the burnt-out crew as soon as possible.

We entered the bay—upon the shore of which the town is built—about 10 a.m. on the second day after our last meeting with the *Vestale*, and, anchoring in ten fathoms, lowered a boat, in which Mr Richards and his crew were landed, Captain Vernon going on shore with them. The skipper remained on shore until 4 p.m., and when he came off it was easy to see that he was deeply preoccupied. The boat was at once hoisted in, the messenger passed, the anchor hove up, and away we went again, crowding sail for the Congo. As soon as the ship was clear of the Loando reef and fairly at sea once more, Captain Vernon summoned the first and second lieutenants to his cabin, where the three remained closeted with him for some time, indeed the two officers dined with him; but, whatever the matter might be, neither Mr Austin nor Mr Smellie let fall a word as to its nature, though it was evident from their manner that it was deemed of considerable import.

When I turned in that night I felt very greatly dissatisfied with myself. Those outrageous suspicions, upon which I have dwelt so much in the last few pages, seemed to be gathering new strength every day in spite of my utmost endeavours to dissipate them, and that, too, without the occurrence of anything fresh to confirm them. I accordingly took myself severely to task; subjected myself to a rigid self-examination, looking the matter square in the face; and the conclusions to which I came were—first, that I had allowed myself to be deluded into the belief that the *Vestale* herself was the craft which had committed the act of piracy of which poor Richards and his crew were the victims; and second, that I had been an unmitigated idiot for suffering myself to be so deluded. On going thoroughly over the whole question I was forced to admit to myself that there was not a particle of evidence incriminating the French gun-brig save what I had manufactured out of my own too vivid imagination; and I clearly foresaw that unless I could get rid of, or, at all events, conquer, this hallucination, I should be doing or saying something which would get me into a serious scrape. And, having at last thus settled the question—as I thought— to my own satisfaction, I rolled over in my hammock and went to sleep.

The breeze held fresh during the whole of that night; and the *Daphne* made such good progress that by eight o'clock on the following morning we found ourselves once more abreast of Padron Point at the entrance to the Congo. Sail was now shortened; the ship hove-to, and the men sent to their breakfasts; the officers also being requested to get theirs at the same time.

At 8:30 the hands were turned up, the main topsail filled, and, under topsails, jib, and spanker, and with a leadsman in the fore-chains on each side, the sloop proceeded boldly to enter the river, under the pilotage of the master, who stationed himself for the purpose on the fore-topsail yard. This was a most unusual, almost an un-heard-of, proceeding at that time, the river never having been, up to that period, properly surveyed; so we came to the conclusion that there was something to the fore a trifle out of the common; a conclusion which was very fully verified a little later on.

It was just low water as we came abreast of Shark Point— which we passed at a distance of about a mile—but we found plenty of water everywhere; and, stretching across the river's mouth, the *Daphne* finally entered Banana Creek, and anchored in six fathoms close to a smart-looking little barque of unquestionable American nationality. The sails were furled, the yards squared, ropes coiled down, and decks cleared up; and then the first cutter was piped away, Mr Smellie at the same time receiving a summons to the skipper's cabin.

The conference between the captain and the second lieutenant was but a short one; and when the latter again appeared on deck he beckoned me to him and instructed me to don my dirk, as I was to accompany him on a visit to the barque. Just as we were about to go down over the side Captain Vernon appeared on deck, and, addressing the second "luff," said.

"Whatever you do, Mr Smellie, keep my caution in mind, and do not provoke the man. Remember, that if he *is* an American—of which I have very little doubt—we cannot touch him, even if he has his hold full of slaves; so be as civil to him as you can, please; and get all the information you can out of him."

"Ay, ay, sir; I'll do my best to stroke his fur the right way, never fear," answered Smellie laughingly; and away we went.

A couple of minutes later we shot alongside the barque; and Smellie and I clambered up her side-ladder to the deck, where we were received by a lanky cadaverous-looking individual arrayed in a by no means spotless suit of white nankin topped by a very dilapidated broad-brimmed Panama straw-hat.

"Mornin', gentlemen," observed this individual, in response to our salutation; "powerful hot; ain't it?"

"Very," returned Smellie in his most amicable manner,

"but"—pointing to the awning spread fore and aft, "I see you know how to make yourselves comfortable. Your ship, I observe, is called the *Pensacola* of New Orleans. I have come on board to go through the formality of looking at your papers. You have no objection, I presume?"

"Nary objection, stranger. Look at 'em and welcome," was the reply. "I guess I'll have to trouble you to come below, though."

With this he led the way down the companion-ladder, and we followed; eventually bringing-up on the comfortably-cushioned lockers of a fine spacious airy cabin very nicely fitted up.

Seating himself opposite us, the skipper struck a hand-bell which stood on the cabin table; in response to which summons a black steward, clad, like his master, in dingy white, made his appearance from the neighbouring pantry. Our host thereupon formed his right hand into the shape of a cup and raised it to his mouth, at the same time exhibiting three fingers of his left hand; and the steward, nodding and grinning his comprehension of the mute order, withdrew, to reappear next moment with a case-bottle of rum, three glasses, and a water-monkey, or porous earthen jar, full of what proved, on our pouring it out, to be a very doubtful-looking liquid.

"Help yourselves, gentlemen," said our host, pushing the rum-bottle and water-monkey towards us. "I ain't got no wine aboard to offer you, but the liquor is real old Jamaica, and the water is genuine Mississippi; they make a first-grade mixture. But perhaps you prefer to take your liquor 'straight;' I always do."

And he forthwith practically illustrated the process of taking liquor "straight" by half-filling his tumbler with neat rum, which he swallowed at a single gulp. He then rose and retired to his state-room in search of his papers; leaving us to sip our five-water grog meanwhile.

The papers were produced, examined, and found to be perfectly correct; after which Smellie set himself to the task of "pumping" our new acquaintance; without much result, though we certainly managed to obtain one bit of valuable information from him.

"Whether there's slavers or no in this rivulet, I'll just leave you to find out, stranger," he remarked, in answer to a question of Smellie's; "I'm here about my own business, and you're here about yourn; you can't interfere with me; and I won't interfere with you. But I don't mind tellin' you that if you'd been here five days ago you'd have had a chance of nabbin' the *Black Venus*, the smartest slaver, I guess, that's ever visited this section of our sublunary sphere."

"Indeed!" exclaimed Smellie eagerly. "What sort of a craft is she? What is she like?"

"She is a brig,"—I pricked up my ears at this, and so, too, I could see, did Smellie—"of about three hundred tons register; long, and low in the water; mounts fourteen guns, seven of a side, and a long 32-pounder on her forecastle. Has very tall sticks, with a rake aft; and a tremendous spread of 'caliker.' And she's the fastest craft in all creation. *Your* ship looks as if she could travel; but I 'low she ain't a carcumstance to the *Black Venus*."

"How is she painted?" asked Smellie. "Is she all black, or does she sometimes sport a white riband?"

"Aha!" thought I; "that looks as though my suspicions are at last shared by somebody else. Richards' communication to the skipper has surely borne fruit."

"Wall," replied the Yankee with a knowing twinkle in his eye, "*when she sailed from here* she was black right down to her copper. But that ain't much to go by; I guess her skipper knows a trick or two."

"You think, then, he might alter her appearance as soon as he got outside?" insinuated Smellie.

"He might—and he mightn't," was the cautious reply.

"Um!" observed Smellie. Then, as if inspired with a sudden suspicion, he asked:

"Have you seen any men-o'-war in here lately?"

I could see by the knowing look in our Yankee friend's eyes that he read poor Smellie like a book.

"Wall," he replied. "Come to speak of it, there *was* a brig in here a few days ago that looked like a man-o'-war. She were flyin' French colours—when she flew any at all—and called herself the *Vestale*."

"Ah!" ejaculated Smellie. "Did any of her people board you?"

"You bet!" was the somewhat ambiguous answer. Not that the reply was at all ambiguous in itself; it was the peculiar emphasis with which the words were spoken, and the peculiar expression of the man's countenance as he uttered them, which constituted the ambiguity; the *words* simply implied that the *Pensacola* had been boarded; the *look* spoke volumes, but the volumes were written in an unknown tongue, so far as we at least were concerned.

"What is the *Vestale* like?" was Smellie's next question.

"Just as like the *Black Venus* as two peas in a pod," was the reply, given with evident quiet amusement.

"And how was *she* painted?" persisted Smellie. "Ah, there now, stranger, you've puzzled me!" was the unexpected answer.

"Why? Did you not say you saw her?" queried Smellie sharply.

"No, I guess not; I didn't say anything of the sort. I was ashore when her people boarded me. It was my mate that told me about it."

"Your mate? Can we see him?" exclaimed Smellie eagerly.

"Yes, I reckon," was the reply. "He's ashore now; but you've only to pull about five miles up the creek, and I calculate you'll find him somewheres."

"Thanks!" answered Smellie. "I'm afraid we can't spare the time for that. Can you tell me which of the two brigs—the *Vestale* or the *Black Venus*—sailed first from the river?"

"Wall, stranger, I'd like to help you all I could, I really would; but," with his hand wandering thoughtfully over his forehead, "I really *can't* for the life of me remember just now which of 'em it was."

The fellow was lying; I could see it, and so could Smellie; but we could not, of course, tell him so; and we accordingly thanked him for his information and rose to go, with an

uncomfortable feeling that we had received certain information, part of which was probably true whilst part was
undoubtedly false, and that we were wholly without the
means of distinguishing the one from the other.

We returned to the *Daphne* with our information, such as it
was; and Smellie at once made his report to the skipper. A
consultation followed in which the first lieutenant took part,
and at the end of half an hour the three officers reappeared
on deck, and the captain's gig was piped away.

Being suspicious, as I have already remarked, that something
unusual was brewing, I remained on deck during the
progress of this conference, so as to be at hand in the event
of my services being required; and the *Pensacola* happening
to be the most prominent object in the landscape, she
naturally came in for a large share of my attention during the
progress of the discussion above referred to. She was flying
no colours when we anchored in such close proximity to her,
a circumstance which I attributed to the fact that she was, to
all appearance, the only vessel in the river, and I was,
therefore, not much surprised when, a short time after our
visit to her, I observed her skipper go aft and run up the
American ensign to his gaff-end. But I *was* a little surprised
when he followed this up by hoisting a small red swallow-
tailed flag to his main-royal-mast-head. I asked myself what
could be the meaning of this move on his part, and it did not
take me very long to arrive at the conclusion that it was
undoubtedly meant as a signal of some sort to somebody or
other. He was scarcely likely to do such a thing for the
gratification of a mere whim. And if it was a signal, what did
it mean's and to whom was it made? There was of course the
possibility that it was a prearranged signal to his absent
mate; but, taken in conjunction with the fact that it was
exhibited almost immediately after our visit to his ship,
coupled with the other fact of his obvious attempt to keep us

in the dark with respect to certain matters, I was greatly disposed to regard it rather as a warning signal to a vessel or vessels concealed in one or other of the numerous creeks which we knew to exist in our immediate vicinity. Accordingly, on the reappearance of the second lieutenant on deck, I stepped up to him and directed his attention to the suspicious-looking red flag, and mentioned my surmises as to its meaning.

"Thank you, Mr Hawkesley," said he. "I have no doubt it *is* a signal of some kind; but what it means we have no possible method of ascertaining, and, moreover, it suits our purpose just now to take no notice of it. By the way, are you anything of a shot?"

"Pretty fair," I replied. "I can generally bring down a bird upon the wing if it is not a very long shot."

"Then put your pistols in your belt, provide yourself with a fowling-piece (I will lend you one), and be in readiness to go with us in the gig. We are bound upon a sporting expedition."

I needed no second invitation, but hurried away at once to make the necessary preparations; albeit there was a something in Mr Smellie's manner which led me to think that sport was perhaps after all a mere pretext, and that the actual object of our cruise was something much more serious.

A few minutes sufficed to complete my preparations, and when I again stepped on deck, gun in hand, Captain Vernon and Mr Smellie were standing near the gangway rather ostentatiously engaged—in full view of the American skipper—in examining their gun-locks, snapping off caps, and so on; whilst the steward was in the act of passing down over the side—with strict injunctions to those in the boat to be careful in the handling of it—a capacious basket of provisions with a snow-white cloth protruding out over its sides. The precious basket being at length safely deposited in the gig's stern-sheets, I followed it down the side; the second lieutenant came next, and the skipper bringing up the rear, we hoisted our lug-sail, the sea-breeze blowing strongly up the river, and shoved off; our motions being intently scrutinised by the Yankee skipper as long as we could make him out.

We had scarcely gone a quarter of a mile before a noble crane came sailing across our course with his head tucked in between his shoulders, his long stilt-like legs projecting astern of him, and his slowly-flapping wings almost touching the water at every stroke.

"There's a chance for you, Hawkesley," exclaimed our genial second luff; "let drive at him. All is fish that comes to our net so long as we are within range of the Yankee's telescope; fire at everything you see."

I raised my gun, pulled the trigger, and down dropped the crane into the water with a broken wing.

"Very neatly done," exclaimed the skipper approvingly. "Pick up the bird, Thomson,"—to the coxswain.

The unfortunate bird was duly picked up and hauled into the boat, though not without inflicting a rather severe wound with its long sharp beak on the hand of the man who grasped it; and we continued our course.

On reaching the mouth of the creek we hauled sharp round the projecting point, and shaped a course up and across toward the opposite side of the stream, steering for a low densely-wooded spit which jutted out into the river some eight miles distant. The tide, which was rising, was in our favour, and in an hour from the time of emerging from the creek into the main stream we had reached our destination; the boat shot into a water-way about a cable's length in width, the sail was lowered, the mast unstepped, and the men, taking to their oars, proceeded to paddle the boat gently up the creek.

We proceeded up this creek a distance of about two miles, when, coming suddenly upon a small branch, or tributary, well suited as a place of concealment for the boat, she was headed into it, and—after proceeding along the narrow canal for a distance of perhaps one hundred yards—hauled alongside the bank and secured.

CHAPTER SEVEN

MR. SMELLIE MAKES A LITTLE SURVEY

Giving the gig's crew strict injunctions not to leave their boat for a moment upon any consideration, but to hold themselves in readiness to shove off on the instant of our rejoining them—should a precipitate retreat prove necessary—Captain Vernon and Mr Smellie stepped ashore with a request that I would accompany them.

The channel or canal in which the gig was now lying was about fifty feet wide, with a depth of water of about eight feet at the point to which we had reached. Its banks were composed of soft black foetid mud in a semi-liquid state, *so* that in order to land it was necessary for us to make our way as best we could for a distance of some two hundred feet over the roots of the mangrove trees which thickly bordered the stream, before we were enabled to place our feet on solid ground.

Beyond the belt of mangroves the soil was densely covered with that heterogeneous jumble of parasitic creepers of all descriptions spoken of in Africa by the generic denomination of "bush," thickly interspersed with trees, many of which were of large size. Path there was none, not even the faintest traces of a footprint in the dry sandy soil to show that humanity had ever passed over the ground before us. It may be that ours *were* the first human footsteps which had ever pressed the soil in that particular spot; at all events it looked very much like it, and we had not travelled one hundred feet before we became fully impressed with the necessity for carefully marking our route if we had the slightest desire to find our way back again. This task was intrusted to me, and I accomplished it by cutting a twig half through, and then bending it downwards until a long light strip of the inner wood was exposed. This I did at distances of about a yard apart all along our route, whilst the skipper and Smellie went ahead and forced a passage for the party through the thick undergrowth.

The general direction of our route was about south-south-west, as nearly as the skipper could hit it off with the aid of a pocket-compass, and it took us more than two hours to accomplish a journey of as many miles through the thick tangled undergrowth. This brought us out close to the water's edge again, and we saw before us a canal about a cable's length across, which the skipper said he was certain was a continuation of the one we had entered in the gig. About a mile distant, on the opposite side of the canal, could be seen the tops of the hills which we had noticed on the occasion of our first exploration of the river.

Here, as at the point of our landing, the banks of the canal consisted of black slimy foetid mud, out of which grew a belt of mangroves, their curious twisted roots straggling in a thick complicated mass of net-work over the slime beneath.

The sun was shining brilliantly down through the richly variegated foliage on the opposite bank of the stream, and lighting up the surface of the thick turbid water as it rolled sluggishly past; but where we stood—just on the inner edge of the mangrove-swamp—everything was enshrouded in a sombre green twilight, and an absolute silence prevailed all round us, which was positively oppressive in its intensity.

Breathless, perspiring, and exhausted with our unwonted exertions, we flung ourselves upon the ground for a moment's rest, during which the skipper and Smellie sought solace and refreshment in a cigar. As for me, not having at that time contracted the habit of smoking, I was contented to sit still and gaze with admiring eyes upon the weird beauty of my surroundings.

For perhaps a quarter of an hour my companions gave themselves up to the silent enjoyment of their cigars, but at the end of that time the skipper, turning to Smellie, said:

"I think this must be the creek to which we have been directed; but there are so many of these inlets, creeks, and canals on this side of the river—and on the other side also for that matter—that one cannot be at all certain about it. I would have explored the place thoroughly in the gig, and so have saved the labour of all this scrambling through the bush, but for the fact that if we are right, and any slave-craft happen to be lurking here—as our Yankee friend's suspicious conduct leads me to believe may be the case—there would be a great risk of our stumbling upon them unawares, and so giving them the alarm. And even if we escaped that mischance I have no doubt but that they keep sentinels posted here and there on the look-out, and we could hardly hope that the boat would escape being sighted by one or other of them. If there *are* any craft hereabout, we may rest assured that they are fully aware of the presence of the *Daphne* in the river; but I am in hopes that our *ruse* of openly starting as upon a sporting expedition has thrown dust in their eyes for once, and that we may be able to steal near enough to get a sight of them without exciting their suspicions."

Harry Collingwood

"It would be worth all our trouble if we *amid* do so," responded Smellie. "But I don't half like this blind groping about in the bush; to say nothing of the tremendously hard work which it involves there is a very good chance, it seems to me, of our losing ourselves when we attempt to make our way back. And then, again, we are quite uncertain how much further we may have to go in order to complete our search satisfactorily. Do you not think it would be a good plan for one of us to shin up a tree and take a look round before we go any further? There are some fine tall trees here close at hand, from the higher branches of which one ought to be able to get a pretty extensive view."

"A very capital idea!" assented the skipper. "We will act upon it at once. There, now," pointing to a perfect forest giant only a few yards distant, "is a tree admirably suited to our purpose. Come, Mr Hawkesley, you are the youngest, and ought therefore to be the most active of the trio; give us a specimen of your tree-climbing powers. Just shin up aloft as high as you can go, take a good look round, and let us know if you can see anything worth looking at."

"Ay ay, sir," I responded; "but—" with a somewhat blank look at the tall, straight, smooth stem to which he pointed, "where are the ratlines?"

"Ratlines, you impudent young monkey!" responded the skipper with a laugh; "why, an active young fellow like you ought to make nothing of going up a spar like that."

But when we reached the tree it became evident that the task of climbing it was not likely to prove so easy as the skipper had imagined; for the bole was fully fifteen feet in circumference, with not a branch or protuberance of any description for the first sixty feet.

The second lieutenant, however, was equal to the occasion, and soon showed me how the thing might be done. Whipping out his knife, he quickly cut a long length of "monkey-rope" or creeper, and twisting the tough pliant stem into a grummet round the trunk of the tree, he bade me pass the bight over my shoulders, and then showed me how, with its aid, I might work myself gradually upward.

Accordingly, acting under his directions I placed myself within the bight, and tucking it well up under my arm-pits, slid the grummet up the trunk as high as it would go. Then bearing back upon it, so that it supported my whole weight, I worked my body upwards by pressing against the tree-trunk with my knees. By this means I rose about two feet from the ground. Then pressing against the tree firmly with my feet I gave the grummet a quick jerk upward and again worked myself up the trunk with my knees as before. In this way I got along very well, and after an awkward slip or two, in which my knees suffered somewhat and my breeches still more, soon acquired the knack of the thing, and speedily reached the lowermost branch, after which the rest of my ascent was of course easy.

On reaching the topmost branches I found that the tree I had climbed was indeed, as the skipper had aptly described it, a forest giant; it was by far the most lofty tree in the neighbourhood, and from my commanding position I had a fine uninterrupted prospect of many miles extent all round me, except to the southward, where the chain of hills before-mentioned shut in the view.

Away to the northward and eastward, in which direction I happened to be facing when I at length paused to look around me, I could catch glimpses of the river, over and between the intervening tree-tops, for a distance of quite twenty miles, and from what I saw I came to the conclusion that in that direction the river must widen out considerably and be thickly studded with islands, among which I thought it probable might be found many a snug lurking-place for slave-craft. On the extreme verge of the horizon I also distinctly made out a small group of hills, which I conjectured to be situate on the northern or right bank of the river. From these hills all the way round northerly, to about north-north-west, the country was flat and pretty well covered with bush; although at a distance of from two to four miles inland I could detect here and there large open patches of grassland. Bearing about north-north-west from my point of observation was another chain of hills which stretched along the sea-coast outside the river's mouth, and extended beyond the horizon. To the left of them again, or about north-west from me, lay Banana Creek, its entrance about eleven miles distant, and over the intervening tree-tops on Boolambemba Island I could, so clear was the atmosphere just then, distinctly make out the royal-mast-heads of the *Daphne* and the American barque; I could even occasionally detect the gleam of the sloop's pennant as it waved idly in the sluggish breeze. Still further to the left there lay the river's mouth, with the ripple which marked the junction between the fresh and the salt water clearly visible. Next came Shark Point, with the open sea stretching mile after mile away beyond it, until its gleaming surface became lost in the ruddy afternoon haze, and on the inner side of the point I could trace, without much difficulty, the course of the various creeks which we had explored in the boat on the occasion of our first visit. Looking below me, I allowed my eye to travel along the course of the stream or canal which flowed past almost under my feet, and following it along I saw that it forked at a point about three miles to the westward, and turned suddenly northward at a point about three miles further on, the branch and the stream itself eventually joining the river, and forming with it two islands of about five and three miles in length respectively, the larger of the two being that which we had so laboriously crossed that same afternoon.

The view which lay spread out below and around me was beautiful as a dream; it would have formed a fascinating study for a painter; but whatever art-instincts may have been awakened within me upon my first glance round were quickly put to flight by a scene which presented itself at a point only some three miles away. At that distance the channel or stream below me forked, as I have already said, and at the point of divergence of the two branches the water way broadened out until it became quite a mile wide, forming as snug a little harbour as one need wish to see. And in this harbour, perfectly concealed from all prying eyes which might happen to pass up or down the river, lay a brig, a brigantine, and a schooner, three as rakish-looking craft as could well be met with. Their appearance alone was almost sufficient to condemn them; but a huge barracoon standing in a cleared space close at hand, and a crowd of blacks huddled together on the adjacent bank, apparently in course of shipment on board one or other of the craft in sight, put their character quite beyond question.

A hail from below reminded me that there were others who would feel an interest in my discovery.

"Well, Mr Hawkesley, is there anything in sight, from your perch aloft there, worth looking at?" came floating up to me in the skipper's voice.

"Yes, sir, indeed there is. There are three craft in the creek away yonder, in the very act of shipping negroes at this moment," I replied.

"The deuce there are!" ejaculated the skipper. "Which do you think will be the easier plan of the two: to climb the tree, or to make our way through the bush to the spot?"

"You will find it much easier to climb the tree, I think, sir. You can be alongside me in five minutes, whilst it will take us nearly two hours, I should say, to make our way to them through the bush," I replied.

"Very well; hold on where you are then. We will tackle the tree," returned the skipper.

And, looking down, I saw him and the second lieutenant forthwith whip out their knives and begin hacking away at a creeper, wherewith to make grummets to assist them in their attempt at tree-climbing.

In a few minutes the twain were alongside me, and—in happy forgetfulness of the ruin wrought upon their unmentionables in the process of "shinning" aloft—eagerly noting through their telescopes the operations in progress on board the slavers.

"They seem very busy there," observed the skipper with his eye still peering through the tube of his telescope. "You may depend on it, Mr Smellie, the rascals have got wind of our presence in the river, and intend trying to slip out past us to-night as soon as the fog settles down. I'll be bound they know every inch of the river, and could find their way out blindfold?"

"No doubt of it, sir," answered the second luff. "But it is not high-water until two o'clock to-morrow morning, so that I suspect they will not endeavour to make a move until about an hour after midnight. That will enable them to go out on the top of the flood, and with a strong land-breeze in their favour."

"So much the better," returned Captain Vernon, with sparkling eyes. "But we will take care to have the boats in the creek in good time. You never know where to have these fellows; they are as cunning as foxes. Please note their position as accurately as you can, Mr Smellie, for I intend you to lead the attack to-night."

"Thank you, sir," answered Smellie delightedly; and planting himself comfortably astride a branch, he drew out a pencil and paper and proceeded to make a very careful sketch-chart of the river-mouth, Banana Creek, and the creek in which the slavers were lying; noting the bearings carefully with the aid of a pocket-compass.

"There, sir," said he, when he had finished, showing the sketch to the skipper; "that will enable me to find them, I think, let the night be as dark or as thick as it may. How do you think it looks for accuracy?"

"Capital!" answered Captain Vernon approvingly; "you really have a splendid eye for proportion and distance, Mr Smellie. That little chart might almost have been drawn to scale, so correct does it look. How in the world do you manage it?"

"It is all custom," was the reply. "I make it an invariable rule to devote time and care enough to such sketches as this to ensure their being as nearly accurate as possible. I have devised a few rules upon which I always work; and the result is generally a very near approximation to absolute accuracy. But the sun is getting low; had we not better be moving, sir?"

"By all means, if you are sure you have all the information you need," was the reply. "I would not miss my way in that confounded jungle to-night for anything. It would completely upset all our arrangements."

"To say nothing of the possibility of our affording a meal to some of the hungry carnivora which probably lurk in the depths of the said jungle," thought I. But I held my peace, and dutifully assisted my superior officers to effect their descent.

It was decidedly easier to go up than to go down; but we accomplished our descent without accident, and after a long and wearisome tramp back through the bush found ourselves once more on board the gig just as the last rays of the sun were gilding the tree-tops. The tide had now turned, and was therefore again in our favour; and in an hour from the time of our emerging upon the main stream we reached the sloop, just as the first faint mist-wreaths began to gather upon the bosom of the river.

I was exceedingly anxious to be allowed to take part in the forthcoming expedition and had been eagerly watching, all the way across the river, for an opportunity to ask the necessary permission; but Captain Vernon had been so earnestly engaged in discussing with Smellie the details and arrangements for the projected attack that I had been unable to do so. On reaching the ship, however, the opportunity came. As we went up over the side the skipper turned and said:

"By the way, Mr Smellie, I hope you—and you also, Mr Hawkesley—will give me the pleasure of your company to dinner this evening?"

Smellie duly bowed his acceptance of the invitation and I was about to follow suit when an idea struck me and I said:

"I shall be most happy, sir, if my acceptance of your kind invitation will not interfere with my taking part in to-night's boat expedition. I have been watching for an opportunity to ask your permission, and I hope you will not refuse me."

"Oh! that's it, is it?" laughed the skipper. "I thought you seemed confoundedly fidgety in the boat. Well—I scarcely know what to say about it; it will be anything but child's play, I can assure you. Still, you are tall and strong, and—there, I suppose I must say 'yes.' And now run away and shift your damaged rigging as quickly as possible; dinner will be on the table in ten minutes."

I murmured my thanks and forthwith dived below to bend a fresh pair of pantaloons, those I had on being in so dilapidated a condition—what with the tree-climbing and our battle with the thorns and briars of the bush—as to be in fact scarcely decent.

The conversation at the dinner-table that night was of a very animated character, but as it referred entirely to the projected attack upon the slavers I will not inflict any portion of it upon the reader. Mr Austin, the first lieutenant, was at first very much disappointed when he found he was not to lead the boat expedition; but he brightened up a bit when the skipper pointed out to him that in all probability the slavers would slip their cables and endeavour to make their escape from the river on finding themselves attacked by the boats; in which case the cream of the fun would fall to the share of those left on board the sloop.

Mr Smellie—who was at all times an abstemious man—contented himself with a couple of glasses of wine after dinner, and, the moment that the conversation took a general turn, rose from the table, excusing himself upon the plea that he had several matters to attend to in connection with the expedition. As he rose he caught my eye and beckoned me to follow him, which I did after duly making my bow to the company.

When we reached the deck the fog was so thick that it was as much as we could do to see the length of the ship.

"Just as I expected," remarked my companion. "How are we to find the creek in such weather as this, Mr Hawkesley?"

"I am sure I don't know, sir," I replied, looking round me in bewilderment. "I suppose the expedition will have to be postponed until it clears a bit."

"Not if I can prevent it," said he with energy. "Although," he added, a little doubtfully, "it certainly *is very* thick, and with the slightest deviation from our course we should be irretrievably lost. Whereaway do you suppose the creek to be?"

"Oh, somewhere in that direction!" said I, pointing over the starboard quarter.

"You are wrong," remarked my companion, looking into the binnacle. "The tide is slackening, whilst the land-breeze is freshening; so that the ship has swung with her head to the eastward, and the direction in which you pointed leads straight out to sea. Now, if you want to learn a good useful lesson—one which may prove of the utmost value to you in after-life—come below with me to the master, and between us we will show you how to find that creek in the fog."

"Thank you," said I, "I shall be very glad to learn. Why, you do not even know its compass-bearing."

"No," said Smellie, "but we will soon find it out." With that we descended to the master's cabin, where we found the owner in his shirt-sleeves and with a pipe in his mouth, poring over a chart of the coast on which was shown the mouth of the river only, its inland course being shown by two dotted lines, indicating that the portion thus marked had never been properly surveyed. He was busily engaged as we entered laying down in pencil upon this chart certain corrections and remarks with reference to the ebb and flow of the tidal current.

"Good evening, gentlemen!" said he as we entered. "Well, Mr Smellie, so you are going to lead the attack upon the slavers to-night, I hear."

"Yes," said Smellie, unconsciously straightening himself up, "yes, if this fog does not baffle us. And in order that it may not, I have come to invoke your assistance, Mr Mildmay."

"All right, sir!" said old Mildmay. "I expected you; I was waiting for you, sir."

"That's all right," said the second lieutenant. "Now, Mildmay," bending over the chart, "whereabouts is the *Daphne*?"

"*There* she is," replied the master, placing the point of his pencil carefully down on the chart and twisting it round so as to produce a black mark.

"Very good," assented Smellie. "Now, look here, Mr Hawkesley, this is where your lesson begins." And he produced the sketch-chart he had made that afternoon and spread it out on the table.

"You will see from this sketch," he proceeded, "that the *Daphne* bore exactly north-north-west from the tree in which we were perched when I made it. Which is equivalent to saying that the tree bears south-south-east from the *Daphne*; is it not?"

I assented.

"Very well, then," continued Smellie. "Be so good, Mr

Mildmay, as to draw a line south-south-east from that pencil-mark which represents the *Daphne* on your chart."

The master took his parallel ruler and did so.

"So far, so good," resumed the second lieutenant. "Now my sketch shows that the outer extremity of Shark Point bore from the tree north-west 1/4 west. In other words, the tree bears from Shark Point south-east 1/4 east. Lay off that bearing, Mildmay, if you please."

"Very good," he continued, when this second line had been drawn. "Now it is evident that the point where these two lines intersect must be the position of the tree. But, as a check upon these two bearings I took a third to that sharp projecting point at the mouth of Banana Creek," indicating with the pencil on the chart the point in question. "That point bears north-west by north; consequently the tree bears from it south-east by south. Mark that off also, Mildmay, if you please."

The master did so, and the three lines were found to intersect each other at exactly the same point. "Capital!" exclaimed Smellie, in high good-humour. "That satisfactorily establishes the exact position of the tree. Now for the next step. The slave fleet bears north-west 1/4 west from the tree; and the western entrance to the creek (that by which we shall advance to the attack to-night) bears exactly north-west from the same point. Let us lay down these two bearings on the chart—thus. Now it is evident that the slave fleet and the entrance to the creek are situate *somewhere or other* on these two lines; the question is—*where*? I will show you how I ascertained those two very important bits of information if you will step to my cabin and bring me the telescope which you will find hanging against the bulkhead."

Intensely interested in this valuable practical lesson in surveying I hurried away to do his bidding, and speedily returned with the glass, a small but very powerful instrument, which I had often greatly admired.

Taking the telescope from my hand he drew it open and directed my attention to a long series of neat little numbered lines scratched on the polished brass tube.

"You see these scratches?" he said. "Very well; now I will explain to you what they are. When I was a midshipman it was my good fortune to be engaged for a time on certain surveying work, during which I acquired a tolerably clear insight of the science. And after the work was over and done with, it occurred to me that my knowledge might be of the greatest use in cases similar to the present. Now I may tell you, by way of explanation, that surveying consists, broadly, in the measurement of angles and lines. The angles are, as you have already seen, very easily taken by means of a pocket-compass; but the measurement of the lines bothered me very considerably for a long time. Of course you can measure a line with perfect accuracy by means of a surveyor's chain, but I wanted something which, if not quite so accurate as that, would be sufficiently correct, while not occupying more than a few seconds in the operation of measurement. So I set to work and trained myself to judge distances by the eye alone; and by constant diligent practice I acquired quite a surprising amount of proficiency. And let me say here, I would very strongly recommend you and every young officer to practise the same thing; you will be surprised when you discover in how many unexpected ways it will be found useful. Well, I managed to do a great deal of serviceable work even in this rough-and-ready way; but after a time I grew dissatisfied with it—I wanted some means of measuring which should be just as rapid but a great deal more accurate. I thought the matter over for a long time, and

Harry Collingwood

at last hit upon the idea of turning the telescope to account. The way I did it was this. You have, of course, found that if you look through your telescope at an object, say, half a mile away, and then direct the instrument to another object, say, four miles off, you have to alter the focus of the glass before you can see the second object distinctly. It was this peculiarity which I pressed into my service as a means of measuring distances. My first step was to secure a small, handy, but first-rate telescope—the best I could procure for money; and, provided with this, I commenced operations by looking through it at objects, the exact distances of which from me I knew. I focused the glass upon them carefully, and then made a little scratch on the tube showing how far it had been necessary to draw it out in order to see the object distinctly; and then I marked the scratch with the distance of the object. You see," pointing to the tube, "I have a regular scale of distances here, from one hundred yards up to ten miles; and these scratches, let me tell you, represent the expenditure of a vast amount of time and labour. But they are worth it all. For instance, I want to ascertain the distance of an object. I direct the telescope toward it, focus the instrument carefully, and find that I can see it most clearly when the tube is drawn out to, say, this distance," suiting the action to the word. "I then look at the scale scratched on the tube, and find that it reads six thousand one hundred feet— which is a few feet over one nautical mile. And thus I measure all my distances, and am so enabled to make a really satisfactory little survey in a few minutes as in the case of this afternoon. You must not suppose, however, that I am able to measure in this way with absolute accuracy; I am not; but I manage to get a very near approximation to it, near enough for such purposes as the present. Thus, within the distance of a quarter of a mile I have found that I can always measure within two feet of the actual distance; beyond that and up to half a mile I can measure within four feet of the actual distance; and so on up to ten miles, which distance I can measure to within four hundred feet.

"And now to return to the business in hand. My telescope informed me that the slave fleet was anchored at a distance of eighteen thousand three hundred feet (or a shade over three nautical miles) from the tree, and that the western entrance to the creek is twenty-eight thousand nine hundred feet (or about four and three-quarter nautical miles) from the same spot. We have now only to mark off these two distances on the two compass-bearings which we last laid down on the chart: thus,"—measuring and marking off the distances as he spoke—"and here we have the position of the slavers and of the entrance to the creek; and by a moment's use of Mildmay's parallel ruler—thus—we get the compass-bearing of the entrance from the *Daphne*. There it is—south-east by east; and now we measure the distance from one to the other, and find it to be—eight miles, as nearly as it is possible to measure it. Thus, you see, my rough-and ready survey of this afternoon affords us the means of ascertaining our course and distance from the *Daphne* to a point for which we should otherwise have been obliged to search, and which we could not possibly have hoped to find in the impenetrable fog which now overspreads the river."

"Thank you, Mr Smellie," said I, highly delighted with the lesson I had received; "if it will not be troubling you too much I think I must ask you to give me a lesson or two in surveying when you can spare the time."

"I shall be very pleased," was the reply. "Never hesitate to come to me for any information or instruction which you think I may be able to afford you. I shall always be happy to help you on in your studies to the utmost extent of my ability. But we have not quite finished yet, and it is now, Mildmay, that I think *you* may perhaps be able to help us. You see we shall have to pull—or sail, as the case may be—

across the current, and it will therefore be necessary to make some allowance for its set. Now do you happen to know anything about the speed of the current in the river?"

"Not half so much as I should like," replied the master; "but a hint which the skipper dropped this morning caused me to take the dinghy and go away out in mid-stream *to spend the day in fishing*—ha—ha—ha! The Yankee had his glass turned full upon me, off and on, the whole morning—so I'm told—and if so I daresay he saw that I had some fairly good sport. But I wasn't so busy with my hooks and lines but that I found time to ascertain that the ebb-stream runs at a rate of about four knots at half-tide; and just abreast of us it flows to seaward at the rate of about one knot at half-flood; the salt water flowing *into* the river along the bottom, and the fresh water continuing to flow *outwards* on the surface. Now, at what time do you propose to start?"

"About half-past nine to-night," answered Smellie.

Old Mildmay referred to a book by his side, and then said:

"Ah, then you will have about two hours' ebb to contend with—the last two hours of the ebb-tide. Now let me see,"— and he produced a sheet of paper on which were some calculations, evidently the result of his observations whilst "Sshing." He ran over these carefully, and then said:

"How long do you expect it will take you to cross?"

"Two hours, if we have to pull across—as I expect we shall," answered the second lieutenant.

"Two hours!" mused the master. "Two hours! Then you'll have to make allowance, sir, for an average set to seaward of two miles an hour all the way across, or four miles in all."

"Very well," said Smellie. "Then to counteract that we must shape our course for a point four miles *above* that which marks the entrance to the creek—must we not, Mr Hawkesley?"

"Certainly," I said; "that is quite clear."

"Then be so good as to lay that course down on the chart."

I measured off a distance of four miles with the dividers, and marked it off *above* the mouth of the creek; then applied the parallel ruler and found the course.

"It is exactly south-east," said I; "and it will take us close past the southern extremity of this small island."

"That is quite right," remarked Smellie, who had been watching me; "and if we happen to sight the land in passing that point it will be an assurance that, so far, we have been steering our proper course. But—bless me,"—looking at his watch—"it is a quarter after nine. I had no idea it was so late. Run away, Mr Hawkesley, and make your preparations. Put on your worst suit of clothes, and throw your pea-jacket into the boat. You may be glad to have it when we get into the thick of that damp fog. Bring your pistols, but not your dirk; a ship's cutlass, with which the armourer will supply you, will be much more serviceable for the work we have in hand to-night."

I hastened away, and reached the deck again just in time to see the men going down the side into the boats after undergoing inspection.

CHAPTER EIGHT

WE ATTACK THE SLAVERS

The attacking flotilla was composed of the launch, under Mr Smellie, with me for an *aide*; the first cutter, in charge of Mr Armitage, the third lieutenant; and the second cutter, in charge of Mr Williams, the master's mate; the force consisting of forty seamen and four officers—quite strong enough, in Captain Vernon's opinion, to give a satisfactory account of the three slavers, which, it was arranged, we were to attack simultaneously, one boat to each vessel.

The last parting instructions having been given to Smellie by the skipper, and rounded off with a hearty hand-shake and an earnest exclamation of "I wish you success;" with a still more hearty hand-shake and a "Good-bye, Harold, old boy; good luck attend you!" from Mr Austin, the second lieutenant motioned me into the launch; followed me closely down; the word to shove off was given, and away we went punctually at half-past nine to the minute.

The fog was still as thick as ever; so thick, indeed, that it was as much as we could do to see one end of the boat from the other; and, notwithstanding the care with which, as I had had an opportunity of seeing, the second lieutenant had worked out all his calculations, I own that it seemed to me quite hopeless to expect that we should find the place of which we were in search. Nevertheless, we pushed out boldly into the opaque darkness, and the boats' heads were at once laid in the required direction, each coxswain steering by compass, the lighted binnacle containing which had been previously masked with the utmost care. Our object being to take the slavers by surprise the oars were of course muffled, and the strictest silence enjoined. Thus there was neither light nor sound to betray our whereabouts, and we slid over the placid surface of the river almost as noiselessly as so many mist-wreaths.

In so dense a fog it was necessary to adopt unusual precautions in order to prevent the boats from parting company. We therefore proceeded in single file, the launch leading, with the first cutter attached by her painter, the second cutter, in her turn, attached by her painter to the first cutter, bringing up the rear. The cutters were ordered to regulate their speed so that the connecting rope between each and the boat ahead should be just slack enough to dip into the water and no more, thus insuring that each boat's crew should do its own fair share of work at the oars.

Once fairly away from the ship's side we were immediately swallowed up by the impenetrable mist; and for a considerable time the flotilla glided gently along, without a sight or sound to tell us whether we were going right or wrong; without the utterance of a word on board either of the boats; and with only the slight muffled sound of the oars in the rowlocks and the gurgle of the water along the boats' sides to tell that we were moving at all. The silence would have been oppressive but for the slight murmuring swirl and ripple of the great river and the chirping of the countless millions of insects which swarmed in the bush on both banks of the stream. The latter sent forth so remarkable a volume of sound that when first told it was created by insects alone I

Harry Collingwood

found my credulity taxed to its utmost limit; and it was not until I was solemnly assured by Mr Austin that such was the case that I quite believed it. It was not unlike the "whirr" of machinery, save that it rose and fell in distinct cadences, and occasionally—as if by preconcerted arrangement on the part of every individual insect in the district—stopped altogether for a few moments. Then, indeed, the silence became weird, oppressive, uncanny; making one involuntarily shuffle nearer to one's neighbour and glance half-fearfully over one's shoulder. Then, after a slight interval, a faint, far-off signal *chirp! chirp!* would be heard, and in an instant the whole insect-world would burst into full chorus once more, and the air would fairly vibrate with sound. But the night had other voices than this. Mingled with the *chirr* of the insects there would occasionally float off to us the snarling roar of some forest savage, the barking call of the deer, the yelping of a jackal, the blood-curdling cry of a hyena, the grunt of a hippopotamus, the weird cry of some night-bird; and—nearer at hand, sometimes apparently within a yard or so of the boats—sundry mysterious puffings and blowings, and sudden faint splashings of the water, which latter made me for one, and probably many of the others who heard them, feel particularly uncomfortable, especially if they happened to occur in one of the brief intervals of silence on shore. Once, in particular, during one of those silent intervals, my hair fairly bristled as the boat was suddenly but silently brought up all standing by coming into violent collision with some object which broke water directly under our bows; the shock being instantly followed by a long moaning sigh and a tremendous swirl of the water as the creature—whatever it was—sank again beneath the surface of the river.

The men in the launch were, like myself, considerably startled at the circumstance, and one of them—an Irishman—exclaimed, in the first paroxysm of his dismay:

"Howly ropeyarns! what was that? Is it shipwrecked, stranded, and cast away we are on the back of a say-crocodile? Thin, Misther Crocodile, let me tell yez at wanst that I'm not good to ate; I'm so sthrongly flavoured wid the tibaccy that I'd be shure to disagray wid yez."

This absurd exclamation appealed so forcibly to the men's sense of the ridiculous that it had the instant effect of steadying their nerves and raising a hearty laugh, which, however, was as instantly checked by Smellie, who, though he could not restrain a smile, exclaimed sharply:

"Silence, fore and aft! How dare you cry out in that ridiculous fashion, Flanaghan? I have a good mind to report you, sir, as soon as we return to the ship."

"*Who shall say how many of us will live to return?*"

"Merciful God! who spoke?" hoarsely cried the second lieutenant. And well he might. The words were uttered in a sound scarcely above a whisper, in so low a tone, indeed, that but for Smellie's startled ejaculation I should almost have been inclined to accept them as prompted by my own excited imagination; yet I saw in an instant that every man in the boat had heard them and was as much startled as myself. Who had uttered them, indeed? Every man's look, as his horrified glance sought his neighbour's face, asked the same question. Nobody seemed to have recognised or to be able to identify the voice; and the strangest thing about it was that it did not appear to have been spoken in the boat at all, but from a point close at hand.

The men had, with one accord, laid upon their oars in the first shock of this new surprise, and before they had recovered themselves the first cutter had ranged up alongside.

"Did anyone speak on board you, Armitage?" asked Smellie.

"No, certainly not," was the reply.

"Did you hear anyone speak on board the second cutter then?" followed.

"No; I heard nothing. Why?"

"No matter," muttered the second lieutenant. Then, in a low but somewhat louder tone:

"Give way, launches; someone has been trying to play a trick upon us."

The men resumed their work at the oars; but an occasional scarcely heard whisper reaching my ears and suggesting rather than conveying such fragmentary sentences as "Some of us doomed"—"Lose the number of our mess," etcetera, etcetera, showed that a very unfortunate impression had been made by the strange incident.

As we proceeded the second lieutenant began to consult his watch, and at last, turning to me as he slipped it back into his fob, he whispered:

"A quarter after tea. We ought now to be close to Boolambemba Point, but the fog keeps so dense that I am afraid there is no chance of our sighting it."

The insect chorus had been silent for an unusually long time when he spoke; but as the words left Smellie's lips the sounds burst out once more, this time in startling proximity to our larboard hand.

"By George! there it is, though, sure enough," continued

Smellie. "By the sharpness of the sound we must be close aboard of the point. How is her head, coxswain?"

Before the man could reply there came in a low murmur from the men pulling the port oars:

"We're stirring up the mud here, sir, on the port hand."

And at the same moment, looking up, we became aware that the darkness was deeper—more intense and opaque, as it were, on our port hand than anywhere else.

"All right!" answered Smellie; "that is the point, sure enough, and very prettily we have hit it off. If we can only make as good a shot at the mouth of the creek I shall be more than satisfied. How have you been steering, coxswain?"

"South-east, sir, as straight as ever I could keep her."

"That's all right. South-east is your course all the way across. Now we are beginning to draw off from the point and out into mid-stream, and there must be no more talking upon any pretence whatever. The noise of the insects will tell us when we are drawing in with the other bank. On a night like this one has to be guided in a great measure by sound, and even the chirp of the grasshoppers may be made useful, Mr Hawkesley."

I murmured a whispered assent as in duty bound, and then all hands relapsed into silence once more.

The men worked steadily away at the oars, not exerting themselves to any great extent, but keeping the boat moving at the rate of about four knots per hour. According to our time-reckoning, and the fact that the volume of sound proceeding from the southern bank of the river had overpowered that from the northern bank, we had accomplished rather more than the half of our passage across the stream, when, happening to raise my head upon emerging from a brown study into which I had fallen, I thought I caught a momentary glimpse of some object looming through the fog broad on our port beam. I looked more earnestly still, and presently felt convinced that there *was* something there.

Laying my hand on the second lieutenant's arm to call his attention, I whispered:

"Can you see anything out there, sir, abreast of us on our port hand?"

Smellie looked eagerly in the indicated direction for some moments, and then turning to the coxswain, whispered:

"Starboard—hard!"

The boat's helm was put over, her bows swept round; and then I was certain *that we were being watched*, for as the launch swerved out of her course the object became suddenly more distinct, only to vanish completely into the fog next moment, however, its course being as suddenly and promptly altered as our own, thus proving that there were other eyes at least as sharp as ours. But that single momentary glance had been sufficient to show me that the object was a native canoe containing three persons.

The second lieutenant was seriously disconcerted at this discovery, and was evidently in great doubt as to whether it would be more prudent to push on or to turn back. If the occupants of the canoe happened to be associated with the slavers, and had been sent out as scouts in anticipation of an attack from us, then there could be little doubt that it would be wiser to turn back, since a light craft like a canoe could easily reach the creek far enough ahead of us to give the alarm, in which case we should find a warm reception prepared for us; and in so dense a fog all the advantage would be on the side of those manning the slave fleet.

On the other hand, the *rencontre* might possibly have been purely accidental, and its occupants supremely indifferent to the movements of ourselves and the slavers alike, in which case it would be not only mortifying in the extreme but possibly fatal to Smellie's prospects in the service if he allowed himself to be frightened out of the advantage of so excellent an opportunity for effecting a surprise.

It was a most embarrassing problem with which he thus suddenly found himself brought face to face; but with a brave man the question could not long remain an open one; a few seconds sufficed him to determine on proceeding and taking our chance.

The sounds from the shore now rapidly increased in intensity, and by and by we suddenly found that they proceeded from both sides of the boats. Smellie drew out his watch and consulted it by the light of the boat's binnacle.

"Twenty minutes to twelve! and we are now entering the creek," he whispered to me.

The slavers, we knew, were anchored about two miles up the creek, and the conviction suddenly smote me that in another half-hour I should in all probability be engaged in a fierce and deadly struggle. Somehow up to that moment I had only regarded the attack as a remote possibility—a something which *might* but was not very likely to happen. I suppose I had unconsciously been entertaining a doubt as to the possibility of our finding the creek. Yet, there we were in it, and nothing could now avert a combat, and more or less bloodshed. Nothing, that is, except the exceedingly unlikely circumstance of our finding the birds flown.

Did I wish this? Was I *afraid*?

Honestly, I am unable to say whether I was or not; but I am inclined to acquit myself of the charge of cowardice. My sensations were peculiar and rather unpleasant, I freely admit; but looking back upon them now in the light of long years of experience, I am disposed to attribute them entirely to nervous excitement. Hitherto my nostrils had never sniffed the odour of powder burned in anger; I was about to undergo a perfectly new experience; I was about to engage with my fellow-men in mortal combat; to come face to face with and within arm's-length of those who, if the opportunity occurred, would take my life deliberately and without a moment's hesitation. In a short half-hour I might be dying— or *dead*. As this disagreeable and inopportune reflection flashed through my mind my heart throbbed violently, the blood rushed to my head, and my breathing became so laboured that I felt as though I was stifling. These disagree- able—indeed I might more truthfully call them *painful*— sensations lasted in their intensity perhaps as long as five minutes, after which they rapidly subsided, to be succeeded by a feverish longing and impatience for the moment of action. My excitement ceased; my breathing again became regular; but the period of suspense—that period which only a few minutes before had seemed so short—now felt as though it were lengthening out to a veritable eternity. I wanted to begin at once, to know the worst, and to get it over.

I had not much longer to wait. We had advanced about a mile up the creek when a deep hoarse voice was heard shouting something from the shore.

"Oars!" exclaimed Smellie; and the men ceased pulling. "What was it the fellow said?" continued the second lieutenant, turning to me.

"Haven't the slightest idea, but it sounded like Spanish," I replied.

The hail was repeated, but we could make nothing of it. Mr Armitage, however, who boasted a slight knowledge of Spanish, informed us—the first cutter having by this time drifted up abreast of us—that it was a caution to us to return at once or take the consequences.

"Oh! that's it, is it?" remarked Smellie. "Well, it seems that we are discovered, so any further attempt at a surprise is useless. Cast the boats adrift from each other, and we will make a dash for it. Our best chance now is to board and carry the three craft simultaneously with a rush—if we can. Give way, lads!"

The boats' painters were cast off; the crews with a ringing cheer plunged their oars simultaneously into the water, and away we went at racing speed through the dense fog along the channel.

We had scarcely pulled half a dozen strokes when the report of a musket rang out from the bank on our starboard hand; and at the same instant a line of tiny sparks of fire appeared on either hand through the thick haze, rapidly increasing in size and luminosity until they stood revealed as huge fires of dry brushwood. They were twelve in number, six on either bank of the channel, and were spaced about three hundred yards apart. So large were they that they rendered the fog quite luminous; and it seemed pretty evident that they had been built and lighted for the express purpose of illuminating the channel and revealing our exact whereabouts. I was congratulating myself upon the circumstance that the dense fog would to a considerable extent defeat their purpose, when, in an instant, as though we had passed out through a solid wall, we emerged from the fog, and there lay the three slave-craft before us, moored with springs on their cables, boarding-nettings triced up, and guns run out, evidently quite ready to receive us.

The three craft were moored athwart the channel in a slightly curved line, with their bows pointing to the eastward, the brig being ahead, the schooner next, and the brigantine the sternmost of the line. Thus moored, their broadsides commanded the whole channel in the direction of our advance, and could, if required, be concentrated upon any one point in it.

"Hurrah!" shouted Smellie, rising to his feet and drawing his sword; "hurrah, lads, there is our game! Give way and go at them. I'll take the brig, Armitage; you tackle the brigantine, and leave Williams to deal with the schooner. Now bend your backs, launches; there is a glass of grog all round waiting for you if we are alongside first."

"Hurroo! pull, bhoys, and let's shecure that grog annyhow," exclaimed the irrepressible Flanaghan; and with another cheer and a hearty laugh the men stretched themselves out and plied the stout ashen oars until the water fairly buzzed again under the launch's bows, and it almost seemed as though they would lift her bodily out of the water.

As for Armitage and Williams, they were evidently quite determined not to be beaten in the race if they could help it. Both were on their feet, their drawn swords in their right hands, pistols in their left, and their bodies bobbing energetically forward, in approved racing fashion, at every stroke of the oars; whilst the voice of first one and then the other could be heard encouraging their respective crews with such exclamations as:

"Pull now! pull *hard! There* she lifts! *Now* she travels! There we draw ahead. *Well* pulled; again so," and so on, she men all the while straining at the oars with a zeal and energy which left in the wake of each boat a long line of swirling, foamy whirlpools.

We were within about eighty yards of the slavers—the launch leading by a good half length—when a voice on board the brig uttered some word of command, and that same instant—*crash*! came a broadside at us, fired simultaneously from the three ships. The guns were well-aimed, the shot flying close over and all round us, tearing and thrashing up the placid surface of the water about the boats, and sprinkling us to such an extent that, for the moment, we seemed to be passing through a heavy shower; yet, strange to say, no damage was done.

Before the guns could be again loaded we were alongside, and then ensued—so far at least as the launch was concerned—a few minutes of such desperate hand-to-hand fighting as I have never since witnessed. We dashed alongside the brig in the wake of her larboard main rigging, and as the boat's side touched that of the slaver every man dropped his oar, seized his cutlass, and sprang for the main channels. Here, however, we were received so warmly that it was found utterly impossible to make good our footing, the men springing up only to fall back again into the boat wounded with pike-thrust, pistol-bullet, or cutlass-gash. Smellie and I happened to make a dash for the same spot, but being the lighter of the two I was jostled aside by him and narrowly avoided tumbling overboard. He succeeded in gaining a temporary footing on the chain-plate, and was evidently about to scramble thence upon the sheer-pole, when I saw a pike thrust out at him from over the topgallant bulwarks. The point struck him in the right shoulder, passing completely through it; the thrust upset his balance, and down he came by the run into the boat. Our lads meanwhile were cutting and hacking most desperately at the boarding netting, endeavouring to make a passage-way through it, but unfortunately they had emptied their pistols in the first rush, and, unable to reach their enemies through the netting, were completely at their mercy. In less than three minutes all hands were back in the boat, every one of us more or less hurt, and no nearer to getting on board than we had been before the beginning of the attack.

The cutters had evidently fared no better, for they were already hauling off, discomfited; seeing which, Smellie, who seemed scarcely conscious of his wound, reluctantly gave the order for us to follow their example, which we promptly did. Poor Smellie! I pitied him, for I could see he was deeply mortified at our defeat. The three boats converged toward each other as they hauled off, and as soon as we were within speaking distance of them the second lieutenant inquired of Armitage and Williams whether they had suffered much.

"We have one man killed, and I think none of us have escaped quite scot-free," was Armitage's reply; whilst Williams reported that two of his men were seriously hurt and seven others slightly wounded.

"Well," said Smellie, "it is evident that we can do nothing with them unless we change our tactics. We will, therefore, all three of us attack the schooner, the two cutters boarding her, one on each bow, whilst we in the launch will make a feint of attacking the brigantine, passing her, however, at the last moment, and boarding the schooner aft. Now—away we go!"

The boats upon this were quickly swept round, and off we dashed toward our respective points of attack. We were still fully a hundred yards distant when another broadside was poured into us, this time with very destructive effect so far as the launch was concerned. We were struck by no less than five nine-pound shot, two of which played havoc with our oars on the starboard side, a third tore out about twelve feet of planking and gunwale on the same side, and the remaining two struck the boat's stem close together, completely demolishing the bows and, worst of all, killing three men.

The launch was now a wreck and sinking. Smellie, therefore, conceiving it to be our best chance under the circumstances, gave orders to steer straight for the schooner's main-chains. We succeeded in reaching our quarry before the boat sank, and that was all, the launch capsizing alongside as we sprang from her gunwale to that of the schooner. Very fortunately for us, the two cutters had arrived nearly a minute before us, and when we boarded the entire crew of the schooner was on her forecastle fully occupied in the endeavour to repel their attack. Taking advantage of this we quietly but rapidly slipped in on deck through her open ports aft, and then made a furious charge forward, attacking the Spaniards in their rear. Our presence on board seemed to take them considerably by surprise. They wavered and hesitated, but, incited by a burly ruffian who forced his way through the crowd, rallied once more and attacked us hotly. This was exactly what we wanted. Our fellows, by Smellie's order, contented themselves with acting for the time being strictly on the defensive, giving way gradually before the impetuous attack of the Spaniards, and drawing them by degrees away from the forecastle. A diversion was thus effected in favour of the cutters' crews, of which they were not slow to avail themselves; and in less than five minutes after the attack of the launch's crew our entire party had gained a footing upon the schooner's deck. Even then the Spanish crew continued to fight desperately, inflicting several very severe wounds upon our lads, until at last, thoroughly roused by such obstinacy, the blue-jackets made such a determined charge that they cleared the decks by actually and literally driving their opponents overboard. Not that this entailed much loss upon the Spaniards, however; for they all, or very nearly all, swam either to the brig or the brigantine, where they were promptly hauled on board.

On our side Smellie lost not a moment in availing himself to the fullest extent of our partial victory. He ordered the cutters to be dropped under the schooner's stern, and whilst this was being done the springs were veered away and hauled upon until the schooner was brought broadside-on to her former consorts, now her antagonists. This done our lads went to the guns, double-shotted them, and succeeded in delivering an awfully destructive raking broadside fore and aft along the decks of both the brig and the brigantine. The frightful outcries and the confusion which ensued on board these craft assured us that our fire had wrought a tremendous amount of execution among the men crowding their decks; but they were too wise to give us an opportunity to repeat the dose. Their springs were promptly manned, and by the time that the schooner's batteries were again loaded our antagonists had brought their broadsides to bear upon us.

Once more was our double-shotted broadside hurled upon the foe, and then, before our lads had time to run-in their guns, we received the combined fire of the brig and the brigantine in return. Through the sharp ringing explosion of our antagonists' nine-pounders we distinctly heard the crashing of the shot through the schooner's timbers, and then—O God! I shall never forget it—the piercing shrieks and groans of mortal agony which uprose beneath our feet! Not a man of us upon the schooner's decks was injured by that terrible double broadside; for the Spaniards, resolved to sink the craft, had depressed the muzzles of their guns and sent their shot through the schooner's sides just above the water-line on the one side and out through her bottom on the other, regardless of the fact that *the vessel's hold was packed full of slaves.* The slaughter which resulted among these unhappy creatures, thus closely huddled together, I must leave to the reader's imagination—it was simply indescribable.

For a moment all hands of us on board the schooner were struck dumb and motionless with horror at this act of cowardice and wanton barbarity; then, with a yell of righteous fury our lads turned again to their guns, which thenceforward were loaded and fired independently, and as rapidly as possible. The slavers on their part were not behindhand in alacrity, and presently we received another broadside from the brig, closely followed by one from the brigantine, the guns being in both cases aimed as before, with similar murderous results, and with a repetition of those heart-rending shrieks of agony and despair.

"My God! I can't bear this!" I heard Smellie exclaim, as the dying shrieks of the negroes below again pealed out upon the startled air. "Mr Williams, take half a dozen men below and free those unhappy blacks. I don't know whether I am acting prudently or not, but I cannot leave them chained helplessly down there to be cut to pieces by the shot of those Spanish fiends. Let them come on deck and take their chance with us. Some of them at least may possibly effect their escape, either in the schooner's boats or by swimming to the shore."

Williams lost no time in setting about his perilous work of mercy; and a few minutes after his disappearance down the main hatchway the unhappy slaves began to make their appearance on deck, where they first stared in terrified wonder about them, and then crouched down helplessly on the deck wherever they might happen to find themselves.

In the meantime the cannonade was kept briskly up on both

sides, and presently the Spaniards began to pepper us with musketry in addition. The bullets, fired at short range, flew thickly about us; and the casualties quickly increased, several of the unfortunate blacks falling victims to the first discharge. Seeing this, Smellie ordered the schooner's boats, three in number, to be lowered and the slaves passed into them. This was done, our lads leaving the guns for a few minutes for the purpose; but—will it be credited? The Spaniards no sooner became aware of our purpose than they directed their fire upon the boats and their hapless occupants; so that we were compelled to quickly drag the unhappy blacks back on board the schooner again, to save them from being ruthlessly slaughtered. The worst of it was, that though Williams had succeeded in freeing many of them from the heavy chains with which they were secured together in the schooner's hold, most of them still wore heavy fetters on their ankles. These we now proceeded to knock off as fast as we could, afterwards pitching the poor wretches overboard—with scant ceremony, I fear—to take their chances of being able to reach the shore. And during all this the Spaniards never ceased firing upon us for an instant; so there we were in the midst of a perfect hailstorm of round-shot and bullets; the air about us thick and suffocating with the smoke from the guns, our only light the quick intermittent flashes of the cannon and musketry; the whole atmosphere vibrating with the roar and rattle of the fusillade, the shouts of the combatants, and the shrieks of the wounded and dying; struggling with the unhappy negroes who, driven almost frantic with the unwonted sights and sounds around them, seemed quite unable to comprehend our intentions, and resisted to the utmost our well-meant endeavours to pass them over the ship's side into the water.

In the midst of all this tumult and confusion we were suddenly confronted by an additional horror—Williams, badly wounded in the head by a splinter, staggering on deck, closely followed by his men, with the news that the schooner was rapidly sinking, and that it was impossible to free any more of the blacks.

I glanced down the hatchway. Merciful Heaven! shall I ever forget the sight which met my eyes in that brief glimpse! The intelligence was only too literally true. By the dim light of a horn lantern which Williams had suspended from the beams I could see the black water welling and bubbling rapidly up from the shot-holes below, and the wretched negroes, still chained below, surrounded by the mangled corpses of their companions and already immersed to their chins, with their heads thrown as far back as possible so as to keep their mouths and nostrils free until the last possible moment, their faces contorted and their eyes protruding from their sockets with mortal fear.

One of the unhappy creatures was a woman—a mother. Actuated by that loving and devoted instinct which cons-trains all animals to seek the safety of their helpless offspring before their own, she had raised her infant in her arms as high as possible above the surface of the bubbling water, and had fixed her dying gaze yearningly upon the little creature's face with an expression of despairing love which it was truly pitiful to see. I could not bear it. The mother was lost—chained as she was to the submerged deck, nothing could then save her—but the child might still be preserved. I sprang down the hatchway and, splashing through the rapidly-rising water, seized the child, and, as gently as possible, tried to disengage it from the mother's grasp. The woman turned her eyes upon me, looked steadfastly at me for a moment as though she would read my very soul, and then—possibly because she saw the flood of compassion which was welling up from my heart into my eyes—pressed her child's lips once rapidly and convulsively to her own already submerged mouth, loosed her grasp upon its body,

Harry Collingwood

and with a wild shriek of bitter anguish and despair threw herself backwards beneath the flood.

My heart was bursting with grief and indignation—grief for the miserable dying wretches around me, and indignation at our utter inability to prevent such wholesale human suffering. But there was no time to lose; the schooner was already settling down beneath our feet, and I saw that it would very soon be "Every man for himself and God for us all;" so I passed my charge on deck and quickly followed it myself.

I was just in time to see Smellie spinning the schooner's wheel hard over to port and lashing it there. Divining in an instant that he hoped by this manoeuvre to sheer the schooner alongside the brig, I seized the child I had brought up from below, dropped it into one of our own boats astern, and then stood by to make a spring for the brig with the rest of our party. Half a minute more and the sides of the two ships touched.

"Now, lads, follow me! Spring for your lives—the schooner is sinking!" I heard Smellie shout; and away we went—Armitage leading one party forward, and Smellie showing the way to the rest of them aft. And, even as we made our spring, the schooner heeled over and sank alongside.

We were met, as before, by so stubborn a resistance that I believe every one of us received some fresh hurt more or less serious before we actually reached the deck of the brig; but our lads were by this time fully aroused—neither boarding-nettings nor anything else could any longer restrain them; and in a few seconds, though more than one poor fellow fell back dead, we were in possession of the brig, the crew, in obedience to an order from their captain, suddenly flinging down their weapons and tumbling headlong into their boats, which for some reason—a reason we were soon to learn—

they had lowered into the water.

To our surprise our antagonists, instead of taking refuge on board the brigantine, as we fully expected they would, took to their oars and pulled in frantic haste up the creek. In the dense darkness which now ensued consequent upon the cessation of firing it was impossible to send a shot after them with any chance of success; and so they were allowed to go free.

The hot pungent fumes which arose through the grating of the brig's main hatchway very convincingly testified to the presence of slaves on board that craft also; and, warned by his recent experience on board the schooner, Smellie resolved to warp the brig in alongside the bank and land the unfortunate creatures before resuming hostilities. A gang of men was accordingly sent forward to clear away the necessary warps and so on; and I was directed to go with a boat's crew into one of the cutters to run the ends of the warps on shore.

The boats, it will be remembered, had been passed astern of the schooner, and there they still remained uninjured, that craft having settled down in water so shallow that her deck was only submerged to a depth of about eighteen inches. In order to reach either of the boats, however, it was necessary to pass along the deck of the sunken craft; and I was just climbing down the brig's side to do so—the men having preceded me—when the bulwarks to which I was clinging suddenly burst outward, the brig's hull was rent open by a tremendous explosion, and, enveloped for an instant in a sheet of blinding flame, I felt myself whirled upwards and outwards for a considerable distance, to fall finally, stunned, scorched, and half-blinded, into the agitated waters of the creek. Moved more by instinct than anything else I at once struck out mechanically for the shore. It was at no great distance from me, and I had almost reached it when some object—probably a piece of falling wreckage from the dismembered brig—struck me a violent blow on the back of the head, and I knew no more.

CHAPTER NINE

DOOMED TO THE TORTURE

Consciousness at length began, slowly and with seeming reluctance, to return to me; and so exceedingly disagreeable was the process, that if I could have had my own way just then, I think I should have preferred to die. My first sensation was that of excessive stiffness in every part of my body, with distracting headache. Then, as my nerves more fully recovered their functions, ensued a burning fever which scorched my body and sent the blood rushing through my throbbing veins like a torrent of molten metal. And finally, as I made an unsuccessful effort to move, I became aware, first of all by sundry sharp smarting sensations, that I had been wounded in three or four places; and secondly, by a feeling of severe compression about the wrists and ankles, that I was bound—a prisoner!

With complete restoration to consciousness my sufferings rapidly grew more acute; and at length, with a groan of exquisite agony, I opened my eyes and looked about me.

"Where was I?"

Somewhere on shore, evidently.

Overhead was the deep brilliantly blue sky, with the sun, almost in the zenith, darting his burning beams directly down upon my uncovered head and my upturned face. Turning my head aside to escape the dazzling brightness which smote upon my aching eyeballs with a sensation of positive torture, I discovered that I was lying in about the centre of an extensive forest clearing of nearly circular shape and about five hundred yards in diameter, hemmed in on all sides by a dense growth of jungle and forest trees, and carpeted thickly with short verdant grass.

Near me lay the apparently inanimate body of poor Mr Smellie, bound hand and foot, like myself; and dotted about here and there on the grass, mostly in a sitting posture and also bound, were some fifteen or twenty negroes, who, from their wretched plight, I conjectured to be survivors from the sunken slave schooner. Turning my head in the opposite direction I discovered at a few yards distance a party of negroes, some fifty in number, much finer-looking and more athletic men than those in bonds round about me, who, from the weapons they bore, I at once concluded to be our captors. This surmise was soon afterwards proved to be correct; for, upon the completion of the meal which they were busily discussing when I first made them out, they approached us, and with sufficiently significant gestures gave us to understand that we must rise and march.

The captive blacks rose to their feet stolidly and without any apparent difficulty; but so far as I was concerned this was an impossibility, my feet as well as my hands being secured. One great hulking black fellow, noticing that neither Smellie nor I showed any signs of obedience, deliberately proceeded to prod us here and there with the point of his spear. Upon Smellie these delicate attentions produced no effect whatever, he evidently being either dead or insensible; but they aroused in me a very lively feeling of indignation, under the influence of which I launched such a vigorous kick at the unreasonable darky's shins as made him howl with pain and sent him hopping out of range in double-quick time—a proceeding which raised a hearty laugh at his expense among his companions. A moment later, however, he returned, his eyes sparkling with rage, and would have transfixed me with the light javelin he carried had not another of the party interfered. By the order of this last individual Smellie and I were presently raised from the ground, and each borne by two men, were carried off in the rear of the column of captive blacks, our captors taking up such positions along the line on either side as effectually precluded all possibility of escape.

Passing across the open space, we presently plunged into the jungle, traversing a bush-path just wide enough to allow of two men walking abreast. I had not much opportunity, however, for noting any of the incidents of our journey, for, owing to the clumsy way in which I was being carried, my wounds burst open afresh, and I soon fainted from loss of blood.

When next I recovered consciousness I found that we were afloat, no doubt on the river, though I had no means of ascertaining this for certain, as I was lying in the bottom of the canoe, and could see nothing but blue sky beyond either of the gunwales. Smellie was lying beside me, and, to my great joy, I found that he was not only alive but a great deal better than I could have thought possible after witnessing his former desperate condition. Of course we at once exchanged congratulations each at the other's escape; and then began to compare notes. My companion in misfortune had, it seemed, just started to go forward when the explosion occurred on board the brig; the shock had rendered him unconscious; and when he recovered he found himself on board the canoe with me beside him. Poor fellow! he was in a sad plight. He was severely wounded in no less than four different parts of his body; his face and hands were badly scorched; his clothing—about which he was always very particular—hung upon him in tatters; and lastly, he was greatly distressed in mind at the disastrous failure of the expedition, at the fearfully heavy casualties which we knew had befallen the attacking party, and at the extreme probability that those casualties had been very largely increased by the blowing up of the brig. I said what I could to comfort him, but, alas! that was not much; and it was a relief to us both to change the subject, even though we naturally turned at once to the discussion of our own problematical future.

The craft in which we found ourselves was a war-canoe, about sixty feet long and five feet beam, manned by about forty of our captors, who sat two abreast close to the gunwales, paddling vigorously; the negro prisoners, as well as ourselves, being stowed along the middle of the canoe, fore and aft. A fresh fair breeze was blowing, and full advantage was being taken of this circumstance, a huge mat sail being hoisted on the craft which must inevitably have capsized her had it happened to jibe. From the sharp rushing sound of the water along the sides and bottom of the canoe, and the swift strokes of the paddles, I judged that we must be travelling through the water at a rapid rate, a conjecture the truth of which was afterwards very disagreeably verified. We sped on thus until sunset, when the sail was suddenly lowered and with loud shouts, which were re-echoed from the shore, the canoe's course was altered, the craft grounding a few minutes afterwards on a beach where all hands of us landed.

Smellie and I were by this time quite able to walk, but before we could set foot to the ground a couple of stalwart blacks were told off to each of us, and we were carried along as before. On this occasion, however, our journey was but a short one, not more, perhaps, than five or six hundred yards altogether. Arrived, apparently, at our destination, we were set down, and immediately bound with *llianos* or monkey-rope to the bole of a huge tree. Looking about us, we discovered that we were in a native village of considerable size, built in a semicircular shape, having in its centre a structure of considerable architectural pretensions in a barbaric sort of way, which structure we conjectured—from the presence of a hideous idol in front of it—must be a sort of temple. Looking about us still further, we noticed that the remainder of the prisoners were being bound to trees like ourselves. There was a peculiarity about the disposition of the prisoners which I certainly did not like; there might be no motive for it, but it struck me that our being ranged in a semicircle in front of this idol had a rather sinister appearance.

Having secured the prisoners to their satisfaction, our captors left us; and we were speedily surrounded by a curious crowd consisting chiefly of women and children, who came and stared persistently with open-mouthed curiosity at the captives, and especially at Smellie and myself, greatly attracted by the apparently novel sight of our white skins. The old women were, for the most part, hideously ugly, wrinkled, and bent, their grizzled wool plastered with grease and dirt, and their bodies positively *encrusted* with filth. The young women, on the other hand—those, that is to say, whose ages seemed to range between thirteen and sixteen or seventeen—were by no means destitute of personal attractions, which—to do them justice—they exhibited with the most boundless liberality. They were all possessed of plump well-made figures; their limbs were, in many cases, very finely moulded; they had an upright graceful carriage; the expression of their features was amiable and gentle; and, notwithstanding their rather prominent lips, a few of them were actually pretty.

One of these damsels, a perfect little sable Hebe, seemed to be greatly attracted by us, walking round and round the tree to which we were secured—first at a respectful distance, and then nearer and nearer. Finally, after studying our countenances intently for nearly a minute, she boldly approached and laid her finger upon my cheek, apparently to ascertain whether or no it was genuine flesh and blood. Satisfied that it was so, she backed off to take another look at us, and I thought an expression of pity overspread her face. Finally she addressed us. We were, of course, quite unable to understand the words she uttered, but her actions, graceful as they were, were significant enough; she was evidently asking whether we were hungry or thirsty. To this inquiry Smellie nodded a prompt affirmative, which I backed up with the single word "*Rather*," uttered so expressively that I am certain she quite understood me. At all events, she tripped lightly away, returning in a few minutes with a small finely-woven basket containing about two quarts of fresh palm-juice, which she presented first to Smellie's lips, and then to mine. Need I say that, between us, we emptied it? Our hostess laughed gaily as she glanced at the empty basket, evidently pleased at the success of her attempt to converse with us; and then, with a reassuring word or two, she tripped away again. Only to return, however, about a quarter of an hour later, with the same basket, filled this time with a kind of porridge, which, though not particularly tasty, was acceptable enough after our long fast. This, our fair, or rather our *dark* friend administered to us alternately by means of a flat wooden spatula. This feeding process had not passed, it need hardly be said, unobserved; and by the time that our meal was concluded quite a large audience of women had gathered round to witness the performance. The animated jabber and hearty ringing laughter of several of the younger women and the somewhat abashed yet pleased expression of our own particular friend seemed to indicate that *badinage* was not altogether unknown, even in this obscure African village. But everything of that kind was brought abruptly to an end by a loud discordant blowing of horns and the hollow *tub, tub, tub* of a number of rude drums; at which sounds the crowd around us broke up at once and retired, our little Hebe casting back at us more than one glance strongly indicative, as it seemed to me, of compassion.

A fire had been kindled in front of the idol, or *fetish*, during the feeding process above referred to, and now that the curious crowd of women and girls who then surrounded us had retired we were able to see a little more of what was going on. The horn-blowing and drum-beating emanated from a group of entirely naked savages who were marching in a kind of procession round the idol. This ceremony lasted about ten minutes, when another negro made his appearance upon the scene, emerging from the temple, if such it actually was, bearing in his hands a queer-looking construction, the nature of which I was at first unable to distinguish. After marching solemnly round the idol three times this individual seated himself tailor-fashion before it, laid the instrument on his knees, and began to hammer upon it with a couple of sticks; whereupon we became aware that he was playing upon a rude imitation of a child's harmonicon, the keys of which appeared to be constructed of hard wood, out of which he managed to beat a very fair specimen of barbaric music. This music seemed to be the overture to some impending entertainment; for upon the sound of the first notes the inhabitants began to pour out of their huts and to gather in a promiscuous crowd round the giant tree-stump upon which the hideous fetish was mounted. When the gathering was apparently complete the music ceased, the drumming and horn-blowing burst out afresh, and the crowd immediately divided into two sections, the smaller, and I presume the more select division squatting on the ground in a semicircle in front of the image, whilst the remainder of the inhabitants ranged themselves into two quadrants about thirty feet apart, one on each side and in front of their deity. Through this open space between the two quadrants it appeared probable that we should obtain a very good, if rather distant view of the ceremonies which were evidently about to take place.

The audience having arranged themselves in position, the horn-blowing ceased, and the musicians stepped inside the inner circle and seated themselves to the right and left of the fetish. A pause of perhaps a couple of minutes ensued, and then horns, drums, and harmonicon suddenly burst out with a loud confused fantasia, each man apparently doing his utmost to drown the noise of the others. Louder and louder blared the horns; the drummers pounded upon their long narrow drums until it seemed as though at every stroke the drum-heads must inevitably be beaten in; whilst the harmonicon-man hammered away at his instrument with a vigour and rapidity which must have been truly gratifying to his friends.

In the midst of this wild hullabaloo a blood-curdling yell rang out upon the still night air, and from the open door of the temple or fetish-house there bounded into the inner circle a most extraordinary figure, clad from head to heel in monkey skins, his head adorned with a coronet of beads and feathers, a bead necklace round his neck, a living snake encircling his waist as a girdle, and bearing in his hand a red and black wand about four feet long.

Upon the appearance of this individual the uproar suddenly ceased, then the *maestro* who presided at the harmonicon struck up a low accompaniment, and the last comer burst into a subdued monotonous chant, pointing and gesticulating from time to time with his wand.

I watched the proceedings with a great deal of interest, and was beginning to wonder what would happen next, when Smellie turned to me and quietly asked:

"Mr Hawkesley, do you ever say your prayers?"

"Sir?" I ejaculated in unutterable surprise at so impertinent a question, as it seemed to me.

"I asked whether you ever said your prayers: I ought to have said, rather, do you ever pray? There is often a very great difference between the two acts," he returned quietly.

"Well—ah—yes—that is—certainly, sir, I do," stammered I.

"Then," said Smellie, "let me recommend you to pray *now*— to pray with all the earnestness and sincerity of which you are capable. Make your peace with God, if you have not already done so, whilst you have the opportunity, for, unless I am very greatly mistaken, *it is our doom to die to-night*."

I was so shocked, so completely knocked off my balance, by this unlooked-for communication, that, for the moment I lost all power of speech, my tongue clave to the roof of my mouth, and I could only stare at my fellow-prisoner in horrified incredulity.

"My poor boy," he said compassionately, "I am afraid I have spoken to you too abruptly. I ought to have prepared you gradually for so momentous a piece of intelligence, to have *broken* the news to you. But, there, what matters? You are a plucky lad, Hawkesley—your conduct last night abundantly proved that—and I am sure that, if the occasion should come, you will stand up and face death in the presence of these savages as an Englishman should; I am not afraid of that. But, my dear boy, are you prepared to die? Are you in a fit state to meet your God? You are very young, quite a lad in fact, and a *good* lad too; you cannot yet have erred very grievously. Thoughtless, careless, indifferent you may have been, but your conscience can hardly charge you with any *very* serious offence, I should think; and you may therefore well hope for pardon and mercy. Seek both at once, my dear boy."

"But—Mr Smellie—I—I don't understand; *you* don't appear to be afraid or—or disturbed at—the near prospect of death."

"No," he replied, raising his eyes heavenward for a moment; "no, thank God, I am *not* afraid. My mother—" his lips quivered, his voice faltered and almost broke for an instant, and by the red glare of the fire I saw the tears well up into his eyes as he spoke that revered name. But he steadied himself again directly, and went on—"my dear mother taught me to be ready for death at any moment; taught me so lovingly and so thoroughly that I can regard with perfect calmness to-night, as I have a score of times before, the approach of the Last Enemy. But let us not waste the precious moments in conversation. Time soon will be for us no more; and—ah! see, there comes the vile high-priest of a loathsome idolatry to claim his first victim. Should you by any chance escape the coming horrors of this night, Hawkesley, and live to reach England once more, seek out my mother—Austin will instruct you as to where she may be found—and tell her that her son died as she would wish him to die, a sincere Christian. I am to be the first victim it would appear. Farewell, my dear boy! God bless you, and grant us a happy meeting at His right hand on the last Great Day!"

I strove in vain to reply to his solemnly affectionate farewell. I wanted to let him know how inexpressibly precious to me were the few words of exhortation and encouragement he had spoken; to say were it only a single word to cheer his last moments with the assurance that he had not spoken in vain; but my emotion was too great. I felt that in the effort to speak I should inevitably burst into tears, and so, perhaps, unman him, and disgrace him and myself in the eyes of these inhuman savages. So, perforce, I held my peace, and watched with a wildly-beating heart to see how a brave man should die.

In the meantime the fetish-man had concluded his chant, and, in the midst of a breathless silence on the part of his audience, stood looking intently round the circle at the group of prisoners secured to the trees. He glanced keenly at each of us in turn, and at length pointed his wand straight at Smellie. It was this action which caused the second lieutenant to announce to me his belief that it was he who was to be the first victim of the impending sacrificial cere-mony. Keeping his wand pointed directly at my companion, the uncouth figure slowly and with a quite undescribable undulatory dancing motion, advanced toward our tree, the crowd hastily making way for him, and four members of the inner circle rising to their feet and following him at a touch from his finger.

Overcoming by a strong effort the horrible fascination which this loathsome wretch exercised over me, I turned to look at my companion.

He seemed to be utterly unconscious of his surroundings. His eyes were raised to heaven, his lips moved from time to time, and it was manifest that he was holding the most solemn and momentous communion which it is possible for man to hold even with his Maker. Pale, haggard, and worn with mental and physical suffering, his crisp brown curly hair stiff and matted with blood, his face streaked with ensanguined stains, and his scorched clothing hanging about him in blood-stained rags, I nevertheless thought it would be difficult to picture a more perfect embodiment of a good, noble, and brave man.

Slowly and sinuously, like a serpent stealing upon his prey, the fetish-man or witch-doctor advanced until he stood within a yard of his intended victim, with the fatal wand still pointing straight at Smellie's breast. He stood thus for a full minute or more, seemingly striving to wring from the bound and helpless prisoner some sign of panic or at least of discomposure. In vain. His last most solemn act of duty done, Smellie at length turned his eyes upon those of his enemy, regarding him with a gaze so calmly steadfast, so palpably devoid of fear, that the savage, mortified at his utter failure, suddenly, with an exclamation unmistakably indicative of rage and chagrin, dropped the point of his wand, to raise it again instantly and direct it toward my breast.

But the cool intrepidity which I had just witnessed was contagious; in my sublime admiration of it my soul soared far above and beyond the reach of so debasing a feeling as fear, and in my turn I met the cruel sinister gaze of the crafty savage with one as calm as Smellie's own.

For perhaps a full minute—it may have been more, it may have been less; it is difficult to estimate the lapse of time under such trying circumstances—the fetish-man did his best to disconcert me; then, baffled once more, with a furious and threatening gesture he passed on to the next prisoner.

"We are reprieved for the time being," said Smellie, as the gesticulating witch-doctor and his myrmidons passed on, "but only to become the victims of a more refined and protracted torture at last. Having failed to exhibit any signs of fear in the first instance we are spared to witness the cumulative sufferings of those who are to precede us, in order that by the sight of their exquisite torments our courage may be quelled by the anticipation of our own. I imagine, from what I have read of the customs of this people, that we are about to witness and become participants in a ceremony undertaken to avert or remove some great calamity—a ceremony involving the sacrifice of many victims, each of whom is put to death with more refined barbarity than that dealt out to the victim preceding him. Ah! see there—a worthy victim has at last been found with which to begin the sacrifice."

I looked in the direction his eyes indicated, and, sure enough, the light but fatal stroke with the wand was just in the act of being struck upon the naked breast of one of the negro prisoners. As the blow fell a loud shriek of despair rang out from the lips of the wretched man; the fetish-man's four assistants sprang upon their prey, his bonds were cut, and in another moment he was dragged, struggling desperately and shrieking with mortal fear, into the inner circle and up to the broad tree-stump which supported the fetish or idol.

In the meantime the fire had been bountifully replenished with wood and now blazed up fiercely. By its ruddy light I saw the fetish-man retire to the interior of the temple or fetish-house, to appear immediately afterwards with a rude stone hammer in one hand and what looked like four or five large spike-nails in the other. He stood for a moment gloating over the agonised countenance of his victim, and then nodded his head. At the signal his four assistants seized their prisoner, and, despite his terrible struggles, rapidly placed him, head downwards, with his back against the tree-stump, and his limbs extended as far as they would go round it, when the fetish-man proceeded with cruel deliberation to secure him in position by *nailing him there*, the spikes taken from the fetish-house being used for the purpose.

The horns, drums, and harmonicon now broke forth afresh into a hideous clamour, which, however, was powerless to drown the dismal shrieks of the victim; and the fetish-man, arming himself with a large broad-bladed and most murderous-looking knife, began to dance slowly, with most extraordinary contortions of visage and body, round the idol. Gradually his gyrations grew more rapid, his gestures more extravagant; the knife was flourished in the air in an increasingly threatening manner, and at length, as the weird dancer whirled rapidly round the tree-stump, the weapon was at each revolution plunged ruthlessly into the writhing body of the hapless victim, the utmost care being taken, I noticed, to avoid any vital part. Finally, when the dancer had apparently danced himself into a frenzy—when his gyrations had become so rapid that it almost made me giddy to look at him, and when his contortions of body grew so extravagant that it was difficult to say whether he was dancing on his head or on his heels—there flashed a sudden lightning-like gleam of the knife, and the head of the miserable victim fell to the ground, to be snatched up instantly and, with still twitching features, nailed between the feet of the body.

A loud murmur of applause from the spectators greeted this effort of the fetish-man, in the midst of which he retired for a few minutes to the interior of the fetish-house, probably to recruit his somewhat exhausted energies.

CHAPTER TEN

A FIENDISH CEREMONIAL

"Now," said Smellie as he turned once more to me, "we shall probably be again threatened on the reappearance of that bloodthirsty villain. But whatever you do, Hawkesley, maintain a bold front; let him see no sign or trace whatever of weakness or discomposure in you. The fellow's thirst for blood is by this time fully aroused, and every succeeding victim will be subjected to greater refinements of torture; all that diabolical scoundrel's fiendish ingenuity will now be exercised to devise for his victims increasingly atrocious and protracted agonies. There is one, and only one hope for us, which is that by a persistent refusal to be terrorised by him, and a judiciously scornful demeanour, we may at last exasperate him out of his self-control, and thus provoke him into inflicting upon us the *coup-de-grace* at once and without any of the preliminary torments. Here he comes again. Now, for your own sake, dear lad, remember and act upon my advice."

The first act of the wretch was to despatch his four assistants into the forest, whence they returned in a short time with three long slender poles and a considerable quantity of creeper or monkey-rope. With these, under the fetish-man's superintendence, a very tolerable set of light shears was speedily constructed, which, when finished, was erected immediately over the fire—now an immense mass of glowing smokeless cinders—in front of the idol. The entire arrangement was so unmistakably suggestive that I could not restrain a violent shudder as it occurred to me that it might possibly be my fate to be subjected to the fiery torment.

All being ready, a dead silence once more fell upon the assembly, and the chief actor in the inhuman ceremonial once more looked keenly around him for a victim.

As in the first instance, so now again was the wand pointed at Smellie's breast, and once more the cruel crafty bearer of it advanced on tip-toe with a stealthy cat-like tread toward us. He approached thus until he had reached to within about ten feet of the tree, when he once more paused in front of us, gesticulating with the wand and making as though about to strike with it the light blow which seemed to be the stroke of doom, keenly watching all the while for some sign of trepidation on the part of his victim. Then, whilst the wretch was in the very midst of his fantastic genuflexions before us, Smellie turned to me with a smile and observed:

"Just picture to yourself, Hawkesley, the way in which that fellow would be made to jump if Tom Collins, the boatswain's mate, could only approach him from behind now, and freshen his way with just one touch of his 'cat.'"

There was perhaps not much in it; but the picture thus suggested to my abnormally excited imagination seemed so supremely ridiculous that I incontinently burst into a violent and uncontrollable fit of hysterical laughter (the precise effect which I afterwards ascertained Smellie was anxious to produce); so highly exasperating the fetish-man that, with eyes fairly sparkling with rage, he advanced and struck me a violent blow on the mouth with his filthy hand, passing on immediately afterwards to seek elsewhere for a victim.

He had not far to seek; the miserable wretch next me on my left was so paralysed with fear that he was deemed a fit and proper person to become the next sacrifice, and almost unresistingly—until resistance was all too late—he was dragged forward into the inner circle, thrown flat upon his stomach, and his hands and feet bound securely together behind him. Then, indeed, he seemed suddenly to awake to a sense of his horrid fate; and his superhuman struggles for freedom and his ear-splitting yells were simply dreadful beyond all description to see and hear. The fetish-man and his assistants, confident of the reliable character of their work, stood back and looked on quietly at the miserable wretch's unavailing struggles; they seemed to be regarded as quite a part of the entertainment, and the unhappy creature was allowed to continue them unmolested until they ceased from exhaustion. Then, when he lay quite still, panting and breathless, with his eyes starting from their sockets and the perspiration streaming from every pore, the fetish-man approached him and deftly bending on to his fettered limbs an end of stout monkey-rope, he was dragged along the ground into the fire, and thence triced in an instant up to the shears, whence he hung suspended at the height of about a foot immediately over the glowing embers.

The miserable sufferer bore the torment as long as he could, and I shall never forget the awful sight his distorted features presented as, drawing back his head as far as he could from the fierce heat, he glared round the circle seeking perchance for a hand merciful enough to put him out of his misery—but after the first minute of suffering his stoicism abandoned him, and he writhed so violently that the fetish-man and his assistants had to steady the shears in order to prevent them from capsizing altogether. And with every writhe of the victim the slender poles bent and gave, letting the miserable sufferer sink down some three or four inches nearer the fire. The superhuman struggles, the frightful contortions and writhings of the man, his ear-splitting yells, the horrible smell of roasting flesh—oh, God! it was awful beyond all attempt at description. I pray that I may never look upon such a ghastly sight again.

The fiendish exhibition had probably reached its most appalling phase, and I was wondering, shudderingly, what form of torture could possibly exceed it in cruelty, when there was a sudden slight movement of my bonds; they slackened and fell away from the tree-trunk against which I leaned, and *I was free*. Not a moment was allowed me in which to get over the first shock of my bewilderment; a soft plump hand grasped mine and gently drew me round behind the tree, so rapidly that I had only time to note the fact that apparently every eye in the assembly was fixed upon the writhing figure suspended over the fire—and before I had fairly realised what was happening I found myself a dozen yards away from my starting-point, gliding rapidly and noiselessly through the deep shadows cast by the tree-trunks, towards the outer darkness which prevailed beyond the range of the fire-light; with our little black Hebe friend of a few hours before dragging me along on one side of her and Smellie on the other.

Five minutes later we had left the village so far behind us that the barbarous sounds of horn and drum, mingled with the yells of anguish from the tortured victim, momentarily becoming more and more softened by our increasing distance, were the sole evidences that remained to us of its existence, and we found ourselves hurrying along through the rank grass, threading the mazes of the park-like clumps of lofty timber, and forcing a passage through the thickly clustering festoons of parasitic orchids, under the subdued light of the mellow stars alone.

With almost breathless rapidity our tender-hearted little deliverer hurried us forward, frequently exclaiming in low urgent accents, "Zola-ku! zola-ku," so expressively uttered that we had no difficulty in interpreting the words to mean that there was the most extreme necessity for rapid movement on our part. We accordingly hastened our steps to the utmost limit of our capacity, and in about ten minutes from the moment of our liberation emerged upon a long narrow strip of sandy beach, with the noble river sweeping grandly to seaward before us. Here our guide paused for a moment, apparently pondering as to what it would next be best to do. Glancing down the river I saw indistinctly, at about two hundred yards distance, some shapeless objects which I took to be canoes drawn up on the beach, and pointing to them I exclaimed to Smellie:

"Are not those canoes? If they are, what is to prevent our seizing one and making our way down the river without further ado?"

Our little Hebe glanced in the direction I had indicated, and seemed quite to understand the nature of my suggestion, for she shook her head violently and exclaimed rapidly in accents of very decided dissent, "Ve! *Ve*!! Ve!!!" pointing at the same time to Smellie's and my own untended wounds.

At that moment a loud confused shouting arose in the distant village, strongly suggestive of the discovery of our flight. The sounds apparently helped our guide to a decision as to her next step, for, seizing our hands afresh, she led us straight into the river until the water was up to our knees, and then turned sharply to the right or up stream. Pressing forward rapidly, our way freshened very decidedly by unmistakable shouts of pursuit emanating from the neighbourhood of the village, we reached, after about a quarter of an hour of arduous toil, a small creek some forty yards wide. Pausing here for a moment, our guide made with her hands and arms the motion of swimming, pointed across the creek, touched Smellie on the breast with the query "Yenu?" and then rapidly repeated the same process with me. We took this to mean an inquiry as to our ability to swim the creek, and both replied "Yes" with affirmative nods. Whereupon our guide, raising her finger to express the necessity for extreme caution, and uttering a warning "Ngandu" as she next pointed to the waters of the creek, waded gently and without raising a ripple into the deep water, Smellie and I following, and with a few quiet strokes we happily reached the other side in safety, to plunge forthwith into the friendly shadows of the forest. Had we known then—what we learned afterwards— that the word "Ngandu" is Congoese for "crocodile," and that it was uttered as an intimation to us that the river and its creeks literally swarm with these reptiles, it is possible that our swim, short though it was, would not have been undertaken with quite so much composure.

Once fairly in the forest, it became so dark that it was quite impossible for us to see whither we were going, but our guide seemed to be well acquainted with the route, which, from the comparatively few obstacles met with, seemed to be a tolerably well-beaten path, so we crowded sail and pressed along with tolerable rapidity behind the slender black and almost indistinguishable figure of our leader. The pursuit, too, was hotly maintained, as we could tell by the occasional shouts and the sudden *swishings* of branches at no great distance from us in the bush; but at length, after a most wearisome and painful tramp of fully nine miles, we got fairly out of reach of all these sounds, and finally, at a sign from our deliverer, flung ourselves down in the midst of a thick growth of ferns at the foot of a giant tree, and, despite the increasing anguish of our wounds, soon went to sleep.

We awoke at daybreak, to find ourselves alone: our guide of

the previous night had vanished. We were greatly disconcerted at this, for we felt that we should like to have done
something—though we scarcely knew what—to mark our
appreciation of her extremely important services of the
preceding night. Besides, somehow, we had both taken the
notion into our heads that in liberating us, she had committed
an unpardonable sin against her former friends, and that
when she crossed the creek and plunged into the forest with
us she was virtually cutting herself adrift from her own
people and casting in her lot with us. In which case, if we
should succeed in making good our escape and finding our
way back to the ship, we had little doubt about our ability to
make such arrangements on her behalf as should cause her to
rejoice for the remainder of her life at having befriended us.
However, it seemed as though, having conducted us to a
place of temporary safety, she had returned to the village,
doubtless hoping to escape all suspicion of having had a
hand in our liberation.

It was a glorious morning. The sun was darting his early
beams through the richly variegated foliage, and touching
here and there with gold the giant trunks and limbs of the
forest trees. The earth around us was thickly carpeted with
long grass interspersed with dense fern-brakes, and here and
there a magnificent clump of aloes, their long waxy leaves
and delicate white blossoms standing out in strong relief
against the blaze of intense scarlet or the rich vivid green of
a neighbouring bush. The early morning air was cool, pure,
and refreshing as it gently fanned our fevered temples and
wafted to us a thousand delicate perfumes. The birds,
glancing like living gems between the clumps of foliage,
were saluting each other blithely as they set out upon their
diurnal quest for food. The bees were already busy among
the gorgeous flowers; butterflies—more lovely even than the
delicate blossoms above which they poised themselves—
flitted merrily about from bough to bough; all nature, in fact,

was rejoicing at the advent of a new day. And ill, suffering though we were, we could not but in some measure take part in the general joy, as with hearts overflowing with gratitude we remembered that we had escaped the horrors of the previous night.

A glance or two about us and we scrambled to our feet, intent, in the first instance, upon an immediate search for water. We had just settled the question as to which direction seemed most promising for the commencement of our quest when a clear musical call floated toward us, and looking in the direction from whence it came, we beheld our black Hebe approaching us, dragging a small dead antelope by the heels after her. So she had not abandoned us after all; on the contrary, she had probably spent a good part of the night arranging for the capture of the creature which was to furnish us with a breakfast.

On joining us she held up her prize for our inspection, and then, with a joyous laugh at our approving remarks—at the meaning of which she could, of course, only make the roughest of guesses—she set to work deftly to clear away and lay bare a space upon which to start a fire, in which task, as soon as we saw what she wanted, we assisted her to the best of our poor ability. This done, she went groping about beneath the trees apparently in search of something; soon returning with two pieces of dry stick, one of which, I noticed, had a hole in it. A quantity of dry leaves and sticks was next collected, having arranged which to her satisfaction, she knelt down, and inserting the pointed end of one stick in the hole of the other, twirled it rapidly between the palms of her hands, producing by the friction thus set up, first a slight wreath of smoke, and ultimately a tiny flame, which was carefully communicated to the dry leaves, and then gently fanned by her breath into a blaze. And in this way a capital fire for cooking purposes was speedily obtained.

In the meantime Smellie and I had produced our knives and had undertaken to skin and cut up the animal, some juicy steaks from which were soon spluttering on pointed sticks before the fire. The cooking operations being thus put in satisfactory progress, our little black friend borrowed my knife and plunged once more into the forest depths, to return again shortly afterwards with a huge gourd full of deliciously clear cool water.

The antelope steaks were by this time ready, and we all sat down to breakfast together. For my own part, I must say I thoroughly enjoyed the meal; but I was sorry to observe that Smellie ate with but little appetite, drinking large quantities of water, however. The poor fellow made no complaint, but I could tell by his haggard look, his flushed cheeks, and his glittering eyes that it was quite time his wounds were attended to, or we should be having him down with fever in the bush, and then Heaven alone could tell when we should—if ever—be able to rejoin the *Daphne*.

But we were not to be allowed to sink tamely into a state of despondency or apprehension; our sable lady friend proved to be, like the rest of her sex, a great talker, and she seized the opportunity afforded by the discussion of breakfast to plunge into an animated conversation. She began by intro-ducing herself, which she managed in quite an original fashion. Pausing for a moment, with a piece of steak poised daintily on a large thorn, she pointed to herself and remarked "Mono;" then touched Smellie and me lightly on the breast and added "Ingeya;" "Ingeya." We nodded gravely to signify that we understood, or thought we did; upon which she pointed to herself once more and observed, "Mono Lubembabemba."

"Which, being interpreted, means, as I take it, that her lady-ship's name is Lubem by—something. Your most obedient servant, Miss Lubin by—"

She laughed a very pretty musical little laugh at Smellie's elaborate assumption of mock gallantry and his bungling efforts to pronounce the name.

"Lubem-ba-bemba," she corrected him; and this time the gallant second lieutenant managed to stumble through it correctly, at which there was more laughter and rejoicing on the lady's part. Then I was called upon to repeat the name, which, having paid the most praiseworthy attention whilst Smellie was receiving his lesson, I managed to do very fairly.

Then, flushed with her success, Miss Lubembabemba made a further attempt at conversation. Pointing to herself and repeating her name, she next pointed to Smellie and asked:

"Ingeya?"

Her meaning was so evident that Smellie answered at once, with another elaborate bow:

"Harold Smellie; at your service."

"Halold-smellie-at-o-serveece!" she repeated with wide-opened eyes of wonder at what she doubtless thought a very extraordinary name.

We both burst involuntarily into a laugh at this really clever first attempt to reproduce the second lieutenant's polite speech; at which she first looked decidedly disconcerted, but immediately afterwards joined heartily in the laugh against herself.

"No, no, no," said Smellie, "that won't do; you haven't got it quite right *Harold*; Harold."

"Halold?" she repeated. And after two or three attempts to put her right—attempts which failed from her evident inability to pronounce the "r"—Smellie was obliged to rest content with being henceforward called "Halold."

Then, of course, she turned to me with the same inquiry:

"Ingeya!"

"Dick," said I.

This time she caught the name accurately, and then, to show that she clearly understood the whole proceeding, pointed to Smellie, to me, and to herself in rotation, pronouncing our respective names.

"Yes," commented Smellie approvingly, "you have learned your lesson very well indeed, my dear; but we shall never be able to remember that extraordinary name of yours—Lubemba—what is it—you know; besides, it will take us a dog-watch to pronounce it in full; so I propose that we change it and re-christen you after the ship, eh? Call you 'Daphne,' you know. How would you like that? You—Daphne; I—Halold, since you *will* have it so; and this strapping young gentleman, Dick. Would that suit you? Daphne—Halold—Dick;" pointing to each of us in turn.

Her ladyship seemed to take the proposal as a tremendous compliment, for her face lighted up with pleasure, and she kept on pointing round the circle and repeating "Halold—Dick—Daphne" until breakfast was concluded. And thenceforward she refused to answer to any other name than Daphne, assuming an air of the most complete unconsciousness when either of us presumed to address her as "Lubembabemba" (the butterfly).

Breakfast over, I thought it was high time to attend to our wounds. The first requirement was water—plenty of it, and this want I managed with some little difficulty to explain to Miss Daphne. Comprehending my meaning at last she intimated that a stream was to be found at no great distance; and we at once set off in search of it, our little black friend carrying along with her a live ember from the fire, which, by waving it occasionally in the air, she managed to keep glowing.

We had not very far to go—most fortunately, for I saw that Smellie's wounds were momentarily giving him increased uneasiness and pain. A walk of about a quarter of an hour took us to a sequestered and most delightful spot, where we were not only perfectly concealed from chance wanderers, but where we also found a small rocky basin full of deliciously cool and pure water, which flowed into it from a tiny stream meandering down the steep hill-side. In this basin we laved our hurts until they were thoroughly cleansed from the dry hard coagulated blood, and then we set about the task of bandaging them up. Daphne, who, by the way, seemed to have little or no idea of surgery, made herself of great use to us in the bathing process, when once she understood what was required; but when it came to bandaging she found herself unable to help us further, and sorrowfully confessed herself beaten. We were compelled to convert our shirts, the only linen in our possession, into bandages; and poor Daphne, to her evident extreme sorrow, had no linen to sacrifice to our necessities, or indeed any clothing at all to speak of. The costume of a Congoese belle, according to her rendering of it, was a petticoat of parti-coloured bead fringe about twelve inches deep, depending loosely from the hips; the rest of her clothing consisting entirely—as Mike Flanaghan would have said—of jewellery, of which she wore a considerable quantity. I may as well here enumerate her ornaments, for the information and benefit of those who have never enjoyed the acquaintance of an African beauty. In the first place she wore a circular band of metal, about two inches wide, round her head and across her forehead. This band, or coronet, had a plain border of about half an inch wide, and inside this border, for about an inch in width throughout its length, the metal was cut away in very fine lines, forming an intricate and really elegant lace-like pattern. Then she wore also a very large pair of circular ear-rings, similarly ornamented, these ornaments being so large and heavy that they had actually stretched the lobes, and so spoiled the shape of what would otherwise have been a very pretty pair of ears. Upon each of her plump, finely-shaped arms, between the shoulder and the elbow, she wore four or five massive armlets of peculiar but by no means unskilled workmanship; and lastly, round each ankle she wore a single anklet of similar workmanship. On the previous night, when this rather lavish display of jewellery had first attracted my casual notice, I had imagined it to be brass; but now, seeing it again in the full light of day, I discovered it to be *gold*, almost or quite pure, as I judged from its softness.

To return to our subject Daphne's first task on our arrival at the pool had been to kindle another fire; and, after helping us as far as she could to doctor our wounds, she next undertook an exploration of the forest in our immediate neighbourhood, returning in about an hour's time with three long, thin, straight shafts of a kind of bamboo, and three small uprooted saplings. These articles she forthwith plunged into the fire, and after an hour's diligent work manipulated the bamboos into three very effective lances or javelins, and the saplings into three truly formidable clubs, the knotted roots being charred and trimmed until they formed rounded heads as large as one's two fists put together. One of each of these weapons she presented both to Smellie and to me, retaining one of each for herself; and thus armed, we were ready to set out once more upon our travels. But it was high time that our wanderings should be conducted with something like method. Our object was, of course, to rejoin the ship with the least possible delay; and before making a fresh start Smellie thought it would be just as well to acquaint our companion with this our desire. He accordingly undertook to do so, and a very amusing scene resulted; but he succeeded at last in making his wish clearly understood, and this achieved we once more resumed our march.

CHAPTER ELEVEN

FAITHFUL UNTO DEATH

By the time that we were finally ready to start it was about noon, and the heat had become intensely oppressive. The refreshing zephyrs of the morning had died completely away, and the motionless atmosphere, rarefied by the burning rays of the sun, was all a-quiver. Not a beast, bird, or insect was stirring throughout the whole length and breadth of the far-stretching forest aisles. The grass, the flowers, the leaves of the trees, the graceful festoons of parasitic creepers, were all as still as though cut out of iron. The stagnant air was saturated to oppressiveness with a thousand mingled perfumes; and not a sound of any kind broke in upon the death-like stillness of the scene. It was Nature's silent hour, the hour of intensest heat; that short interval about noon when all living things appear to retire into the most sheltered nooks—the darkest, coolest shadows; the one hour out of the twenty-four when absolute, unbroken silence reigns throughout the African forest.

Under Daphne's leadership we struck off on a westerly course through the green shadows of the forest, and toiled laboriously forward until the dusky twilight warned us of the necessity for seeking a resting-place wherein to pass the coming night. This was found at length in the centre of a wide clearing or break in the forest; and Smellie and I, at Daphne's expressively—conveyed pantomimic suggestion, forthwith set about gathering the wherewithal to build a fire, whilst the damsel herself undertook the task of providing a supper for the party. Our task was barely completed when her dusky ladyship returned with three grey parrots and a pair of green pigeons, as well as a large gourd of water, from which we eventually managed to make a very satisfying supper. A circle of fires was then built about our camping-place, and we flung ourselves down in the long grass to sleep, two at least of the party being, as I can vouch, thoroughly done up.

We managed to get perhaps a couple of hours of sleep, and then our rest was completely destroyed for the remainder of the night by a well-sustained attack on the part of countless ticks, ants, and other inquisitive insects, which persisted in perambulating our bodies and busily taking sample bites out of our skins in an evident effort to ascertain the locality of the tenderest portions of our anatomy.

Next morning I discovered with the greatest concern that Smellie was downright ill, so much so that it soon became evident it would be quite impossible for us to prosecute our journey, for that day at least. Daphne's distress at this unfortunate state of affairs was very keen, but she was a pre-eminently sensible little body, seeing almost at a glance what was wanted; and promptly diverting her sympathies into a practical channel, she at once set off in search of a more suitable abiding place than the one we had occupied through the night. This she at length found in an open glade at no great distance; and thither we promptly removed our patient, the rapidly-increasing seriousness of his symptoms admonishing us that there was little room for delay.

Our new camping-place was a lovely spot, being an open

amphitheatre of about ten acres in extent surrounded on all sides by the forest, and having a tiny rivulet of pure sparkling fresh water flowing through it. Daphne of course at once took the lead in the arrangements necessary for what threatened to be a somewhat protracted sojourn; and by her directions (it was singular how rapidly we were learning to make ourselves mutually understood) I proceeded in the first instance to clear away the grass, as far as possible, from a circular space some fifteen feet in diameter, within a few yards of the bank of the stream. Daphne, meanwhile, having borrowed Smellie's knife, went off into the forest, from which she soon afterwards returned with a heavy load of long tough pliant wands. Flinging these upon the ground, she next busied herself in lighting a fire on the partially cleared space, employing me to procure for her the necessary materials; and when a large enough bonfire had been constructed, and the embers were all red-hot, she spread them carefully over the whole of the space upon which I had been working, and thus effectually destroyed what grass I had been unable to remove. This done our next task was to cut all the wands or wattles to a uniform length of about twenty-seven feet and point them at both ends; after which, by driving the ends into the soil on opposite sides of our cleared circle of ground, we soon had complete the framework of a hemi-spherical bee-hive-like structure. A second load of wattles was, however, necessary to strengthen this framework to Daphne's liking, and leaving poor Smellie for the nonce to take care of himself, the pair of us set out to procure them. Daphne led me to a dense brake wherein immense numbers of these wattles were to be found, and leaving me to cut as many as I could carry, proceeded further afield in quest of building material of another sort I had completed my task and was back in camp preparing my load for use when Daphne returned; and this time she came staggering in under a tremendous load of palm-leaves, which I rightly guessed were to be used for thatch. So we toiled on during the whole of that day, which, like the preceding, was intensely hot, and by dusk our hut was so far complete as to be capable of affording us a shelter during the succeeding night. By mid-day of the following day it was quite finished; and an efficient shelter having thus been provided for Smellie from the scorching rays of the sun, we were then in a position to give him our undivided attention, of which he by that time stood in most urgent need.

The ensuing fortnight was one of ceaseless anxiety to Daphne and myself, poor Smellie being prostrate with raging fever and utterly helpless during the whole of that time. Fugitives as we were, and in a savage country, it was quite out of our power to procure assistance, medical or otherwise. We were thrown completely upon our own resources, and we had nothing whatever to guide us in our inexperience. Daphne, to my surprise, appeared to possess no knowledge whatever of the healing art; and thus the treatment of our patient devolved solely upon me. And what could I do?

I had no drugs; and had I had access to the best appointed apothecary's shop I should still have lacked the knowledge requisite for a right use of its contents. So we were obliged, no doubt fortunately for the patient, to allow Nature to take her course, merely adopting such simple precautionary measures as would suggest themselves to anyone possessed of average common sense. We provided for our patient a comfortable, fragrant, springy bed of a species of heather; cleansed and dressed his wounds as often as seemed necessary; kept him as cool as possible, and fed him entirely upon fruits of a mild and agreeable acid flavour. During that fortnight Smellie was undoubtedly hovering on the border-land between life and death, and but for the tireless and tender solicitude of Daphne I am convinced he would have passed across the dividing line and entered the land of shadows. I soon saw that this poor ignorant black girl, this unsophisticated savage, had, all unknowingly to Smellie, yielded up her simple untutored heart a willing captive to the charm of his genial manner and gallant bearing; and as the crisis approached which was to decide the question of life or death with him, the unhappy girl established herself beside him and seemed to enter upon a blind, dogged, obstinate struggle with the Grim Destroyer, with the life of the unconscious patient as the stake.

As for me, I was wretched, miserable beyond all power of description. Knowing but little of Smellie, save as my superior officer, until the terrible night when we found ourselves fellow-captives doomed to a cruel death together, I had since then seen so much that was noble and good in him that I had speedily learned to *love* him with all my heart, ay, with the same love which David bore to Jonathan. And there he lay, sick unto death, and I was powerless to help him.

At length, leaving him one day under Daphne's care, I sallied forth to seek a fresh supply of fruit for him, and, wandering farther than usual afield in my misery and abstraction, I discovered a fruit-bearing tree quite new to me. The fruit—a kind of nut somewhat similar to a walnut—had a very strong, but by no means unpleasant, bitter taste, and it suddenly occurred to me that possibly this fruit might prove to be a not altogether ineffective substitute for quinine. At all events, I was resolved to try it, on myself first, if necessary, and I gathered as many of the nuts as I could conveniently carry.

On my arrival at the hut I showed them to Daphne, and tried to find out whether she knew anything about them; but for once we failed to comprehend each other, and I was obliged to carry out my original intention of experimenting upon myself. With this object I opened the nuts and set the kernels to steep in water in a gourd basin (upon setting up house-keeping we soon accumulated quite a number of gourd

Harry Collingwood

utensils). I observed with satisfaction that the water soon began to acquire a brown colour; and after my decoction had stood for about three hours I found that its flavour had become quite as strong as was desirable. Fearing to take much at the outset, lest I should unwittingly be swallowing poison, I drank about a quarter of a pint, and then, with some anxiety, awaited the result. It was about noon when I swallowed the potion, and two hours afterwards I was more hungry than I remembered to have ever been before. So far, good; I determined to wait until night, and then, if no worse result than hunger revealed itself, try the effect of my new medicine upon Smellie. By sunset I had come to the conclusion, that whatever else my decoction might be, it was not a poison, and with, I must confess, a certain amount of fear and trepidation, I at last prevailed upon myself to administer the draught, sitting down forthwith to watch and await the result. By midnight the most that could be said of our patient was that he was no worse; and, encouraged on the whole by this negative result, I then administered a second and larger dose. Next morning I thought I detected signs of improvement, and by sundown the improvement was no longer doubtful; the dry, scorching feeling of the skin had given place to a cool healthy moisture; the pulse was slower; the fevered and excited brain at length found rest, and the patient at last even pleaded guilty to a feeling of hunger.

Jubilation now reigned supreme in our palm-leaf hut; the fatted calf (in the shape of a parrot of gorgeous plumage) was killed—and devoured by the patient with something approaching to relish—and my reputation as a great medicine-man was thenceforth fully established.

From this time Smellie began to slowly mend, thanks as much, probably, to Daphne's tireless nursing and assiduous care as to the relentless perseverance with which I administered my new medicine; and in little more than a week he was able, with assistance, to totter into the open air and sit for half an hour or so under the shadow of a rough awning of thatch which Daphne and I had with some difficulty contrived to rig up for him.

Our little black friend still continued to devote herself wholly to Smellie, waiting upon him hand and foot, watching beside him night and day, fanning him with a palm-leaf, or feeding him on delicious fruit whilst he lay awake under his rude shelter drawing in fresh life and renewed health at every inspiration of the delicious, perfume-laden air, and snatching brief intervals of rest only whilst he slept. In consequence of this arrangement the furnishing of the larder devolved wholly upon me, and I soon acquired a considerable amount of skill in bringing down my game, principally birds, either by a dexterous cast of my club, or by means of a long reed tube, like an exaggerated pea-shooter, from which I puffed little reed darts to a great distance with considerable force.

About a fortnight after Smellie had exhibited the first symptoms of improvement I went out foraging as usual, and, having secured the necessary supplies, was within a quarter of a mile of our hut, on my return journey, when I suddenly discovered a negro stealing cautiously along from tree to tree before me. His actions were so suspicious that my curiosity was aroused, and, placing myself in ambush behind the nearest tree, I resolved to watch him. He was making straight for our hut, dodging from tree to tree, and lurking behind each until he had apparently satisfied himself that the coast ahead was perfectly clear. Such excessive caution on the stranger's part, coupled with the fact that he carried four broad-pointed spears, seemed to me to indicate a purpose the direct reverse of friendly, and I came to the conclusion that it would be well to shorten the distance between him and myself a trifle, if possible. This, however, was not by any means easy to do until the skulking savage had arrived within sight of the hut, when he paused long enough to allow of my creeping up to within a dozen yards of him, when the reason for his hesitation became apparent. Smellie and Daphne were under the awning outside the hut, and my mysterious friend could advance no further without passing into the open clearing, and so revealing himself.

We remained thus for fully half an hour, the savage so intently watching the couple under the awning that he had not the remotest suspicion of being himself watched. At the end of that time, the sun having set meanwhile, Smellie staggered to his feet, and, leaning on Daphne's shoulder, passed into the hut.

My mysterious neighbour maintained his position for some five minutes longer, and then, springing from his hiding-place, made a dash for the hut at full speed, I following. When I emerged from the forest into the open amphitheatre in the centre of which stood our hut, the savage was some fifty yards ahead of me, running like a hunted deer. I began to fear that he was bent on mischief of some kind, and—now that it was too late—keenly regretted the indecision which had allowed him to remain so long unchallenged. In my anxiety to check his speed I raised a shout. At the sound he glanced over his shoulder, saw me in hot pursuit, and paused for an instant, dashing forward the next moment, however, more rapidly than ever.

My shout was evidently heard by the occupants of the hut, for Daphne immediately afterwards appeared at the entrance. At the sight of the figure bounding toward her she uttered a little cry and put out her hands protestingly, calling out to him at the same time. I could not catch the words she uttered, and if I could have done so it is very improbable that I should have understood them, but it struck me that they conveyed either a warning or an appeal. Whatever they were, he paid no attention to them, but still rushed forward, brandishing a spear threateningly. In another second or two he reached the hut and endeavoured to force an entrance. To this, however, Daphne offered the most energetic opposition, obstinately maintaining her position in the doorway. The savage then strove to *force* his way in, but Daphne still persisting in her opposition he drew back a pace, and, raising his arm with a savage cry, drove the broad-bladed javelin with all his brutal strength down into her bare bosom. The poor girl staggered under the force of the blow, and with a stifled shriek and an appealing cry to "Halold," reeled backward, and fell to the ground inside the hut. Meanwhile, the savage, leaving the javelin quivering in the body of his victim, turned to meet me, snatching another javelin with his right hand from his left at the same instant; and as he did so I recognised our former enemy, the fetish-man or witch-doctor of Daphne's village. I was by this time within arm's-length of him, and, quick as light, he made a lunge at me. By a happy chance I succeeded in parrying the stroke with the blow-pipe which I held in my left hand, and then, springing in upon him, I dealt him so tremendous a blow with my heavy, knotted, hard-wood club that his skull crashed under it like an egg-shell, and he fell a brainless corpse at my feet.

Entering the hut I found Smellie on his knees beside the lifeless body of Daphne.

"Too late, Hawkesley! you were just too late to save this poor devoted girl," he murmured. "Only a few seconds earlier, and you would have been in time to arrest the murderous blow. She is quite dead; indeed her death must have been instantaneous. See, the blade of the javelin is quite a foot long, and it was completely buried in her body; it must have passed clean through her heart. Poor girl! she was indeed faithful unto death, for it was my life that yonder murderous wretch thirsted for. You doubtless recognised him—the fetish-man who strove so hard to terrify us on the night of the sacrifice in the village! I am convinced that, in his anger and chagrin at our escape, he has patiently hunted us down, determined to make us feel his vengeance in one way if he failed in the other. Poor Daphne clearly read his intention, I am sure; and it was her resistance, her defence of poor helpless me, that brought this cruel death upon her. Well, God's will be done! The poor girl was only an ignorant savage, and it is hardly possible that she can ever have heard His holy name mentioned; but for all that she had pity upon the stranger and him who had no helper, and I cannot but believe that she will therefore receive her full reward. It only remains now to so dispose of her body that it shall be secure from violation by the birds of the air and the beasts of the field. But how is that to be done?"

He might well ask. We had neither shovel nor any other appliance wherewith to dig a grave, and it was obviously impossible to do so with our bare hands alone. We at length decided to burn both the bodies, and I forthwith set about the construction of a funeral pyre. Fortunately, we had the forest close at hand; the ground beneath the trees was abundantly strewn with dry leaves, twigs, and branches, and thus I had not far to go for fuel. By the time that darkness closed in I had accumulated a goodly pile close to the edge of the open amphitheatre, and thither I at length conveyed both the bodies, laid them on the top of the pyre, and finally ignited the heap of dried leaves which I had arranged in the centre.

This done, Smellie came out of the hut, and we stood side by side mournfully watching the crematory process. Naturally, we were very keenly distressed at the untimely and tragic fate which had overtaken our staunch little friend Daphne. She had been so cheerful, so helpful, and—particularly during Smellie's illness—so tender, so gentle, so sympathetic, and so tireless in her ministrations, that, unconsciously to ourselves, we had acquired for her quite a fraternal affection. As I stood there watching the fierce, bright flames which were steadily reducing her body to ashes, and recalled to mind the countless services she had rendered us during the short period of our mutual wanderings, and, above all, the fervent compassion which had moved her to a voluntary and permanent abandonment of home and friends for the sake of two helpless strangers of a race entirely alien to her own, my heart felt as though it would burst with sorrow at her cruel fate. As for Smellie, trembling with weakness and depressed in spirits as he was after his recent sharp attack of fever, he completely broke down, and, laying his head upon my shoulder, sobbed like a child. Poor Daphne! it seemed hard that she should thus, in the first bright flush and glory of her maidenhood, be struck down, and the light of her life extinguished by the ruthless hand of a murderer; and yet, perhaps, after all, it was better so, better that she should enjoy the bliss of laying down her life for the sake of the man she loved, rather than that, living on, she should see the day when all the vague, indefinite hopes and aspirations of her innocent, unsophisticated heart would crumble into ashes in a moment, and the man who, all unknowingly, had become the autocrat of her fate and the recipient of her blind, passionate, unreasoning love should lightly and smilingly bid her an eternal farewell.

At length the fire died down: the crematory process was completed; nothing remained of the pyre and its burden but a smouldering heap of grey, flaky ashes; and we returned sorrowfully to our hut, there to forget in sleep, if we could, the grievous loss we had sustained.

The painful incident of Daphne's death produced so distressing an effect upon Smellie in his feeble condition that another week passed away before he was sufficiently recovered to admit of our resuming our journey. By the end of that time, however, his strength had in some measure returned, and a feverish anxiety to get away from the scene of the tragedy having taken possession of him, we made what few preparations we had it in our power to make and got under weigh directly after breakfast on one of the most delightful mornings it has ever been my good fortune to witness.

Our progress was, of course, painfully slow; but by this time speed was a matter of merely secondary importance, since we knew that we must long since have been given up by our shipmates as dead; and that the *Daphne* was, in all probability, hundreds of miles away in an unknown direction. It was quite possible that on reaching the river's mouth we might have to wait weeks, or even months, before she would again make her appearance and give us an opportunity to rejoin.

Day after day we plodded on through the glorious forest, following no pathway, but shaping a course as directly west as circumstances would permit, meeting with no incidents worthy of mention, picking up a sufficient subsistence without much trouble, our way beguiled by glorious prospects of wood and river, and our curiosity fed by the countless strange glimpses into the secrets of nature afforded us as we wended our way through that lonely wilderness. We slept well at night in spite of the babel of sounds which rose and fell around us; awoke in the morning refreshed and hungry; and so entered upon another day. The life was by no means one of hardship; and what was most important of all, Smellie was slowly but steadily regaining strength and progressing toward recovery.

At length, late in the afternoon of the fifth day from that which had witnessed the resumption of our journey, our wanderings came unexpectedly to an end, for a time at least, by our stumbling, in the most unexpected manner in the world, upon a human habitation. And the strangest as well as the most fortunate part of it was that the habitation in question was the abode of *civilised* humanity. We had been travelling, almost uninterruptedly, along the ridge of a range of hills, and on the afternoon in question had reached a spot where the range took an abrupt turn to the southward, curving round in a sort of arm which encircled a basin or valley of perhaps half a mile in width, open to the river on the north side. The hill-side sloped gently down to the valley bottom on the eastern, southern, and western sides, and was much more thickly wooded than the country through which we had hitherto been passing. In the very thickest part of the wood, however, and about half-way down the slope, was a clearing of some ten acres in extent, and in the centre of the clearing a very neat and pretty-looking house, with a verandah running all round it, and a thatched roof. The clearing itself appeared to be in a high state of cultivation, a flower-garden of about an acre in extent lying immediately in front of the house, whilst the remainder of the ground was thickly planted with coffee, peach, banana, orange, and various other fruit-trees.

We lost no time in making our way to this very desirable haven, and had scarcely passed through the gate in the fence which surrounded the clearing when we were fortunate enough to encounter the proprietor himself. He was a very fine handsome specimen of a man, with snow-white hair and moustache, both closely cropped, and an otherwise clean-shaven face, which, with his neck and hands, were deeply bronzed by exposure to the vertical rays of the sun. He was clad in white flannel, his head being protected by a light and very finely-woven grass hat with an enormous brim, whilst his feet were encased in a pair of slippers of soft untanned leather. He was busily engaged among his coffee-trees when he first caught sight of us; and his start of surprise at our extraordinary appearance was closely followed up by a profound bow as he at once came forward and courteously addressed us in Spanish. Unhappily neither Smellie nor I understood a word of the language, so the second lieutenant answered the hail in French. The old gentleman shook his head and, I thought, looked rather annoyed, whereupon Smellie tried him in English, to which, very much to my surprise, I must confess, he responded with scarcely a trace of accent.

"Welcome, gentlemen, welcome!" he exclaimed, with outstretched hand. "So you are English? Well, after all, I might have guessed it. I am glad you are not French—*very* glad. Do me the honour to consider my house and everything it contains as your own. You have met with some serious misfortune, I grieve to see; but if you will allow him, Manuel Carnero will do his best to repair it. You have evidently suffered much, and appear to be in as urgent need of medical attendance as you are of clothing. Fortunately, I can supply you with both, and shall be only too happy to do so; I have a very great regard for the English. Come, gentlemen, allow me to conduct you to the house."

So saying, he escorted us up the pathway until the house was reached, when, stepping quickly before us, he passed through the open doorway, and then, turning round, once more bade us welcome to his roof.

CHAPTER TWELVE

DONA ANTONIA

The ceremony of bidding us formal welcome having been duly performed to Don Manuel's satisfaction, he turned once more and called in stentorian tones for some invisible individual named Pedro, who, quickly making his appearance in the shape of a grave decorous-looking elderly manservant, received certain instructions in Spanish; after which our host, turning to us, informed us that his valet would have the honour of showing us to our rooms. Thereupon the sedate and respectful Pedro, who was far too well-trained a servant to betray the slightest symptom of surprise at our exceedingly disreputable appearance, led the way to two small but pleasantly situated rooms adjoining each other, and, bowing profoundly to each of us as we passed into our respective apartments, closed the doors and withdrew.

The rooms in question were furnished with bed, washstand, dressing-table, etcetera, precisely in the English fashion, but the floors, instead of being covered with carpets, were bare, save for a large and handsome grass mat which occupied the centre of the room. I flung myself into a chair and was gazing complacently about me, congratulating myself upon the good fortune which had guided our wandering feet to such exceedingly comfortable quarters, when I heard

Smellie's door open, and the next moment caught the tones of Don Manuel's voice. Directly afterwards a knock came to my own door, and upon my shouting "Come in," Pedro reappeared bearing upon his arm what proved to be a complete rig-out from stem to stern, including even a hat and a pair of shoes. These he spread out upon the bed, and then once more withdrew.

I took the garments up and looked at them. They were just about my size, a trifle large, perhaps, but nothing worth speaking about; they had evidently been worn before, but were in excellent condition, beautifully clean, and altogether so inviting that I lost no time in exchanging them for my rags. This exchange, in addition to a pretty thorough ablution, made quite a new man of me; I felt actually comfortable once more, for the first time since leaving the *Daphne* on the occasion of that unfortunate night attack.

Smellie was still in his room, for I could hear him moving about, so I went in, curious to know whether he had fared equally well with myself. I found him struggling, with Pedro's assistance, slowly and rather painfully into a some-what similar suit to that which I had donned; but the poor fellow, though still very thin and haggard, looked brighter, better, and altogether more comfortable than I had seen him for a long time, our new friend Don Manuel having personally dressed his wounds for him before turning him over to the hands of Pedro.

The second lieutenant looked at me in astonishment. "Why, Hawkesley, is that you?" he exclaimed. "Upon my word, young gentleman, you look vastly comfortable and vastly well, too, in your borrowed plumes. Why, you are worth a dozen dead men yet."

"I think I may say the same of you, my dear sir," I replied. "I am heartily glad to see so great a change in your appearance."

"Thank you very much," he returned. "Yes, I feel actually comfortable once more. Don Manuel has dressed and bound up my wounds, applying soothing salves to them, and altogether tinkering me up until I am pretty nearly as good as new. But, Hawkesley, my dear boy, are we in our sober senses, or is this only a delightful dream? I can scarcely realise that I am awake; that we are actually among our fellow-men once more; and that I am surrounded by the walls and sheltered by the roof of a material house, in which, as it seems to me, we are likely to enjoy a good many of the comforts of civilisation. But come," as he settled himself into a loose white flannel jacket, "let us join our host, who, I have reason to believe, is awaiting our presence at his dinner-table. Heave ahead, Pedro, my lad; we're quite ready to weigh."

Pedro might have understood Smellie's every word, so promptly did he fling open the door and bow us to follow him. Leading us along a cool and rather dark corridor, he conducted us to the front part of the house, and throwing open the door of a large and very handsomely furnished apartment, loudly announced us in Spanish as what I took to be "the English hidalgos."

Don Manuel was awaiting us in this room, and on our entrance rose to greet us with that lofty yet graceful courtesy which seems peculiar to the Spaniard. Then, turning slightly, he said:

"Allow me, gentlemen, to present to you my daughter Antonia, the only member of my family remaining to me. Antonia, these are two English gentlemen who, I trust, will honour us so far as to remain our guests for some time to come."

We duly bowed in response to her graceful curtsey, and her few words of welcome, spoken in the most piquant and charming of broken English, and then, I believe, went in to dinner. I say, I *believe* we went in to dinner on that eventful evening, because I know it was intended that we should; but I have no recollection whatever of having partaken of the meal. For the rest of that evening I was conscious of but one thing—the presence of Antonia Carnero.

How shall I describe her?

She was of medium height, with a superbly moulded figure, neither too stout nor too slim; a small well-poised head crowned with an immense quantity of very dark wavy chestnut hair having a golden gleam where the light fell upon it but black as night in its shadows; dark finely-arched eyebrows surmounting a pair of perfectly glorious brilliant dark-brown eyes, now sparkling with merriment and anon melting with deepest tenderness; very long thick dark eyelashes; a nose the merest trifle *retrousse*; a daintily-shaped mouth with full ripe ruddy lips; and a prettily rounded chin with a well-developed dimple in its centre. Her voice was musical as that of a bird; her complexion was a clear pale olive; her movements were as graceful and unrestrained as those of a gazelle; and she was only eighteen years of age, though she looked more like two-and-twenty.

We were a very pleasant party at dinner that evening. Don Manuel was simply perfect as a host, courteously and watchfully attentive to our slightest wants, and frankness itself in his voluntary explanation of the why and the wherefore of his establishment of himself in such an out-of-the-way place. Antonia, whilst not taking any very prominent part in the conversation, struck in now and then with a suggestive, explanatory, or playful remark, showing that she was was both attentive to and interested in the conversation. Smellie, more easy and comfortable, both in mind and body, than he had been for many a day, abandoned himself to the pleasant influences of his surroundings and bore his part like the cultured English gentleman he was; his deep rich melodious voice, easy graceful bearing, commanding figure, and handsome face, still pale and wan from his recent sufferings, evidently proving immensely attractive to Dona Antonia, much to my secret disgust. As for me, I am afraid I did little more than sit a silent worshipper at the shrine of this sylvan beauty upon whom we had so unexpectedly stumbled.

Don Manuel informed us that, though a Spaniard by birth, he had spent so many years in England that all his tastes and sympathies had become thoroughly Anglicised; that his second wife, Dona Antonia's mother, had been an Englishwoman; that he was an enthusiastic naturalist; and that he had chosen the banks of the Congo for his home principally in order that he might be able to study fully and at his leisure the fauna and flora of that little-known region; adding parenthetically that he had found the step not only a thoroughly agreeable but also a fairly profitable one, by doing a little occasional business with the whites who frequented the river on the one hand and with the natives on the other. I thought he looked a trifle discomposed when Smellie informed him that we were English naval officers, and I am quite sure he did when he was further informed that we had been in the hands of the natives. A very perceptible shade of anxiety clouded his features when Smellie recounted our adventures from the moment of our leaving the *Daphne*; and once or twice he shook his head in a manner which seemed to suggest the idea that he thought we might perhaps prove to be rather dangerous guests, under all the circumstances. If, however, any such idea really entered his mind he was careful to restrain all expression of it, and at the end of Smellie's narrative he uttered just the few courteous phrases of polite concern which seemed appropriate to the occasion and then allowed the subject to drop. Dona Antonia, on the contrary, evinced a most lively interest in the story, her face lighting up and her eyes flashing as she asked question after question, and her parted lips quivering with excitement and sympathetic apprehension as Smellie lightly touched upon the critical situations in which we had once or twice found ourselves. To my great surprise, and, I may add, disappointment, however, she did not exhibit very much sympathy in poor Daphne's tragic fate; on the contrary, she appeared to me to listen with a feeling closely akin to impatience to all that part of the story with which the negro girl was connected; and Smellie's frequent mention of the poor unfortunate creature actually elicited once or twice a slight but quite unmistakable shrug of the lovely shoulders and a decidedly contemptuous flash from the glorious eyes of his fair auditor.

I may as well at once confess frankly that, with the usual susceptibility of callow youth, I promptly became captivated by the charms of our lovely hostess; and I may as well complete my confession by stating that, with the equally usual overweening conceit of callow youth, I quite expected to find my clumsy and ill-timed efforts to render myself agreeable to my charmer speedily successful. In this expectation, however, I was doomed to be grievously disappointed; for I soon discovered that, whilst Dona Antonia was good-natured enough to receive my awkward attentions with unvarying patience and politeness, it was *Smellie's* footstep and the sound of *his* voice which caused her eyes to sparkle, her cheek to flush, and her bosom to heave tumultuously. So, in extreme disgust at the lady's deplorable lack of taste and discernment, I was fain to abandon my efforts to fascinate her, attaching myself to her father instead and accompanying him, gun in hand, on his frequent rambles through the forest in search of "specimens."

Returning to the house one evening rather late, we found a stranger awaiting Don Manuel's arrival. That is to say, he was a stranger to Smellie and myself, but he was evidently a tolerably intimate acquaintance of our host and hostess. He was a tall, dark, handsome, well-built man, evidently a Spaniard, with black restless gleaming eyes, a well-knit figure, and a manner so very free-and-easy as to be almost offensive. His attire consisted of a loose jacket of fine blue cloth garnished with gold buttons, a fine linen shirt of snowy whiteness, loose white nankeen trousers confined at the waist by a crimson silk sash, and a pair of canvas slippers on his otherwise naked feet. He wore a pair of gold rings in his small well-shaped ears, and the gold-mounted horn handle of what was doubtless a stiletto peeped unobtrusively from among the folds of his sash. A crimson cap of knitted silk with a tassel of the same depending from its pointed crown lay on a chair near him, and completed a costume which, whilst it undoubtedly set off his very fine figure to advantage, struck me as being of a somewhat theatrical character. Don Manuel greeted him in Spanish with effusion, and yet with—I thought;—a faint suspicion of uneasiness, on our entrance, and then introduced him to Smellie and me in English, as Senor Garcia Madera. He bowed stiffly in acknowledgment, murmured something to the effect that he "no speak Inglese," and then rather rudely turned his back upon us, and addressing Dona Antonia in Spanish, evidently laid himself out to play the agreeable to her.

I think we all—except Senor Madera,—felt slightly uncomfortable at dinner and for the remainder of that evening. Don Manuel indeed strove with all his might to promote and encourage general conversation, but his behaviour lacked that graceful ease which usually characterised it, his manner was constrained; he was obviously making an effort to dissipate the slight suggestion of discord which obstinately asserted itself in the social atmosphere, and I could see that he was a little ruffled at finding his efforts unsuccessful. As for Antonia, it was easy to see that the new guest was to her an unwelcome one, and his persevering attentions distasteful to her; yet, either because he *was* a guest or for some other cogent reason, she evidently did her best to be agreeable and conciliatory to the man, casting, however, slight furtive deprecatory glances in Smellie's direction, from time to time, as she did so.

Senor Madera—who was evidently a seaman and not improbably the master of a slaver—remained the guest of Don Manuel for the night, sleeping under his roof, and taking his departure very early next morning, before either Smellie or I had turned out, in fact. On our making our appearance Don Manuel referred to his late visitor, explaining that he commanded a ship which traded regularly to the river, and was one of the few individuals through whom he maintained communication with his native country. He apologised very gracefully for his acquaintance's brusque behaviour of the night before, which, whilst deprecating, he explained by attributing it to a feeling of jealousy, Madera having, it would appear, exhibited a decided disposition to pay serious attention to Dona Antonia during his last two or three visits. And—Don Manuel suggested—being like the rest of his countrymen, of an exceedingly jealous disposition, it was possible that he would feel somewhat annoyed at finding two gentlemen domiciled beneath the same roof as his *inamorata*. At this Smellie drew himself up rather haughtily, and was beginning to express his profound regret that our presence in the house should prove the means of introducing a discordant element into an affair of so delicate a nature, when Don Manuel interrupted him by assuring us both that he regarded the circumstance as rather fortunate than otherwise, since, however much he might esteem Senor Madera as an acquaintance and a man of business, he was by no means the class of person to whom he would be disposed to confide the happiness of his daughter.

This little apology and explanation having been made, the party separated, Smellie retiring to the verandah with a book to study Spanish, while Don Manuel and I trudged off with our guns and butterfly-nets as usual.

On our return we found that Madera had again put in an appearance, and another evening of constraint and irritation was the result. This occurred also on the third evening, after which for a short time Senor Madera, apparently conscious of the fact that his company was not altogether desirable, relieved us of his presence.

Just at this time it happened unfortunately—or fortunately rather, as the event proved—that Don Manuel was confined to the house, his hand having been badly stung by some poisonous insect, and I availed myself of the opportunity to make an exploration of the neighbourhood. We had of course taken an early opportunity to acquaint Don Manuel with our expectation that the *Daphne* would again visit the river at no very distant period, and that whenever such an event occurred we should make a very strenuous effort to rejoin her; and he had promised to use every means that lay in his power to procure for us timely notice of her arrival, pointing out at the same time the paucity of his sources of information, and suggesting that whilst it would afford him unmingled pleasure to retain us as his guests for an indefinite period it would be well for us when we were quite tired of our sojourn ashore to ourselves keep a look-out for the appearance of the ship. So on the occasion of Don Manuel's accident, finding Smellie unwilling—as indeed he was still unable—to take a long walk, I determined, as I have already said, to make a thorough exploration of the neighbourhood, and at the same time endeavour to ascertain whether the *Daphne* was once more in the river.

Madera's appearance at Don Manuel's house, coupled with the evident fact that he was a seaman, had at once suggested to me the strong probability that there must be a navigable creek at no very great distance; and I thought it might be useful to ascertain whether such actually was or was not the case, and—in the event of this question being decided in the affirmative—also to ascertain the precise locality of the said creek. Of course it would have been a very simple matter to put the question directly to Don Manuel; but he had evinced such very palpable embarrassment and reticence whenever Madera's name had been mentioned that I thought it would be better to rely, in the first instance at all events, upon my own personal investigations. So when I left the house that morning it was with the determination to settle this question before turning my attention to anything else.

At a distance of about half a mile from the house the level ridge of the chain of hills was interrupted by a lofty hummock rising some two hundred feet higher than the hills themselves, affording a capital look-out; and to this spot I first of all directed my steps. On arriving at the place, however, I found the growth of timber to be so thick as to completely exclude the prospect; and the only means whereby I could take advantage of my superior elevation, therefore, was to climb a tree. I accordingly looked about me, and at last picked out an immense fellow whose towering height seemed to promise me an uninterrupted view; and, aided by the tough rope-like creepers which depended from its branches, I soon reached its top. From this commanding position I obtained, as I had expected, an unbroken view of the country all round me for a distance of at least thirty miles. The river was naturally a prominent object in the landscape, and, exactly opposite me, was about three miles in width, though, in consequence of the numerous islands which crowded its channel, the water-way was scarcely anywhere more than half a mile in width. These islands ceased about four miles lower down the river, leaving the channel perfectly clear; but they extended up the river in an unbroken chain to the very limits of my horizon. But what gratified me most was the discovery that in clear weather, such as happened to prevail just then, I could see right down to the mouth of the river, Shark Point being just discernible on the western horizon. Boolambemba Point was clearly defined; and I felt convinced that, on a fine day and with a good telescope, I should be able to see and even to identify the *Daphne*, should she happen to be at anchor in Banana Creek at the time.

This important point settled, I turned my attention to matters nearer at hand, and began to look about me for the creek, the existence of which I so strongly suspected. For a few minutes I was unable to locate it; but suddenly my eye, wandering over the vast sea of vegetation which lay spread out beneath me, became arrested by the appearance of a slender straight object projecting a few feet above the tree-tops. A careful scrutiny of this object satisfied me that it must be the mast-head of a ship; and where the ship was, there, too, would be the creek. Doubtless the craft lying there so snug, and in so suspiciously secret a harbour, was the one to which our rather insolent acquaintance Madera belonged; and curiosity strongly prompted me to have a look at her. Accordingly, taking her bearings by the position of the sun, I descended the tree and set out upon my quest I estimated that she was distant from my view-point about two miles, and about one mile from Don Manuel's house. A walk of perhaps three-quarters of an hour conducted me to the edge of a mangrove-swamp; and I knew then that the creek must be at no great distance. Plunging boldly into the swamp, I made my way as best I could over the tangled roots in what I deemed the proper direction, and after a toilsome scramble of another quarter of an hour found myself at the water's edge.

The creek was precisely similar in character to all the others with which I had previously made acquaintance; but so narrow and shallow at the point where I had hit it off that I saw at once, to my vexation, that I must have a further scramble among the mangrove-roots, exposed all the while to the attacks of countless hosts of bloodthirsty mosquitoes, if I would gratify my desire to see Senor Madera's vessel. And, having gone so far, I determined not to turn back until I had satisfied my curiosity; so on I went. My pace over such broken ground was naturally not very brisk, so that it was fully an hour later before I found myself standing—well concealed behind an intervening tree-trunk—opposite a small but beautifully-modelled schooner, moored head and stern close alongside the opposite bank. She was a craft of about one hundred and twenty tons register, painted grey, with very lofty spars, topsail-rigged forward, very little standing rigging, and a most wicked look all over.

When I put in my unobtrusive appearance the crew were busy with a couple of long untrimmed pine spars, the ends of which they were getting ashore. A few minutes' observation sufficed to satisfy me that they were rigging a gangway; and, settling myself comfortably in a position where my presence could not be detected, I determined to see the matter out. I looked carefully for Senor Madera on board, but was unable to detect his presence; I therefore concluded that, unlikely as such a supposition seemed, he had left the ship to make an early call upon Don Manuel.

The gangway was soon rigged, and after testing it by passing along it three or four times one of the schooner's crew disappeared in the bush. A quarter of an hour later he returned, closely followed by a number of armed natives in charge of a gang of slaves, who—poor wretches—were secured together in pairs by means of heavy logs of wood lashed to their necks. These slaves were mostly men; but there were a few young women with them, two or three of whom carried quite young babies lashed on their backs. And every slave, not excepting the women with children, was loaded with one large or two small tusks of ivory. These unfortunates were driven straight on board the schooner, the ivory was taken from them as they reached the deck, and they were then driven below; the *clink, clink* of hammers which immediately afterwards proceeded from the schooner's hold bearing witness to the business-like promptitude with which the unhappy creatures were being secured. I counted them as they passed in over the gangway; they numbered sixty-three; and, judging from the schooner's size, I calculated that she had accommodation for about one hundred and fifty; her cargo being therefore incomplete, I feared we should be called upon to endure Senor Madera's presence for at least another day or two. The wretches who constituted the schooner's crew were a very noisy set, laughing, chattering, and shouting at the top of their voices, and altogether exhibiting by their utter carelessness a perfect consciousness of the fact that there were no men-o'-war just then anywhere near the river. How heartily I wished there had been a pennant of some sort at hand; I felt that I would not have cared what might be its nationality, I would have found means to board the craft, conveying the news of that wretched slaver's whereabouts, and afterwards assisting, if possible, in her capture.

I remained snugly ensconced in my hiding-place until the clearing up and washing down of the decks informed me that work was over on board the schooner for that day, and then set out cautiously to return to the house. I managed to effect a retreat into the cover of the bush without betraying myself; and then, moved by a quite uncontrollable impulse, bent my steps once more in the direction of the hill-top, from which I had that morning effected my reconnaissance—though it took me considerably out of my way—determined to have just one more look round before settling myself for the evening.

It was about four o'clock p.m. by the position of the sun when I once more stood beneath the overshadowing foliage of the tree which I had used as an observatory; and ten minutes later I found myself among its topmost branches. The atmosphere was luckily still quite clear, a fresh breeze from the eastward having prevailed during the whole of that day; but a purplish haze was gathering on the western horizon, and my heart leapt into my mouth—to make use of a well-worn figure of speech—when, standing out in clear relief against this soft purple-grey background, I saw, far away in the south-western board, the gleaming white sails of a ship stretching in toward the land *under easy canvas*.

It was this latter fact, of the ship being under easy canvas, which so greatly gratified me. A slaver or an ordinary trader would have been pressing in under every stitch that would draw—as indeed would a man-o'-war if she were upon some definite errand—but *only* a man-o'-war would approach the land in that leisurely manner with evening close at hand. The stranger was a long distance off—perhaps as much as twenty miles—and it was, of course, impossible to see more than that she *was* a ship of some sort; but I had by that time acquired experience enough to know, from the tiny white speck which gleamed up against the haze, that she was coming in under topsails only. What would I not have given just then to have held my trusty telescope in my hand once more just for an hour or *so*!

Suddenly I remembered having one day seen a very fine instrument belonging to Don Manuel in his own especial den. It was really an astronomical telescope; but, like many similar instruments, it was also provided with a terrestrial eye-piece, for I had looked through it across the river, and had marvelled at its far-reaching power. It was fitted to a tripod stand, but could be disconnected at will; and the bold idea presented itself to me of borrowing this instrument for a short time in order to ascertain, if possible, the nationality of the stranger. It was of course just possible that she might be English, in which event it would manifestly be Smellie's and my own duty to attempt to join her.

Full of this idea I descended hastily to the ground and made my way with all speed in the direction of Don Manuel's house. The telescope was fortunately in the place where I expected to find it; and, disconnecting it from the stand and tucking it into its leather case, I set out again for the look-out tree. Arrived there, I slung the instrument over my shoulder by means of the stout leather strap attached to the case, and at once ascended to the topmost branches of the tree, where, selecting a good substantial limb for a seat, with another conveniently situated to serve as a rest for the telescope, I comfortably settled myself in position, determined to ascertain definitely, if possible, before sunset, what the intentions of the strange sail might be.

I lost no time in extricating the instrument from its case and bringing it to bear upon the white speck, which, even during the short period of my absence, had perceptibly changed its position, thus proving the craft to be a smart vessel under her canvas. I soon had her focused, but found to my intense disappointment that, owing to her great distance and the rarefied condition of the atmosphere due to the intense heat of the day, I was unable to make out very much more in the shape of detail than was possible with the naked eye; the craft, as seen through the telescope, appearing to be merely a wavering blot of creamy white, with another wavering blot of dark colour, representing the hull, below it; a dark line with a spiral motion to it, which made it look like a corkscrew, representing above the sails the bare topgallant and royal-masts. This was vexatious, but the sun was still fully an hour high. By the time that he would reach the horizon the craft would probably be some seven or eight miles nearer; the atmosphere was cooling and becoming less rarefied every minute, and I was sanguine that before darkness set in I should succeed in getting such a view of the stranger as would enable me to form a tolerably accurate opinion as to her nationality and intentions.

Of course I kept my eye glued almost uninterruptedly to the eye-piece of the instrument, merely withdrawing it for a minute or so occasionally to give the visual organ a rest. And gradually, as I watched, the wavering motion of the white and dark blots decreased, they grew less blot-like and more defined in their outlines, and finally I succeeded in detecting the fact that the craft sported a broad white ribbon along her sides. Then I made out that she carried a white figure-head under the heel of her bowsprit; next, that her boats were painted black to their water-lines and white below, and so one detail after another emerged into clear definition until the entire craft stood distinctly revealed in the field of the instrument. By this time I was all a-quiver with excitement, for as the approaching ship showed with ever-increasing distinctness, a growing conviction forced itself upon me that many of her details were familiar to me. Finally, just as the sun was hovering for a moment like a great ball of fire upon the extreme verge of the purple horizon, the stranger tacked. The smartness with which she was manoeuvred was alone almost sufficient to proclaim her as English, but the point was definitely settled by my catching a momentary glimpse of Saint George's ensign fluttering at her peak as it gleamed in the last rays of the setting sun. In another moment she glided gracefully across the golden track of the sinking luminary, her every spar and rope clearly defined and black as ebony, her sharply outlined sails a deep rich purple against the gold, and the broad white ribbon round her shapely hull just distinguishable. The sun vanished, and though the western horizon immediately in his wake was all aglow with gold and crimson, the light at once began to fade rapidly away. I looked again at the ship: she was already a mass of pearly grey, with a row of little dark grey dots along her side, indicating the position of her ports. I took advantage of the last gleam of twilight to count these dots twice over. There were fourteen of them along her starboard broadside, indicating that she was a 28-gun ship; she was ship-rigged, and this, in conjunction with several little peculiarities which I had recognised connected with her spars and rigging, convinced me that she was actually none other than the *Daphne*. Another look—I could just distinguish her against the soft velvety blue-black background of the darkening sea, but I saw enough to satisfy me of the correctness of my surmise, and saw, too, that—happy chance—she was clewing up her courses as though about to lay-to or anchor off the mouth of the river for the night. Then, as she faded more and more and finally vanished from the field of the telescope, I closed the instrument and proceeded to carefully replace it in its case. By the time that I had done this the glow of the western horizon had faded into sober grey, the sky overhead had deepened into a magnificent sapphire blue and was already becoming thickly studded with stars, the forest around and below me had merged into a great shapeless mass of olive-black foliage, out of the depths of which arose the deafening *whir* of countless millions of insects; and the conclusion forced itself upon me that it was high time I should see about effecting a descent from my lofty perch if I wished to do so in safety. I had no sooner scrambled down into the body of the tree than I found myself in complete darkness, and it was with the utmost difficulty and no little danger that I accomplished the remainder of the descent. However, I managed at last to reach the ground without mishap, and, taking up my gun—which I had placed against the trunk of the tree, and without which, acting upon

Don Manuel's advice, I never ventured into the forest—I turned my face homeward, anxious to find Smellie and acquaint him with the state of affairs without a moment's unnecessary delay.

In due time I reached the gate in the palisading which surrounded Don Manuel's garden and passed through. In the brilliant star-light the sandy path which led up to the house was distinctly visible between the rows of coffee and other trees, and so also were two figures, a short distance ahead of me, sauntering along it toward the house, with their backs turned to me. They were evidently male and female, and were walking very closely together, so much so indeed that I felt almost certain that the arm of the taller of the two figures must be encircling the waist of the other, and from the height of the one and the white gleaming garments of the other I at once came to the conclusion that they were Smellie and Dona Antonia. My footsteps were of course quite inaudible on the light sandy soil, and the couple in front of me were consequently in a state of blissful ignorance as to my presence. Had they been aware of it I am little doubtful now as to whether it would have very greatly disturbed their equanimity. Be that as it may, I felt a certain amount of delicacy about advancing, and so showing them that I had been an involuntary witness of their philandering, so I softly stepped aside off the pathway and ensconsed myself behind a coffee-bush, thinking that perhaps they would go on and enter the house, in which case I could follow them in at a respectful distance. If, on the other hand, they did not enter, they would at all events be at such a distance from me when they turned that I might safely show myself without much fear of disconcerting either of them. So thinking, I continued to watch their receding figures, intending to step back into the pathway as soon as they were at a sufficient distance from me.

But before they had traversed half the distance between the gate and the house I was startled at seeing a group of figures suddenly and noiselessly emerge upon the pathway close behind them.

Harry Collingwood

CHAPTER THIRTEEN

AN EVENTFUL NIGHT

What did it mean? Who were they, and what could they possibly want? I could see them clearly enough to distinguish that they wore the garments of civilisation; but they did not belong to the house: Don Manuel had only two men in his service; whereas, so far as I could distinguish in the uncertain light, there were five men in the group before me. Then, too, their actions were suspicious, their movements were stealthy, and it looked very much as though they were dogging the footsteps of the couple ahead of them for no good purpose. I did not at all like the aspect of affairs, so quietly disencumbering myself of the telescope, which I deposited on the ground, I grasped my gun, and, stepping into the pathway, shouted warningly to the second lieutenant:

"Look out, Mr Smellie, you are being followed!" Immediately there was a shout, in Spanish, of "Come on, men, give it him!" and the group made a dash at Smellie and his companion. Then followed an exclamation of surprise and anger in Smellie's well-known voice, a single stifled scream from Dona Antonia, and a most unmistakable affray. With a shout I dashed up the path, and in another minute or less plunged into the thick of the melee. Smellie was beset by three of the ruffians, who were slashing viciously at him with long ugly-looking knives, and he was maintaining a gallant defence with the aid of a stout stick, the assistance of which he had not up to then been wholly able to discard in walking. I saw that if he was to be saved from a serious, perhaps even a fatal, stab, prompt action was necessary, so without waiting for further developments I cocked my gun, and, making a lunge with it at the man who seemed to be Smellie's most formidable antagonist, pulled the trigger just as the muzzle struck his side, and poured the contents of the barrel into his body. At such very close quarters the charge of shot took effect like a bullet, and the fellow staggered backwards and fell to the ground with an oath and an agonised exclamation in Spanish of:

"Help, my men, help; I am shot!"

The remaining two who had been attacking Smellie turned at this to assist their wounded companion; and the second lieutenant and I thereupon dashed down the path after the other two, who were hurrying off the scene with all speed, carrying Dona Antonia bodily away with them. A dozen bounds or so and we were up with them. With an inarticulate cry of rage Smellie sprang upon the man nearest him and brought his stick down upon the fellow's head with such tremendous force that the stout cudgel shivered to pieces in his hand, whilst the recipient of the blow dropped prone without a groan or cry of any kind upon the pathway. The other meanwhile had dropped his share of their joint burden and seemed inclined to resume hostilities, but a well-aimed sweep of the butt-end of my gun took all the fight out of him, and he beat a hasty retreat, leaving his companion to our tender mercies. Smellie, however, had something else to think about, for there, upon the pathway, her white dress already stained with the blood of the prostrate ruffian beside her, lay the senseless body of Dona Antonia. Raising her in his arms my companion at once made for the house, despatching Pedro, who had just put in an alarmed appearance, in advance to summon the assistance of Old Madre Dolores, Antonia's special attendant.

I convoyed the pair as far as the door, and then retraced my steps down the pathway, intent on recovering the telescope, and also to reconnoitre the scene of action and ascertain whether or no the enemy had beaten a final retreat. The ground proved to be clear; so I presume that the fellow whose head Smellie had broken was not after all quite so seriously injured as he at first appeared to be.

On my return to the house I found the whole place in confusion, as might naturally be expected, and Don Manuel, with his damaged hand in a sling, anxiously inquiring of Smellie whether he had any idea as to the identity of the perpetrators of the outrage.

"I certainly *have* an idea who was the leader," answered Smellie; "but I scarcely like to give utterance to my suspicions. Here comes Hawkesley; let us see whether his opinion upon the matter coincides with mine. Hawkesley, do you think you ever met either of those men before?"

"Yes," I replied unhesitatingly; "unless I am greatly mistaken, the man who was so pertinacious in his attack upon you, and whom I shot, was Senor Madera."

"Exactly so," coincided Smellie. "I recognised him directly; but it was so very dark down there among the trees that I scarcely cared to say as much without first having my conviction verified. I very much fear, Don Manuel, you have been grossly deceived by that fellow; if I am not greatly mistaken he is a thorough rascal. I do not say this because of his cowardly attack upon me—that I can quite account for after your explanation of a night or two ago; but his daring outrage upon your daughter is quite another matter."

"Yes, yes," exclaimed Don Manuel excitedly; "the fellow is a villain, there is no doubt about that. I have never entertained a very high opinion of him, it is true; but I must admit that I was quite unprepared for any such high-handed behaviour as that of to-night."

"Well," said Smellie cheerfully, "I think Hawkesley has given his ardour a cooling for some time to come, at all events; and for the rest, you will have to be very carefully on your guard for the future, my dear sir. I do not think he will venture a second attempt so long as we remain under your roof, but after we are gone—"

"Which I hope will not be for some time to come," hospitably interrupted Don Manuel. "But have no fear for us, my dear Don Harold; 'forewarned is forearmed,' as you say in your England, and I shall take care to render any further attack upon my daughter's liberty impossible. But come, dinner awaits us, and we can further discuss the matter, if need be, over the—what is that you call it?—ah, yes, 'the social board!'"

Thereupon we filed into the dining-room, and took our places at the table. And there, before the conversation had an opportunity to drift back into its former channel, I detailed my day's doings, and apprised Smellie of the important fact that the *Daphne* was in the offing.

"This is momentous news, indeed," remarked Smellie when I had finished. "We must leave you to-night, I fear, Don Manuel, reluctant as we both must be to cut short so very agreeable an acquaintance. But I trust we shall have many opportunities of visiting you again, and so keeping alive the friendship established between us; and as to Senor Madera—

Harry Collingwood

if Hawkesley is only correct in his conjectures as to the schooner he saw—why, I trust we may be able to effectually and permanently relieve you of his disagreeable attentions before twenty-four hours have passed over our heads."

Don Manuel bowed. "If Senor Madera is indeed the captain of a slave-ship, as I have sometimes felt inclined to believe he is," said he, "I beg that you will not permit the accident of having encountered him under my roof to influence you in any way in his favour. As I have already said, he is only an acquaintance—not a friend of mine—and if he is a transgressor against the laws relating to the slave-trade, make him suffer for it, if you can lay hands upon him. With regard to your proposed attempt to rejoin your ship to-night, I very much regret that I am only able to offer you the most meagre assistance; such as it is, however, you are heartily welcome to it. I have a canoe down in the creek yonder, and you are very welcome to take her; but she is only a small affair, and as I presume you are not very much accustomed to the handling of canoes, you will have to be exceedingly careful or you may meet with an upset. And that, let me tell you, may possibly prove a very serious affair, since the creek, ay, and the river itself, swarms with crocodiles."

Smellie duly expressed his thankful acceptance of Don Manuel's kind offer, and the conversation then became general. At the conclusion of the meal Smellie requested the favour of a few minutes' private conversation with Don Manuel; and that gentleman, with a somewhat questioning and surprised look, bowed an affirmative and at once led the way to his own especial sanctum.

I never actually heard what was the nature of the momentous communication which the gallant second lieutenant wished so suddenly to make to his host; but from the length of time that they remained closeted together, and the remark of Don

Manuel when they at length reappeared—"Very well, my dear sir, then that is settled; upon the conditions I have named you can have her,"—I made a pretty shrewd guess at it.

In the meantime Dona Antonia had reappeared, very little the worse for her adventure; she was very pale, it is true, and she became perceptibly paler when, with that want of tact which is one of my most marked characteristics, I abruptly told her that we were on the point of leaving her to rejoin our ship. But she amply redeemed this want of colour by the deep rosy flush with which she greeted Smellie's approach and the low whispered request in response to which she placed her hand on his arm and retired with him to the verandah.

It was about 9:30 p.m. when they reappeared, Smellie looking very grave, but at the same time rather exultant, and poor Antonia in tears, which she made no attempt whatever to conceal. I was, of course, all ready to start at a moment's notice. We had no preparations to make, in fact, and we at once proceeded to the disagreeable task of saying farewell to our kind and generous host. It was a painful business; for though we had not known Don Manuel and his daughter very long, we had still known them quite long enough to have acquired for them both a very large measure of esteem and regard—in Smellie's case there could no longer be the least doubt that his feelings toward his hostess were even warmer than this—so we hurried over the leave-taking with all speed, and then set off down the pathway, under Pedro's guidance, on our road to the creek.

It was by this time pitch dark. The stars had all disappeared; the sky had become obscured by a heavy pall of thunder-cloud; and away to the eastward the lightning was already beginning to flash and the thunder to growl ominously. Before we reached the gate in the palisading Pedro had volunteered the prognostication of a stormy night, utterly unfit for such an expedition as that upon which we were bound, and had strongly urged us more than once to follow his counsel and postpone the attempt. But to this proposition we could not, of course, listen for a moment. If we missed the present opportunity to rejoin the *Daphne* it was impossible to conjecture when another might offer; and pleasant though our sojourn under Don Manuel's hospitable roof had undoubtedly been, it was not *business*; every day so spent was a day distinctly lost in the pursuit of our professional interests. So we plodded steadily on, and in about half an hour's time reached the head of the creek, where, carefully housed under a low thatch covering, we found the canoe.

She was, indeed, a frail craft in which to undertake such a journey as ours, being only some two feet six inches beam, by about sixteen inches deep, and twenty feet long; hollowed out of a single log. She had no thwarts, and the paddlers were therefore compelled to squat tailor-fashion in the bottom of her, looking forward. This was, so far, fortunate; since she was so frightfully crank that, with such unaccustomed canoeists as ourselves, it was only by keeping our centres of gravity low down that we prevented her capsizing the moment we stepped into her. Pedro, worthy soul, detained us about twenty minutes whilst he explained the peculiarities of the craft and the proper mode of handling the paddles; and then, with Smellie aft and me forward, we bade the old fellow good-bye and boldly shoved off down the creek.

The channel here being narrow, and overarched to a great extent with trees, the darkness was quite as intense as it had been on our journey from the house through the wood and down to the creek; so dark was it, indeed, that but for the lightning which now flashed around us with rapidly-increasing frequency, it would have been quite impossible for us to see where we were going. This stygian darkness, whilst it proved an obstacle to our rapid progress, promised to afford us, by way of compensation, most valuable assistance in another way, since we hoped to slip past the schooner undetected in the impenetrable obscurity; our desire just then being to avoid anything like a renewal of our acquaintance with Senor Madera so soon after our very recent little misunderstanding. Unfortunately there were two or three phenomena which combined to render this feat a matter of difficulty. The first was the vivid lightning which, at increasingly brief intervals, lit up the channel with noontide distinctness. The next was the failure of the wind; a stark breathless calm having fallen upon the face of nature like a pall, in the which not so much as a single leaf stirred; and the whole insect-world, contrary to its usual custom, awaiting in hushed expectancy the outburst of the coming storm, a great and death-like silence prevailed, through which the slightest sound which we might accidentally make would have been heard for a long distance. And another, and perhaps the worst of all, was the highly phosphorescent state of the water. This was so excessive that the slightest ripple under the bows of the canoe, along her sides, and for some distance in her wake, together with the faint swirls created by our paddles, produced long trailing lines and eddies of vivid silvery light which could scarcely fail to attract the attention of a vigilant look-out and so betray our whereabouts. We were thus compelled to observe the utmost circumspection in our advance, which was made, as far as was practicable, through the deepest shadows of the overhanging foliage.

We were creeping slowly down the channel in this cautious fashion when a slight and almost imperceptible splash from the opposite bank attracted my attention. Glancing across in that direction I noticed a slowly spreading circle of luminous ripples, and beneath them a curious patch of pale phosphorescent light rapidly advancing toward us. In a few seconds it was almost directly underneath the canoe and keeping pace with her. To my consternation I then saw that it was a crocodile about the same length, "over all," as the canoe, the phosphorescence of the water causing his scaly carcass to gleam like a watery moon and distinctly revealing his every movement. We could even see his upturned eyes maintaining a vigilant watch upon us.

"Do you see that, sir?" I whispered.

"I do, indeed," murmured Smellie; "and I only hope the brute is completely ignorant of his ability to capsize us with a single whisk of his tail, if he should choose to do so. Phew! what a flash!"

What a flash, indeed! It seemed as though the entire vault of heaven had exploded into living flame; the whole atmosphere was for a moment irradiated; our surroundings leapt out of the darkness and stood for a single instant vividly revealed; and there, too, away ahead of us, at a distance of perhaps half a mile, appeared the schooner, her hull, spars, and rigging showing black as ebony against the brilliantly— illuminated background of foliage and cloud. Simultaneously with the lightning-flash there came a terrific peal of thunder, which crackled and crashed and roared and rumbled about us with such an awful percussion of sound that I was absolutely deafened for a minute or two. When I recovered my hearing the wild creatures of the forest were still giving vent to their terror in a chorus of roars and howls and screams of dismay. The crocodile, evidently not caring to be out in such weather, had happily vanished. We had scarcely gathered our wits once more about us when the flood-gates of heaven were opened and down came the rain. I had heard a great deal, at one time and another, about the violence of tropical rain-storms, but this exceeded far beyond all bounds the utmost that I had thereby been led to anticipate. It came, not in drops or sheets, or even the metaphorical "buckets-full," but in an absolute *deluge* of such volume that not only were we drenched to the skin in a single instant, but almost before I was aware of it the water had risen in the bottom of the canoe to a depth of at least four inches. I was actually compelled to lean forward in a stooping posture to catch my breath.

For fully five minutes this overwhelming deluge continued to descend upon us, and then it relaxed somewhat and settled down into a steady downpour.

"Was that object which we caught sight of some distance ahead, just now, the schooner?" asked Smellie as soon as the rushing sound of the rain had so far abated as to permit of our hearing each other's voices.

"It was, sir," I replied.

"Then now is the time for us to make a dash past her; they will scarcely be keeping a very bright look-out in such rain as this," he remarked.

We accordingly hauled out into the centre of the stream and plied our paddles as rapidly as possible. We had been working hard for perhaps five minutes when Smellie said in a low cautious tone of voice:

"Hawkesley!"

"Sir?"

"Do you know, the fancy has seized upon me to have a look in on the deck of that schooner. If we are duly cautious I really believe it might be managed without very much risk. Somehow I do not think they will be keeping a particularly bright look-out on board her just now. The look-out may even be stowed away comfortably in the galley out of the rain. Have you nerve enough for the adventure?"

"Certainly I have, sir," I replied, a bold idea flashing at that instant through my brain.

"Then keep a sharp look-out for her, and, when you see her, work your paddle so as to drop the canoe alongside under her main-chains, and stand by to catch a turn with your painter."

"Ay, ay, sir," I replied; and we once more relapsed into silence and renewed paddling.

Five minutes later a shapeless object loomed up close aboard of us on our port bow, and, sheering the canoe sharply to larboard, we dropped her handsomely and without a sound alongside the schooner just in the wake of her main-chains. I rapidly took a turn with the painter round the foremost channel-iron, and in another moment stood alongside my superior officer in the schooner's main-chains.

Placing our heads close to the dead-eyes of the rigging, so as to expose ourselves as little as possible, we waited patiently for another flash of lightning—Smellie looking aft and I looking forward, by hastily-whispered agreement. Presently the flash came.

"Did you catch sight of the look-out?" whispered Smellie to me.

"No, sir," I whispered back; "did you?"

"No; but I noticed that the skylight and companion are both closed and the slide drawn over—probably to exclude the rain. I fancy most of the people must have turned in."

"Very probably," I acquiesced; "there is not much to tempt them to remain out of their bunks on such a night as this."

"True," remarked Smellie, still in the most cautious of whispers. "I feel more than half-inclined to climb inboard and make a tour of the decks."

"All right, sir!" I agreed. "Let us slip off our shoes and get on board at once. You take the starboard side of the deck; I'll take the port side. We can meet again on the forecastle."

"Agreed," was the reply; and slipping off our shoes forthwith we waited for another flash of lightning, and then, in the succeeding darkness, scrambled noiselessly in on deck and proceeded on our tour of investigation.

On reaching the schooner's deck we separated, and I made it my first business to carefully examine the skylight and companion. In the profound darkness it was quite impossible to *see* anything; but by careful manipulation I soon ascertained that the former was shut down, and that the doors of the latter were closed and the slide drawn over within about six inches, as Smellie had said. It must have been frightfully hot down in the cabin, but the officers apparently preferred that to having a deluge of rain beating down below. The cabin was dimly lighted by a swinging lamp turned down very low; but I could see no one, nor was there any sound of movement down there—at which I was considerably surprised, because if the schooner really belonged to Senor Madera, as I had supposed, one would have expected to find one or two persons at least on the alert in attendance upon the wounded man.

Having learned all that it was possible to learn in this quarter, I next proceeded aft as far as the taffrail, where I found the deck encumbered on both sides by two big coils of mooring hawser, the other ends of which were secured, as I had noticed earlier in the day, to a couple of tree-trunks on shore.

I next proceeded leisurely forward, noting on my way the fact that the schooner mounted a battery of four brass nine-pounders on her starboard side—and of course her port battery would be the same. The main hatchway was securely covered in with a grating, up through which arose the unmistakable odour which betrays the presence of slaves in a ship's hold. All was quiet, however, below—the poor wretches down there having probably obtained in sleep a temporary forgetfulness of their miserable condition. On reaching the galley I found that the door on the port side was closed; but on applying my ear to the chink I fancied I could detect, through the steady *swish* of the rain, the sounds of regular breathing, as of a slumbering man. Forward of the galley was the foremast, and on clearing this a faint gleam of light indicated the position of the fore-scuttle; and whilst I was still glancing round in an endeavour to discover the presence of a possible anchor-watch the light was suddenly obscured by the interposition of the second lieutenant's body, as he cautiously peered down into the forecastle. I advanced to his side and laid my hand upon his arm, at the same time mentioning his name to apprise him of my presence.

"Well," he whispered, first drawing me away from the open scuttle, "what have you discovered?"

I told him, adding that I thought the anchor-watch must have taken refuge in the galley from the rain, and there have fallen asleep.

"Yes," whispered Smellie; "he is safe enough there, and sound asleep, for I accidentally touched him without disturbing his slumber."

I thought the time had now arrived for the propounding of my brilliant idea.

"What is to prevent our *seizing the schooner*, sir?" I asked.

"Nothing whatever," was the reply. "I have been thinking of such a thing myself. She is already virtually in our possession, and a very little labour and patience would make her actually so. I think we are men enough to get her under canvas and to handle her afterwards, for she is only a very small craft. The great—and indeed only—danger connected with the affair consists in the possibility of their firing a pistol into the powder-magazine when they discover that they are prisoners, and so sending the ship and all hands sky-high together."

"They *might* possibly do such a thing," I assented; "but I am willing to take the risk, sir, if you are."

"Well done, Hawkesley! you are made of the right stuff for a sailor," was Smellie's encouraging remark. "Then we'll do it," he continued. "The first thing is to close and fasten the fore-scuttle, which, I have already ascertained, is secured with a hasp and staple. A belaying-pin will secure it effectually; so that is the first thing we need."

A loose belaying-pin was soon found; and, provided with this, we then returned to the fore-scuttle, noiselessly placed the cover in position, and thrust the pin through the staple thus effectually imprisoning the crew.

"Now another belaying-pin and a rope's-end—a fathom or so off the end of the topgallant halliards will do—to secure this vigilant look-out in the galley."

Armed with the necessary gear we next crept toward the

galley. The question was, how to secure the man effectually in the intense darkness and confined space, and at the same time prevent his raising an alarm. The only thing was to lure him out on deck; and accordingly, whilst Smellie awaited him at the door, I went in, and grasping him by the shoulder shook him roughly, retiring again promptly as soon as I found that I had aroused him. The fellow rose to his feet hurriedly, evidently under the impression that one of the officers had caught him napping, and, scarcely half-awake, stumbled out on deck muttering in Spanish a few incoherent words which he no doubt intended for an explanation of his presence in the galley. As he emerged from the door I promptly—and I fear rather roughly—forced the belaying-pin between his teeth and secured it there with the aid of my pocket handkerchief, Smellie at the same moment pinioning him from the other side so effectually that he was rendered quite incapable of resistance. A very short time sufficed us to secure him beyond the possibility of escape; and then the next thing demanding our attention was the skylight and companion. I had already thought of a means by which these might be made perfectly secure, and I now offered the idea to Smellie for whatever it might be worth. My suggestion met with his most unqualified approval, and we forthwith set about carrying it out. There was an abundance of firewood in the galley; and, selecting suitable pieces, we lost no time in hacking out half-a-dozen wedges. Armed with these we went aft, and noiselessly closing the companion slide to its full extent firmly wedged it there. A short piece of planking wedged tightly in between the binnacle and the companion doors made the latter perfectly secure; and when we had further heaped upon the skylight lid as many heavy articles as we could find about the decks and conveniently handle between us, the crew were effectually imprisoned below, fore and aft, and the work of seizing the schooner was complete.

We were not a moment too soon. The thunderstorm had all

this while been raging with little if any diminution of fury, the rain continuing to pour down upon us in a steady torrent. But hitherto there had been no wind. We had barely completed our task of making matters secure fore and aft, however, when the lightning and rain ceased all in an instant.

"Now look out for the wind, sir," said I to Smellie.

"When the rain comes *before* the wind. Stand by and well your topsails mind."

"Let the breeze come as soon as it likes," was the cheerful reply; "we shall want a breeze to help us out of the creek presently. But we may as well get the canvas on her whilst the calm lasts, if possible; so run your knife along the lashing of that mainsail, whilst I overhaul the sheet and cast adrift the halliards."

So said, so done, and in another minute the sail was loose. We then tailed on to the halliards, and after a long and weary drag managed to get the sail set after a fashion. But we had hardly begun this task before the squall burst upon us, and well was it for us then that the schooner happened to be moored in so completely sheltered a position. The wind careered, roaring and howling past us overhead, swaying and bending the stoutest forest giants as though they were pliant reeds; but down in the narrow channel, under the lee of the trees, we felt no more than a mere *scuffle*, which, however, was sufficient to make the mainsail flap heavily, and this effectually roused all hands below.

The first intimation we received of this state of things was a loud battering against the inside of the companion doors, accompanied by muffled ejaculations of anger. To this, however, we paid not the slightest heed; we knew that our prisoners were safe for a time at least, so as soon as we had

Harry Collingwood

set the mainsail to our satisfaction I skimmed out on the jib-boom and cast loose the jib, then slipped inboard again and helped Smellie to hoist it. This done, by Smellie's order I went aft to the wheel, whilst he, armed with the cook's axe, cut the hawsers fore and aft by which the schooner was secured to the bank.

The wind was very baffling just where we were; moreover we happened, unfortunately, to be on the lee side of the canal, and for a couple of minutes after cutting adrift we were in imminent danger of taking the ground after all our trouble. Between us, however, we succeeded in so far flattening in the main-sheet as to cant her bows to windward, and though the schooner's keel actually stirred up the mud for a distance of quite fifty yards, we at last had the gratification of seeing her draw off the bank. The moment that she was fairly under weigh I drew Smellie's attention to the violent pounding at the companion doors, and suggested as a precautionary measure that we should run one of the guns up against the doors in case of any attempt to batter them down, which we accordingly did; the wheel being lashed for the short period necessary to enable us to accomplish this task.

Very fortunately for us the wind had by this time broken up the dense black canopy of cloud overhead, permitting a star or two to peep through the rents here and there; the moon, too, just past her second quarter, had risen, so that we now had a fair amount of light to aid us. The navigation of the narrow creek was, however, so difficult that a look-out was absolutely necessary, and Smellie accordingly went forward and stationed himself on the stem-head to con the ship.

CHAPTER FOURTEEN

WE REJOIN THE "DAPHNE"

The people in the cabin, finding that no good result followed their violent pounding upon the inside of the companion doors, soon abandoned so unprofitable an amusement, and I was just beginning to hope that they had philosophically made up their minds to submit with a good grace to the inevitable, when *crash* came a bullet through the teak doors and past my head in most uncomfortable proximity to my starboard ear.

Smellie looked round at the sound.

"Any damage done, Hawkesley?" he hailed.

"None so far, I thank you," replied I; and as I spoke there was another report, and another bullet went whizzing past, well to port this time for a change. A minute or two passed, and then came a regular fusillade from quite half a dozen pistols discharged simultaneously I should say, one of the bullets knocking off the worsted cap I wore and grazing the skin of my right temple sufficiently to send a thin stream of blood trickling down into the corner of my right eye.

"You seem to be in a warm corner there," hailed Smellie;

"but if you can hold on until we round this point I'll come and relieve you."

"No, thanks, I would very much rather you would continue to con the ship," I replied.

A minute or two later we rounded the point referred to, and, the creek widening out considerably, we began to feel the true breeze, when the schooner, even under the short and ill-set canvas we had been able to give her, at once increased her speed to about six knots. At the same time, however, she began to "gripe" most villainously, and with the helm hard a-weather it was as much as I could possibly do to keep her from running ashore among the bushes on our starboard hand. The people in the cabin were still pertinaciously blazing away through the companion doors at me, and doing some remarkably good shooting, too, taking into consideration the fact that they could only guess at my whereabouts; but I was just then far too busy to pay much attention to them. At length, fearing that, when we got a little lower down and felt the full strength of the breeze, the schooner would, in spite of all my efforts, fairly run away with me, I hailed Smellie, and, briefly explaining the situation to him, asked him to either give her the fore staysail or else come aft and trice up the tack of the mainsail. He chose the latter alternative, as leaving the craft under canvas easily manageable by one hand, and came aft to effect the alteration, hurriedly explaining that he would relieve me as soon as possible; but that there was still some difficult navigation ahead which he wanted to see the schooner safely through.

He triced the tack of the sail close up to the throat of the gaff, and was about to hurry forward again, when the schooner sheering round a bend into a new reach, my attention was suddenly attracted by something ahead and on our lee bow at a distance of perhaps half a mile.

"What is that away there on our lee bow, sir?" I exclaimed; "is it not a craft of some sort?"

Smellie jumped up on the rail to get a better view, and at the same moment a pistol shot rang out from the skylight, the bullet evidently flying close past him. He took not the slightest notice of the shot, but stood there on the rail with his hand shading his eyes, intently examining the object we were rapidly nearing.

"It is a brig," said he, "and unless I am very greatly mistaken—but no, it can't be—and yet it *must* be too—it surely *is* the *Vestale*."

"It looks remarkably like her; but I can't make out— confound those fellows! I wish they would stop firing.—I can't make out the white ribbon round her sides," said I.

"No, nor can I. And yet it is scarcely possible we can be mistaken. Luff you may—a little—do not shave her *too* close. She has no pennant flying, by the way, whoever she may be. Ah! the rascals have pinked me after all," as a rattling volley was discharged at him through the glazed top of the skylight, and I saw him clap his hand to his side.

We were by this time close to the strange brig, on board which lights were burning in the cabin, whilst several persons were visible on deck. As we swept down toward her, hugging her pretty closely, a man sprang into the main rigging and hailed in Spanish:

"*Josefa* ahoy! What's the matter on board? Why are you going to sea without a full cargo? Have matters gone wrong at the head of the creek?"

"No, no," replied Smellie in the same language, which by the way he had been diligently studying with Antonia's assistance during our sojourn under Don Manuel's roof— "no, everything is all right; our cargo—"

Unfortunately he was here interrupted by another volley from the cabin, and at the same time a voice yelled from the schooner's stern windows:

"We are captured; a prize to the accursed Ingleses."

The words were hardly out of the speaker's mouth when three or four muskets were popped at us from the brig, fortunately without effect. We were, however, by that time past her, and her crew, who seemed thoroughly mystified at the whole affair, made no further effort to molest us. Of one thing, however, we were amply assured, she was not the *Vestale*. The craft we had just passed—whilst the *double* of the French gun-brig in every other respect—was painted black down to her copper, and she carried under the heel of her bowsprit a life-size figure of a negress with a scarf striped in various colours round her waist. *A negress?* Ah! there could not be a doubt of it. "Mr Smellie," said I, "do you know that craft?"

"N-n-no, I can't say I do, Hawkesley, under her present disguise."

"Disguise, my dear sir; she is not disguised at all. That is the pirate-brig which destroyed poor Richards' vessel—the *Juliet*. And—yes—there can scarcely be a doubt about it— she must be the notorious *Black Venus* of which the Yankee skipper told us."

Smellie looked at me in great surprise and perplexity for a moment.

"Upon my word, Hawkesley, I verily believe you are right!" he exclaimed at last. "The *Black Venus*—a negress for a figure-head—ha! are you hurt?"

"Not much, I think," stammered I, as I braced myself resolutely against the wheel, determined that I would *not* give in. The fact was, that whilst we were talking another shot had been fired through the companion doors, and had struck me fairly in the right shoulder, inflicting such severe pain that for the moment I felt quite incapable of using my right arm. Fortunately the schooner now steered pretty easily, and I could manage the wheel with one hand.

"We must stop this somehow," said Smellie, again jumping on the rail and taking a long look ahead.

"Do you see that very tall tree shooting up above the rest, almost directly ahead?" he continued, pointing out the object as he turned to me.

I replied that I did.

"Well, steer straight for it then, and I will fetch aft some hatch-covers—there are several forward—and place them against the doors; I think I can perhaps contrive to rig up a bullet-proof screen for you."

"But you are hurt yourself, sir," I protested.

"A mere graze after all, I believe," he replied lightly, and forthwith set about the work of dragging aft the hatch-covers, six of which he soon piled in front of the companion.

"There," he said, as he placed the last one in position, "I think you are reasonably safe now; it was a pity we did not think of that before. Shall I bind up your shoulder for you?

You are bleeding, I see."

"No, thank you," I replied; "it is only a trifling scratch, I think, not worth troubling about now. I would much rather you would go forward and look out; it would never do to plump the schooner ashore now that we have come so far. Besides, there are the men down forward; they ought to be watched, or perhaps they may succeed in breaking out after all."

Smellie looked at me rather doubtfully for almost a full minute. "I believe you are suffering a great deal of pain, Hawkesley," he said; "but you are a thoroughly plucky fellow; and if you can only keep up until we get clear of this confounded creek I will then relieve you. And I will take care, too, to let Captain Vernon know how admirably you have conducted yourself, not only to-night, but from the moment that we left the *Daphne* together. Now I am going forward to see that all is right there. If you want help give me a timely hail."

And he turned and walked forward.

The navigation of the creek still continued to be exceedingly intricate and difficult; the creek itself being winding, and the deep-water channel very much more winding still, running now on one side of the creek, now on the other, besides being studded here and there with shoals, sand-banks, and tiny islets. This, whilst it made the navigation very difficult for strangers, added greatly to the value of the creek as a safe and snug resort for slavers; the multitudinous twists in the channel serving to mask it most artfully, and giving it an appearance of terminating at a point beyond which in reality a long stretch of deep water extended.

At length we luffed sharply round a low sandy spit thickly

covered with mangroves, kept broad away again directly afterwards, and abruptly found ourselves in the main stream of the Congo. Here the true channel was easily discernible by the long regular run of the sea which had been lashed up by the gale; and I had therefore nothing to do but keep the schooner where the sea ran most regularly, and I should be certain to be right. Smellie now gave a little much-needed attention to the party in the forecastle, who had latterly been very noisy and clamourous in their demonstrations of disapproval. Luckily they did not appear to possess any fire-arms: the only fear from them, therefore, was that they would find means to break out; and this the second lieutenant provided against pretty effectually by placing a large wash-deck tub on the cover and coiling down therein the end of one of the mooring hawsers which stood on the deck near the windlass.

Having done this, he came aft to relieve me at the wheel, a relief for which I was by no means sorry.

The party in the cabin had, shortly before this, given up their amusement of popping at me through the closed doors of the companion, having doubtless heard Smellie dragging along the hatch-covers and placing them in position, and having also formed a very shrewd guess that further mischief on their part was thus effectually frustrated. Unfortunately, however, they had made the discovery that my head could be seen over the companion from the fore end of the skylight, and they had thereupon begun to pop at me from this new position. They had grazed me twice when Smellie came aft, and he had scarcely opened his lips to speak to me when another shot came whizzing past us close enough to him to prove that the fellows still had it in their power to undo all our work by a single lucky hit.

"Why, Hawkesley," he exclaimed, "this will never do; we

must put a stop to this somehow. We cannot afford to be hard hit, either of us, for another hour and a half at least. What is to be done? How does your shoulder feel? Can you use your right arm?"

"I am afraid I cannot," I replied; "my shoulder is dreadfully painful, and my arm seems to have no strength in it. But I can steer easily with one hand now?"

"How many people do you think there are in the cabin?" was Smellie's next question.

"I can scarcely say," I replied; "but I have only been able to distinguish *three* voices so far."

"Three, eh? The skipper and two mates, I suppose." He ruminated a little, stepped forward, and presently returned with a rather formidable-looking iron bar he had evidently noticed some time before; and coolly remarked as he began to drag away the hatch-covers from before the companion:

"I am going down below to give those fellows their *quietus*. If I do not, there is no knowing what mischief they may yet perpetrate before we get the—what was it those fellows called her?—ah! the *Josefa*—before we get the *Josefa* under the *Daphne's* guns. Now, choose a star to steer by before I remove any more of this lumber, and then sit down on deck as much on one side as you can get; I shall try to draw their fire and then rush down upon them."

With that he removed his jacket and threw it loosely over the iron bar, which he laid aside for the moment whilst he cleared away the obstructions from before the doors. Then, taking up the coat and holding it well in front of the opening so as to produce in the uncertain light the appearance of a figure standing there, he suddenly flung back the slide and threw open the doors.

The immediate results were a couple of pistol shots and a rush up the companion-ladder, the latter of which Smellie promptly stopped by swinging his somewhat bulky carcass into the opening and letting himself drop plump down upon the individuals who were making it. There was a scuffle at the bottom of the ladder, another pistol shot, two or three dull crushing blows, another brief scuffle, and then Smellie reappeared, with blood flowing freely from his left arm, and a truculent-looking Spaniard in tow. This fellow he dragged on deck, and unceremoniously kicking his feet from under him, lashed him securely with the end of the topgallant brace. This done, he once more dived below, and in due time two more Spaniards, senseless and bleeding, were brought up out of the cabin and secured.

"There," he said, wiping the perspiration from his forehead, "I think we shall now manage to make the rest of our trip unmolested, and without having constantly before our eyes the fear of being blown clear across the Congo. Let me take the wheel; I am sure you must be sadly in need of a spell. But before you do anything else I will get you to clap a bandage of some sort round my arm here; I am bleeding so profusely that I think the bullet must have severed an artery. Here is my handkerchief, clap it round the arm and haul it as taut as you can; the great thing just now is to stop the bleeding; Doctor Burnett will do all that is necessary for us when we reach the sloop."

I bound up his arm after a fashion, making a good enough job of it to stop the bleeding, and then went forward to keep a look-out. We were foaming down the river at a tremendous pace, the gale being almost dead fair for us, and having the additional impetus of a red-hot tide under foot we swept down past the land as though we had been a steamer. Sooth to say, however, I scarcely felt in cue just then either to admire the *Josefa's* paces or to take much note of the wonderful picture presented by the river, with its brown mud-tinted waters lashed into fury by the breath of the tropical tempest and chequered here and there with the shadows of the scurrying clouds, or lighted up by the phosphorescence which tipped each wave with a crest of scintillating silvery stars. The wound in my shoulder was every moment becoming more excruciatingly painful and more exacting in its demands upon my attention; my interest seemed to centre itself upon the *Daphne* and her surgeon; and it was with a feeling of ineffable relief that, on jibing round Shark Point, about an hour and a half after clearing the creek, I saw at a distance of about seven miles away an indistinct object off Padron Point which I knew must be the *Daphne* at anchor.

"Do you see the sloop, sir?" I hailed.

"No," returned Smellie from his post at the wheel, stooping and peering straight into the darkness. "I cannot make her out from here. Do you see her?"

"Yes, sir," I replied joyously; "there she is, broad on our port bow. Luff, sir, you may."

"Luff," I heard Smellie return; and the schooner's bows swept round until they pointed fair for the distant object. "Steady, sir!"

"Steady it is," replied Smellie, his voice sounding weird and mournful above the roar of the wind and the wash of the sea. I managed to trim over the jib-sheet without assistance, and then leaned over the bulwarks watching the gradual way in which the small dark blot on the horizon swelled and developed into a stately ship with lofty masts, long yards, and a delicate maze of rigging all as neat and trig as though she had but just emerged from the dockyard.

The sea being quite smooth after we had once rounded Shark Point, we made the run down to the sloop in about an hour, passing to windward of her, and then jibing over and rounding-to on her lee quarter, with our jib-sheet to windward.

As we approached the sloop I noticed that lights were still burning in the skipper's cabin, and I thought I could detect a human face or two peering curiously out at us from the ports. The dear old hooker was of course riding head to wind, and as we swept down across her bows within easy hailing distance a figure suddenly appeared standing on the knight-heads, and Armitage's voice rang out across the water with the hail of:

"Schooner ahoy!"

"Hillo!" responded Smellie.

A slight and barely perceptible pause; and then—

"What schooner is that?"

"The *Josefa*, slave schooner. Is that Mr Armitage?"

"Ay, ay, it is. Who may you be, pray?"

I had by this time gone aft and was standing by Smellie's side. The schooner was just jibing over and darting along on the *Daphne's* starboard side.

"Armitage evidently has not recognised my voice as yet," remarked Smellie, "or else," he added, "they have given us up on board as dead, and he is unable so suddenly to realise the fact of our being still alive."

Then, as we finally rounded-to under the *Daphne's* quarter, Armitage reappeared aft, and the confab was renewed, Smellie this time taking the lead.

"*Daphne* ahoy!" he hailed, "has Captain Vernon yet retired for the night?"

"I think not," was the reply. "What do you want?"

"Kindly pass the word to him that Mr Smellie and Mr Hawkesley are alongside in a captured slaver: and say we shall feel greatly obliged if he will send a prize crew on board us to take possession."

"Ay, ay! I will."

Armitage thereupon disappeared, and, we being at the time to leeward of the sloop, a slight but distinct commotion became perceptible on board her. Presently a figure appeared in the fore-rigging, and a deep, gruff, hoarse voice hailed:

"Schooner ahoy! Did you say as Mr Smellie and Mr Hawkesley was on board you?"

"Yes I did. Do you not recognise my voice, Collins?"

"Ay, ay, sir! in course I does *now*," was the boatswain's hearty response. Then there followed, in lower tones, certain remarks of which we could only catch such fragments as:

"—lieutenant hisself, by—reefer, too;—man—rigging, you sea-dogs—give—sailors' welcome."

Then in an instant the lower rigging became black with the

figures of the men, and, with Collins as fugleman, they greeted our unexpected return with three as hearty cheers as ever pealed from the throats of British seamen.

For the life of me I could not just then have spoken a word had it been ever so necessary. That hearty ringing British cheer gave me the first convincing assurance that I was once more *safe* and among friends, and, at the same time, enabled me to *fully* realise, as I never had before, the extreme peril to which I had been exposed since I last saw the craft that lay there rolling gracefully upon the ground-swell, within a biscuit toss of us.

The men were just clearing the rigging when a small slight figure appeared on the sloop's quarter, and Captain Vernon's voice hailed us through the speaking-trumpet:

"Schooner ahoy! How many hands shall I send you?"

"A dozen men will be sufficient, sir," replied Smellie. "And I shall feel obliged if you will send with them the necessary officers to relieve us. We are both hurt, and in need of the doctor's services."

"You shall have the men at once," was the reply. "Shall I send Burnett to you, or can you come on board the sloop?"

"We will rejoin the sloop, sir, thank you. Our injuries are not very serious," replied Smellie.

"Very well, be it so," returned the skipper; and there the conversation ended.

The next moment the clear *tee-tee-tweetle-tweetle-weetle-wee-e-e* of the boatswain's whistle came floating down to us, followed by his gruff "Cutters away!" and presently we saw the boat glide down the ship's side, and, after a very brief delay, shove off and come sweeping down toward us.

Five minutes later the prize crew, under Williams, the master's mate, with young Peters, a fellow mid of mine, as his second in command, stood upon the schooner's deck, and Mr Austin, who had accompanied them, was wringing our hands as though he would wring them off.

Smellie saw the exquisite agony which our warm-hearted "first luff" was unconsciously inflicting upon *me* by his effusive greeting, and thoughtfully interposed with a—

"Gently, Edgar, old fellow. I am afraid you are handling poor Hawkesley a little roughly. He has received rather a bad hurt in the right shoulder to-night in our fight with the schooner's people."

"Fight!—schooner's people! I beg your pardon, Hawkesley; I hope I haven't hurt you. Why, you never mean to say you have had to *fight* for the schooner?" Austin interrupted, aghast. "Well, we *took* her by surprise; but her people proved very troublesome, and very pertinacious in their efforts to get her back again," Smellie replied. "But, come, let us get on board the old *Daphne* once more. I long to set foot on her planks again; and, like Hawkesley here, I shall not be sorry to renew my acquaintance with Burnett."

So said, so done. We made our way into the boat, leaving the prize crew to secure the prisoners, and a few minutes later stood once more safe, if not altogether sound, on the deck of the dear old *Daphne*.

CHAPTER FIFTEEN

A STERN CHASE—AND A FRUITLESS ONE

"Welcome back to the *Daphne*, gentlemen!" exclaimed Captain Vernon as he met us at the gangway and extended his hand, first to Smellie and then to me. "This is indeed a pleasant surprise—for all hands, I will venture to say, though Armitage loses his step, at least *pro tem.*, in consequence of your reappearance, Mr Smellie. But he is a good-hearted fellow, and when he entered my cabin to report you alongside, though he seemed a trifle incredulous as to your personality, he was as delighted as a schoolboy at the prospect of a holiday."

Smellie took the skipper's extended hand, and after replying suitably to his greeting, said:

"I must beg you will excuse Hawkesley, sir, if he gives you his left instead of his right hand. His starboard shoulder has been disabled to-night by a pistol-bullet whilst supporting me most intrepidly in the task of bringing out the schooner."

The skipper seized my left hand with his right, and pressing it earnestly yet gently, said:

"I am proud and pleased to hear so gratifying an account of

you, Hawkesley. Mr Armitage has already borne witness to your gallantry during the night attack upon the slavers; and it was with deep and sincere sorrow that I received the news of your being, with Mr Smellie, missing. I fear, gentlemen, your friends at home will suffer a great deal of, happily unnecessary, sorrow at the news which I felt it my duty to send home; but that can all be repaired by your personally despatching to them the agreeable intelligence of your both being still in the land of the living. But what of your hurts? Are they too serious to be attended to in my cabin? They are not? I am glad to hear that. Then follow me, both of you, please; for I long to hear where you have been, what doing all this time, and how you happened to turn up so opportunely here to-night I will send for Burnett to bring his tools into my cabin; and you can satisfy my curiosity whilst he is doing the needful for you. Will you join us, Austin? I'll be bound your ears are tingling to hear what has befallen these wandering knights."

Thereupon we filed down below in the skipper's wake—I for one being most heartily thankful to find myself where I could once more sit down and rest my aching limbs. The skipper's steward brought out some wine and glasses, and then at Burnett's request—that individual having promptly turned up—went away to get ready some warm water.

"I think," said our genial medico, turning to me, "*you* look in most urgent need of my services, so I will begin with you, young gentleman, if you please. Now whereabouts are your hurts?"

I told him, and he straightway began to cut away the sleeve of my coat and shirt, preparatory to more serious operations; whilst Smellie, drawing his chair up to the table, helped himself to a glass of wine, and then said:

"Before I begin my story, sir, will you permit me to ask what was the ultimate result of that most disastrous expedition against the slavers? I am naturally anxious to know, of course, seeing that upon my shoulders rests the odium of our failure."

Captain Vernon stared hard at the second lieutenant for a minute, and then said:

"My dear Smellie, what in the world are you talking about? Disaster! Odium! Why, man, the expedition was a *success*, not a failure. I admit that there was, most unfortunately, a very serious loss of life among the unhappy slaves; but we took the brigantine and afterwards raised the schooner, with a loss to ourselves of only four killed—now that you two have turned up. It was a most dashing affair, and admirably conducted, when we take into consideration the elaborate preparations which had been evidently made for your reception; and the *ultimate result* about which you inquire so anxiously will, I hope, be a nice little bit of prize-money to all hands, and richly deserved promotion to yourself, Armitage, and young Williams."

It was now Smellie's turn to look surprised.

"You astonish me, sir," he said. "The last I remember of the affair is that, after a most stubborn and protracted fight, in which the schooner was sunk, we succeeded in gaining possession of the brig, only to be blown out of her a few minutes later, however; and my own impression—and Hawkesley's too, for that matter, as I afterwards discovered on comparing notes with him—was that our losses must have amounted to at least half of the men composing the expedition."

"Well," said Captain Vernon, "I am happy to tell you that you were mistaken. Our total loss over that affair amounts to four men killed; but the severity of the fight is amply testified to by the fact that not one man out of the whole number escaped without a wound of some kind, more or less serious. They have all recovered, however, I am happy to say, and we have not at present a sick man in the ship. There can be no doubt that the slavers somehow received timely notice of our presence in the river, through the instrumentality of your fair-speaking friend, the skipper of the *Pensacola*, I strongly suspect, and that they made the best possible use of the time at their disposal. Had I been as wise then as I am now my arrangements would have been very different. However, it is easy to be wise after the event; and I am thankful that matters turned out so well. And now, I think we are fairly entitled to hear your story."

Thereupon Smellie launched out into a detailed recital of all that had befallen us from the moment of the explosion on board the brig up to our unexpected arrival that same night alongside the *Daphne*. He was interrupted by countless exclamations of astonishment and sympathy; and when he had finished there seemed to be no end to the questions which one and another was anxious to put to him. In the midst of it all, however, Burnett broke in with the announcement that, having finished with me, he was ready to attend to the second lieutenant.

The worthy medico's attentions to me had been, as may be gathered from the fact that they outlasted Smellie's story, of somewhat protracted duration, and that they were of an exceedingly painful character I can abundantly testify, the ball having broken my shoulder-blade and then buried itself among the muscles of the shoulder, whence Burnett insisted on extracting it, in spite of my protestations that I was quite willing to postpone that operation to a more convenient season. After much groping and probing about, however, utterly regardless of the excruciating agony he thus inflicted upon me, the conscientious Burnett had at last succeeded in extracting the ball, which he kindly presented to me as a memento, and then the rest of the work was, comparatively speaking, plain sailing. My wound was washed, dressed, and made comfortable; and I was dismissed with a strict injunction to turn-in at once.

To this the skipper moved, as an amendment, that I be permitted to drink a single glass of wine before retiring; and whilst I was sipping this they turned upon me with their questions, with the result that I soon forgot all about my hammock. At length Captain Vernon said:

"By-the-by, Hawkesley, what sort of a young lady is this Dona Antonia whom Mr Smellie has mentioned once or twice?"

"She is simply the most lovely creature I have ever seen, sir," I replied enthusiastically.

"—And my promised wife," jerked in Smellie, in a tone which warned all hands that there must be no jocularity in connection with the mention of the dona's name.

"Ho, ho!" ejaculated the skipper with a whistle of surprise. "That is how the wind blows, is it? Upon my word, Smellie, I heartily congratulate you upon your conquest. Quite a romantic affair, really. And pray, Mr Hawkesley, what success have *you* met with in Cupid's warfare?"

"None whatever, sir," I replied with a laugh. "The only other lady in Don Manuel's household was old Dolores, Dona Antonia's attendant, and I was positively afraid to try the effect of my fascinations upon her."

"Lest you should prove only *too* successful," laughed the

skipper. "By the way, Smellie, do you think this Don Manuel was quite plain and above-board with you? I suppose *he* does nothing in the slave-trading business, eh?"

"I think not, sir; though he undoubtedly possesses the acquaintance of a certain Senor Madera, a most suspicious-looking character, whose name I have already mentioned to you—by the way, Hawkesley, you were evidently mistaken as to the *Josefa* belonging to Madera; he was nowhere to be found on board her."

"What is it, Mr Armitage?" said the skipper just then, as the third lieutenant made his appearance at the door.

"A vessel, apparently a brig, sir, has just come into view under the northern shore, evidently having just left the river. She is hugging the land very closely, keeping well under its shadow, in fact, and has all the appearance of being anxious to avoid attracting our attention."

The skipper glanced interrogatively at Smellie, who at once responded to the look by saying:

"The *Black Venus*, without doubt. I expect that our running away with the *Josefa* has given them the alarm, and they have determined to slip out whilst the option remains to them, and take their chance of being able to give us the slip."

"They shall not do that if I can help it," remarked the skipper energetically; and, rising to his feet, he gave orders for all hands to be called forthwith. This broke up the party in the cabin, much to the gratification of Burnett, who now insisted that both Smellie and I should retire to our hammocks forthwith, and on no account presume to leave them again until we had his permission.

I was not very long in undressing, having secured the services of a marine to assist me in the operation; but before I had gained my hammock I was rejoined by Keene, a brother mid, whose watch it was below, and who brought me down the news that the sloop was under weigh and fairly after the stranger, who, as soon as our canvas dropped from the yards, had squared away on a westerly course with the wind on her quarter and a whole cloud of studding-sails set to windward.

What with the excitement of finding myself once more among so many friends and the pain of my wound it was some time before I succeeded in getting to sleep that night; and before I did so the *Daphne* was rolling like an empty hogshead, showing how rapidly she had run off the land and into the sea knocked up by the gale.

When I awoke next morning the wind had dropped to a considerable extent, the sea had gone down, and the ship was a great deal steadier under her canvas. I was most anxious to leave my hammock and go on deck, but this Burnett would not for a moment consent to; my wound was very much inflamed and exceedingly painful, the result, doubtless, of the probing for the bullet on the night before; and instead of being allowed to turn out I was removed in my hammock, just as I was, to the sick bay. I was ordered to keep very quiet, but I managed to learn, nevertheless, that the chase was still in sight directly ahead, about nine miles distant, and that, though she certainly was not running away from us, there seemed to be little hope of our overtaking her for some time to come.

Matters remained in this unsatisfactory state for the next five days, the *Daphne* keeping the chase in sight during the whole of that time, but failing to come up with her. The distance between the two vessels varied according to the weather, the chase appearing to have the best of it in a strong breeze, whilst the *Daphne* was slightly the faster of the two in light airs. Unfortunately for us, the wind continued very nearly dead fair, or about three points on our starboard quarter, whereas the sloop seemed to do best with the wind abeam. We would not have objected even to a moderate breeze dead in our teeth, our craft being remarkably fast on a taut bowline; and as day after day went by without any apparent prospect of an end of the chase the barometer was anxiously watched, in the hope that before long we should be favoured with a change of weather.

On the morning of the fifth day I was so much better that, acceding to my urgent request, Burnett consented, with many doubtful shakes of the head, to my leaving my hammock and taking the air on deck for an hour or two. I accordingly dressed as rapidly as possible, and got on deck just in time to catch sight of the chase, about six miles distant, before a sea mist settled down on the scene, which soon effectually concealed her from our view. This was particularly exasperating, since, the wind having dropped to about a five-knot breeze, we had been slowly but perceptibly gaining on her for the last three or four hours; and now, when at length there appeared a prospect of overtaking her, a chance to elude us in the fog had presented itself. Of course it was utterly impossible to guess what ruse so wary a foe would resort to, but that he would have recourse to one of some kind was a moral certainty. Captain Vernon at once took counsel with his first and second lieutenants as to what course it would be most advisable to adopt under the circumstances, and it was at last decided to put the ship upon a wind, and make short tacks to the eastward until the fog should clear, it being thought highly probable that the chase would likewise double back upon her former course in the hope of our running past her in the fog.

The studding-sails were accordingly taken in, and the ship brought to the wind on the starboard tack. We made short reaches, tacking every hour, and had gone about for the third time when, just as the men were coiling up the ropes fore and aft, the look-out reported:

"Sail, ho! straight ahead. Hard up, sir, or you will be into her."

Mr Austin, who had charge of the deck, sprang upon a gun, and peered out eagerly ahead.

"Hard over, my man, *hard* over!" he exclaimed excitedly; then continued, after a moment of breathless suspense:

"All clear, all clear! we have *just* missed her, and that is all. By Jove, Hawkesley, that was a narrow squeak, eh? Why, it is surely the *Vestale*! *Vestale* ahoy!"

"Hillo!" was the response from the other craft, indubitably the brig which we had fallen in with shortly after our first look into the Congo, and which we had been given to understand was the *Vestale*, French gun-brig.

"Have you sighted a sail of any kind to-day?" hailed Austin.

"Non, mon Dieu! We have not nevaire seen a sail until now since we leave Sierra Leone four weeks ago."

This ended the communication between the two ships, the *Vestale*—or whatever she was—disappearing again into the fog before the last words of the reply to our question had been uttered.

"Well," said Mr Austin, as he jumped down off the gun, "I am disappointed. When I first caught sight of that craft close under our bows I thought for a moment that we had made a clever guess; that the chase had doubled on her track, and that, by a lucky accident, we had stumbled fairly upon her in the fog. But as soon as I caught sight of the white figure-head and the streak round her sides I saw that I was mistaken. Well, we *may* drop upon the fellow yet. I would give a ten-pound note this instant if the fog would only lift."

"I cannot understand it for the life of me," I replied in a dazed sort of way, as I stepped gingerly down off the gun upon which I, like the first lieutenant, had jumped in the first of the excitement.

Mr Austin looked at me questioningly.

"What is it that you cannot understand, Hawkesley?" he asked.

"That brig—the *Vestale*, as she calls herself—and all connected with her," I answered.

"Why, what *is* there to understand about her? Or rather, what is there that is incomprehensible about her?" he asked sharply.

"*Everything*," I replied eagerly. "In the first place, we have only the statement of one man—and he a member of her own crew—that she actually *is* the veritable *Vestale*, French gun-brig, which we know to be cruising in these waters. Secondly, her very extraordinary resemblance to the *Black Venus*, which, as you are aware, I have seen, absolutely *compels* me, against my better judgment, to the belief that the two brigs are, in some mysterious way, intimately associated together, if, indeed, they are not absolutely *one and the same vessel*. And thirdly, my suspicion that the latter is the case receives strong confirmation from the fact that on *both* occasions when we have been after the one—the *Black Venus*—we have encountered the other—the *Vestale*."

Mr Austin stared at me in a very peculiar way for a few minutes, and then said:

"Well, Hawkesley, your last assertion is undoubtedly true; but what does it prove? It can be nothing more than a curious coincidence."

"So I have assured myself over and over again, when my suspicions were strengthened by the first occurrence of the coincidence; and so I shall doubtless assure myself over and over again during the next few days," I replied. "But if a coincidence only it is certainly curious that it should have occurred on two occasions."

"I am not quite prepared to admit that," said the first lieutenant. "And, then, as to the remarkable resemblance between the two vessels, do you not think, now, honestly, Hawkesley, that your very extraordinary suspicions may have magnified that resemblance?"

"No," said I; "I do not. I only wish Mr Smellie had been on deck just now to have caught a glimpse of that inexplicable brig; he would have borne convincing testimony to the marvellous likeness between them. Why, sir, but for the white ribbon round the one, and the difference in the figure-heads, the two craft would be positively indistinguishable; so completely so, indeed, that poor Richards was actually unable to believe the evidence of his own senses, and, I firmly believe, was convinced of the identity of the two vessels."

"Indeed!" said Mr Austin in a tone of great surprise. "That is news to me. So Richards shared your suspicions, did he?"

"He did, indeed, sir," I replied. "It was, in fact, his extra-ordinary demeanour on the occasion of our second encounter with the *Vestale*—you will remember the circumstance, sir?—which confirmed my suspicions; suspicions which, up to then, I had attributed solely to some aberration of fancy on my part. Then, again, when we questioned the skipper of the *Pensacola* relative to the *Black Venus* and the *Vestale*, how evasive were his replies!"

"Look here, Hawkesley; you have interested me in spite of myself," said Mr Austin. "If you are not too tired I should like you to tell me the whole history of these singular suspicions of yours from the very moment of their birth."

"I will, sir, with pleasure. They arose with Monsieur Le Breton's visit to us on the occasion of our first falling in with the *Vestale*," I replied. And then having at last finally broached the subject which had been for so long a secret source of mental disquiet to me, I fully detailed to the first luff all those suspicious circumstances—trifling in them-selves but important when regarded collectively—which I have already confided to the reader. When I had finished he remained silent for a long time, nearly a quarter of an hour I should think, with his hands clasped behind his back and his eyes bent on the deck, evidently cogitating deeply. Finally he emerged from his abstraction with a start, cast an eye aloft at the sails, and then turning to me said:

"You have given me something to think about now with a vengeance, Hawkesley. If indeed your suspicions as to the honesty of the *Vestale* should prove well-founded, your mention of them and the acute perception which caused you in the first instance to entertain them will constitute a very valuable service—for which I will take care that you get full credit—and may very possibly lead to the final detection and suppression of a series of hitherto utterly unaccountable transactions of a most nefarious character. At all events we can do no harm by keeping a wary eye upon this alleged *Vestale* for the future, and I will make it my business to invent some plausible pretext for boarding her on the first opportunity which presents itself. And now I think you have been on deck quite as long as is good for you, so away you go below again and get back to your hammock. Such a wound as yours is not to be trifled with in this abominable climate; and you know,"—with a smile half good-humoured and half satirical—"we must take every possible care of a young gentleman who seems destined to teach us, from the captain downwards, our business. There, now, don't look hurt, my lad; you did quite right in speaking to me, and I am very much obliged to you for so doing; I only regret that you did not earlier make me your confidant. Now away you go below at once."

I of course did dutifully as I was bidden, and, truth to tell, was by no means sorry to regain my hammock, having soon found that my strength was by no means as great as I had expected. That same night I suffered from a considerable accession of fever, and in fine was confined to my hammock for rather more than three weeks from that date, at the end of which I became once more convalescent, and—this time observing proper precautions and a strict adherence to the doctor's orders—finally managed to get myself reported as once more fit for duty six weeks from the day on which Smellie and I rejoined the *Daphne*. I may as well here mention that the fog which so inopportunely enveloped us on the day of my conversation with Mr Austin did not clear away until just before sunset; and when it did the horizon was clear all round us, no trace of a sail being visible in any direction from our main-royal yard.

CHAPTER SIXTEEN

A VERY MYSTERIOUS OCCURRENCE

In extreme disgust at the loss of the notorious *Black Venus* Captain Vernon reluctantly gave orders for the resumption of the cruise, and the *Daphne* was once more headed in for the land, it being the skipper's intention to give a look in at all the likely places along the coast as far north as the Bight of Benin.

This was terribly tedious and particularly trying to the men, it being all boat work. The exploration of the Fernan Vas river occupied thirty hours, whilst in the case of the Ogowe river the boats were away from the ship for four days and three nights; the result being that when at last we went into Sierra Leone we had ten men down with fever, and had lost four more from the same cause. The worst of it all was that our labour had been wholly in vain, not a single prize being taken nor a suspicious craft fallen in with. Here we found Williams and the prize crew of the *Josefa* awaiting us according to instructions; so shipping them and landing the sick men Captain Vernon lost no time in putting to sea once more.

On leaving Sierra Leone a course was shaped for the Congo, and after a long and very tedious passage, during the whole of which we had to contend against light head-winds, we found ourselves once more within sight of the river at daybreak.

It was stark calm, with a cloudless sky, and a long lazy swell came creeping in from the southward and eastward causing the sloop to roll most uncomfortably. We were about twelve miles off the land; and at about half-way between us and it, becalmed like ourselves, there lay a brig, which our telescopes informed us was the *Vestale*. On this fact being decisively ascertained Mr Austin came up to me and said:

"There is your *bete noire*, the *Vestale*, once more, you see, Hawkesley. I have been thinking a great deal about what you said to me some time ago respecting her, and I have come to the conclusion that it is quite worth our while to look into the matter, at least so far as will enable us to judge whether your suspicions are wholly groundless or not. If they are—if, in fact, the craft proves to be what she professes herself—well and good; we can dismiss the affair finally and for ever from our minds and give our undivided attention to other matters. But I confess you have to a certain extent imbued me with your own doubts as to the strict integrity of yonder brig; there are one or two little matters you mentioned which escaped my notice end which certainly have rather a suspicious appearance. I therefore intend—if the craft is bound into the river like ourselves—to make an early opportunity to pay her a visit on some pretext or other."

"Have you mentioned the matter to Captain Vernon yet, sir?" I inquired.

"No, not yet," was the reply. "I must have something a little more definite to say before I broach the matter to him. But here comes the breeze at last, a *sea* breeze, too, thank Heaven! Man the braces fore and aft; square away the yards and brail in the mizen. Hard up with your helm, my man, and keep her dead away for the mouth of the river."

The faint blue line along the western horizon came creeping gradually down toward us, and presently a catspaw or two ruffled the glassy surface of the water for a moment and disappeared. Then a deliciously cool and refreshing draught of air fanned our faces and swelled out the light upper canvas for an instant, died away, came again a trifle stronger and lasted for perhaps half a minute, then with a flap the canvas collapsed, filled again, the sloop gathered way and paid off with her head to the eastward; a bubble or two floated past her sides, a faint ripple arose under her bows, grew larger, became audible, the glassy surface of the water grew gently ruffled and assumed an exquisite cerulean tint, the wheel began to press against the helmsman's hand, and away we went straight for the mouth of the river—and the brig.

The breeze, gentle though it was, reached our neighbour long before we did, and as soon as she felt it she too bore up, squared her yards, and headed direct for Boolambemba Point. She was about three miles ahead of us when the breeze reached her, and I felt very curious to see where she would finally come to an anchor. The only *safe* anchorage is in Banana Creek, and though slavers constantly resort to the numerous other creeks and inlets higher up the river no captain of a man-of-war would think for a moment of risking his ship in any of them unless the emergency happened to be very pressing, nor even then unless his vessel happened to be of exceedingly light draught. If therefore the brig anchored in Banana Creek I should accept it as a point in favour of her honesty; if not, my suspicions would be stronger than ever.

It so happened that she *did* anchor in Banana Creek, but fully a quarter of a mile higher up it than old Mildmay the master thought it prudent for us to venture, though in obedience to a hint from Mr Austin he took us much further in than where we had anchored on our previous visit. The brig got in fully half an hour before us, her canvas was consequently stowed, her yards squared, ropes hauled taut and coiled down, and her boats in the water when our anchor at length plunged into the muddy opaque-looking water of the creek.

We were barely brought up—and indeed the hands were still aloft stowing the canvas—when a gig shoved off from the brig and pulled down the creek. A few minutes later she dashed alongside and Monsieur Le Breton once more presented himself upon our quarter-deck, cap in had, bowing, smiling, and grimacing as only a Frenchman can. His visit, though such a singularly precipitate one, was, it soon turned out, merely a visit of ceremony, which he prolonged to such an extent that Captain Vernon was perforce obliged to invite him down below to breakfast, Mr Austin and I being also the skipper's guests on that particular morning. In the course of the meal he made several very complimentary remarks as to the appearance of the *Daphne*, and finally—when I suppose he saw that he had thus completely won poor Austin's heart—he very politely expressed his extreme desire to take a look through the ship, a desire which the first luff with equal politeness assured him it would give him great pleasure to gratify.

The fellow certainly had a wonderfully plausible and winning way with him, there was no denying that, and I saw that under its influence the slight suspicions which I had imparted to poor honest-hearted, straightforward Mr Austin were melting like snowflakes under a summer sun. Still, under all the plausibility, the delicate flattery, and the elaborate politeness of the man, there was a vague indefi-nable *something* to which I found it quite impossible to reconcile myself; and I watched him as a cat does a mouse, anxious to note whatever suspicious circumstances might transpire, in order that I might be fully prepared for the talk with the first luff which I felt certain would closely follow upon our visitor's departure. To my chagrin, however, I was on this occasion wholly unable to detect anything whatever out of the common, and Monsieur Le Breton's broken English, upon which I had laid such stress in my former conversation with Mr Austin, was now quite consistent and irreproachable. He was taken through the ship and shown every nook and corner in her, and finally, about noon, took his leave. Just before going down over the side he apologised for the non-appearance of "Captain Dubosc" upon the plea that that gentleman was confined to his hammock with a severe attack of dysentery; but if the officers of the *Daphne* would honour the *estate's* ward-room with their presence at dinner that evening Monsieur Le Breton and his brother officers would be "enchanted." And, apparently as an after-thought, when his foot was on the top step of the gangway ladder, this very agreeable gentleman urgently requested the pleasure of Mr Austin's company on a sporting expedition which he and one or two more were about to undertake that afternoon. This latter invitation was declined upon the plea of stress of work; but the invitation to dinner was accepted conditionally upon the work being in a sufficiently forward state to allow of the officers leaving the ship.

We were indeed exceedingly busy that day, Mr Austin having determined to take advantage of the opportunity which our being at anchor afforded him to lift the rigging off the mastheads and give it and them a thorough overhaul.

As for me, I was engaged during the whole of the day in charge of a boat's crew filling up our water casks and tanks and foraging in the adjacent forest for a supply of fruit, not a single native canoe having approached us during the entire day. It was, consequently, not until late in the afternoon, when the neck of the day's work was broken, that I had an opportunity of exchanging a word or two with the first lieutenant on the subject of our neighbour, the brig, and then it was only a word or two. Mr Austin opened the conversation with:

"Well, Hawkesley, what do you think of our friend Monsieur Le Breton, now that you have had an opportunity of bettering your acquaintance with him?"

"Well, sir," I replied; "on the whole I am inclined to think that there is just a bare possibility of my having been mistaken in my estimate of him and of the character of the brig. Still—"

"Still your mind is not yet quite easy," Mr Austin laughingly interrupted me. "Now, what could you possibly have noticed of a suspicious character in the poor fellow's conduct this morning?"

"Nothing," I was obliged to acknowledge. "I am quite prepared to admit, sir, a total absence of those peculiarities of manner which *I am certain* existed during his first visit to the ship. But did you not think it strange that he should be in such a tremendous hurry to come on board us this morning? At first I was inclined to think his object might be to prevent a visit from some of us to the brig; but that supposition is met, to some extent, by his invitation to us for this evening. The delay may, of course, have afforded them an opportunity to make arrangements for our reception by putting out of sight any—"

"Any tell-tale evidences of their dishonesty," laughed the first luff. "Really, Hawkesley, I must say I think you are deceiving yourself and worrying yourself unnecessarily. Of course I can quite understand how, having harboured those extraordinary suspicions of yours for so great a length of time, you now find it difficult to dismiss them all in a moment; but have patience for a few hours more; an excellent opportunity is now offered us for satisfying ourselves as to the brig's *bona fides*, and you may rest assured that I shall make the very best use of it. I find I shall be the only guest of the Frenchmen to-night—the rest of the officers are far too busy to leave the ship, and indeed *I* can hardly be spared, and would not go but for the fact that it would look uncivil if we in a body declined their invitation; but I will see that to-morrow you have an opportunity of going on board and investigating for yourself. And now I must be off to make myself presentable, or I shall be keeping my hosts waiting, and perhaps spoil their dinner."

With that he dived below; and I turned away to attend to some little matter connected with the progress of the work. A quarter of an hour later he reappeared on deck, clean-shaven, and looking very handsome and seamanlike in his best suit of uniform; and, the gig being piped away, he went down over the side, giving me a parting nod as he did so. I watched the boat dash up alongside the brig; noted that the side was manned in due form, that our worthy "first" was received by a group of officers on the quarter-deck, conspicuous among whom I could make out with the aid of my glass Monsieur Le Breton, evidently performing the ceremony of intro-duction; and then the work being finished, ropes coiled down, and everything once more restored to its proper place, the hands were piped to tea, and I descended to the midshipmen's den, thoroughly tired out with my unwonted exertion.

When I again went on deck, about an hour later, the stars were shining brilliantly; the moon, about three days old, was gleaming with a soft subdued radiance through the topmost branches of the trees on the adjacent shore; and the night-mist was already gathering so thickly on the bosom of the river that the brig loomed through it vague, shadowy, and indistinct as a phantom craft. The tide was ebbing, and her stern was turned toward us, but no lights appeared gleaming through her cabin windows, which struck me as being a little strange until I remembered that Monsieur Le Breton had spoken of her captain being ill. A few of our lads were amusing themselves on the forecastle, dancing to the enlivening strains of the cook's fiddle, or singing songs; and an occasional round of applause or an answering song came floating down upon the gentle night-breeze from the brig; but as the fog grew thicker these sounds gradually ceased, we lost sight of her altogether, and so far as sound or sight was concerned we might have been the only craft in the entire river. Our own lads also quieted down; and finally the only sounds which broke the solemn stillness of the night were the sighing of the breeze, the gentle rustle of the foliage, and the loud sonorous *chirr, chirr, chirr* of the insects.

It was about half-past nine o'clock, and I was just thinking of going below to turn-in when I became conscious of the sounds of a commotion of some sort; a muffled cry, which seemed to me like a call for "help;" a dull thud, as of a falling body, and *a splash*! The sounds certainly proceeded from the direction of the brig; and I thought that they must have emanated from a spot at about her distance from the *Daphne*. The slight feeling of drowsiness which had possessed me took flight at once; all my senses became instantly upon the alert; and I awaited in keen expectancy to hear if anything further followed. In vain; the minutes sped past, and neither sight nor sound occurred to elucidate the mystery. I began to feel anxious and alarmed; my old suspicions rose up again like a strong man aroused from sleep; and I walked aft to Mr Armitage, who was leaning against a gun with his arms folded, and his chin sunk upon his breast evidently in deep meditation. He started up as he heard my footstep approaching; and on my asking if he had heard anything peculiar ahead of us, somewhat shortly acknowledged that he had not. I thereupon told him what I had heard; but he evidently attached no importance to my statement, suggesting that *if anything* it was doubtless some of the Frenchmen amusing themselves. I was by no means satisfied with this, and, my uneasiness increasing every moment, I went forward to ascertain whether any of the hands on the forecastle had heard the mysterious sounds. I found them all listening open-mouthed to some weird and marvellous yarn which one of the topmen was spinning for their edification; and from them also I failed to elicit anything satisfactory. Finally, it suddenly occurred to me that, in my wanderings ashore, I had often noticed how low the night-mists lay upon the surface of the river; and it now struck me that by going aloft I might get sight of something which would tend to explain the disquieting occurrence. To act upon the idea was the work of a moment; I sprang into the main rigging and made my way aloft as rapidly as if my life depended upon it, utterly heedless of the fact that the rigging had been freshly tarred down that day; and in less than a minute had reached the maintopmast crosstrees. As I had anticipated I was here almost clear of the mist; and I eagerly looked ahead to see if all was right in that quarter. The first objects which caught my eye were the mastheads of the brig, broad on our starboard bow instead of directly ahead, as I had expected to find them. This of itself struck me as being somewhat strange; but, what was stranger still, *they seemed to be unaccountably near to us.* I rubbed my eyes and looked at them again. They were just in a line with the tops of a clump of trees which rose like islands out of the silvery mist, and as I looked I saw that the spars were moving, gliding slowly and almost imperceptibly past the trees toward the river. *The brig was adrift.* I listened intently for quite five minutes without hearing the faintest sound from the craft, and during that time she had neared us almost a cable's length. In another minute or two she would be abreast of and within a couple of ships' lengths of us. What could it mean? She could not by any possibility have struck adrift accidentally. And if her berth was being intentionally shifted for any reason, why was the operation carried out under cover of the fog and in such profound silence? There had been no sound of lifting the anchor; nor could I hear anything to indicate that they were running out warps; it looked very much as though they had slipped their cable, and were allowing the tide to carry them silently out to sea. And where was Mr Austin during this stealthy movement? Was he aware of it? Why, if my suspicions were correct, had they invited the officers of the *Daphne* on board to dinner? Was it merely a blind, a temporary resort to the usual courtesies adopted for the purpose of giving colour to their assumed character of a French man-o'-war, or was it a diabolical scheme to get us all into their power and so deprive a formidable antagonist of its head, so to speak, and thus cripple it?

All these surmises and many others equally wild flashed through my bewildered brain as I stood there on the crosstrees watching the stealthy phantom-like movement of the brig's upper spars; and the conclusion to which I finally came was that Captain Vernon ought to be informed forthwith of what was going on. I accordingly descended to the deck and once more sought out the third lieutenant.

"Mr Armitage," said I, in a low cautious tone of voice, "the brig is adrift, and driving down past us with the tide in the direction of the river."

"The brig adrift!" he repeated incredulously. "Nonsense, Mr Hawkesley, you must be dreaming!"

"Indeed I am not, sir, I assure you," I replied earnestly. "I have this moment come from aloft, and I saw her topgallant-masts most distinctly over the top of the mist. She is away over in that direction, and scarcely a cable's length distant from us."

"Are you *quite sure?*" he asked, aroused at last by my earnest manner to something like interest. "I can hear no sound of her."

"No, sir," I replied; "and that, in conjunction with the sounds which I undoubtedly heard just now makes me think that something must be wrong on board her. Do you not think the matter ought to be reported to Captain Vernon?"

"Most certainly it ought," he agreed. "Is it possible that the crew have taken the ship from their officers, think you?"

"I scarcely know *what* to think," I replied. "Let us speak to the captain at once, and hear what he has to say about it."

Thereupon the third lieutenant directed Keene, one of the midshipmen, to take temporary charge of the deck; and we at once dived below.

"Well, Mr Armitage, what is it?" asked Captain Vernon, as we presented ourselves in the cabin and discovered him and Mr Smellie chatting together over their wine and cigars.

"I must apologise for intruding upon you, sir," said Armitage; "but Hawkesley here has come to me with a very extraordinary story which I think you had better hear from his own lips."

"Oh! Well, what is it, Mr—. Why, Hawkesley, where in the world have you been, and what doing, man? You are positively smothered in tar."

"Yes, sir," I replied, glancing at myself and discovering for the first time by the brilliant light of the cabin lamp the woeful ruin wrought upon my uniform. "I really beg your pardon, sir, for presenting myself in this plight, but the urgent nature of my business must be my excuse." And I forthwith plunged *in medias res* and told what I had heard and seen.

"The noise of a scuffle and the brig adrift!" exclaimed the skipper. "The crew surely cannot have risen upon their officers and taken the ship!" the same idea promptly presenting itself to him as had occurred to the third lieutenant.

"No, sir," said I. "I do not believe that is it at all; the commotion was not great enough or prolonged enough for that; *all* the officers would not be likely to be taken by surprise, but *one man might be.*"

"One man! What do you mean? I don't understand you," rapped out the skipper.

"Well, then, sir, to speak the whole of my mind plainly, I am greatly afraid that Mr Austin has met with foul play on board that brig, and that she is not a French man-o'-war at all, as she professes to be," I exclaimed.

I saw Smellie start; and he was about to speak when:

"Mr Austin! Foul play! Not a French man-o'-war!!" gasped the skipper. "Why, Good Heavens! the boy is *mad*!"

"If I am, sir, I can only say that I have been so for the last four months," I retorted. "For it is fully as long as that, or longer, that I have had my suspicions about that brig and her crew."

"What!" exclaimed Smellie. "Have *you*, too, suspected the brig?"

"I have, indeed, sir," I replied.

"Take a chair, Hawkesley," interrupted the skipper; "pour yourself out a glass of wine, and let us have your story in the fewest possible words. Mr Armitage, do me the favour to ascertain the brig's present whereabouts and let me know. Now, Hawkesley, we are ready to listen to you."

As the skipper ceased, Armitage bowed and withdrew, whilst I very hastily sketched the rise and progress of my suspicions, from Monsieur Le Breton's first visit up to that present moment.

Before I had proceeded very far, however, Armitage returned with the intelligence that the brig was undoubtedly adrift and already some distance astern of us, and that the topman, who had been aloft to inspect, had reported that he thought he could detect men on her yards.

"Turn up the hands at once then, sir, if you please, and see everything ready for slipping our cable and making sail at a moment's notice. But let everything be done in absolute silence; and keep a hand aloft to watch the brig and report anything further he may notice on board her; it really looks as though we were on the brink of some important discovery. Now go ahead with your story, Hawkesley," said the skipper.

I proceeded as rapidly as possible, merely stating what suspicious circumstances had come under my own notice, and leaving Captain Vernon to draw his own deductions. When I had finished, the skipper turned to Smellie and said:

"Am I to understand, from your remark made a short time

ago, that you, too, have suspected this mysterious brig, Mr Smellie?"

"Yes," answered Smellie, "I certainly had a vague feeling that there was something queer about her; but my suspicions were not nearly so clear and strong as Hawkesley's, and subsequent events quite drove the matter out of my mind."

"Um!" remarked the skipper meditatively; "it is strange, *very* strange. *I* never noticed anything peculiar about the craft."

"The brig is now about half a mile distant, sir, and is making sail," reported Armitage at that moment, presenting himself again at the cabin door.

"Then wait until the hands are out of his rigging; then slip, and we will be after him. I intend to see to the bottom of this," returned the skipper sharply. "There is undoubtedly something wrong or poor Austin would have turned up on board before matters had reached this stage. But, mind, let the work be carried on without an unnecessary sound of any kind."

As Armitage again withdrew and Smellie rose to his feet, Captain Vernon turned to me and said:

"I am very greatly obliged to you for the zeal and discretion you have manifested in this most delicate matter, Hawkesley; whatever comes of it I shall remember that you have acted throughout to the very best of your ability, not coming to me precipitately with a vague unconnected story, but waiting patiently until you had accumulated a sufficiency of convincing evidence for us to act upon; though, even now we must be very cautious as to what we do. And let me also add that Mr Smellie has spoken to me in the highest terms of your conduct throughout that trying time when you and he were ashore together; indeed he assures me that to you, under God, he is indebted for the actual preservation of his life. I have watched you carefully from the moment of your first coming on board, and I have been highly gratified with your conduct throughout. Go on as you have begun, young sir, and you will prove an ornament to the service. And now, gentlemen, to business."

CHAPTER SEVENTEEN

POOR AUSTIN'S FATE

I hurried on deck, highly gratified at the very handsome compliment paid me by the skipper, and found that the hands were aloft, casting loose the canvas. Presently, without a word having been spoken above a whisper, or a shout uttered, they came down again; the topsail halliards were manned, the yards mast-headed, the jib run up, the cable slipped, and we were under weigh; the fog all the time being as thick as a hedge, so thick indeed that it was impossible to see the jib-boom end from the quarter-deck. Old Mildmay, the master, was conning the ship; but of course in such a fog it was all guess-work, and the old fellow was terribly nervous and anxious, as indeed was also Captain Vernon. It struck me that the ship might be better conned from aloft, and I stepped up to the skipper and with due modesty mentioned my idea.

"A very happy thought," exclaimed the master, who happened to overhear me. "I'll just step up as far as the crosstrees myself."

"Very good, Mr Mildmay; do so by all means," said Captain Vernon. "But the wind is light, and what little of it there is will carry the sound of your voice down to the brig if you hail the deck, and so apprise them of our approach. We must avoid that if possible; I want to get alongside the craft and take her by surprise, and we may have some trouble in accomplishing that if they suspect that we are after them. The *Daphne* is a fast ship, but so also is the brig, and I am by no means certain that she has not the heels of us. We must devise a little code of signals from you to the deck, so as to obviate any necessity for hailing. Can anyone suggest anything?"

A very simple plan had occurred to me whilst the skipper was speaking, and as no one else seemed to have a suggestion to make, I offered mine.

"If the pennant halliards were cast adrift down here on deck, sir, and held by one of us," I said, "Mr Mildmay could get hold of them aloft, and one tug upon them might mean 'port,' two tugs 'starboard,' and three 'steady.'"

"Excellent!" exclaimed the skipper, "and perfectly simple; we will adopt it forthwith, and you shall attend to the deck-end of the halliards, Mr Hawkesley, with Mr Keene and Mr Peters to pass the word from you along the deck to the helmsman. Place us in a good weatherly position, Mr Mildmay, if you please, so that when we run clear of the fog the brig may have no chance to dodge us."

"Ay ay, sir, never fear for me," answered Old Mildmay as he swung nimbly into the main rigging, and in a few seconds his body disappeared in the mist.

The old fellow soon put us in the right course, and away we went, crowding sail after the invisible brig. An anxious half-hour followed, and then we ran out of the fog and found ourselves creeping along parallel with the land to the northward of the river-mouth, with the brig about half a mile ahead of us under every stitch of canvas she could show to the freshening land-breeze. We had gained on her considerably, the master having kept a keen eye upon her gleaming upper canvas whilst piloting us out of the river and steering in such a direction as to very nearly cut her off altogether. He of course came down on deck as soon as we had cleared the fog, and Captain Vernon at once ordered the crew to quarters.

The men were not long in getting to their stations, and when all was ready a gun was fired after the flying brig, as a polite request for her to heave-to, and the ensign hoisted to the peak. I was naturally very anxious to see what notice would be taken of this, since the somewhat high-handed course we were taking with the craft had been adopted entirely upon the strength of my representations; and if the brig should, after all, turn out to be the *Vestale* French gun-brig as she had pretended to be, our skipper might perhaps involve himself in a considerable amount of trouble. It was therefore with a sigh of real and genuine relief that I heard a shot come whistling close past us from the brig in reply to our own.

Captain Vernon, too, was evidently much relieved, for he ejaculated in tones of great satisfaction:

"Good! she has fired a shotted gun at us and refuses to show her colours. *Now* my course is perfectly clear. Try the effect of another gun on her, Mr Armitage, and aim at her spars; she is skimming along there like a witch, and if we are not careful will give us the slip yet."

Armitage, who was in charge of the battery forward, upon this began peppering away at her in earnest; but though the shot made daylight through her canvas every time, no damage was done either to her spars or rigging, and it began to be only too evident that she was gradually creeping away from us. To make matters worse, too, her crew were just as smart with their guns as we were with ours, in fact a trifle more so, for before a quarter of an hour had passed several of our ropes, fortunately unimportant ones, had been cut; and at length a thud and a crack aloft turned all eyes in that direction, to see the fore royal-mast topple over to leeward.

Captain Vernon stamped upon the deck in the height of his vexation.

"Away aloft, there, and clear the wreck," he exclaimed, "and, for Heaven's sake, Mr Armitage, see if you cannot cripple the fellow. Ten minutes more and he will be out of range; then 'good-bye' to him. I wish to goodness our people at home would condescend to take a lesson in shipbuilding from the men who turn out these slavers; we should then have a chance of making a capture occasionally."

Whilst the skipper had been thus giving vent to his rapidly-increasing chagrin, Smellie had walked forward; and presently I caught sight of him stooping down and squinting along the sights of the gun which had just been re-loaded and run out. A few seconds of anxious suspense followed, and then came a flash and a sharp report, followed the next moment by a ringing cheer from the men on the forecastle. The brig's fore-yard had been shot away in the slings.

The craft at once shot up into the wind and lay apparently at our mercy.

"Ram us alongside him, Mildmay," exclaimed the skipper in an ecstasy of delight. "Stand by with the grappling-irons fore and aft. Mr Smellie, stand by to lead a party on board him forward; I will attend to matters aft here."

It really looked for a moment as though we actually had the brig; but a chill of disappointment thrilled through me when

I saw how splendidly she was handled. The man who commanded her was evidently equal to any emergency, for no sooner did the craft begin to luff into the wind than he let fly his after braces, shivered his main topsail, and hauled his head sheets over to windward, and—after a pause which must have sent the hearts of all on board into their mouths—the brig began to pay off again, until, by a deft and dainty manipulation of her canvas, she was actually got dead before the wind, when the main yard was squared and away she went once more but little the worse for her serious mishap.

If her skipper, however, was a thorough seaman, so too was old Mildmay. That experienced veteran soon saw how matters were tending, and though he was unable to "ram" us alongside in accordance with Captain Vernon's energetically expressed desire, he placed the *Daphne* square in the wake and to windward of the brig, and within half a cable's length of her, thus, to some extent, taking the wind out of her sails, the effect of which was that we immediately began to gain upon her.

The crew of the brig now worked at their stern-chasers with redoubled energy, and our running-gear soon began to suffer. But though we might to some extent have avoided this by sheering away on to one or other of the brig's quarters, the position we then held was so commanding that the skipper resolved to maintain it. "We must grin and bear it," said he, "it will not be for long; another five minutes will place us alongside. Edge down a trifle toward his port quarter, Mildmay, as though we intended to board him on that side, then, at the last moment, sheer sharply across his stern and range up on his starboard side, it *may* possibly save us a broadside as we board. Mr Smellie, kindly load both batteries with round and grape, if you please; we will deliver our broadside and board in the smoke."

Within the specified five minutes we ranged up alongside the brig, delivered our broadside, receiving hers in return, her hands proving too smart to let us escape that; our grappling-irons were securely hooked into her rigging, and away we went on board her fore and aft, being perhaps a second ahead of the brig's crew, who actually had the hardihood to attempt to board *us*. We were stoutly met by as motley, and, at the same time, as ruffianly a set of men as it has ever been my lot to encounter; and a most desperate struggle forthwith ensued. Captain Vernon of course took care to be first on board; but I stuck close to his coat-tails, and almost the first individual we encountered was no less a personage than our old acquaintance Monsieur Le Breton himself. He pressed fiercely forward and at once crossed swords with the skipper, who exchanged two or three passes with him; but the two were soon separated by the surging crowd of combatants, and then I found myself face to face with him. I was by no means a skilled swordsman, and to tell the truth felt somewhat nervous for a moment as his blade jarred and rasped upon mine. By great good fortune, however, I succeeded in parrying his first thrust, and the next instant—how it happened I could not possibly say—he reeled backwards with my sword-blade right through his body. Leaving him dying, as I thought, on deck, I immediately pressed forward after the skipper, and for a few minutes was kept pretty busy, first with one antagonist and then another. Finally, after a fiercely maintained struggle of some twelve minutes or so, the brig's crew began to give way before our own lads, until, finding themselves hemmed in on all sides, they flung down their arms and begged for quarter, which was of course given them. Upon this, seeing that the skipper and Smellie were both safe, I turned to go below, thinking that I should perhaps discover poor Austin in durance vile in one of the state-rooms. I descended the cabin staircase, and was about to pass into the saloon when I happened to catch sight, out of the corner of my eye, of some dark object moving in an obscure corner under the staircase. Turning to take a more direct look at it I to my great surprise discovered it to be Monsieur Le Breton, who, instead of being dead as I had quite imagined he must be, was alive, and, seemingly, not very much the worse for his wound. He carried a pistol in his hand, and was in the very act of lowering himself down through a trap in the flooring when I grasped him by the collar and invited him to explain his intentions. He quietly allowed me to drag him out of the opening, rose to his feet, and then suddenly closed with me, aiming fierce blows at my uncovered head—I had lost my hat somehow in the struggle on deck—with the heavy brass-mounted butt of his pistol. In such an encounter as this I did not feel very much afraid of him, being tall for my age, and having developed a fair share of muscular strength since leaving England; but it was as much as I could do to hold him and at the same time prevent his inflicting some serious injury upon me. His wound, however, told upon him at last, and I eventually succeeded in dragging him back to the deck, though not until after he had ineffectually emptied his pistol at me.

On regaining the deck I found our lads busy securing the prisoners, and Monsieur Le Breton was soon made as safe as the rest of them.

He was loudly protesting against the indignity of being bound, when Captain Vernon approached.

"Oh! here you are, Hawkesley!" he exclaimed. "I was looking for you, and began to fear that you had met with a mishap. Do me the favour to step below and see if you can discover anything of Mr Austin."

"I have already once been below with that object, sir," I replied; "but, discovering this man—Le Breton as he calls himself—acting in a very suspicious manner, I deemed it my duty to see him safe on deck before proceeding further in my quest."

"What was he doing?" asked the skipper sharply.

"I vill tell you, sare, vat I was doing," interrupted Le Breton recklessly. "I vas on my vay to ze *soute aux poudres* to blow you and all ze people to ze devil to keep company wiz your inqueezatif first leftenant. And I would have done eet, too, but for zat pestilent midshipman, who have ze gripe of ze devil himself. *Peste!* you Eengleesh, you are like ze bouledogue, ven you take hold you not nevare let go again."

"There, Hawkesley, what do you think of that for a compliment?" laughed the skipper. "So, monsieur," he resumed, "you were about to blow us up, eh? Very kind of you, I'm sure. Perhaps you will increase our obligation to you by informing me what you have done with Mr Austin?"

"Done wiz him!" reiterated Le Breton with a diabolical sneer. "Why, I have sent him to ze bottom of ze creek, where I would have sent you all if you had not been too cautious to accept my polite invitation."

"Do I understand you to mean that you have *murdered* him?" thundered the skipper.

"Yes," was the reckless answer; "drowned him or murdered him, call it what you will."

"You treacherous scoundrel!" ejaculated the skipper hoarsely; "you shall be made to bitterly account for this unprovoked outrage; clap him in irons," turning to the master-at-arms, who happened to be close at hand. "Poor Austin!" he continued. "Your suspicions, Hawkesley, have proved only too correct; the craft is, unquestionably, a slaver—or worse. We must have her thoroughly overhauled; possibly some documents of great value to us may be found stowed away somewhere or other. I'll see to it at once." And he forthwith dived below.

The prisoners having been secured, the dead and wounded were next attended to, the former being lashed up in their hammocks ready for burial, whilst the latter were carefully conveyed below to receive such attention as the surgeon and his assistant could bestow. The brig's loss was very severe, sixteen of her men having been killed and twenty-two wounded—principally by our final broadside—out of a total of sixty hands. Our own loss was light, considering the determination with which the enemy had fought, amounting to only eleven wounded. As soon as a sufficiency of hands could be spared for the purpose, the brig's square canvas was furled, a prize crew was told off to take charge of her, and the two craft then made sail in company—the brig under her fore-and-aft canvas only—for the anchorage under Padron Point, where we brought up about a couple of hours later. Captain Vernon then returned to the *Daphne* in the brig's gig, bringing with him a bundle of papers, and leaving Smellie in charge of the prize; an anchor-watch was set, and all hands then turned in, pretty well tired but highly elated at the result of our evening's work.

At daybreak next morning both vessels weighed and returned to their former berths in Banana Creek, the *Daphne* picking up the cable which she had slipped on the previous night. The dead were then buried on the little island which lies on the east side of the creek; after which the carpenter and boatswain with their mates were set to work upon the necessary repairs to the brig. This craft now proved to be English built, having been turned out of a Shoreham shipyard, and originally registered under the name of the *Virginia*; but how she had come to get into the hands of the individuals from whom we took her there was nothing to show. She was completely fitted for carrying on the business of a slaver; but from the nature of the goods discovered in her after hold—which was quite separate from her main hold—there could be no doubt that she had also done a little piracy whenever a convenient opportunity had presented itself.

I was sent away directly after breakfast that morning in charge of a couple of boats with orders to drag the creek for poor Mr Austin's body, and in little more than an hour we fortunately found it quite uninjured. The poor fellow had evidently been taken completely by surprise, a gag being in his mouth, and his hands manacled behind him, with a stout canvas bag containing two 18-pound shot lashed to his feet. We took the body on board the *Daphne*, and it was at once conveyed below to his own cabin, pending the construction of a coffin, the ensign being at the same time hoisted half up to the peak.

This melancholy duty performed I was again sent away to drag for the anchor and cable slipped by the *Virginia* on the previous evening, and these also I found, weighed, and conveyed on board the prize, where, under Smellie's able supervision, the work of repairing and refitting was going on apace.

About noon that same day a strange brig entered the river with the French flag flying at her peak, and brought up in the creek about a cable's length astern of us. We were at once struck with the marked resemblance which the stranger bore to the *Virginia*—though it was by no means so striking as the similarity between our prize and the *Black Venus*—and we forthwith came to the conclusion that we now at last beheld the veritable *Vestale*—the real Simon Pure—before us. And so, upon Armitage boarding her, she proved to be; her captain, upon hearing of the extraordinary personation of his craft so successfully played off upon us by the *Virginia*, actually producing his commission to prove his *bona fides*. During the course of this somewhat eventful day, also, one of our lads learned from one of the prisoners that on the occasion of our second encounter with the *Virginia*—when she so cleverly pretended to be in pursuit of the *Black Venus*—she was actually making the best of her way to Havana with the three hundred slaves on board which she had accused her sister-ship of carrying off, and that her elaborate signalling on that occasion was merely resorted to for the purpose of hoodwinking us.

At four o'clock that afternoon, Mr Austin's body having been deposited in the coffin which had been prepared for it, the hands were mustered on deck in their clean clothes, the boats were hoisted out, and the body was deposited in the launch, with the union-jack spread over the coffin as a pall, and the ensign hoisted half-mast high on the staff in the boat's stern. Just as the procession was on the point of shoving off from the ship's side, the officers of the *Vestale*, who had incidentally learned the particulars of Austin's murder, approached in their two gigs, with the French flag floating at half-mast from the ensign-staves in the sterns of their boats, and took up a position in the rear. We then shoved off; the first and second cutters taking the launch in tow, and proceeding up the creek in charge of old Mildmay, the master, the captain and officers following in the two gigs. As soon as we were clear of the ship's side the *Daphne* began firing minute-guns, to which the *Vestale*, hoisting her ensign half up to the peak, replied; and so we moved slowly up the creek, the minute-guns continuing as long as the boats remained within sight of the ship. We proceeded for a distance of about two miles, which brought us to a lovely spot selected by the skipper, who had himself sought it out during the morning, and there we landed. The body was then passed out of the launch and shouldered by six petty officers;

Smellie and I supporting the pall on one side, whilst Armitage and old Mildmay performed a like duty on the other; the skipper leading the way to the grave and reading the burial service as he went, whilst the remaining officers and men, followed by the contingent from the *Vestale*, formed in the rear of the coffin. Arrived at the grave, the coffin was placed on the ground, the ropes for lowering it to the bottom were adjusted, and finally it was gently and reverently deposited in its last resting-place, the skipper meanwhile reading impressively those solemn sentences beginning with "Man that is born of a woman hath but a short time to live," etcetera. A slight pause was made at the conclusion of these passages, and Smellie, deeply affected, stepped forward and threw the first earth upon the body of his dear friend and brother officer, after which the service again proceeded and soon came to an end. The firing party of marines next formed on each side of the grave and rendered the last honours to the dead; the grave was filled in, a wooden cross being temporarily planted at its head, and we turned sorrowfully away, entered the boats, and with the ensigns now hoisted to the staff-heads, returned to the ship realising *fully*, perhaps for the first time, the fact that we had lost for ever a genial, brave, devoted, and sympathetic friend. "In the midst of life we are in death." Never did I so thoroughly realise the absolute literal truth of this as whilst sitting in the gig, silently struggling with my feelings, on our return from poor Austin's funeral. We had just laid him in his lonely grave on a foreign shore, far away from all that he held dearest and best on earth, in a spot consecrated only by the solemn service which had just been performed over it, a spot which could never be watered by a mother's or a sister's tears, where his last resting-place would be at the mercy of the stranger and the savage, and where in the course of a very few years it would only too probably be obliterated beyond all possibility of recognition. Yet twenty-four short hours ago he was alive and well, rejoicing in the strength of his lusty manhood, and with, apparently, the promise of many years of life before him, never suspecting, as he went down over the ship's side, with a cheery smile and a reassuring nod to me, that he was going thus gaily to meet treachery and death. Poor Austin! I struggled successfully with my feelings whilst the eyes of others were upon me, but I am not ashamed to admit that I wept long and bitterly that night when I reflected in privacy upon his untimely and cruel fate. Nor am I ashamed to acknowledge that I then also prayed, more earnestly perhaps than I had ever prayed before, that I might be taught so to number my days that I might incline mine heart unto that truest of all wisdom, the wisdom which teaches us how to live in such a way that death may never find us unprepared.

On passing the *Virginia* it was seen that her new fore-yard was slung and rigged, the sail bent, and the other repairs completed, so that she was once more ready for sea. Smellie shortly afterwards shifted his traps over into her, returning to the *Daphne* to dine with Captain Vernon and to receive his final instructions.

These given, Mr Armitage and I were summoned to the cabin; and upon our arrival there, the skipper, after speaking regretfully upon the loss which the ship and all hands, himself especially, as he said, had sustained through the first lieutenant's death, informed us that Mr Smellie having received charge of the prize to deliver over to the admiral of the station with an earnest recommendation that she should be turned over to the navy and given to Smellie with the rank of commander, it now became necessary to appoint an acting first lieutenant to the *Daphne*. A few words of commendation to Armitage then followed, and he was presented with an acting order.

The skipper then turned to me.

"It next becomes necessary to appoint an acting second lieutenant," said he, "and after giving the subject my most serious attention, I have determined, Hawkesley, to appoint *you*. Nay, no thanks, young gentleman; you will discover before many hours have passed over your head that you have very little to be thankful for. You will exchange your present easy and irresponsible position for one of very grave and unceasing responsibility; the safety of the ship and of all hands will daily, during your watch, be confided to your care, and many other onerous duties will devolve upon you, every one of which will demand your most unceasing attention and your utmost skill in their proper discharge. Henceforward you will have time to think of nothing but *duty*, duty must wholly engage your thoughts by day, ay, and your very dreams by night; it is no post of mere empty honour which I am about to confer upon you. But, as I once before remarked to you, I have had my eye upon you ever since you came on board the ship, and, young as you are, and short as has been your term of probation, I have sufficient confidence in you to believe that you will do credit to my judgment. I presume, of course, that it is unnecessary to point out to you that this appointment can be only *temporary*; the *Virginia* will doubtless bring back with her from Sierra Leone officers of the admiral's appointment to fill the posts of second and third lieutenant; but if, as I have no doubt, you discharge your temporary duties with anything like the ability I anticipate, your promotion, upon the completion of your time, will be sure and rapid."

So saying, the skipper extended his hand to me and gave mine a hearty shake, Smellie and Armitage following his example and offering me their congratulations.

It being, by this time, rather late, Smellie shortly afterwards rose, and bidding adieu at the gangway to his old shipmates, repaired on board his new command, which was under orders to sail next morning at daybreak.

As for me, I went off to the midshipmen's berth, which, through Keene, Woods, and Williams, the master's mate, being drafted on board the *Virginia*, was now almost empty, and shifted my few traps forthwith into the cabin recently vacated by Smellie, scarcely knowing meanwhile whether I was standing upon my head or my heels.

CHAPTER EIGHTEEN

THE CUTTERS BESET

On the following morning Captain Dubosc and Lieutenant Le Breton (we now discovered that the *Virginia's* people had assumed the names of the officers of the *Vestale* in addition to appropriating the name of the ship) came on board the *Daphne* to breakfast; Armitage and old Mildmay being invited to meet them.

The meal appeared to be a protracted one, for it was served punctually at eight o'clock and the participants did not appear on deck until half-past ten. The secret, however, soon came out, for when they did at length put in an appearance it became perfectly evident, from sundry disjointed remarks which passed between them, that something of importance was on the *tapis*. The Frenchmen's gig was awaiting them, and they soon passed down over the side, Captain Dubosc's last words being:

"Well, then, *mon ami*, it is all settled, and our contingent shall be ready for a start punctually at two o'clock *Au revoir*."

I was not left long in ignorance of the precise nature of the arrangement which had just been concluded, for as soon as the French gig was fairly away from our vessel's side, Captain Vernon beckoned me to him and said:

"Just step down below with me, Hawkesley; I want to have a talk with you."

I followed him down into his cabin, whereupon he directed me to be seated, drew a chair up to the table for himself, and laying his hand upon a bundle of papers, said:

"These are some of the papers which I discovered the night before last on board the *Virginia*; and as I anticipated would be the case, they contain several items of exceedingly important information. One of these items has reference to the existence, on an island some forty miles up the river, of an immense slave depot, as also of a slave hulk, in both of which, if the information here given happens to be reliable, a large number of slaves are at this moment awaiting embarkation. The papers seem also to imply that there is a very snug anchorage close to this island, with a navigable channel leading right up to it.

"Now I am exceedingly anxious, for many reasons, to test the truth of this information, and I have therefore arranged with Captain Dubosc to send a joint expedition up the river to survey the alleged channel, to destroy the depot and the hulk, if such are found to exist, and to free any slaves which may happen to be therein.

"From certain remarks to be found here and there in these documents, I infer that the depot and hulk are in charge of white men, but it is, unfortunately, nowhere stated how many these white men number. They cannot, however, muster very strongly there; they probably do not number above a dozen altogether; the expedition, therefore, will only be a small one, consisting only of our own cutter and that of the

Vestale. I have determined to give the command of our people to Mr Mildmay, he being the most experienced officer at surveying now remaining to us, with you to lend a hand. The French boat will be under the command of Monsieur Saint Croix, the second lieutenant of the *Vestale*; and both boats, though of course under independent commands, will act in concert. This paper," placing one before me, "is, as you will perceive, a sketch-chart of the river, and the two crosses in red ink indicate the positions of the depot and the hulk. It differs somewhat, you will notice, from the admiralty chart," to which he pointed as he spoke, "and it will really be a great point to ascertain which, if either, of the two is correct. To an individual unacquainted with the river, the channel there on the larboard hand going up would naturally suggest itself as the preferable one, being so much wider than the other, but the soundings marked on this sketch go to show that the water is much deeper in the *south* channel. This is one of the points I want cleared up. And another is the bearings and compass courses along the deepest water in each reach of the channel. I have already explained all this to Mildmay of course; but I thought I would also explain it to you, because, knowing exactly what I want, you will be able to render more intelligent assistance than would be possible were you working in the dark. There is only one thing more. You are a tolerably good hand with your pencil, I know; do you think you could make an exact copy of this sketch-chart to take with you, so as to leave the original behind with me?"

I assured the skipper that I both could and would, whereupon he furnished me with the necessary materials and left me in solitude to perform my task, going on deck himself to superintend the preparations for our trip.

The sketch-chart found among the papers on board the *Virginia* was only a small affair, drawn upon a sheet of foolscap paper; but it was so carefully executed that I felt sure it must be the work of an experienced hand, and consequently, in all probability, perfectly accurate. My copy, therefore, to be of any value at all, would have to be, not a free-hand happy-go-lucky sketch, but an absolute *facsimile*. There was a great deal of work in it, and not much time wherein to do it; so, after a little thought, I hit upon the plan of fastening the outspread original with wafers to the glass of one of the stern windows, and watering a thin sheet of paper over it. The strong daylight reflected up from the surface of the water through the glass rendered the two sheets of paper sufficiently transparent to enable me to see every line and mark of the original with tolerable clearness through the sheet upon which I proposed to make my copy; and with the aid of a fine-pointed pencil I soon had it complete, going over it afterwards with pen and ink to make it indelible.

Mildmay and I lunched with the skipper that day, and during the course of the meal we received our final instructions, which were, however, little more than a recapitulation of those given me in the morning.

The meal over, the cutter's crew were paraded, fully armed, in the waist of the ship; their ammunition was served out to them, and they were ordered down into the boat, which lay alongside with a 12-pounder carronade in her bows, together with the necessary powder and shot for the same, spare ammunition for the men's muskets, four days' provisions and water, and, in fact, every necessary for the successful carrying out of the undertaking upon which we were bound. The skipper then shook hands with Mildmay and me, wishing us prosperity and success; we went down over the side into the boat, and the little expedition started. Three minutes later we were joined by Monsieur Saint Croix in the *Vestale's* cutter, when the canvas was set in both boats, the wind, though dead in our teeth for the passage up the river, being free enough to carry us as far as Boolambemba Point.

For the remainder of that day and up to about 4 p.m. on the day following, the expedition progressed without incident of any kind worth mentioning. Our progress was steady but slow, Mildmay's whole energies being devoted to the making of a thoroughly satisfactory and trustworthy survey of the river channel up which we were passing; and in the accomplishment of this duty I was pleased to find that the studies I had been diligently pursuing under Mr Smellie's auspices enabled me to render him substantial assistance. Saint Croix, who kept about a quarter of a mile in our wake, was making a perfectly independent survey, which he compared with ours at the conclusion of each day's work. The first incident of note, though we attached no importance whatever to it at the moment, occurred about four o'clock in the afternoon on the day following our departure from Banana Creek, and it consisted merely in the fact that a large native canoe passed us upward bound, without its occupants bestowing upon us any notice whatever. We had previously encountered several canoes—small craft carrying from two to half-a-dozen natives—and the occupants of these, who seemed to be engaged for the most part in fishing, had invariably greeted us with vociferous ejaculations, which, from the hearty laughter immediately following them, were doubtless choice examples of Congoese wit. But the particular canoe now in question swept past us without a sound. She was a large, well-shaped craft, propelled by twenty-four paddles, and she dashed ahead of us as if we had been at anchor, her occupants—and especially four individuals who sat in the stern-sheets, or at all events where the stern-sheets ought to be, and who, from their display of feathers, bead necklaces, and leopard-skin robes, must have been very bigwigs indeed—looking straight ahead of them and vouchsafing not the faintest indication that they were conscious of our presence. This absurd assumption of dignity greatly tickled us at the moment, we attributing it entirely to the existence in the native mind of a profound conviction of their own immeasurable superiority; but subsequent events tended to give another and a more sinister aspect to the incident. We pressed diligently on with our work until six o'clock, at which time we found ourselves abreast a small native village. Here Mildmay proposed to effect a landing, both for the purpose of procuring some fruit and also to satisfy his very natural curiosity to see what a native village was like. But on pulling in toward the bank the natives assembled, making such unmistakable warlike demonstrations that we deemed it advisable to abandon our purpose. We could, of course, have easily dispersed the hostile blacks had we been so disposed; and Saint Croix, who was a particularly high-spirited, fiery-tempered young fellow, strongly advocated our doing so. But Captain Vernon's orders to us to avoid all collision with the natives had been most stringent, and old Mildmay was far too experienced and seasoned a hand to engage in an affray for the mere "fun" of the thing. He therefore sturdily refused to aid or abet Saint Croix in any such unrighteous undertaking; and we passed the night instead upon a small islet whereon there was nothing more formidable than a few water-fowl and a flock of green parrots to dispute our landing.

We had not been at work above an hour or so on the following morning before we had reason to suspect that some at least of the unusual number of canoes around us were suspiciously watching our movements, if not actually following us up the river. This, however, for the time being caused us little or no uneasiness, as we felt assured that, should their attentions become inconveniently obtrusive, a bullet or two, or failing that, a round-shot from our carronade, fired over their heads, would promptly send them to the right-about. Later on in the day, however, I must confess that I for one began to experience a slight qualm of anxiety as I noticed the steadily increasing number of canoes, *some* of them carrying as many as ten or a dozen men, in our vicinity. They were all ostensibly engaged in fishing, it is true; but that this was only a pretence, or that they were meeting with unusually bad luck, was evident from the small number of fish captured. Still, up to noon, though the behaviour of the natives had been steadily growing more suspicious and unsatisfactory, no actual hostile demonstration had been made; and we landed upon a small bare, sandy islet to cook and despatch our dinner.

During all this time we had, of course, been carefully checking the chart of the river copied by me from the one found on board the *Virginia*, and comparing it with our own survey; the general result being to prove that it was very fairly accurate, quite sufficiently so at least to serve as a safe guide to any vessel of light draught, say up to ten feet or so, making for the island on which was the alleged slave depot. This chart told us that we had now arrived within a distance of some six miles of the island in question, a statement verified to some extent by the fact that on an island situate at about that distance from us we could make out, with the aid of our glasses, an object which might very well pass for a large building of some kind. The river channel between us and this island was entirely free of visible obstructions, and we therefore hoped that, by a little extra exertion, we might succeed in completing our survey right up to the island, and gaining possession of it and the hulk—thus achieving the full object of the expedition—before nightfall.

By the time that we were ready to make a start once more, however, the canoes had mustered in such numbers that even old Mildmay, who had hitherto poo-poohed my suggestions as to the possibility of a contemplated attack, began to look serious, and at last actually went the length of acknowledging that perhaps there might be mischief brewing after all. Saint Croix, however, treated the matter lightly, roundly asserting that the extraordinary gathering was due to nothing more serious than the native curiosity to behold the unwonted sight of a white man, and to watch our mysterious operations. There was undoubtedly a certain degree of probability about this suggestion, and most unfortunately we gave to it a larger share of credence than the event justified, shoving off from our sand-bank and resuming our surveying operations without first adopting those precautionary measures which prudence obviously dictated.

At two o'clock p.m., by which time we had passed over about three of the six miles which lay between the sand-bank and our supposed goal, the French boat being at the time about half a mile astern of us, a loud shouting arose from one of the largest canoes in the flotilla, her paddles were suddenly elevated in the air, and the whole fleet with one accord rapidly closed in between us and the Frenchmen, completely cutting us off the one from the other.

"Hillo!" exclaimed Mildmay, "what's the meaning of this? Just clap a round-shot into the carronade there, you Tom, and pitch it well over the heads of those black rascals. Pull port, back starboard, and slue the boat round with her nose toward them. That's your sort! Now, Tom, are you ready there, for'ard? Then well elevate the muzzle and stand by to fire when I give the word. Hold water, starboard oars, and port oars pull a stroke; we're pointing straight for the Frenchmen just now. Well of all; now we're clear, and no chance of hitting our friends. Fire!"

The carronade rang out its report from the bows of the boat, and the shot went screaming away far over the heads of those in the canoes, the Frenchmen firing in like manner at almost the same moment. A yell of dismay immediately arose from the canoes, and half a dozen of those nearest us dashed their paddles into the water and began paddling precipitately away. Their panic, however, was only momentary; they appeared to have seen and heard artillery before, and as soon as they saw that no damage had been done they arrested their flight, and a contingent of canoes, numbering quite a hundred, began cautiously to advance toward us, spreading out on our right and left in a manner which showed that they meditated an attempt to surround us.

"Give 'em another pill, Tom, and slap it right into the thick of 'em this time; we mustn't let 'em surround us at no price," exclaimed old Mildmay. "Turn round on your thwarts, lads, and pull the boat gently up stream, starn first, so's to keep our bull-dog forward there facing 'em. Now, as soon as you're ready there with the gun let 'em have it." Once again the carronade spoke out, and this time its voice conveyed a death-message to some of the belligerent blacks, the shot striking one of the canoes fair in the stem, knocking her into match-wood, and killing or maiming several of her occupants. We naturally expected that this severe lesson would have the effect of sending our troublesome neighbours to the right-about *en masse*, but to our surprise and discomfiture this was by no means the case; on the contrary, it appeared to have thoroughly aroused their most savage instincts, and with a loud shout they dashed their paddles into the water and advanced menacingly toward us.

"Load your muskets, lads!" exclaimed Mildmay, as, with eyes gleaming and nostrils dilated, the old war-horse snuffed the approaching battle; "load your muskets, and then take to your oars again and back her steadily up stream. Sharp's the word and quick's the action; if those rascals 'outflank' us—as the sodgers call it—we may say 'good-bye' to old England. Mr Hawkesley, d'ye think you can pitch a bullet into that long chap that's creeping up there on our larboard beam? I'm about to try my hand and see if I can't stop the gallop of this fellow who's in such a tremendous hurry away here to the nor'ard of us. Take good aim, now; we haven't a single bullet that we can afford to throw away. Ah! that's *well* done," as I bowled over the individual who was handling the steering paddle in the canoe indicated to me. "Now let's see what an old man can do." He raised his piece to his shoulder, took a long steady aim, and fired. A white spot instantly appeared on the side of the canoe; and one of its occupants sprang convulsively to his feet and fell headlong into the river, nearly capsizing the frail craft as he did so.

This certainly checked the impetuosity of the two particular canoes, the occupants of which had suffered from our fire; but the others only pressed forward with increased eagerness.

"Hang it!" exclaimed the master pettishly, "I don't *want* to do it, but I shall have to give 'em a dose of grape yet. Why won't the stupid donkeys take a hint? And why, in the name of fortune, should they want to interfere with us at all? Try 'em with grape this time, Tom; let's see what they think of 'the fruit of the vine.'"

Meanwhile the French boat had also become actively engaged, the report of her carronade ringing out much more frequently than our own, whilst rattling volleys of musketry breezed up from her at brief intervals; but from the steadily decreasing sharpness of the reports it soon became evident, somewhat, I must confess, to our dismay, that she was *retiring*. It might, of course, be merely a strategic movement on Saint Croix's part; but if, on the other hand, he happened to be situated like ourselves, with all his work cut out to defend himself, and a way open to him *down* stream only, as we had a clear road before us *up* stream only, then indeed matters were beginning to look extremely serious for us. So far as he was concerned, if he could only avoid being surrounded he was comparatively safe; the way would be open for his retreat, and a fine breeze happening to be blowing down the river, he could, with the aid of his sails easily outpace the canoes. But with us the matter was very different; our retreat was cut off, and unless we could beat off the canoes the only course open to us seemed to be that of taking to dry land, intrenching ourselves as best we might, and patiently waiting until assistance should arrive. Meanwhile, in accordance with Mildmay's instructions, our carronade had been loaded with grape, and Tom, taking steady aim, applied the match to his piece. A flash, a roar, a volume of smoke, and away went the grape lashing up the surface of the water fair in line with a thick cluster of canoes, through which the iron shower next moment tore with disastrous effect. One canoe was literally rent to pieces, every one of its occupants, so far as we could see, being killed; two other canoes, one on each side of the first, were so seriously damaged that they immediately swamped, leaving their occupants squattering in the water like so many lame ducks; and three or four others were hit, with serious casualties to their crews. This effectually checked the advance of the blacks for a few minutes, during which we made good use of our oars in urging the boat, still stern foremost, in the direction of the island to which we were bound, and upon which we were now able to distinctly make out the shape of a huge wooden barrack-like structure.

As we pressed on toward the island we became cognisant of the fact that its occupants were in a great state of confusion, and a few minutes later we saw a long procession of blacks, who, from their constrained movements, were apparently manacled, emerge from the barrack and move off toward the opposite side of the island. We were enabled, with the aid of our glasses, to detect on the island the presence of some ten or a dozen white men, and these individuals, carrying each a musket in one hand and a whip in the other, seemed to be very freely using the latter to expedite the movements of the unhappy blacks.

We were, however, allowed but scanty time in which to take note of these matters, for the native canoes soon began to press forward upon us once more, evidently with the fixed determination to surround us if possible, and thus prevent our approach to the island. We knew that if this object were once accomplished our doom was certain, for in such a case, fight as desperately as we might, we must soon be overpowered by sheer force of numbers, and it consequently soon became, so far as we were concerned, an absolute race for life.

On swept the boat, our men pulling her through the water, though still stern foremost, at a pace such as she had rarely travelled before, and on crowded the canoes after us, spread out athwart the stream in the form of a crescent. Luckily for us, the channel at this point was not very wide, and by keeping in the middle of it we were able to throw a musket-shot clear across to either side, otherwise we should soon have found ourselves in a parlous case. The greater number of the canoes obstinately maintained a position in mid-stream ahead of us, thus presenting an insuperable barrier to our retreat down stream, whilst those on the outer wings to port and starboard of us hugged the bank of the stream, two or three of the larger craft making a big spurt ahead of the others now and then in an endeavour to outflank us, which endeavour, however, a well-directed volley of musketry always sufficed to check for the time being.

At length we reached a point where the stream widened out considerably, enabling the canoes on each side to spread out sufficiently far to be beyond musket-shot, and we saw that upon the question whether we or the canoes passed this point first, hinged our fate. The natives, though evidently entertaining a wholesome dread of our carronade, were by no means so dismayed by the execution it wrought among them as we had hoped they would be, and indeed exhibited a decidedly growing disposition to close upon us in spite of our fire; in fact, our position was at every moment growing more critical.

Very fortunately for us we happened to have a few rounds of canister in the boat, and Mildmay now resolved to try the effect of these upon the pertinacious natives. A charge of grape with one of canister on the top of it, was accordingly rammed home and sent flying into the thickest of the crowd of canoes immediately ahead of us, immediately succeeded by a like dose to the right and left wings of the flotilla. The canoes were just at about the right distance to give these murderous discharges their utmost possible effect, and the carnage among the thickly-crowded craft was simply indescribable. The effect was not only to check their advance effectually, but to actually put them to flight, and whilst a similar charge was again rammed home by those in charge of the gun the rest of the men slewed the boat round on her centre, and with a loud cheer gave way at top speed for the island.

We were within a hundred yards of the low shingly beach when, to our astonishment, the roar of artillery from the island greeted our ears, and at the same instant half a dozen round-shot came flying about our ears. Fortunately no damage was done beyond the smashing of a couple of oars and the incontinent precipitation backwards into the bottom of the boat of the pullers thereof, amidst the uproarious laughter of all hands, and before these unfortunates had fairly picked themselves up, the cutter was sent surging half her length high and dry up on the beach, the carronade belched forth its contents, and out we jumped, master and man, and charged up to the sod battery which had fired upon us. We were greeted with a volley of musketry, which, however, never stopped us in our rush a single instant, and as we clambered in at one side we had the satisfaction of seeing the rascally Spaniards go flying out at the other, whence they made short miles of it to a boat which lay awaiting them on the beach at the opposite side of the island, some two or three hundred yards away. We sent a few ineffectual flying shots after them, but attempted no pursuit, as we now found ourselves to some extent masters of the situation; in so far, that is to say, that we found the battery admirably adapted as a place wherein to make a stand until such time as we could see our way clear to once more take offensive measures. As for the Spaniards, they made good their retreat to a large hulk which lay securely moored at a distance of some twenty yards from the steeply sloping eastern shore of the island, and which—floating high out of the water as she did, with channel-plates removed and no gear whatever about her sides to aid us in boarding should we make the attempt—would, I foresaw, prove rather a hard nut for us to crack. Our footing thus made good upon the island and in the battery, we had a moment or two in which to look about us, and the first discovery made was that poor old Mildmay, the master, had been wounded, and was lying helpless, face downwards on the sward outside the battery. The next was, that the natives had recovered from their panic and were actually once more advancing against us, spreading out on all sides so as to completely encircle the island.

The first object demanding our attention was, of course, the master. Directing the man Tom, our chief artilleryman, to look into the state of the guns belonging to the battery, and to load them afresh, I called a couple of men and took them with me to bring in the master. The poor old fellow was lying upon the grass face downwards, and when we gently raised him it became apparent that he had been bleeding rather profusely at the mouth. He was senseless and ghastly pale, and for the moment I feared he was dead. A low moan, however, as the men began to move with him, gave us the assurance that life was not quite extinct, and as gently as we could we lifted him over the low earth parapet, and laid him down under its shelter in comparative safety.

The command of the party now devolved upon me, and a very serious responsibility under the circumstances I found it. Here we were cooped up in a small sod battery, wholly ineffectual to resist a determined assault; with a perfect cloud of hostile natives hovering about us apparently determined to be satisfied with nothing short of our absolute extermination; with a dozen vindictive Spaniards on board the hulk close at hand, doubtless as anxious as the natives to sweep us from the face of the earth; the French boat having vanished from the scene; and—though there was drinkable water in abundance in the river so long as we might be able to get at it—*with only one day's provisions left.*

CHAPTER NINETEEN

THE SITUATION BECOMES DESPERATE

"Well, Tom," said I, "what about the guns?—are they loaded?"

"Yes, sir, they is," answered Tom; "and a most fort'nate circumstance it were that you ordered them guns to be loaded when you did, otherwise we should have been sent sky-high by this time."

"Ah, indeed! how is that?"

"Why, you see, sir, when I was ordered to load the guns I nat'rally looks round for the ammunition for to do it with; and though this is the first time as I've ever found myself aboard a reg'lar genewine land-battery, it didn't take me long for to make up my mind that if there was any ammunition anywheres aboard the thing, it must be in one of them there corner lockers. So I goes away and tries to open the door, which in course I finds locked. It didn't take Ned and me mor'n a jiffy, hows'ever, to prise off the lock; and when I looked in, there sure enough was the powder—a goodish quantity—all made up into cartridges, and there, too, I sees the black stump of a fuze with a red spark on the end fizzing and smoking away—a good un. I knowed what that meant in a second, Mr Hawkesley; so I whips out my knife, sings out to Ned to prise open the other two doors, and cuts off the live end of the fuze at once, and just in time. There warn't more nor an inch of it left. And when we got the other two doors open it were just the same, sir—half a minute more 'd ha' done for the lot of us, sir."

"But you have taken care to see that the magazines are now all right?—that there are no more live fuzes in them?" I exclaimed in considerable alarm.

"Ay, ay, sir; never fear for me," answered Tom with a quiet grin. "They are safe enough now, sir; we gave 'em a good overhaul before doing anything else, sir."

"Thank you, Tom," I replied; "you have rendered a most important service, which, if I live to get out of this scrape, I will not fail to report to Captain Vernon. But I should like to take a squint into these magazines myself."

"Certingly, sir, by all means," returned Tom; and leading the way to the magazines he pointed out the manner in which the fuzes had been placed, and graphically redescribed the manner in which a terrible catastrophe had been averted.

We had, indeed, had a frightfully narrow escape from destruction; for the magazines, of which there were three, one in each angle of the triangular-shaped battery, contained about one hundred cartridges each—quite sufficient to have completely destroyed the battery and all in it.

Having satisfied myself that all was safe here, I at once turned my attention to the next most pressing business of the moment, which was to secure the muskets, ammunition, provisions, and water in the cutter, and to make the craft herself as safe as possible. This was likely to prove a somewhat hazardous task, as the canoes were now close to the beach and pressing rapidly in on all sides. I felt greatly averse to further slaughter; but in this case I scarcely saw how it was to be averted, the natives being so pertinacious in their attacks. It was quite evident that we must either kill or be killed. I therefore most reluctantly gave the order for the discharge of the six nine-pounders which the battery mounted right into the thickest of the crowd—the men to immediately afterwards rush for the boat, secure their muskets and ammunition, and at once return to the battery. This was done; and without pausing an instant to note the effect away we all went down to the boat, seized as much as we could conveniently carry, and immediately scampered back again. The whole operation did not occupy more than a couple of minutes; and I had the satisfaction of seeing all hands scramble back into the battery before the natives had recovered from the check of our last discharge.

So far so good; but a great many things still remained in the boat, especially the provisions and water, which it was absolutely necessary that we should secure; so I called for volunteers to accompany me on a second trip to the cutter. All hands proving equally willing to go, I picked half-a-dozen, leaving the remainder in the battery to cover us with their muskets.

Leaping the low sod parapet of the battery we once more made a dash for the boat; and the natives, catching sight of us, instantly raised a terrific yell and came paddling toward us at top speed.

"Out with your cutlasses, men!" I exclaimed; "we shall have to fight our way back this time, I believe. Now each man seize as much as he can carry in one hand, and keep close together. Now are you all ready? Then march. Ah! capital!" as the lads in the battery bowled over three or four blacks who had landed and were rushing down upon us. "Now *run for it*!"

Away we went, helter-skelter, and once more got safely within the compass of our sheltering walls, though not until I—who, of course, had to be last in seeking cover—had been overtaken and surrounded by some half-a-dozen furious blacks, two of whom I succeeded in disabling with my sword, whilst the remaining four were promptly placed *hors-de-combat* by the muskets of those who were covering our retreat.

Taking fresh courage, perhaps, at our limited number, and possibly also feeling more at home in a fight on dry land than when in their canoes, the natives now closed in upon us on all sides, effecting a landing on the island and pressing forward, with loud cries and much brandishing of spears, to attack the battery. This battery, it may be well to explain, was a small equilateral triangular affair built of sods, and measuring about thirty-five feet on each of its sides. It mounted six nine-pounder brass guns, two to each side; and its walls rose to a height of about seven feet above the ground outside, a ledge about three feet wide on the inside being raised some three feet all round the interior of the walls, thus enabling those on the inside to fire over the low parapet. The guns were mounted on ordinary ship carriages and were unprovided with tackles, being placed upon wooden platforms slightly sloping forward, so that when loaded they could be easily run out by hand, the recoil of the discharge sending them back up the slight slope into loading position. The three angles of the battery were, as has already been intimated, occupied by the magazines.

The natives advanced boldly to the attack, and for the moment I must confess that I felt almost dismayed as I looked around me and got a clear idea of their overwhelming numbers. However, there was no escape—we were completely hemmed in on every side; and if we were to die I thought we might as well die fighting; so, waiting until they were within a few yards only of the walls, I gave the order to fire, and the report of the six nine-pounders rang sharply out upon the evening air. Each man then seized his loaded musket, saw that his naked cutlass was ready to his hand, and waited breathlessly for the inevitable rush.

The round-shot ploughed six well-defined lanes through the approaching phalanx; but our persevering foes had apparently become accustomed to the effects of artillery fire by this time, seeming to regard it as a disagreeable concomitant to the struggle which *must* be faced, but which, after all, was not so very formidable. They had already acquired the knowledge that the guns, once fired, were perfectly harmless until they could be re-loaded, and that the operation of reloading required a certain amount of time. The moment, therefore, that they received our fire they charged down upon the battery, evidently feeling that the worst was over and that it now amounted to no more than an ordinary hand-to-hand fight. "Here they come, lads, with a vengeance!" I exclaimed. "Take your muskets and *aim low*—make every bullet do double or treble duty if you can. Keep cool, and be careful not to throw a single shot away."

This was excellent advice to give, especially as the giver thereof needed it perhaps more than any of those around him; but it was spoken with a calm and steady voice, and the lads responded to it with a hearty and inspiring cheer. They levelled their muskets carefully and steadily over the top of the sod parapet, selecting a particular mark and firing only when they felt sure of their aim, though at the moment a perfect cloud of spears came flying into the battery. The next instant our foes were upon us, and then commenced a furious, breathless, desperate hand-to-hand fight which lasted fully ten minutes—the blacks leaping upward or assisting each other in their efforts to surmount the parapet, and we cutting and slashing right and left without a moment's breathing-space in an equally determined effort to keep them out.

During the very thick of the fight light thin jets of smoke were seen to issue from the joints and crevices in the wooden walls of the huge barrack-like structure to windward of us, the jets rapidly growing in numbers and volume and being speedily succeeded by thin arrowy tongues of flame which shot into view for a moment, disappeared, and then appeared again, darting along the surface of the wood and uniting with others, until the entire building became completely enveloped in the flames, which no doubt the Spaniards had kindled on their retreat, in order to make assurance doubly sure, as it were, and in the event of their little scheme for the destruction of the battery miscarrying, to deprive us of what would have afforded us an excellent retreat in which to have withstood a siege.

The smoke, thick, pungent, and suffocating, from the tar and pitch with which the roof and sides of the building had been from time to time liberally coated, drifted down directly upon us in such dense volumes that it was difficult to see an arm's-length ahead, making the act of breathing next to an impossibility, and causing our eyes to stream with water, whilst the heat soon became almost insupportable. Our enemies, however, did not seem to be in the slightest degree incommoded either by the heat or the smoke, but, perceiving how greatly it embarrassed us, pressed forward more eagerly than ever to the attack. We, however, were fighting for our lives, and it is astonishing how much men can do under such circumstances. We actually succeeded in keeping the foe outside our three walls, and finally, after a prolonged effort which inspired us with a most profound sense of their individual intrepidity, they retired, carrying off their dead and wounded with them. They made a most daring attempt to carry off the cutter also with them in their retreat, but fortunately she was secured by a chain attached to the anchor, the latter being firmly embedded in the soil among the long grass; and the idea of pulling it up not seeming to present itself to any of them, they were compelled to abandon the attempt, owing to the galling musketry fire which we maintained upon them.

Exhausted, breathless, with our lips black with powder from the bitten ends of the cartridges, our skins begrimed with smoke, and with the perspiration streaming down our bodies, we now had a moment's breathing-space to look about us. The ground inside the battery literally *bristled* with the spears which had been launched at us, but, marvellous to relate, only three of our number had been hurt in the recent scuffle, and that but very slightly. The injuries, such as they were, were promptly attended to, I at the same time doing what I could for poor old Mildmay; the guns and muskets were re-loaded, and then, placing a look-out at each angle of the battery, we sank down upon the ground and snatched such a hasty meal as was possible under the circumstances.

I embraced the opportunity afforded by this interval of tranquillity to point out to my small command the necessity for placing them upon a short allowance of food. I reminded them that, at the conclusion of the meal which we were then discussing, only one clear day's rations would remain to us, and that, though the French boat had doubtless made good her escape down the river—and, in that case, would probably reach the creek early enough that same evening to make Captain Vernon acquainted with our critical situation—we could scarcely reckon upon the appearance of a relief expedition under twenty-four hours from the time of speaking. I added that, further, it would be only wise to allow another twenty-four hours for possible unforeseen delays, rendering it not improbable that we should have to pass forty-eight hours in our present position, and that I had therefore decided, for these prudential reasons, that it would be necessary to place the party for that period on half rations. The men accepted this decision of mine with the utmost readiness, and, in fact, seemed agreeably surprised to find that I considered it likely we should be rescued in so short a time.

By the time that we had concluded our hasty meal the barrack—which after all, and notwithstanding its size, was a mere wooden shell of a place—had become a shapeless heap of smouldering ruins, and we were consequently to a great extent relieved of the annoyance from the heat and smoke. Now that the place was actually destroyed I was glad rather than otherwise, for standing as it did so close to the battery, it would, had it remained in existence, have afforded splendid "cover" for the enemy, behind which they would have been enabled to steal close up to us unobserved, necessitating a most unremitting watch, in spite of which a sudden unexpected rush might have put them in possession of the battery. Now, however, nothing in the nature of a surprise could well occur, for by the destruction of the barrack we were enabled to obtain an uninterrupted view from the battery all over the diminutive islet upon which it stood.

Half an hour after the conclusion of our meal the wind dropped away to a flat calm, the sun went down behind the low range of hills which stretched away to the westward of us, the landscape assumed a tint of rapidly deepening, all-pervading grey, the mist-wreaths rose from the bosom of the whirling river and stealthily gathered about the island like a beleaguering army of phantoms, and the solemn hush of night was broken only by the loud *chirr* of the insects and the lapping ripple of the rushing stream.

Thicker and thicker gathered the mist about us until at last it became impossible to see across from one side of the battery to the other, and then ensued an anxious time indeed for all of us, and especially so for me, upon whom rested the responsibility of directing what steps should be taken for the safety and preservation of the little force under me. Would the natives attempt another attack that night under cover of the fog? I thought it highly probable that they would, seeing how important an advantage it would be to them to have the power of arranging their forces and creeping up to the very walls of the battery undetected. The idea indeed occurred to me, that under cover of that same fog it might be possible for us to take once more to the cutter, and, letting her drift with the current, in that way slip unobserved away down the river. But a very few minutes' consideration of that scheme sufficed to convince me of its impracticability. I felt convinced that our enemies were quite shrewd enough to anticipate and make due provision for any such attempt on our part. I felt certain, indeed, that would the fog but lift for a moment, of which, however, there was not the most remote probability, we should find ourselves completely hemmed in by a cordon of canoes lying silently and patiently in waiting for the undertaking of some such attempt on our part. And, doubtless, all their arrangements were so framed that, in the event of our making any such attempt, a simple signal would announce our whereabouts and enable the entire flotilla to close in at once upon us; in which case our fate must be certain and speedy. No, I decided, the risk was altogether too great and the prospects of success too infinitesimal to justify any such attempt.

Then as to the expected attack. They would probably wait an hour or two, in the hope of tempting us to venture afloat; then, failing that, they would cautiously close in upon the island, land, steal up as close as possible to the battery, and then endeavour to overpower us with a sudden rush.

Fortunately it was not absolutely dark, notwithstanding the fog, there being a moon in her first quarter, which, though invisible, imparted a certain luminous quality to the haze; and two or three stars of the first magnitude were faintly visible in the zenith, so that if any fighting had to be done we should at least have light enough to distinguish between friend and foe.

This anticipation of an attempted surprise of course necessitated the maintenance of a keen and incessant look-out I accordingly posted half my small command round the walls, with instructions to fire unhesitatingly at any moving object which might come within their range of vision. But I did not expect an *immediate* attack; indeed, the more I weighed the chances of such a thing the less did they appear to be, and in the meantime we were in urgent need of water, our stock being almost exhausted. Hitherto we had refrained from drinking the river water, it having a peculiar sweetish taste which scarcely suited our palates, but very soon it would be "river water or nothing," and I thought that probably this pause of expectation, as it were, would afford us as good an opportunity as we were likely to have for refilling our breakers.

I therefore directed the party who were not engaged upon sentry duty to make ready for a trip to the river with two of the empty breakers. But before engaging so large a portion of my little force in an expedition which, though of the briefest, might expose them to great, because unexpected, dangers, I resolved to reconnoitre the ground in person, and with this object in view slipped noiselessly over the parapet to the ground outside, and throwing myself at full length upon the grass, already wet with the heavy dew, commenced a slow and disagreeable journey to the water side. I intended at first to take a look at the cutter *en passant*, but a moment's thought decided me against this course, it being just possible that I might find a few savages either already established in possession or keeping a stealthy watch upon the boat in readiness to pounce upon any incautious white man who might venture to approach her. I accordingly set out in a direction about at right angles to that which would have led me down to the boat, and though this entailed a considerably longer journey I regarded it as also a very much safer one.

After a somewhat long and tedious journey—long, that is to say, in point of time, though the distance traversed was very short—I reached the water's edge without adventure, and without having seen the slightest sign indicating the presence of savages upon the island. I therefore hastened back to the battery—narrowly escaping being shot by one of our people, who, in his excessive alertness, fired upon me without first giving the challenge—and hastily gathering together the watering-party led them to the brink of the river and succeeded in securing a couple of breakers of water, which I considered would be sufficient to last us for the next twenty-four hours.

Then ensued a long period of tense, incessant, and painful watching for the enemy, who, I anticipated, might make their appearance at any moment. But hour after hour dragged laggingly away, the whole force kept incessantly on the *qui vive* to guard against the expected attempt at surprise, the men, wearied out by their excessive exertions of the previous day, needing a continuous, uninterrupted round of visits from me to prevent their falling asleep upon their arms.

And thus the long night at length wore itself away; a faint glimmer of dawn appeared in the eastern sky, rapidly brightening, the fog assumed a rosy flush, and presently up rose the glorious sun, gleaming like a white-hot ball through the haze, a faint breeze from the westward sprang up, the mist rolled away like a curtain, and there lay the noble river around us, sparkling like a sheet of molten silver under the morning sunbeams. And there, too, lay the flotilla of canoes, completely hemming us in on every side, thus fully justifying the caution which had prevented my attempting to effect an escape down the river during the preceding night.

It was exasperating now to the last degree to know that our night's rest had been thrown away for nothing, and that, for all the benefit our vigilance had been to us, all hands might just as well have lain down and gone to sleep all night; but repining was of no use; we had naturally expected an attack and had held ourselves in readiness to meet it, and the only thing that remained was to snatch what rest we could during the day. It was a great advantage to be able to once more *see* our enemies; and as there seemed to be no immediate disposition on their part to make a move, I gave orders for breakfast to be got under weigh as speedily as possible, stationing a look-out at each angle of the battery during the discussion of the meal. We had scarcely settled ourselves when the alarm was given that the canoes were advancing, and, leaping to our feet, we found that such was indeed the case, the whole fleet having tripped their anchors and begun paddling in toward the island.

We at once opened fire upon them from the nine-pounders as a matter of course, but the rascals had not only learned wisdom but had also evidently very sharp eyes, for at the moment when the match was about to be applied to the guns the canoes immediately in the line of fire smartly swerved from their course and the shot went hissing harmlessly past, missing their mark by the merest hair's-breadth.

Before we had time to load again the savages had effected a landing upon the beach, and then ensued a repetition of the previous day's fighting, excepting that our antagonists fought with their energies renewed by a quiet night's rest and more obstinately than ever, whilst we were weary and fagged by our long and fruitless watch. During the desperate struggle which consumed the next quarter of an hour half a dozen natives managed at different times to actually force their way into the battery, but luckily for us they got in only one at a time and they were promptly despatched.

At last they were beaten off and compelled to retire to their canoes as before, carrying away with them their killed and wounded—of whom I counted no less than thirty being borne away by their comrades—our lads "freshening their way" for them with a hot musketry fire so long as they remained within range.

Then followed another brief interval during which we finished our scanty breakfast, after which, having seen the guns and muskets loaded afresh, I undertook to maintain a look-out, and ordered the men to lie down and snatch such rest as they could get.

But our foes, wily as savages always are, had evidently in their recent hand-to-hand struggle with us detected the evidences of our extreme fatigue, and were by no means disposed to allow us much time or opportunity to recuperate our exhausted energies, for the men had scarcely flung themselves upon the ground, where sleep instantly seized upon them, when the canoes were once more put in motion and again the unhappy blue-jackets were called upon to resist an attack. I now began to feel a strong suspicion that the enemy had quite counted upon our being kept upon the alert during the whole of the previous night, the perfect silence which they had maintained being, as they very probably surmised, rather a harassing than a reassuring circumstance to us, and that they fully intended to take the fullest possible advantage of this during the ensuing day. But their heavy losses in killed and wounded had at the same time made them increasingly wary, and for the next hour or two they contented themselves with a continuous series of demonstrations which drew our fire and kept us incessantly on the alert, without actually renewing their attack.

At length the wind dropped away to a flat calm and the rays of the unclouded sun beat remorselessly down upon us with a fierce intensity which in our exhausted condition was positive agony. A burning unquenchable thirst took possession of us, and the men resorted to the water-kegs so incessantly that the water diminished with startling rapidity, and foreseeing the possible difficulty of obtaining a further supply I was at last reluctantly compelled to put them upon an allowance, so that very speedily we had thirst added to our other miseries. And during all this time our aching eyes were every moment directed down the river in the hope, which grew less and less as the day wore on, of detecting the approach of the boats which we felt certain were on their way to effect our rescue.

CHAPTER TWENTY

RESCUED

Finally the long, harassing, anxious day drew to a close, the sun set, the night-mists gathered once more about us, and the hoped-for rescue had not appeared.

We were by this time completely worn out, and I foresaw that unless the men could obtain a little rest our pertinacious enemies must inevitably prove victorious.

Of course in this matter of rest everything depended upon the behaviour of the foe. If from principle or superstition, or for any other reason, it was their invariable habit to abstain from fighting at night all might yet be well with us, for though our stock of provisions and water was getting low, and the ammunition for our muskets was getting short, I felt convinced that, could our lads but secure three or tour hours of unbroken rest, they were quite equal to holding the battery for another twenty-four hours at least. Unfortunately I knew nothing whatever about the fighting customs of the natives, and was consequently quite without a guide of any kind beyond my own reason. I felt convinced that the blacks had fully realised the advantage to them of our fagged condition during the past day, and had little doubt but that they were acute enough to trace it to its correct source; the question

Harry Collingwood

then was, would they allow us to pass an undisturbed night and thus sacrifice an important advantage? I greatly doubted it. But they might allow a few hours' cessation of hostilities in the hope of lulling us into a feeling of false security, and thus making us the victims of an easy, yet well-executed surprise. The more I thought about the matter the more probable did this course of action appear; and at last I resolved to put it to the test by dividing the men into watches and allowing them an hour's sleep at a time.

But before doing this I thought I would repeat my experiment of the previous night and endeavour to secure a little more water, and this I did with such signal success that we actually refilled all our breakers, besides giving every man an opportunity to completely slake his thirst.

It was just eight o'clock p.m. by the time that we had completed our preparations, and I then made half the men lie down, which they did, falling instantly asleep. This of course necessitated increased vigilance on the part of the watchers, each of whom had to guard a double length of parapet; but the first hour passed peacefully away, and the sleepers were awakened in order that we might have our turn. It was really amusing, notwithstanding the gravity of our situation, to hear each man protest as he sat up and rubbed his eyes that we had not treated them fairly, and that they had only that moment fallen asleep. But when assured to the contrary they roused up at once, and I was greatly gratified to see that, short as had been their period of rest, it had undoubtedly done them a world of good. The "watch on deck" was placed under the command of the man Tom who had done such good service with the carronade on board the cutter, he being, in my opinion, the most trustworthy man in the party; and giving him the most stringent orders to keep a bright look-out, to fire at once and unhesitatingly on any moving object which might make its appearance, and to call me in the event of anything taking place out of the common, I flung myself upon the ground with my back to the sod parapet, and in the act of folding my arms across my chest fell asleep.

To be cruelly awakened the next instant, almost before I had had time to fully realise the blessedness of the gift of sleep.

"Well, Tom, what is it? Has the enemy hove in sight!" I exclaimed pettishly, rubbing away at my eyes to force them open.

"No, sir; everything's still quiet, thank God."

"Then what did you wake me for, in Heaven's name!"

"Four bells, sir; our turn for a spell of sleep again, sir," was the exasperating reply.

"Four bells! Nonsense!"

I could not believe it. As in the case of the others it really seemed as though I had not actually had time to get to sleep at all, yet I had slept soundly for an hour, and on staggering to my feet, though the abrupt awakening had inflicted upon me positive suffering, I found when fairly awake, that I was very distinctly the better for my short nap, which seemed to have made up, at least partially, in soundness what it lacked in duration.

Another hour passed peacefully—and this time not quite so laggingly—away; our turn again arrived for a rest; and once more did we enjoy for a brief space the bliss of perfect oblivion. At midnight we were called again, Tom reporting that neither sight nor sound had occurred during his watch to disturb him. We now began to feel really refreshed, and during the next hour some of the men in my watch actually found superfluous energy enough to hum under their breath a snatch or two of a forecastle song as they paced vigilantly to and fro over the short stretch of ground which constituted their "beat."

As the silent hour flitted away without disquieting sight or sound of any kind I began to feel sanguine that we were going to be blessed with uninterrupted peace for the remainder of the night, and inwardly resolved that if matters still continued satisfactory after my watch had had its next hour's sleep I would extend the period of sleep to two hours for the next watch, which, with what they had already had, ought to put them in excellent trim for the fatigues of the succeeding day, whatever they might be. And with this resolve still uppermost in my mind I laid down and once more dropped to sleep when my turn came at one o'clock a.m.

Two o'clock arrived, our watch was called, and still there had been no sign of the enemy. I thought we might now safely reckon upon being allowed to pass the remainder of the night undisturbed; I accordingly informed the retiring watch that unless we happened to be attacked in the interim they would now be allowed to sleep for a spell of two hours instead of one, and they forthwith composed themselves for a good long nap.

But it was not to be. An hour later one of the men startled us all into instant wakefulness by sharply giving the challenge, which was instantly repeated all round the battery, and peering anxiously into the fog I detected the indistinct presence of several shapeless objects lying prone upon the ground where I knew that nothing of the kind ought to be. These objects were quite motionless; but the man who had first given the challenge assured me that his attention had first been attracted to them by a stealthy movement. Ordering the man to at once rouse the sleepers, cautioning them individually to take up their proper stations an noiselessly behind the parapet, I waited until every man had gained his post, and then taking a steady aim at one of the objects I discharged my musket. With a shriek of pain the object at which I had fired half raised itself to an erect position and then fell heavily forward. At the same moment a loud blood-curdling yell resounded upon the heavy night air, and the foggy background instantly became alive with the forms of the savages who sprang to their feet and came bounding toward the battery, hurling their spears as they came.

"Take steady aim, my men; select your mark, and each bring down your man if possible; keep cool now. Ah! I am hit!" I exclaimed, as a spear came whizzing in over the parapet, passing clean through the fleshy part of my right thigh. In the excitement of the moment it did not take me a second to relieve myself of my unpleasant encumbrance by drawing the spear shaft right through the wound; and the next moment I found myself engaged with the rest in resisting the hottest and most determined assault to which we had hitherto been subjected. Luckily for us the battery was only a small affair, and our party was therefore large enough to take pretty good care of it, otherwise that night attack would have ended the business. But our men had now had the benefit and refreshment of three hours' sound sleep, and they fought with such renewed energy, such dogged determination, that the assault again failed, and the savages were once more driven off. That satisfied them for the time being. They had deferred their attack until the early hours of the morning, doubtless hoping to find us worn out with ceaseless watching, and perchance at length overcome with sleep; and instead of that we had been found more alert than ever; in their anxiety to take us unawares they had rather overdone it, in fact, and the result was that they left us undisturbed for the short remainder of the night.

There was, however, no more rest for us; after this well-planned attempt at a surprise I dare not allow any of my small party to again go off duty, and sunrise found us still anxiously watching for another attack. When the mist at length cleared away we discovered the hostile canoes still closely hemming us in; but they now seemed to have tired of their fruitless efforts to take the battery by assault, and had apparently made up their minds to try the effect of a regular siege. This was bad enough; for our provisions, though husbanded with the utmost care, were only sufficient to allow us a mere mouthful each for two meals during that day; but to be spared the fatigue of constantly fighting was something to be grateful for; and I felt certain that the relief expedition *must* appear before the lapse of many hours longer. We consequently sat down to our scanty morning meal not only with excellent appetites but also in very fair spirits, considering what we had lately been called upon to endure; and, the meal over, I next devoted my attention to the wounded, of whom there were by this time several, and did what I could to make them and myself as comfortable as possible.

About an hour after sunrise a little air from the eastward sprang up, and by nine a.m. it was blowing quite a free breeze, which, though it certainly refreshed us greatly, and was in pleasing contrast to the suffocating heat of the day before, I was rather sorry to see; for I knew that, combined with the current, it would seriously retard the advance of our friends up the river. To tell the truth, I was getting to be a trifle anxious about this matter; I could not at all understand why it was that we had been left to take care of ourselves so long. If the French boat had reached the creek in safety she would doubtless arrive about ten or eleven p.m., or a few hours only after our establishment of ourselves upon the island. Forty hours or thereabouts had elapsed since then, yet there was no sign of help. Could it be possible that the

Frenchmen had *not* escaped after all? In that case we might have to wait another day, or even a couple of days; for I thought it scarcely probable that Captain Vernon would take alarm on the instant of our becoming overdue. I was anxiously weighing all these surmises in my mind, and endeavouring to arrive at a fair and reasonable estimate of the longest possible time we might still be expected to hold out, when the look-out men raised a simultaneous cheer, followed by a joyous shout of—

"The boats! The boats! Here they come. *Hurrah*!" With one bound I reached the parapet; and, sure enough, at a distance of only three-quarters of a mile away, and just sweeping fairly into view from behind the next island below us, the launch, pinnace, and second cutter of the *Daphne* appeared, with their ensigns streaming in the breeze and the quick-flashing oar-blades and the bayonets of the "jollies" gleaming brightly in the sun.

"Up, lads! and give them a cheer, just to let them know where we are," I exclaimed exultantly; and at the word up scrambled the whole of our little party except poor old Mildmay, who was too seriously hurt to move without assistance—and from the top of the parapet we sent echoing down to them upon the wings of the breeze three such ringing cheers as must have assured them of the sincerity of our delight at their appearance. As the sound reached the boats I saw the officers rise in the stern-sheets and wave their caps to us in response; the oar-blades flashed quicker in the sun; the foam gathered in increasing volume under the bows of the boats as their crews put on an extra spurt; and presently a flash and a puff of fleecy smoke started out simultaneously from each boat, and the *boom* of the three reports came dull and heavy to us against the opposing breeze.

Of course we fully expected that the mere appearance of the

boats would suffice to put our sable enemies to flight, but nothing of the kind happened; on the contrary, the canoes resolutely faced the new-comers, and evinced a very decided disposition to dispute their passage up the river.

We should beat them to a certainty; no one in their sober senses could for a moment doubt that; but in the meantime, if it actually came to a hand-to-hand tussle between whites and blacks we in the battery, who had already had so many opportunities of observing their perfect fearlessness, knew very well that the latter could make matters decidedly difficult and unpleasant for our friends.

But it was no time just then for cogitation, the moment for decisive action had arrived, and I forthwith took the necessary steps to enable our party to do their share of the work in hand.

"That will do, lads," I exclaimed, as the men on the parapet paused to recover the breath they had expended in their vociferous greeting to the boats. "Jump down and man the guns. Load and double shot them; and you, Tom, place the remainder of those fuzes in the magazine in such a way that they will do their work effectually when required. We will give the canoes another broadside, just to 'freshen their way' and show them that we are in earnest; and then I shall abandon and blow up the battery previous to shoving off to join our lads yonder."

The men turned to with a will; the guns were loaded; and I then went with Tom to personally inspect the arrangement of the fuzes.

When all was ready I gave the word to fire; the six guns belched forth their contents simultaneously; and without waiting to see what damage had been done, the men seized their muskets, the water-kegs, and our few other belongings; and with two hands specially detailed to convey the master carefully down to the boat, all hands, excepting Tom and myself, left the battery and made the best of their way down to the cutter, which, after depositing poor old Mildmay as comfortably as possible in the stern-sheets, they got afloat.

"Step your mast," I shouted, "and see all ready for hoisting the sail."

We waited patiently until we saw that everything was ready on board the cutter; and then Tom and I ignited the fuzes in the three magazines. It was awfully risky work, as the fuzes were fearfully short; but it had to be done, and it was done coolly and smartly, after which we bounded over the low parapet and ran for our lives down to the boat. "Shove off and give way for your lives, men," I panted, as we tumbled in over the gunwale with a considerable loss of shin-leather; and in another instant we were surging away from the island as fast as the oars and sail would drive us. The men were just belaying the halliards of the lug when—*boom*—a dull heavy report came from the battery; a great black cloud of smoke and dust, liberally intermixed with clods and stones and masses of earth, shot up into the air; and when it cleared away *the battery was gone.*

"Now, Tom, jump forward, my man, and get that carronade loaded with grape or canister or langridge, *anything* you happen to have handy, and be smart about it, my fine fellow," I exclaimed, as I saw a group of canoes separate themselves from the rest and form in line across our course, evidently for the purpose of opposing our passage and preventing our effecting a junction with our friends. "Load your muskets, men, and draw your cutlasses; we must get through that line of canoes somehow, and I mean to do it."

The men obeyed without a word; their blood was by this time thoroughly aroused; they were all a-quiver with eager excitement; and as I looked at them sitting there upon the thwarts, facing forward, with their naked cutlasses beside them and their loaded muskets firmly grasped in their hands, their fingers just feeling the triggers, their teeth clenched, and their eyes flashing, I felt that nothing short of a frigate with her crew at quarters would stop them.

The rescuing party was by this time smartly engaged with the main body of the canoes, and by their tardy progress I knew that they already had their hands fully occupied. The detachment which had assumed the responsibility of intercepting us had separated itself some distance from the main body, and was now formed in a double line right across our course, altering its position from time to time in such a manner as to keep always square ahead of us. I saw that it would be useless to attempt to dodge them; we had not time for that; so I directed the coxswain to steer straight for the broadside of the midship canoe, the craft, that is to say, which occupied the centre of the opposing line. She was a biggish craft for a canoe, being somewhere about fifty feet long, and manned by forty negroes; the canoe which lay on her starboard side, or beyond her, being about the same size. There were sixteen more canoes in the line; and altogether they presented the appearance of a very formidable barrier. But I had had an opportunity of learning pretty well what they were when Smellie and I, bound hand and foot, took our memorable cruise up the river in one of them, and I knew that they were, after all, but very crank, flimsy, fragile affairs, not to be compared for a moment in strength with the stout boat which carried us at such a gallant pace over the swirling river. So I determined to give our foolhardy opponents the stem, trusting to the weight and momentum of the boat to enable us to break through the line.

On rushed the cutter, the breeze roaring merrily over her, and the broad lag-sail dragging at her like a team of cart-horses; whilst Tom crouched in the bows, squinting along the sights of his piece, and holding himself in readiness to fire at the instant that he should get the order. We were within a hundred feet of the line of canoes when the crew of the big craft began to see danger; they had hoped, by their persistent demonstration of barring our path, to intimidate us, but, now that it was too late, they saw that they had failed, that we meant mischief; and, setting up a loud yell of consternation, they plied their paddles desperately in an effort to avoid the impending collision. It was unavailing; the canoes ahead and astern of them, confused like themselves, and only imperfectly comprehending what their comrade would be at, closed in upon instead of separating from them; and immediate dire confusion was the result. When within twenty yards of them Tom delivered the contents of his carronade; and an immediate outburst of groans, yells, and shrieks bore testimony to the accuracy of his aim. Before the smoke had fairly cleared away the cutter was upon them. The big canoe nearest us had been torn nearly in halves by the discharge of the carronade, and we swept over her almost without feeling it. The other big fellow was, however, afloat and apparently uninjured. Another yell of terror went up from her occupants as our sail overshadowed them; there was a violent shock as our strong iron-bound stem crashed down upon their gunwale; the canoe heeled over; and the cutter leaped upward as she crushed her way through and over this second adversary.

For a few seconds we were involved in a confused medley of canoes and wreckage, of drowning savages wildly clutching at the gunwales of the boat in an ineffectual effort to save themselves; there was a rattling volley of musketry, a flash or two of cutlass blades, and then away sped the cutter once more. *We were through.*

Our carronade was quickly loaded again, but happily further destruction of human life was unnecessary. The savages, who seemed to have depended implicitly upon the power of their detached squadron to stop us, became demoralised when they saw the cutter dash irresistibly through the opposing line, and receiving at the same time very severe treatment at the hands of the rescuing party, they broke up suddenly and beat a precipitate retreat, each canoe seemingly striving to outdo the rest in the speed of its flight. And thus ended victoriously for us the fight which we had been for over forty hours maintaining against such apparently overwhelming odds.

We soon found ourselves alongside the launch; and hearty were the congratulations and eager the questions which were showered upon us by her crew, quickly repeated by those of the other two boats, which joined in almost immediately afterwards.

"You seem to have been in rather a bad fix," exclaimed Armitage, who was in command of the boats, as he shook me heartily by the hand. "Tell us all about it."

I detailed as succinctly as possible all that had transpired since our departure from the ship, and wound up by a suggestion that if they had any spare rations they would be most acceptable.

"Rations!" exclaimed Armitage; "to be sure we have, my boy; but let us adjourn to this island of yours, where we can get them properly cooked. I feel curious to see the spot which you held so pluckily for so long a time. But, by the by, where is the French boat all this time?"

"The French boat? Has she not turned up at the creek?" I exclaimed in surprise. "We felt certain of her escape, and indeed depended upon the information she would convey of our predicament for the despatch of assistance."

"She had not put in an appearance up to the time of our starting at noon yesterday, nor have we seen any sign of her during our passage up the stream," was the reply. "You were due to return, you know, the evening before last, and when yesterday morning came, without your appearance, Captain Vernon became uneasy. He allowed you until noon, however; but when noon passed, leaving you still *non est*, he came to the conclusion that something was amiss, and despatched us in quest of you at once. So this is the scene of the struggle, eh?" as the boats grounded on the beach of the island. "A pretty scene of ruin it is."

And so it was. The battery had been completely obliterated by the explosion, nothing remaining to mark its site but the scattered fragments of the sod walls and the dismounted guns; the charred remains of the barrack, a short distance away, aiding to complete the picture of destruction. An immense number of native spears were lying scattered about all over the ground, and these were promptly collected by the seamen as souvenirs of the struggle.

CHAPTER TWENTY ONE

AN AWFUL CATASTROPHE

Meanwhile the Spaniards were still lying *perdu* on board the hulk as they had remained from the moment of our driving them out the battery. During the discussion of our much-needed meal the question of what steps we should take with regard to them had been canvassed; and, our appetites at length satisfied, Armitage and I walked across the island to make a closer inspection of the position of the craft.

I had wondered greatly, at odd times during our protracted struggle with the savages, how the Spaniards had managed to transfer so rapidly from the barrack to the hulk the large number of slaves which the former must have contained, and now the riddle was solved. On arriving abreast of the hulk we found that a small timber jetty had been constructed from the shore to a point within fifty yards of the hulk, and we could see in a moment that by easing off the moorings of the hulk, the current would carry her fairly alongside this jetty, where, without doubt, she must have been lying when we first hove in sight. The slaves had evidently been marched straight on board her over the jetty, and her bow and stern moorings then hove in until she had been hauled far enough away from the jetty to render her capture by its means impossible.

After a little further conversation with Armitage it was agreed that the Spaniards should be hailed and ordered to surrender, and this was accordingly done. We had no very great hope of success, as we felt sure the Spaniards must be fully aware of the difficulty we should experience in capturing the hulk. As before stated, she towered so high out of the water and her sides were so bare that the Spaniards, small as was their number, could effectually resist all our efforts to capture her by boarding; to fire into and sink her would only result in the destruction of all the slaves on board her; and as she was moored with heavy chains, instead of hemp hawsers, to cut her adrift and let her ground upon the island was quite as impracticable as would have been any attempt to board her.

We were therefore very agreeably surprised when the Spaniards, in response to our hail, at once consented to abandon the hulk, provided we would allow them to depart unmolested in their boat. This arrangement suited us very well, we being just then anything but anxious to hamper ourselves with prisoners, and the required promise was unhesitatingly made. The Spaniards thereupon provisioned their boat, lowered her into the water, and half an hour later disappeared round a bend of the river on their way down stream. Taking immediate possession of the hulk, we dropped her in alongside the jetty once more, and landed the slaves upon the island. They were all, for a wonder, in fairly good condition, having evidently been well taken care of, with the view of fitting them as thoroughly as possible to withstand the terrible hardships of the notorious Middle Passage.

Having at length cleared the hulk we next transferred the slaves in batches to the boats, by which they were conveyed across the stream to the mainland, where they were freed and left to shift for themselves, the provisions found on board the hulk being distributed as evenly as possible among them.

Landed thus in a possibly hostile country—for they were evidently a different race of people from those with whom we had recently had so desperate a struggle—unarmed, and with only a small supply of provisions, their situation was perhaps not very much better than it had been when they lay prisoners on board the hulk, but it was all we had it in our power to do for them under the circumstances, and we could only hope that their wit would prove equal to the task of steering them clear of the many dangers to which they were exposed, and conducting them safely back to their own country. There were rather more than eight hundred of them altogether, counting in the piccaninnies, and the transfer of them to the mainland fully occupied us until within half an hour of sunset. As we were by that time pretty well fagged out, and as it was manifestly too late to make any progress worth speaking of on our way back to the creek that night, we resolved to remain until daylight upon the island, which we did without receiving molestation or annoyance of any kind from anybody.

At eight o'clock on the following morning, having previously breakfasted, we started down the river, keeping a bright look-out for the French boat all the way down, and exploring all the most likely creeks and indentations on the south bank of the river, without discovering any trace of her. This protracted search so seriously delayed our progress that we were two whole days making the passage back to the creek, and on our arrival there we discovered that three survivors of the French party had turned up on board the *Vestale* the previous day, reporting the capture of the boat by the natives, and the massacre of all hands except the three who had managed somehow to slip their bonds and make good their escape in a canoe. They had reported that their capture was due to our *abandonment* of them, it appeared, and the insinuation, which Captain Vernon had indignantly repudiated, had occasioned a very serious outbreak of ill-feeling between the two ships, so much so indeed that the commander of the *Vestale* had left the river in high dudgeon on the morning of the day of our arrival, refusing absolutely to co-operate with us any further. I was, of course, subjected to a very severe cross-examination by Captain Vernon on the subject; but my detailed narrative of the affair, which was confirmed in every particular by poor old Mildmay, soon satisfied him that the fault, if fault there was, rested not with us; and both Mildmay and myself were fully exonerated from all blame. Nay more—the master generously represented my defence of the battery in such a light that I received the skipper's highest commendations and renewed promises of support and assistance in my career.

At sunrise next morning we weighed and stood out to sea, bound on a cruise to the westward.

The next two months passed away in the most drearily uneventful manner, the ship being at sea the whole time. At the end of that period, being in latitude 4 degrees south and longitude 5 degrees east on our way back to the Congo, the ship standing to the northward and eastward at the time, under all plain sail, with light baffling south-easterly airs, the look-out aloft, just before being relieved at noon, reported two sail, close together, hove-to broad on our lee bow. The usual form of questions being duly put by Armitage, who happened to be the officer of the watch, the further information was elicited that one of them was a brig and the other a full-rigged ship, but of what nationality they were it was difficult to say, nothing but the heads of their topgallant-sails being visible above the horizon from our fore-topmast crosstrees. The matter being reported to Captain Vernon, orders were given for our course to be so altered as to allow of our edging down upon the strangers; the fact of their being hove-to so close together having a somewhat suspicious appearance.

By three o'clock p.m. we had neared the two vessels sufficiently to bring their hulls into view from the main-royal-yard; they were then lying broadside-on to us with their heads to the eastward, the ship being between us and the brig; but by the aid of our glasses we were able to make out that they had apparently dropped alongside each other, and the skipper gave it as his decided opinion that foul play was going on on the part of one or the other of the two craft. This opinion was shortly afterwards confirmed by the appearance of thick clouds of black smoke arising from the ship; the brig hauling off and standing to the westward under every stitch of canvas she could spread.

"Undoubtedly a most daring act of piracy, committed under our *very* noses, too," commented the skipper to me as the smoke rose up into the clear atmosphere and hung like a great pall immediately over the doomed ship. We were walking together fore and aft upon the quarter-deck at the time, whistling most earnestly and devoutly for a wind, as indeed were all hands fore and aft. Suddenly Captain Vernon paused, and, wetting the back of his hand, held it up to the air.

"The wind is failing us," he remarked, and abruptly dived below to his cabin.

At the same moment I noticed that the corvette was heading three or four points to the eastward of her course.

"Hard up with your helm, man," I exclaimed impatiently to the man at the wheel. "Where are you taking the ship?"

"The wheel *is* hard over, sir," explained the poor fellow with patient deference; "but she's lost steerage-way."

Just then the skipper returned to the deck.

"Pipe away the first and second cutters, Mr Hawkesley," he exclaimed sharply. "Take charge of them yourself with one of the midshipmen to help you, and pull down to the burning ship. As likely as not you will find that a similar trick has been played there to the one by which that unfortunate man Richards and his crew so nearly lost their lives. Let the crews of the boats take their cutlasses and pistols with them, so as to be prepared in the event of interference from the brig's crew, and make all the haste you can. Your first duty is to save the crew; your next to save the ship if possible. The glass is rising, so there will be no wind; but I shall do what I can to shorten the distance between us and the brig yonder. When you have done all that is possible on board the ship, make a dash for the brig, unless you see the recall signal flying."

Three minutes later the two cutters were darting swiftly away over the long glassy undulations of the ground-swell toward the great cloud of smoke on the horizon which served as a beacon for us; the men pulling a long steady stroke, which, whilst it sent the boats through the water at a very fair pace, could be maintained for three or four hours at least.

We were scarcely a mile away from the *Daphne* when she had the rest of her boats in the water and ahead of her towing, whilst, dangling from the yard-arms aloft, could be seen hammocks and bags of shot suspended there to assist— by the swinging motion imparted to them by the rise and fall of the vessel over the swell—the ship's progress through the water. The brig was hull-down to us; but from the steadiness with which her head was kept pointing to the westward I conjectured that she was either sweeping or being towed by her boats.

The sun set in a perfectly clear and cloudless sky, just as we had brought the ship hull-up; but by that time she was a mass of flame fore and aft, and I began to fear that we should be too late to save her crew or to do any good whatever on board her. We kept steadily on, however, and reached her half an hour later.

The three masts went over the side when we were within a cable's length of the burning ship, and on arriving within fifty feet of her we found it impossible to approach any nearer, owing to the intense heat. It was manifestly impossible that any living thing could be in the midst of that fiercely flaming furnace, so we were compelled to content ourselves with merely ascertaining the name of the unfortunate craft, which with considerable difficulty we at length made out to be the *Highland Chieftain* of Glasgow—after which we left her.

On pulling out clear of the smoke and glare of the flames once more we found ourselves to be about six miles distant from the brig, a distance of about eleven miles intervening between us and the *Daphne*. Night had by this time closed completely down upon us; the deep clear violet sky above us was thickly powdered with stars, which were waveringly reflected in the deep indigo of the water beneath, and away to the eastward the broad disc of the full moon was just rising clear of the horizon and casting a long rippling wake of golden light from the ocean's rim clear down to us.

Our first glance was of course in the direction of the *Daphne*. Her towering spread of canvas alternately appeared and vanished as the enormous idly flapping sails caught and lost again, with the heave of the vessel, the glint of the golden moon-beams; but, save this, all was dark and still on board her; no lanterns flashed in her rigging as a recall signal, so I exultingly gave the order for the boats to be headed straight for the brig, determined to win her if dash and courage could do it.

"Pull steadily, lads," I cautioned, as the two crews bent their backs, and with a ringing cheer started the boats in racing style; "no racing now, we cannot afford the strength for it, all you have will be wanted when we get alongside the chase; she is doubtless well manned with a determined crew who will not give in without a tough struggle, so husband your strength as much as possible. Mr Peters," to the midshipman in charge of the second cutter, "drop in my wake, sir, if you please, and see that your men do not overtask themselves."

The men obediently eased down at once, and we jogged steadily along at a pace of about four knots an hour; but their eagerness soon got the better of them, the pace gradually increased, and I had to constantly check them, or we should soon have been tearing away as fiercely as ever.

This state of things lasted for about half an hour, and then the gleam of lanterns suddenly appeared in the *Daphne's* rigging. It was the recall signal, and the men gave audible vent to their feeling of disappointment in an involuntary groan.

"Never mind, men," I said; "I have no doubt Captain Vernon has some good reason for it. Answer the signal, coxswain. Ah! I told you so; the sloop has a little breeze, and here it comes creeping up astern of us. Step the mast, take the covers off the sails, and get the canvas on the boats. Do you see that bright red star close to the horizon, coxswain? Starboard a bit. So, steady, now you have it fair over the boat's stem. Steer for it, and we shall just drop alongside the loop nicely, without troubling her to wait for us."

The breeze soon reached us, toying coyly with the boat's canvas at first, but gradually bellying out the sails until at last they "went to sleep." The breeze was, after all, merely the gentlest of zephyrs, only just sufficient to give a ship steerage-way; but, very fortunately for us, the boats were provided, by a whim of poor Austin's, with a suit each of enormous lateen sails made of light duck, with yards of such a length that they had to be jointed in the middle to enable them to be stowed in the boats; they were just the thing for light airs, and under their persuasive influence we were soon gliding smoothly through the scarcely ruffled water quite as fast as the men could have propelled us with the oars. An hour later we slid handsomely up alongside the sloop, which by this time was slipping along at the rate of about five knots under studding-sails and everything else that would hold a breath of wind, and the boats were hoisted in without any interruption to the ship's progress.

"Well, Mr Hawkesley, what news from the burning ship?" exclaimed the skipper as I stepped up to him to make my report.

I explained to him the state in which we had found the vessel when we reached her, and gave him her name.

"Ah!" he remarked. "Well, it is a bad job, a very bad business altogether. I can only hope we may find the crew uninjured on board the brig when we catch her; but I think it is rather doubtful. Now run away down into my cabin and tell Baines to give you some dinner. I expect everything will be cleared away in the ward-room by this."

On descending to the cabin I found that the skipper had been considerate enough to give orders that a nice little dinner should be ready for me on my return, and those orders having been carried out to the letter I was enabled to sit down in peace and enjoy the meal for which the long pull in the boats had given me a most voracious appetite. The meal over, it being then my watch below, I turned in.

On relieving Mr Armitage at midnight I found that the

weather was still fine, the wind the merest shade fresher than it had been when I left the deck, and the chase directly ahead, about twelve miles distant, her upper canvas showing distinctly in the brilliant rays of the moon. We had gained upon her about a couple of miles during the four hours I had been below, and Captain Vernon—who had been on deck during the whole of the previous watch, and was just about to retire for the night—was in high spirits, and confident in his belief that, if all went well, we should make the capture before sunset on the following day. The best helmsman in my watch was ordered to the wheel. I made a regular tour of the decks, taking an extra pull at a halliard here, easing off an inch or so of this brace or that sheet, and, in short, doing everything possible to increase the speed of the ship, and so my watch passed away; the *Daphne* having crept another couple of miles nearer to the chase during the interval.

Thus matters went on until noon of the following day, when the wind once more showed symptoms of failing, whilst the sky became overcast, threatening a change of weather. We had by this time shortened the distance between ourselves and the chase until a space of only some seven miles or so separated us, and everybody on board, fore and aft, was in a fever of impatience to get alongside the brig, which our glasses had already assured us was none other than the notorious *Black Venus*. She had already proved herself so slippery a customer that an almost superstitious feeling had sprung up in our breasts with regard to her; we felt that however closely we might succeed in approaching her, however helplessly she might seem to be in our power, there could be no dependence whatever upon appearances, and that until we had absolutely succeeded in placing a prize crew upon her decks, and her own crew in irons, we could not feel by any means certain that she was ours. Hence the extraordinary feeling of excitement and impatience which prevailed on board the *Daphne* on that memorable afternoon.

Harry Collingwood

About two o'clock the wind changed, and we were obliged to take in the studding-sail on the port side and get a pull upon the port braces. Meanwhile a heavy bank of clouds had gathered in the south-western quarter, and was gradually working up against the wind, until by three o'clock p.m. the sun was obscured and the entire heavens blotted out by the huge murky mass of seething vapour. It was my watch below, but, like everybody else, I was much too excited to remain anywhere but on deck, and, to confess the truth, I did not half like the appearance of things in general. According to my notions we were about to experience one of those sudden and violent atmospheric changes which are so frequently met with in the tropics; yet there was the ship with a whole cloud of studding-sails set on the starboard side, as well as every other rag of canvas that could be coaxed to do an ounce of work. "If," thought I, "my knowledge of weather is worth anything, all hands of us will be pretty busy before long, and we shall be lucky indeed if we do not lose some of our spars, as well as an acre or two of those flying-kites up aloft there." I even forgot myself so far as to gently insinuate such a possibility to Mr Armitage, but I was so sharply snubbed for my pains that I determined to interfere no further whilst off duty, but to keep my eyes open and be ready to lend a hand whenever and wherever required.

Captain Vernon was of course on deck, and from the anxious way in which he from time to time glanced, first at the portentous sky overhead, next at the chase, and finally at our immense spread of canvas, I felt sure that he, to some extent, shared my apprehensions.

At length, after a more than usually anxious glance round, he went to the skylight and took a peep apparently at the barometer. I was watching him, and I saw him start and take another keen look at it. Then he suddenly dived down the companion-way into the cabin to make a closer inspection of it, as I conjectured. My curiosity was aroused, and I was walking aft to take a look at the instrument through the skylight on my own account, when the canvas suddenly flapped, and the next second, without further warning of any description, a perfect tornado burst upon us.

The ship was taken flat aback, and over she went, bowing helplessly before the irresistible strength of the hurricane. I thought I heard Armitage's voice shouting an order of some kind, but if such was the case it was impossible to distinguish the words through the deafening rush of the wind, which completely swallowed up all other sounds. As I felt the deck rapidly heeling under my feet I made a desperate scrambling spring for the nearest port on the weather side; for I somehow seemed to realise instinctively that the *Daphne's* brief career was ended—that she would never again recover herself, but would "turn the turtle" altogether. The ominous words of the riggers on that day when, in the first flush of my new-born dignity, I went down to inspect the craft which was to be my future home, recurred to my mind as vividly as though they had that moment been spoken, and I felt that the prophecy lurking behind them was then in the very act of fulfilment. I was fortunate enough to reach and grasp one of the gun-tackles, and drawing myself up to windward by its aid, I passed out through the open port on to the upturned weather side of the ship, where I paused for a moment to glance behind, or rather beneath me. I shall never forget the sight which then met my gaze. The ship was lying over on her beam-ends with her lower yard-arms deeply buried in the sea. The whole of the lee side of the deck was submerged; the water was pouring in tons down the open hatchways, the lee coamings of which were already under water, and the watch below could be seen ineffectually endeavouring to make their way up on deck through these openings, the rush of water down which irresistibly drove them back again at each attempt. As for the watch on deck they were already either swimming about in the sea to leeward or clinging convulsively to the rigging, whither a few had instinctively betaken themselves when the ship first went over. But I had time only for a momentary glance; the sloop had hung stationary in this position for just the barest perceptible space of time; then with a sudden jar she began to settle once more, and I had time only to scramble breathlessly along her wet and slippery sides and on to her bilge when she rolled fairly over and floated keel upwards. And as she did so, a hideous shriek rang out from her interior and became audible even above the awful rush of the gale.

CHAPTER TWENTY TWO

AN ABDUCTION AND AN IMPORTANT CAPTURE

For a few moments I felt bewildered—stunned—by the awful suddenness of this frightful catastrophe; the piercing shrieks of despair, too, which continued to issue from the interior of the vessel, unmanned me, and I crouched there upon the upturned bottom of the fabric like one in a dream. I felt that it *was* a dream; the disaster was too complete and too unexpected to be real, and I waited there, frozen with horror, anxiously looking for the moment when I should awake and be released from the dreadful nightmare.

But the sight of some half-a-dozen men battling for their lives in the water to leeward of the hull, and vainly struggling to reach the main-topgallant-mast—which had gone at the first stroke of the hurricane, and having somehow broken adrift from the topmast-head, now lay floating, with all attached, a few yards away—brought my senses back to me, and abandoning my precarious refuge I sprang into the sea and assisted the men, one after the other, to reach the floating spars. As I looked round me, in the vain hope of discovering further survivors, a few more spars floated up to the surface—a spare topmast, a studding-sail boom or two, the fore-topgallant-mast, with royal-mast, yards, and sails attached; and finally a hen-coop with seven or eight drowned fowls in it. All these I at once took measures to secure, knowing that our only hope of ultimate escape—and a very frail and slender hope it then appeared—rested upon the possibility of our being able to construct a raft with them. In this attempt we were fortunately successful, and sunset found us established on a small but fairly substantial and well-constructed raft. We mustered seven hands all told, six seamen and myself—*seven only out of our entire crew!* And so far we were safe. But as I looked, first at the frail structure which supported us, and then at the boundless waste of angry sea by which we were environed, and upon which we were helplessly tossed to and fro, I thought in my haste that it would have been better after all if we had shared the fate of our comrades, now at rest in their ocean grave and beyond the reach of those sufferings which seemed only too surely to await us. Then better thoughts came to me. I reflected that whilst there was life there was hope, and that the Hand which had been outstretched to preserve us whilst others had been allowed to perish, was also able to save us to the uttermost, if such should be the Divine Will. And was it not our duty to submit to that Will, to endure patiently whatever might be in store for us? Assuredly it was; and I humbly bowed my head in silent thanksgiving and prayer—thanksgiving for my preservation so far, and prayer that I might be given strength and patience to endure whatever privation or sufferings might come to me in the future.

Whilst constructing the raft we had been too busy to note more than the bare fact that we were being gradually but perceptibly swept away from the capsized hull of the unfortunate *Daphne*; but when our work was at length completed and we had a moment to look around us, our first glances were directed to windward in search of the wreck She was nowhere to be seen, and we had no doubt that, whilst we had been so busily employed, the wreck had gradually settled deeper and deeper into the water until she had gone down altogether.

Most fortunately—or most providentially I ought rather to say—for us, the tornado had been as brief in its duration as it had been disastrous in its effects, otherwise we could never have hoped to survive. In little more than ten minutes from the capsizing of the sloop the strength of the hurricane was spent, and the wind dropped to a fresh working breeze. Of this circumstance the *Black Venus* promptly availed herself—her crew having undoubtedly observed the disaster—by bearing up and standing to the eastward under every inch of canvas she could spread. Our first impression on witnessing this manoeuvre was that, animated by some lingering spark of humanity in their breasts, her people were returning in quest of possible survivors; but this hope was speedily extinguished by the sight of the brig sweeping to leeward and passing us at a distance of about half a mile, with her crew busily engaged in the operation of crowding sail upon their vessel. We stood up and waved to her as she passed, and I have no doubt whatever that we *were* seen; but no notice was taken of us, and she soon swept out of sight to leeward. I hardly expected any other result, and was consequently by no means discouraged at this fresh instance of inhumanity; indeed, had they taken it into their heads to rescue us, it is probable that our lot among them would have been little if any better than it was out there on the open ocean, drifting about upon our tiny raft.

When night fell we had had sufficient time to fully realise the peril and hopelessness of our position; and I think most of us fully made up our minds that we were destined to a lingering death from starvation, unless, indeed, the end should happen to be precipitated by the springing up of another gale or some equally fell disaster.

But our gloomy anticipations were destined to be speedily

and pleasantly dissipated, for at dawn on the following morning we were agreeably surprised by the sight of a sail in the northern quarter—the craft evidently heading directly for us. The wind was blowing from the westward at the time, a five-knot breeze; the weather was clear and the sea had gone down, leaving nothing but the swell from the blow of the preceding day. We accordingly set to work and unhesitatingly cut adrift one of the smaller spars of which our raft was constructed, and, hastily securing the crazy fabric afresh, reared the spar on end, with my shirt—the only white one among us—lashed to its upper extremity as a signal.

The hour which followed was one of most agonising suspense. Would she or would she not alter her course before observing our signal? The helmsman was not steering quite as steadily as he might have done, and our hearts went into our mouths and a cry of anguish involuntarily escaped our lips every time the stranger showed a tendency to luff to windward or fall off to leeward of her course. At length, however, our apprehensions were set at rest; for just as her hull was rising above our limited horizon we saw a sudden flash from her side, followed by a puff of white smoke, and a few seconds later the sharp ringing report of a gun came wafted down to us. Then her topgallant-sails and royals fluttered a moment in the cool morning breeze as they were rapidly sheeted-home and mast-headed; and half an hour later the *Virginia*—yes, there could be no doubt about it, it was our latest prize; and there, abaft the main rigging, stood the well-known figure of Smellie himself—the *Virginia* hove-to close to windward of us, a boat was lowered, and we soon found ourselves standing safe and sound on the brig's deck, the cynosure of all eyes and the somewhat bewildered recipients of our former comrades' eager questions.

As for Smellie, with the considerate kindness which was always one of his most prominent characteristics, he first gave orders that the half-a-dozen hands rescued with me should receive every attention, and then carried me off to his own cabin and rigged me in a jury suit of his own clothes—which, by the way, were several sizes too big for me—whilst my own togs were drying; and then, giving orders for breakfast to be served in the cabin at the earliest possible moment, he sat down and listened to my story.

His distress at the loss of so many friends was keen and sincere, but it did not for a moment obscure his sound common sense. A few minutes sufficed me to give him a hasty outline of the disaster and to make him acquainted with the direction of our drift during the night; the which he had no sooner ascertained than he altered the brig's course as much as was necessary to take her over the scene of the catastrophe, at the same time sending three hands aloft to keep a sharp look-out for wreckage or any other indications that we were nearing the spot, and especially for possible survivors.

Half an hour later we passed a grating, then a spare studding-sail boom, then a couple of hen-coops close together; after which fragments of wreckage became increasingly frequent until we reached a spot where one of the *Daphne's* boats was found floating with her stern torn out of her; several hatch-covers, the mizen topgallant-mast and sail, three dead sheep, a wash-deck tub, and other relics being in company; after which the wreckage suddenly ceased. We had evidently passed over the spot where the *Daphne* had gone down. And the brig was immediately hove-to and all the boats despatched upon a search expedition—unhappily a vain one, for not a sign of another survivor could be found, nor even a dead body to which we could give decent and Christian burial.

This melancholy fact at length indubitably established,

Smellie gave the order to make sail, shaping a course for the Congo, whither we felt sure the *Black Venus* had made the best of her way.

Crowding sail upon the *Virginia* we made the passage to the river's mouth in a trifle over five days, during the last three of which the wind was light and variable with us, anchoring in Banana Creek at two p.m. on the fifth day from that on which we had been picked up. The *Virginia* having succeeded in completing her complement of officers and men at Sierra Leone, the half-dozen picked up with me had been acting as supernumeraries on board, whilst I had simply been Smellie's guest. I was very much gratified, therefore, when he invited me to go with him in the boat on a search expedition to ascertain, if possible, the whereabouts of the redoubtable *Black Venus*.

We started in the gig that same afternoon as soon as the ship was moored, Smellie being of opinion that we should find the object of our quest snugly moored within the creek below Don Manuel's house, where we had seen her on the eventful evening when we captured the *Josefa*; and this creek being situate at some distance up the river, it was necessary that we should make an early start in order to be back on board before the rising of the evening mists.

We reached the creek in due course without adventure, and began cautiously to ascend it. Mile after mile we made our way, landing at the extremity of every reach and carefully reconnoitring the succeeding one before entering it with the boat; but our search was in vain—we arrived at the head of the creek without finding a single trace of the brig, or indeed of any other vessel.

Being there, it was only natural that Smellie and I should feel a strong desire to see once more the kind host and gentle hostess who had so generously nursed and entertained us in the time of our sore need. Leaving the boat at the head of the creek, therefore, in charge of the coxswain, with instructions to the latter to fire a couple of muskets in rapid succession should our presence be required, or, in the event of that being inadvisable, to make the best of his way along the footpath and up to the house, we set out—the bright flush on Smellie's bronzed cheek, the joyous sparkle in his eyes, and the eager spring in his elastic footstep betraying plainly enough the pleasurable anticipations which occupied his mind.

Traversing the path with rapid footsteps we soon reached the palisading which inclosed the garden, passed through the gate, and found ourselves in sight of the house. There it stood just as we had last seen it, door and windows wide open, the muslin curtains at the windows waving idly in the fitful breeze, and the bamboo lounging-chairs—one of them overturned—under the verandah.

We stepped briskly out, warm work though we had found it breasting the hill, and passed up the main avenue leading to the front door—Smellie keeping his eyes intently fixed upon the said front door, doubtless in the hope of seeing Dona Antonia emerge, and of enjoying her first glance of surprise and delight. I of course had no such inducement to look straight ahead, and my glances therefore wandered carelessly here and there to the right and left, noting the exquisite shapes and colours of the flowers and fruit and the luxuriant foliage and delightful shade of the trees.

Whilst thus engaged my wandering thoughts were suddenly arrested by the appearance of several large and heavy footprints in the sandy soil of the footpath; and whilst I was still idly wondering what visitors Don Manuel could have so recently had and from whence they could possibly have come, my eye lighted upon a single drop of blood; then

Harry Collingwood

another, then quite a little line of blood-drops. They were, however, only such as would result from a trifling cut or scratch; so I said nothing about it. A little further on, up the pathway, a tall thorny shrub thrust its branches somewhat obtrusively over the border of the path; and one of the twigs—a good stout one—was broken and hung to its parent branch by a scrap of bark only. Curiosity prompted me to pause for a moment to examine the twig; and I then saw that one of the thorns was similarly broken, its point being stained with blood still scarcely dry. This solved the riddle. Someone passing hastily had evidently been caught by the thorn and rather severely scratched. A few paces further on a shred of white muslin hung from another bush; and I began to fear that Dona Antonia had been the sufferer.

Beaching the house we walked unceremoniously in, delighted at the idea of the surprise we should give our friends. Proceeding to the parlour, or usual sitting-room, we found it empty, with, to our great surprise, the table and one or two chairs capsized, a torn scarf lying on the floor, and other evidences of a struggle of some sort. The sight brought us abruptly to a stand-still on the threshold—Smellie and I looking at each other inquiringly, as though each would ask the other what could be the meaning of it all. Then with a quick stride my companion passed in before me, glanced round the room, and uttered a low exclamation of horror. I at once followed, glanced in the direction indicated by Smellie's outstretched finger, and there, behind the door, lay the body of poor Pedro, face downwards on the floor, a little pool of coagulating blood being just visible on the matting beneath his forehead.

Quickly stooping we turned him over on his back. He was quite dead, though not yet cold, the cause of death being clearly indicated by a small bullet-wound fair in the centre of his forehead.

My thoughts flew back in an instant to the night on which we last stood under that same roof, to the attempted abduction of Dona Antonia; and the conviction at once seized upon me that we were now looking upon another piece of Senor Madera's work.

The same thought evidently struck Smellie, for he turned to me and exclaimed breathlessly:

"Dona Antonia!—where can she be?"

And without waiting for an answer he dashed into the passage and began calling loudly:

"Antonia! Antonia mia! where are you, darling! It is I— Harold."

Then, receiving no answer, he shouted alternately for Don Manuel and old Madre Dolores.

This time he was more successful, for as he paused for breath we heard a voice far down the garden-path replying in Spanish, "Hola! Hola! Who calls for me so loudly?"

And looking in that direction we saw Don Manuel sauntering up the path with his gun thrown carelessly over his shoulder and a well-filled bag of "specimens" by his side.

We hastened out to meet him, and received a right joyous and hearty greeting, to which we hastily responded; and then poor Smellie in his anxiety blurted out:

"And where is Dona Antonia?"

"Is she not in the house?" asked Don Manuel.

"I cannot find her anywhere," replied Smellie, "and I greatly fear—" then his natural caution returned to him and he checked himself. "By the way," he continued, "have you seen anything of your friend Senor Madera lately."

"No," answered Don Manuel, "he has never had the assurance to appear here since the night on which he made his audacious attempt to abduct my daughter; but I noticed just now that his ship is in the creek below there, so I hastened home, deeming it only prudent to be on the spot whilst he favours us with his unwelcome proximity."

"His ship in the creek!" exclaimed Smellie incredulously. "Then she must have arrived within the last half-hour, for it is barely that since we passed from the mouth to the head of the creek, and no ship was in it then."

A little cross-questioning, however, elicited the fact that there were *two* creeks near Don Manuel's house; we had explored the western creek, and it was the other which at that moment sheltered Senor Madera's ship.

Smellie then, with infinite tact and patience, gradually broke to the poor old gentleman the news of the tragedy which had been enacted in the house during its owner's brief absence, together with our fears as to the fate which had befallen Dona Antonia.

The poor old fellow was at first most frightfully agitated, as of course might reasonably have been expected; indeed in the first paroxysm of his grief and rage I almost feared he would lose his senses altogether. But Smellie's gentle firmness and sound reasoning soon brought him to a calmer frame of mind, and then we instituted a thorough but fruitless search of the house.

I then thought it time to mention the various little signs I had observed on the garden-path; and we forthwith directed our steps to the several spots, carefully examining the ground foot by foot, with the result that we were soon enabled to arrive at something like a definite conclusion. Our examination showed that at least half a dozen men had visited the house probably not more than half an hour before our arrival; that there had been a struggle, in which the unfortunate Pedro had lost his life; and that Dona Antonia, and also in all probability poor old Madre Dolores, who could nowhere be found, had been forcibly carried off. Having come to this conclusion, we next patiently tracked the footprints, which led us through the wood down to the head of the creek referred to by Don Manuel, on the muddy banks of which we distinctly traced not only the heavy footprints of the abductors, but also the lighter ones of, presumably, Dona Antonia and her nurse, as well as the mark of the boat's keel where she had been grounded. This much determined, Don Manuel next led us to a spot from which he assured us that Senor Madera's vessel could be seen; and there, sure enough, we saw our old foe the *Black Venus* snugly moored in the creek.

A council of war was at once held as to what should be our next proceeding. It was manifestly impossible to attack the brig there and then; our little force was wholly inadequate to the capture of the vessel, and any attempt to do so would only have resulted in putting her crew upon their guard. Don Manuel informed us that, from his knowledge of the creek, he was certain there would not be a sufficient depth of water over the sand-bar at its mouth to allow of the brig sailing before high-water, which would be at about half-past six o'clock that evening; but we were unanimously of opinion that, having secured his prey, Senor Madera *would* sail then. As to what might happen in the interim, it would not bear thinking of, and we could only hope and pray for the best.

Having by this time obtained all the light which it was possible to gain on the matter, we prepared to return to the *Virginia*, Don Manuel eagerly accepting Smellie's invitation to accompany us. But before doing this, there lay before us the melancholy task of burying poor Pedro's body, and with the aid of half a dozen men from the gig this was accomplished as speedily as possible, after which the house was shut up, and we hastened down to the boat and made the best of our way back to our ship.

Poor Smellie behaved most admirably under the very trying circumstances. That he was fearfully agitated and anxious, I, who knew him so well, could easily see; but with a determination and firmness of will which I heartily envied he resolutely put aside all other considerations and devoted all his energies to the solution of the problem of what it would be best to do. We were a silent and thoughtful party as we wended our way back to the ship; but once there, the skipper promptly led the way to his cabin and informed Don Manuel and me that he had decided upon a plan of action.

It was exceedingly simple. He was, he said, more firmly convinced than ever that the *Black Venus* would sail that night. The weather was clear and fine, the barometer high; and we might therefore reckon with certainty upon the springing up of the land-breeze shortly after sunset. This breeze would be a fair wind *out* of the river; but so long as it lasted no ship could re-enter against it and the strong current. Smellie's plan, therefore, was simply to go outside as soon as the evening mists gathered sufficiently to conceal our movements, and there await the *Black Venus*, trusting to the speed of the *Virginia* and our own manoeuvring to enable us to get promptly alongside her.

The plan looked very promising, and it was adopted. The messenger was at once passed, and the ship hove short; after which we awaited with such patience as we could muster for the gathering of the mist. At length, about seven p.m., the anchor was tripped, and the *Virginia* glided gracefully out of the creek to seaward, under topsails, jib, and boom mainsail. We knew almost to a hair's-breadth the course which the *Black Venus* must steer for the first seven or eight miles after clearing Shark Point, and Smellie placed us right across this track, jamming the vessel close upon a wind and wearing short round every twenty minutes; by which plan we were never more than ten minutes sail from the line over which we expected the enemy to pass.

A careful calculation, based upon our knowledge of the *Black Venus's* extraordinary sailing powers, showed that we might look for her about half-past nine o'clock; and half an hour previous to that we began to make our preparations for according to her a suitable reception. The decks were cleared for action, the magazine was opened, arms and ammunition were served out to the crew, who were then sent to quarters; the guns were loaded each with a round-shot and a charge of grape on the top of it, and all the canvas was loosed and made ready for setting at a moment's notice. Then all the sharpest eyes available in the ship were set upon the watch for our slippery foe, and we were ready.

The night-mists to which frequent reference has been made are, it ought to be explained, confined to the river itself; and though on such occasions as that of which we are now treating they are carried out to seaward by the land-breeze a few miles beyond the river's mouth, they soon get dissipated; so that whilst in the river itself the fog may be so thick as to render it impossible to see further than half the ship's length ahead, it will be perfectly clear at a distance of seven or eight miles outside. It was just upon the outer or seaward skirts of the fog-bank that we had taken up our station and were hovering to and fro.

The *Virginia* had just gone round, and was stretching to the southward upon the port tack, when, from my station on the heel of the bowsprit, I thought I detected a sudden thickening of the haze at a spot about three points on the weather-bow. Straining my eyes to their utmost I gazed intently into the darkness; the appearance became more pronounced, more defined every second, and as I watched it assumed the form of an irregularly-shaped truncated pyramid.

"Sail ho! broad on the weather-bow!" I exclaimed joyously; and in a moment half a dozen voices exultingly reiterated the cry of "Sail ho!"

Yes, there could be no mistake about it; for whilst the words were still upon our lips the apparition grew more substantial, assumed the misty outline of a ship in full sail, and finally shot out from among the fog-wreaths clear and well-defined—a brig running before the wind under studding-sails.

I hastened aft to where Smellie stood grasping the maintop-mast backstay, and was greeted by him with the characteristic remark of:

"What a fellow he must be, and what nerve he must have! Fancy a man running out of that river and through the fog under studding-sails." Then, turning to the helmsman, he said:

"*Now* we have him fairly, I think. Up with your helm, my man, and steer for his jib-boom end. Mr Costigan,"—to the first lieutenant—"make sail, if you please."

"Oi, oi, sorr," answered that worthy in a rich Hibernian brogue. "Let go and overhaul the fore and main clewgarnets; board the fore and main tacks and aft wid the sheets. Fore and main topmast-staysail and jib halliards, hoist away. Sheet home and set the fore and main-topgallant-sails, and be smart about it. Aisy now, there, wid that main tack; don't ye see, you spalpeens, that the ship is bearin' up. Man the braces, fore and aft; ease up to leeward and round in to windward as the ship pays off. Well of all, belay, and coil up. Misther Hawkesley, am I to have the pleasure of showin' ye the way on board the hooker yonder?"

"Thanks, no, I think not, Costigan," I answered with a laugh. "I propose to lend my valuable aid to the alter division of the boarders; you are a host in yourself, you know, and can manage very well without me. But I shall keep a look-out for you in the waist of the brig."

"Very well, it's there I'll mate ye, young gintleman, or my name's not Denis Costigan."

And away hurried the impetuous Irishman to place himself at the head of the forward division of boarders.

The brig had sighted us almost as quickly as we had her, and she made one or two attempts to dodge us. But it was of no use, she had run into our arms, as it were; we were much too close together when the vessels became visible to each other to render anything like dodging at all possible; moreover Smellie, standing there on the breach of one of the guns, watched the chase with so unwavering an eye and met any deviation on her part so promptly with a corresponding swerve on the part of the *Virginia*, that Senor Madera soon scornfully gave up the attempt, and held steadily forward upon his course.

The sister brigs, for such they eventually proved to be, now running on almost parallel courses, soon narrowed the space between them to a bare hundred feet, the *Virginia*, however, having been so carefully steered as to give her a slight lead. This seemed to be the moment for which Senor Madera had waited, for he now suddenly threw open his ports, and without attempting the mockery of hoisting an ensign of any kind, poured into us the whole contents of his double-shotted starboard broadside, aiming high, however, with the evident hope of knocking away some of our more important spars. Our lower canvas was immediately riddled and a few unimportant ropes were cut; but beyond this we fortunately sustained no damage.

By way of reply to this, Smellie, without removing his eyes from the chase, waved his hand gently to the helmsman; the wheel was put a half a dozen spokes or so over to port, and the *Virginia* slewed slightly more toward her antagonist.

"Now, steady men," cautioned the skipper. "Do not fire until I give the word, then pour your broadside in upon her decks—not a shot below the sheer-strake for your lives." I well knew of whom he was thinking when he said this; Antonia was doubtless in the cabin, and it was her safety for which he was thus careful. "And as soon as you have fired your broadside," he continued, "draw your cutlasses and stand by to board. Are the grappling-irons all ready?"

"All ready, sir," came the reply from the tars who were standing by to throw them, and then there ensued a few breathless moments of intense silence.

Gradually the two brigs neared each other, until the lap and swirl of the water along our antagonists' sides could be distinctly heard. At that moment a rattling volley of small-arms was discharged from the *Black Venus*, and I saw Smellie start and reel on his elevated perch. The next instant, however, he had recovered himself, and once more waving to the helmsman, he gave the word:

"Fire!"

Prompt at the command, our broadside rattled out, and amid the crashing of timber and the shrieks of the wounded I felt the jar of collision between the two vessels.

"Heave!" shouted Smellie. "Boarders away!" And with a simultaneous spring fore and aft, away we went over the bulwarks and down on to the crowded decks of the *Black Venus*.

The fight was short but stubborn. Our antagonists fought with the desperate bravery of men who already felt the halters settling round their necks; but whoever heard of British tars yielding an enemy's deck when once their feet were firmly planted upon it? Besides, almost every individual man among us felt that we had a long score of disappointments and floutings to wipe out, and steadily but irresistibly we drove the pirates into the waist of their ship, where, huddled closely together, it was impossible for them to use their arms effectively. Finally, Smellie and Madera, after several unsuccessful efforts to get at each other, managed to cross swords, and after a few rapid passes the latter fell, run through the body by the skipper. In the very act of falling, however, he whipped a pistol from his belt and aiming point blank at the skipper, fired, the ball passing through Smellie's lungs. The poor fellow turned blindly, and with the blood spurting from his mouth reeled into my arms.

I knew very little of the fight after this, for summoning a couple of men I at once proceeded to remove the skipper on board his own vessel; but before we had got him fairly down on deck a cheer from our lads told us that victory had once more declared herself on our side, and that the redoubtable *Black Venus* was ours.

Getting Smellie below and into his cot with all speed, I waited until the arrival of the surgeon upon the scene, when, handing the patient over to his tender mercies, I hastened back on board the prize, and went straight below into her cabin. It was a magnificently furnished apartment, and fitted with every luxury, even to a guitar. But it was empty. Could it be possible that we had been deceived, after all, as to the circumstances of Dona Antonia's abduction? Perhaps she was concealed somewhere. I shouted:

"Dona Antonia! Dona Antonia! are you here? Fear not; it is I—Dick Hawkesley. We have captured this vessel; Madera is wounded, if not slain outright; your father is at hand, and you are free."

"Who calls?" I heard a voice—Madre Dolores'—exclaim from an adjacent berth, the door of which was closed. "Who calls?"

"I—Dick Hawkesley," I replied. "Don't you recognise my voice, Madre?"

"Ay, to be sure I do—*rum*" was the reply. A sound of the withdrawal of bolts followed; the door cautiously opened, and the Madre, with her eyes gleaming and a cocked pistol pointed straight in my direction, protruded her head through the opening. One look was sufficient. With a wild cry of delight she dashed the pistol to the floor, exploding it in the act, and sending the ball within a hair's-breadth of my starboard ankle, and rushing forward flung her arms convulsively about my neck, pouring out a torrent of Spanish endearments between the kisses which the poor old soul liberally bestowed upon me. I submitted with a good grace for a moment, and then gently but firmly withdrew myself from her embraces, to meet the glance of Dona Antonia, who stood in the doorway of the state-room, looking on with a curiously mingled expression of fear, doubt, and amusement.

A few words sufficed to fully explain to her the state of affairs, and then hastily enveloping her and old Dolores in the first wraps that came to hand, I conveyed them with all speed on board the *Virginia* and presented them to Don Manuel.

My story is now ended, or nearly so; my adventures on the Congo and the west coast terminating with the capture of the *Black Venus*; a few additional words, therefore, will suffice to fittingly dismiss the principal personages who have figured in this history, and to bring the history itself to a symmetrical conclusion.

We returned with our prize to Banana Creek, on the morning following the action, and there remained for a couple of days to bury the dead, and to refit. Don Manuel embraced this opportunity to make a flying visit to his house, from which he returned after an absence of a few hours only, bringing with him a small but solidly constructed and extremely heavy oak chest, which he explained to me in confidence contained his daughter's dowry, and which eventually proved to be the receptacle of a goodly store of Spanish dollars.

From Banana Creek the two brigs proceeded in company to Sierra Leone, where the *Black Venus* was soon afterwards adjudicated upon and condemned as a pirate, my evidence and that of the other six survivors from the *Daphne* being accepted as conclusive of the fact that she had been guilty of at least *one* act of piracy; namely, in the case of the *Highland Chieftain*. Her crew were committed to prison upon heavy sentences, meted out in proportion to the comparative guilt of the parties; but additional evidence shortly afterwards cropping up—that of poor Richards of the *Juliet* amongst it—additional charges were preferred against them; and

Madera, who proved to be the half-brother of the fictitious Monsieur Le Breton, late of the *Virginia*, with his officers and several of his men, suffered the penalty of death by hanging.

Smellie's wound proving unexpectedly troublesome, he was ordered home that he might have the benefit of a more temperate climate to assist his recovery, and he accordingly took passage for London in a tidy little barque, the *Lilian*, Don Manuel and his daughter, with old Dolores, all of whom had gone on to Sierra Leone with us, also engaging berths in the same vessel. The survivors from the *Daphne* being also ordered home to stand their trial for the loss of that vessel, I thought I could not do better than secure one of the remaining berths in the *Lilian's* cabin—the men being accommodated in the steerage. Thus we had the mutual pleasure of each other's society all the way home.

The passage was a long but uneventful one, and by the time that we arrived in the Chops of the Channel Smellie's wound had taken so favourable a turn that he was almost as well as ever, save and except for a little lingering weakness and shakiness in his lower spars, which, somehow, obstinately continued to need the assistance and support of Dona Antonia's fair arm whenever the two promenaded the deck together. My gallant superior was extremely anxious to be married immediately on the ship's arrival, and after the usual protestations and pleadings for delay with which engaged maidens delight to torment their lovers, Dona Antonia so far yielded as to consent to the wedding taking place on the earliest possible day after my trial, so that I might be present at the ceremony.

And this arrangement was duly carried out; the trial by court-martial being, of course, a mere form, from which I and my fellow-survivors emerged with a full acquittal, accompanied, in my case, by a few very gracious and complimentary remarks from the president on the manner in which I had conducted myself during my short period of service.

As for Smellie, he found himself fully confirmed in his rank of commander, with the gracious intimation that, in appreciation of his valued services, an appointment would be at his disposal whenever he felt himself sufficiently recovered to ask for it, which he did after a six months' sojourn at home with his young wife. I sailed with him in the capacity of midshipman, and in the West Indies and elsewhere we passed through several stirring adventures together, the record of which may possibly be given in the future.

Choose from Thousands of 1stWorldLibrary Classics By

A. M. Barnard
Ada Leverson
Adolphus William Ward
Aesop
Agatha Christie
Alexander Aaronsohn
Alexander Kielland
Alexandre Dumas
Alfred Gatty
Alfred Ollivant
Alice Duer Miller
Alice Turner Curtis
Alice Dunbar
Allen Chapman
Alleyne Ireland
Ambrose Bierce
Amelia E. Barr
Amory H. Bradford
Andrew Lang
Andrew McFarland Davis
Andy Adams
Angela Brazil
Anna Alice Chapin
Anna Sewell
Annie Besant
Annie Hamilton Donnell
Annie Payson Call
Annie Roe Carr
Annonaymous
Anton Chekhov
Archibald Lee Fletcher
Arnold Bennett
Arthur C. Benson
Arthur Conan Doyle
Arthur M. Winfield
Arthur Ransome
Arthur Schnitzler
Arthur Train
Atticus
B.H. Baden-Powell
B. M. Bower
B. C. Chatterjee
Baroness Emmuska Orczy
Baroness Orczy
Basil King
Bayard Taylor
Ben Macomber
Bertha Muzzy Bower
Bjornstjerne Bjornson

Booth Tarkington
Boyd Cable
Bram Stoker
C. Collodi
C. E. Orr
C. M. Ingleby
Carolyn Wells
Catherine Parr Traill
Charles A. Eastman
Charles Amory Beach
Charles Dickens
Charles Dudley Warner
Charles Farrar Browne
Charles Ives
Charles Kingsley
Charles Klein
Charles Hanson Towne
Charles Lathrop Pack
Charles Romyn Dake
Charles Whibley
Charles Willing Beale
Charlotte M. Braeme
Charlotte M. Yonge
Charlotte Perkins Stetson
Clair W. Hayes
Clarence Day Jr.
Clarence E. Mulford
Clemence Housman
Confucius
Coningsby Dawson
Cornelis DeWitt Wilcox
Cyril Burleigh
D. H. Lawrence
Daniel Defoe
David Garnett
Dinah Craik
Don Carlos Janes
Donald Keyhoe
Dorothy Kilner
Dougan Clark
Douglas Fairbanks
E. Nesbit
E. P. Roe
E. Phillips Oppenheim
E. S. Brooks
Earl Barnes
Edgar Rice Burroughs
Edith Van Dyne
Edith Wharton

Edward Everett Hale
Edward J. O'Biren
Edward S. Ellis
Edwin L. Arnold
Eleanor Atkins
Eleanor Hallowell Abbott
Eliot Gregory
Elizabeth Gaskell
Elizabeth McCracken
Elizabeth Von Arnim
Ellem Key
Emerson Hough
Emilie F. Carlen
Emily Bronte
Emily Dickinson
Enid Bagnold
Enilor Macartney Lane
Erasmus W. Jones
Ernie Howard Pie
Ethel May Dell
Ethel Turner
Ethel Watts Mumford
Eugene Sue
Eugenie Foa
Eugene Wood
Eustace Hale Ball
Evelyn Everett-green
Everard Cotes
F. H. Cheley
F. J. Cross
F. Marion Crawford
Fannie E. Newberry
Federick Austin Ogg
Ferdinand Ossendowski
Fergus Hume
Florence A. Kilpatrick
Fremont B. Deering
Francis Bacon
Francis Darwin
Frances Hodgson Burnett
Frances Parkinson Keyes
Frank Gee Patchin
Frank Harris
Frank Jewett Mather
Frank L. Packard
Frank V. Webster
Frederic Stewart Isham
Frederick Trevor Hill
Frederick Winslow Taylor

Friedrich Kerst	Hayden Carruth	James Branch Cabell
Friedrich Nietzsche	Helent Hunt Jackson	James DeMille
Fyodor Dostoyevsky	Helen Nicolay	James Joyce
G.A. Henty	Hendrik Conscience	James Lane Allen
G.K. Chesterton	Hendy David Thoreau	James Lane Allen
Gabrielle E. Jackson	Henri Barbusse	James Oliver Curwood
Garrett P. Serviss	Henrik Ibsen	James Oppenheim
Gaston Leroux	Henry Adams	James Otis
George A. Warren	Henry Ford	James R. Driscoll
George Ade	Henry Frost	Jane Abbott
Geroge Bernard Shaw	Henry James	Jane Austen
George Cary Eggleston	Henry Jones Ford	Jane L. Stewart
George Durston	Henry Seton Merriman	Janet Aldridge
George Ebers	Henry W Longfellow	Jens Peter Jacobsen
George Eliot	Herbert A. Giles	Jerome K. Jerome
George Gissing	Herbert Carter	Jessie Graham Flower
George MacDonald	Herbert N. Casson	John Buchan
George Meredith	Herman Hesse	John Burroughs
George Orwell	Hildegard G. Frey	John Cournos
George Sylvester Viereck	Homer	John F. Kennedy
George Tucker	Honore De Balzac	John Gay
George W. Cable	Horace B. Day	John Glasworthy
George Wharton James	Horace Walpole	John Habberton
Gertrude Atherton	Horatio Alger Jr.	John Joy Bell
Gordon Casserly	Howard Pyle	John Kendrick Bangs
Grace E. King	Howard R. Garis	John Milton
Grace Gallatin	Hugh Lofting	John Philip Sousa
Grace Greenwood	Hugh Walpole	John Taintor Foote
Grant Allen	Humphry Ward	Jonas Lauritz Idemil Lie
Guillermo A. Sherwell	Ian Maclaren	Jonathan Swift
Gulielma Zollinger	Inez Haynes Gillmore	Joseph A. Altsheler
Gustav Flaubert	Irving Bacheller	Joseph Carey
H. A. Cody	Isabel Cecilia Williams	Joseph Conrad
H. B. Irving	Isabel Hornibrook	Joseph E. Badger Jr
H. C. Bailey	Israel Abrahams	Joseph Hergesheimer
H. G. Wells	Ivan Turgenev	Joseph Jacobs
H. H. Munro	J. G.Austin	Jules Vernes
H. Irving Hancock	J. Henri Fabre	Julian Hawthrone
H. R. Naylor	J. M. Barrie	Julie A Lippmann
H. Rider Haggard	J. M. Walsh	Justin Huntly McCarthy
H. W. C. Davis	J. Macdonald Oxley	Kakuzo Okakura
Haldeman Julius	J. R. Miller	Karle Wilson Baker
Hall Caine	J. S. Fletcher	Kate Chopin
Hamilton Wright Mabie	J. S. Knowles	Kenneth Grahame
Hans Christian Andersen	J. Storer Clouston	Kenneth McGaffey
Harold Avery	J. W. Duffield	Kate Langley Bosher
Harold McGrath	Jack London	Kate Langley Bosher
Harriet Beecher Stowe	Jacob Abbott	Katherine Cecil Thurston
Harry Castlemon	James Allen	Katherine Stokes
Harry Coghill	James Andrews	L. A. Abbot
Harry Houidini	James Baldwin	L. T. Meade

L. Frank Baum
Latta Griswold
Laura Dent Crane
Laura Lee Hope
Laurence Housman
Lawrence Beasley
Leo Tolstoy
Leonid Andreyev
Lewis Carroll
Lewis Sperry Chafer
Lilian Bell
Lloyd Osbourne
Louis Hughes
Louis Joseph Vance
Louis Tracy
Louisa May Alcott
Lucy Fitch Perkins
Lucy Maud Montgomery
Luther Benson
Lydia Miller Middleton
Lyndon Orr
M. Corvus
M. H. Adams
Margaret E. Sangster
Margret Howth
Margaret Vandercook
Margaret W. Hungerford
Margret Penrose
Maria Edgeworth
Maria Thompson Daviess
Mariano Azuela
Marion Polk Angellotti
Mark Overton
Mark Twain
Mary Austin
Mary Catherine Crowley
Mary Cole
Mary Hastings Bradley
Mary Roberts Rinehart
Mary Rowlandson
M. Wollstonecraft Shelley
Maud Lindsay
Max Beerbohm
Myra Kelly
Nathaniel Hawthrone
Nicolo Machiavelli
O. F. Walton
Oscar Wilde
Owen Johnson
P.G. Wodehouse
Paul and Mabel Thorne

Paul G. Tomlinson
Paul Severing
Percy Brebner
Percy Keese Fitzhugh
Peter B. Kyne
Plato
Quincy Allen
R. Derby Holmes
R. L. Stevenson
R. S. Ball
Rabindranath Tagore
Rahul Alvares
Ralph Bonehill
Ralph Henry Barbour
Ralph Victor
Ralph Waldo Emmerson
Rene Descartes
Ray Cummings
Rex Beach
Rex E. Beach
Richard Harding Davis
Richard Jefferies
Richard Le Gallienne
Robert Barr
Robert Frost
Robert Gordon Anderson
Robert L. Drake
Robert Lansing
Robert Lynd
Robert Michael Ballantyne
Robert W. Chambers
Rosa Nouchette Carey
Rudyard Kipling
Saint Augustine
Samuel B. Allison
Samuel Hopkins Adams
Sarah Bernhardt
Sarah C. Hallowell
Selma Lagerlof
Sherwood Anderson
Sigmund Freud
Standish O'Grady
Stanley Weyman
Stella Benson
Stella M. Francis
Stephen Crane
Stewart Edward White
Stijn Streuvels
Swami Abhedananda
Swami Parmananda
T. S. Ackland

T. S. Arthur
The Princess Der Ling
Thomas A. Janvier
Thomas A Kempis
Thomas Anderton
Thomas Bailey Aldrich
Thomas Bulfinch
Thomas De Quincey
Thomas Dixon
Thomas H. Huxley
Thomas Hardy
Thomas More
Thornton W. Burgess
U. S. Grant
Upton Sinclair
Valentine Williams
Various Authors
Vaughan Kester
Victor Appleton
Victor G. Durham
Victoria Cross
Virginia Woolf
Wadsworth Camp
Walter Camp
Walter Scott
Washington Irving
Wilbur Lawton
Wilkie Collins
Willa Cather
Willard F. Baker
William Dean Howells
William le Queux
W. Makepeace Thackeray
William W. Walter
William Shakespeare
Winston Churchill
Yei Theodora Ozaki
Yogi Ramacharaka
Young E. Allison
Zane Grey